Eggplant Alley

a novel

By D. M. Cataneo

www.bunkerhillpublishing.com
by Bunker Hill Publishing Inc.
285 River Road, Piermont
New Hampshire 03779, USA

10 9 8 7 6 5 4 3 2 1

Library of Congress Control Number: 2013934778

ISBN 978-1-59373-146-5

Designed by Joe Lops
Printed in China

For Emily

1

Eggplant Alley

Everyone said Eggplant Alley was a lovely place. In the old days.

Way back in the old days, Eggplant Alley was a clean apartment complex tucked into a happy corner of the Bronx. There were thick shade trees in the courtyard and kids everywhere. The kids played jump rope, hopscotch, tag, cowboys and Indians, stickball. Late in the afternoons, the courtyard was scented by suppers cooking. In the blue dusk, the fathers trudged home from work—tired men, carrying empty lunch boxes and afternoon newspapers. They climbed the hill, and they saw the trees and the three red-brick buildings, and they smelled the suppers, and the men knew they were at home in Eggplant Alley. They thought it was the finest place in the world.

All that was long ago, in the old days, in the black-and-white days before Nicky Martini was born.

Also known as the good old days. Nicky was too young to remember these good old days, but he heard an awful lot about them. He was practically an expert.

NICKY WAS a little kid when the changes fell on Eggplant Alley. This happened in the early 1960s. The changes plopped down like water balloons from the heavens, practical jokes from the angels.

First went the trees. Nicky didn't know what kind of trees they were and he didn't catch the name of the disease that killed them. But he watched fascinated on the summer afternoon when the workmen came and sawed the trees down and cut them up. Nicky was just six years old at the time. So he waved bye-bye as the men hauled the pieces out to the trucks.

The landlords of Eggplant Alley replanted. But one night juvenile delinquents swarmed through and ripped the tender little replacements out of the ground and threw them into the street. Just for fun. That was the kind of neighborhood it was becoming. After that, the landlords of Eggplant Alley figured, why bother?

Grandma Martini had three favorite sayings, the third of which applies here:

1. Telling lies is like eating garlic.
2. Never sleep with an itchy dog, unless you intend to scratch.
3. One thing leads to another.

One thing led to another in Eggplant Alley.

A first-floor window was broken and the window was left unfixed. So another window was broken. Tires were slashed. A bike was stolen. The Fuller Brush man was robbed of his brushes. Parcel post packages went missing from welcome mats, and then the welcome mats themselves began to disappear. Someone took up peeing in the elevator. The Rotinos' hot new Pontiac Bonneville convertible was swiped from the parking garage beneath Building B, plucked straight out of the belly of Eggplant Alley.

And one cold February night, the McCarthys—residents of Building C, first floor rear—came home and found a hobo eating Cheez Doodles in Mr. McCarthy's recliner. The man was drunk and stinky, and when he fled, he took the new *TV Guide* with him. No one understood why he needed a *TV Guide* if he didn't have a television. Dad offered, "Maybe he wants to know what he's missing." The incident inspired all first-floor residents to install window bars. And for a few months, Mom flatly refused to purchase snack foods. "They just attract bums," she said.

One thing led to another and another, and before you knew it, nobody wanted to live in Eggplant Alley anymore.

The kids moved away. In one autumn alone, Jimmy Scarole, Bobby Sciatti, Paulie Capicola, and Iggy Schwartz took off with their families. They poured out of Eggplant Alley like refugees fleeing a war zone. They went north to Westchester, west to New Jersey, east to Long Island. Anywhere that wasn't Eggplant Alley.

The day after Nicky's twelfth birthday, the Abbananzos cleared out to California. This was particularly bad luck for Nicky, who had recently noticed Andrea Abbananzo's bluish black hair and the way it shimmered in the elevator light.

Nicky grew accustomed to good-byes. That was one good thing about growing up in Eggplant Alley. You learned how to say good-bye. You got plenty of practice. One day, you play GI Joes and Operation with a kid. Next day, you wave bye-bye at the taillights of his family's Chevrolet as it rolls away, gone forever, down Summit Avenue, Eggplant Alley in their rearview mirror. Everyone said "We'll stay in touch," but no one ever stayed in touch. They preferred to leave Eggplant Alley right where it was, where it belonged—in the rearview mirror.

Nicky was sad to lose playmates, but he did not cry during the good-byes. He'd wave so long, go upstairs, watch *The Soupy Sales Show* on television, eat a grilled cheese and chocolate milk lunch, get over it, move on. This was easy because as far as he was concerned, his best pal was and always would be his big brother, Roy.

2

The Fifth Thing That Ruined Nicky's Childhood

And wouldn't you know it, on a sunny morning in the spring of 1970, when he was thirteen years old, Nicky waved bye-bye to Roy.

That morning Nicky awoke and looked over at Roy's duffel bag, stuffed, lumpy, and zipped on the mussed bed. He inhaled a whiff of Old Spice aftershave, and it all came back to him from the night before.

The shouts. The sobs. The porcelain monkey.

The big argument over the big decision.

Nicky groggily wondered who won the big argument and what was the big decision. Roy was going somewhere. He knew that much. Nicky wanted to know where.

Roy clomped into their room. He wore clunky, shiny black shoes. Army shoes. And now Nicky knew that Roy was going to Vietnam, after all that fuss.

Roy said, "Hey numbskull, you're awake. I thought you were dead. You sleep like a piece of veal."

"You going?"

"I'm a-going."

"Not to Canada?"

"Numbskull. To the airport."

"You going to Vietnam?"

Roy touched his tie and said softly, "No, 'course not. I'm going to the moon. I had a change of orders."

Roy and Mom and Dad and Nicky and their beloved mutt Checkers bunched up at the apartment door. Roy hugged Mom. Roy shook hands with Dad. Roy patted Checkers. Roy scruffled Nicky's hair.

"Stay out of my stuff, numbskull," Roy said, playfully bashing Nicky's backside with the duffel bag.

Nicky wanted to tell Roy how much he would miss him; that Roy was the best friend of his whole life; that he looked up to Roy the way some kids look up to Batman and Mickey Mantle; that Roy was the greatest big brother in the history of the world; that he was afraid of what was happening.

Nicky said, "Okay, Roy."

Nicky pressed his head against the window screen and watched Roy stride across the silent courtyard. From five stories up, Roy looked like one of those plastic army men, the kind they used to buy at the five-and-dime, a hundred to a package.

Roy's duffel bag bounced on his shoulder. His shoes clonked on the cement. Pigeons flapped across the rooftops. The air felt cool and pleasant on Nicky's face. It was a lovely Sunday morning in springtime.

Five stories down, Roy stopped and lifted his face to the sun. He squinted toward the rooftops of Eggplant Alley. He pointed to the sky and shouted, "Hey, numbskull. Great day for stickball!"

Roy's face glowed in the sunshine and he said, "When I get back!"

A hoarse voice bellowed from Building C, "For the love of Mike, put a sock in it!"

Mom touched Nicky's shoulder and said, "Did Roy ask for socks?"

"No, he said it would be a great day for stickball."

Mom made a face and said, "He knows nobody plays stickball around here anymore." She squinted. "Is he smoking?"

A yellow cab rolled to the curb. Roy flicked away his cigarette, opened the back door, pushed in his duffel bag, and climbed in. The cab hesitated, then motored away.

Mom silently drifted out of the room. Nicky dropped onto his bed, across from Roy's tangled blankets and sheets. He looked at the two beds with matching white bedspreads. He looked at the matching yellow oak bureaus, the matching alarm clocks, the matching lamps. He was alone in a room meant for two. He sniffed the air and caught a trace of Roy's aftershave. He counted on his fingers. One, two, three, four, five.

Five.

This was the fifth thing that ruined his childhood.

3

The First Thing That Ruined Nicky's Childhood

That was Nicky's view, that his childhood was a ruin. A wreck. A hole in the ground. He came along, and the good stuff ended. He showed up to play ball, and the ball went down the sewer. He walked into the party, and the ice cream melted.

Have you ever run to catch a bus, and just as you reached the curb, the bus pulled away? There you are, gagging on smelly blue exhaust. That was Nicky's feeling. He missed the bus.

"Stop your whining," Mom said when Nicky whined. "There's always another bus."

Nicky missed the good old days, as described by the lucky ones on hand to witness them. In the good old days, the streets were safe. Eggplant Alley was paradise. Men wore crew cuts. Everyone saluted the flag. The Yankees won the World Series, every year.

"Before you were born," Dad noted.

Instead, Nicky got Eggplant Alley on the slide. Riots in the streets. Revolution in the air. Men with long hair and beards. Cold wars. Hot wars. The Yankees in last place, every stinking year.

"Be thankful you still have a team," Mom said when he complained. "The Dodgers moved clear out of Brooklyn. Broke your grandfather's heart."

In the autumn of seventh grade, while Roy was away in boot camp, Nicky discovered a beautiful new word in Language Arts class. The word was *nostalgic*. The vocabulary workbook said it meant "an abnormal yearning for days gone by." The word touched Nicky deeply, like a love poem, like a new box of crayons, like the smell of garlic frying. Except for the abnormal part, he thought the word described him perfectly.

One rainy, gloomy afternoon, Nicky made the grave mistake of sighing to Mom and Dad, "I sure picked a lousy time to be a kid."

"Are you nuts?" Mom said, flopping a hissing iron onto Roy's school shirt. "You think this is bad? I grew up in the Depression. We didn't have two nickels to rub together. Mrs. Moscowitz! She grew up in Germany, with the Nazis breathing down her neck. Count your blessings."

From his easy chair, from behind the *Daily News,* Dad tossed in, "Don't talk to me about hard times. When I was a kid, my mother would slug me in the mouth so one of my teeth would fall out, so we could leave it under my pillow. We needed the dime from the Tooth Fairy. To buy milk."

"Yeah, yeah," Nicky said. But his true thoughts were: "You forget. The Depression ended. The Nazis are gone. You and Mrs. Moscowitz had happy endings. There were a lot of them in the good old days. Happy endings. I've never seen one of those."

Nicky found comfort counting the opposite of blessings. He built a list of the people and events that ruined his childhood. He did this in secret. No one wanted to hear his complaints, so he wrote them down in the back pages of a composition notebook left over from first grade. On the day Roy left for Vietnam, the list included:

1. John F. Kennedy.
2. The Great Blackout of 1965.
3. The end of stickball.
4. Roy's horrid hippie girlfriend Margalo.

Nicky planned to write at length someday on each entry. He planned to put those vocabulary lessons to work and pour out his heart. He imagined someone would discover his writings long after he was gone. He hoped someone would publish them in a famous book, along the lines of *The Diary of Anne Frank*.

Looking back, with the wisdom that comes from reaching the age of thirteen, Nicky felt silly about Kennedy.

This happened in the autumn of 1963, when Nicky was six. He was fidgeting with Mom in a crowd on Broadway. He was smothered by cloth coats, bopped on the head by vinyl handbags, suffocated by drugstore perfume.

Somebody yelled, "Here he comes!"

Nicky caught a glimpse of President John F. Kennedy, chestnut hair blowing in the wind as he worked down the barricade, grasping hands and grinning and nodding. When Kennedy reached the barricade directly in front of Mom and Nicky, the crowd surged, the way a crowd lunges for a subway car. People yelped and pushed. Mom and Nicky were shoved forward. Kennedy reached into the seething mass to squeeze a flailing hand and a presidential knuckle popped Nicky in the nose.

Nicky wailed. His nose sizzled. Kennedy lightly touched Nicky's head and said, "Sorry," and kept moving.

Nicky hopped up and down. His nose trickled blood. He stomped the asphalt with his Buster Browns. He howled, "I'm going to tell my DAD on you."

Men in suits and sunglasses trailed Kennedy, who passed a handkerchief to one of the men. The man relayed the handkerchief to Mom.

"Ma'am," he said.

"My dad will fix you, too," Nicky said. A droplet of bright red blood brimmed on his upper lip.

Mom fished in her purse for a tissue. She refused to give the president's handkerchief to Nicky. She said, "Who knows where's it's been?"

"I don't wanna TISSUE! I want to tell DAD!" Nicky growled.

Nicky burst into the apartment and calmed down. To him, there was no place like 5-C.

With a tissue jammed up each nostril, Nicky stationed himself at the kitchen window and kept vigil down Groton Avenue, the narrow street that finished in a dead end at the rear of Building B.

At five thirty on the dot, Dad's Yum-E-Cakes delivery van, orange blinker flashing, turned off Lockdale Avenue. The truck roared down Groton, head-on toward Eggplant Alley. Nicky enjoyed the sensation—Dad rushing straight toward him.

The van rolled directly under the kitchen window. Nicky saw his father's wavy brown hair and thick arms behind the windshield. The van was swallowed up by Eggplant Alley's underground garage. Nicky adored the sight—Dad coming home.

Nicky met Dad at the door and pulled him by the finger to the sofa. In a nasally tone, Nicky told the incredible story of the president who punched him in the nose.

Nicky said, "I bled."

"That's bad."

"You're going to beat him up, right, Dad?"

"Sure. But right now, I'm going to read the paper."

"You'll take care of him, right, Daddy? No one hurts your kids and gets away with it, right? You always said that."

Dad stood and touched a hand to Nicky's bristle cut. He said, "Your head's sweaty. Yeah, I'll take care of everything."

"You fix him good."

"Yeah," Dad said from the hallway.

"Fix him."

"You got it, pal. I'll take care of him. The dirty rat," Dad said, fading into the bathroom.

Nicky dropped his moist face onto the plastic slipcover. He sighed in peace. Dad would take care of everything.

Three weeks later, on a Friday afternoon, Nicky stayed home from school with his annual autumn head cold. Mom ironed and stared at a soap opera on the TV, and the screen went black.

Then:

"Here is a bulletin from CBS News. In Dallas, Texas, three shots were fired at President Kennedy's motorcade in downtown Dallas. The first reports say that President Kennedy has been seriously wounded by this shooting."

Mom sat gently next to Nicky on the couch. She made the sign of the cross. Nicky's bottom lip stuck out—his expression when utterly confused. He only wanted Kennedy roughed up a little.

When Roy returned from school, Nicky asked his brother if he had heard the big news about the dead president.

"No, I spent the day on Mars. Didn't hear," Roy said.

"Well," Nicky said, sounding official. "Kennedy was shot and killed, AND I'm pretty sure Dad was behind it."

Roy said, "You better quit eating glue."

Nicky eyed Dad closely during supper. Dad sat calmly in his white T-shirt, arms on the table, and chewed his meat loaf and sipped his can of Ballantine. Same as always.

Nicky thought, "One cool customer."

For a long while, the incident gave Nicky the creeps, the willies, and a first-class case of brain cooties. Starting on November 22, 1963, he questioned everything, from the Tooth Fairy to whether Mr. Ed, the talking horse on television, could really talk. And for the first time in his life, Nicky wondered, with a queasy belly, "What can happen next?"

The answer, of course: plenty.

4

Help

What could happen next? One thing could lead to another. And before you know it, your big brother is off to war in a jungle on the other side of the world. Off to the war they showed on TV every night, in living color, mostly deep greens and bright reds.

That's what.

Nicky sat on his bed, the scent of Roy's aftershave lingering in the spring air. He glanced at his alarm clock, which was alongside Roy's alarm clock. Roy left fifteen minutes ago. Only about ten zillion minutes till Roy came home.

"One year," Nicky thought. "I'm going to need help with this."

He found Dad in the living room. Dad was uneasy in his easy chair. Dad stared at the television, without watching the television. The TV was tuned to a movie musical. On the screen, a man wearing overalls crooned to a woman wearing a straw hat. The woman did leg-kicks on a hay bale.

Nicky asked, "Want me to change this, Dad?"

Nothing.

Nicky thought, "This is bad."

Dad hated musicals. They were on his hit list, along with Blue

Castle hamburgers, cars manufactured by American Motors, the New York Mets, and old man Van Der Woort from the sixth floor, who never held the elevator for you. If Dad's mind was right, he would rather swallow sewing needles than watch a musical.

Nicky said, "Aren't the Yanks playing today?"

Nothing.

Dad was on the premises, but Dad was not there. Dad was in a daze. Nicky had never seen his father in such a state. He had seen Dad happy, angry, tired, disgusted, confused, worried. One time he even saw Dad leave the house wearing two different-colored shoes. That was a famous mistake in family history. But dazed—this was a new one.

Dad wasn't the type. He was unflappable. He was a cool customer. Dad had seen it all, from the Great Depression to World War II. Dad hit the winning basket in the 1947 North Bronx ADC championship game. Dad climbed the fire escape like a superhero when they were locked out of the apartment. Dad laughed—actually laughed!—when he caught the rat in a coffee can the night it stepped off the dumbwaiter into the kitchen. One night, Dad won $62 in a poker game. Dad once saw Babe Ruth stopped at a light in Riverdale and another time shook Dwight Eisenhower's hand at a luncheonette in Yonkers.

But now, with Roy on his way to Vietnam, Dad looked like Superman with a lapful of kryptonite. Dad looked like he did the weekend he had the stomach flu.

"Hey, Dad, I'm gonna go roller-skate on the parkway," Nicky said.

Nothing.

Dad's watery eyes stared at the television. On the screen, a man milked a cow in rhythm to trombone music. Poor Dad. He had always been a world-class worrier when it came to his boys. The highness of fences, the sharpness of scissors, the slipperiness of staircases, the ravages of exotic diseases, the darkness in a stranger's heart—Dad saw potential danger to his kids everywhere. Now his older boy was on his way to war. The airplane ride alone was enough to cause deep, deep worry.

"Dad cannot help me," Nicky muttered.

He found Mom in the kitchen. She stood over the Formica table, peeling garlic. She wore her most massive apron. Her short black hair was wrapped in a red-and-white kerchief. She was dressed to cook.

"What's with the long face?" Mom said. "You're not going to walk around here like that for a whole year. Count your blessings."

Nicky thought, "Okay, let's see. My brother is gone and my father is a zombie. But at least I have not swallowed rat poison; a steam roller has not crushed my skull; a hand grenade has not exploded in my pants . . ."

Nicky fibbed and said, "I have a headache."

"Well, be thankful you have a head," Mom said. "You don't see me sitting around complaining. I'm making myself useful by cooking."

In the small kitchen, garlic sizzled, water boiled, and the oven preheated. Mom toiled amid a pile of peeled potatoes; opened tomato cans, serrated lids up; a pyramid of cream cheese bricks; crumbled crackers on a sheet of waxed paper; a haystack of something green and leafy. The air was hazy with flour.

Nicky thought, "Mom is in bad shape."

When Mom was upset, going over the edge and around the bend, off her rocker, she hit the kitchen and cooked the way some people hit the bars and drank. One night, famous in family lore, Roy disappeared for six hours. He was fourteen and he vanished from the face of the earth. (Turned out Roy and Fishbone Callahan walked the one hundred or so blocks to Yankee Stadium, to stand outside and wait for foul balls.) While Dad frantically searched the dark streets of the Bronx, Mom cooked up a lasagna, baked an apple pie and two pumpkin pies, and churned out five quarts of escarole soup.

Now Nicky stood in the preheated, boiling, sizzling kitchen and he thought, "Roy will be gone for a year. We're gonna need to open a restaurant."

"You won't see me sitting around staring into space," Mom said, chopping something orange. "I lived through World War Two. My two brothers were overseas for almost three years and we didn't sit around staring into space."

Nicky knew the stories of Uncle Dominic and Uncle Vinny the way most kids knew the stories of Curious George and the Cat in the Hat. Uncle Dominic served as an airplane mechanic in Europe. He was shipped home safe and sound in 1945 with a bowel infection. Uncle Vinny was a star second baseman, movie-star-handsome, and industrious enough to go to Fordham for part of one semester. He enlisted in the navy the day after Pearl Harbor and became a frogman. On a mission in the Pacific, he was eaten by a giant clam. His name was listed on the War Memorial plaque, the one recently splashed with graffiti, down in Grant

Park, and Nicky was surprised Mom would bring him up on this night.

Nicky said, "Ma."

Mom said, "I hope we have pot cheese."

Nicky thought, "I wonder what Checkers is up to. Man's best friend."

He found the creaky brown mutt stretched out at the apartment door, graying snout perched on the threshold. Checkers's nose twitched. He was sniffing the hallway air, waiting for Roy to get off the elevator, the way he waited for Roy to come home from school, all those afternoons.

"You can't lie here a whole year, Check," Nicky said, although he did see the attraction of the idea. He rubbed his hand along the dog's back. Checkers shifted, groaned, broke wind.

"Help," Nicky squeaked.

And his plea was answered by a sweet, wonderful sound. The noise was faint, but clear. Nicky moved away from Checkers. He entered the hot kitchen, searching, following. Mom didn't look up. The glorious sounds came from outside. They floated on the spring breeze, drifting through the kitchen curtains, into Nicky's eager ears.

Nicky's Stupid Shenanigans

5

The sounds gently rose from the PS 19 schoolyard, directly below the kitchen window. Boyish shouts. A dull thwock, unmistakably the impact of a stickball bat against a Spaldeen. There is no other sound like it. The clatter of a wooden bat on asphalt, the shriek of a boy, the jangle of a chain-link fence. "Home run," Nicky remembered. "Those were the sounds of a home run." Music to his ears.

Nicky moved past Mom toward the kitchen window, toward the noise. He walked in a trance, as if hypnotized by something beautiful and magical. He was lured to the window. He walked like he did in his dream about Jane Jetson, the one where she blew kisses and crooked her finger at him.

"Do you hear that?" Nicky said to Mom.

"We need eggs," Mom said. She stirred something thick and gloppy in a bowl. She was building up a sweat.

"They're playing stickball out there."

"Don't be crazy," Mom panted, grunting, putting her shoulder into it. "Nobody plays stickball around here anymore."

Nicky parted the curtains and looked out at the sunny day. The schoolyard was empty. Not even a pigeon. And now the schoolyard was silent. The music had stopped. Nicky stared. He stared till his eyeballs ached. He wanted them to be there.

And they emerged, as if out of a fog. Icky Rossilli, pitching. Billy Braggs, hitting. Skipper and Fishbone, pounding their mitts, throwing long shadows onto the gray asphalt. Best of all, out in center field, a tall lanky boy shifted from foot to foot, and spit through his teeth, and tugged at his black baseball cap. Vintage Roy, from the good old days. From the pink of his cheeks to the rolled cuffs of his dungarees, Roy appeared to be roughly age thirteen. Nicky took in this scene from the beloved past, and the sweet sounds—thwock, clatter, shout—rose up again.

"I can really hear them. I can really see them," Nicky said.

"Oh, THAT nonsense," Mom said. She shook her head. "You're starting your stupid shenanigans again."

Mom knew that Nicky was seeing things. Lovely, old things. This was not a recent development. For years, Nicky had conjured scenes out of the past, right before his eyes.

"The last thing we need today is for you to start acting like a nut," said Mom, clopping a knife on the Formica as she diced.

Nicky was sure he was not a nut. The visions didn't haunt him or scare him. They didn't command him to take a hatchet to his family or to eat cockroaches or bark at the milkman. The visions never came on suddenly. They were strictly voluntary. Nicky tuned in to them the way you tune in to a favorite radio program. He enjoyed seeing things from the past. As far as he was concerned, it was no different from looking at old photographs or listening to an old song. No different from remembering the good old days that went along with the photos and the songs. Nicky merely took the reminiscing a few steps closer to the slippery edge.

For example, one Sunday afternoon Dad, Roy, Nicky, and Mr. Greenblatt who lived down on the second floor took in a game together at Yankee Stadium. They sat in cheap seats, high in the third deck. The Yankees were in last place, and they were having a very bad day. They let fly balls dribble out of their mitts and they made throws that were too short or too long and they struck out or popped up whenever the moment called for a big hit. The small crowd on hand booed. It was like being at a party that turned bad.

Dad and Mr. Greenblatt were drinking Ballantine beer. They chattered on and on about the mighty Yankees of the good old days. They spoke of the Great DiMaggio, and their faces softened and their eyes got moist. The way they described him, the Great DiMaggio played center field for the Yankees as if he were a prince with angel wings. Mr. Greenblatt belched and said, "Joltin' Joe was regal." At that moment Nicky peered down at the current Yankee center fielder, who was picking his nose.

So Nicky concentrated and stared until his eyeballs hurt. And out of a fog trotted Joe DiMaggio, in the fluttery flannels from the newsreels. Nicky stared hard around the magnificent stadium and the crowd, no longer booing, was on its feet, cheering with mad delight. Everybody seemed happy. Nicky spelled out this grand vision for Dad, Roy, and Mr. Greenblatt.

"I see Joe D.!" Nicky exclaimed.

Mr. Greenblatt peered into the neck of his Ballantine bottle and said, "Did he get into the beer?"

"Don't mind him. He sees mirages out of the past," Dad said.

"He's just plain nuts," Roy said.

Mr. Greenblatt, who had a huge head and a thick Hell's Kitchen accent, clapped Nicky on the back and said, "Awwww, he's all right. The little fellow just has a craving to give the modern world the slip. Who can blame him?" And Nicky thought Mr. Greenblatt was a genius.

Now, as Mom cooked, Nicky looked out the kitchen window at the boys on the playground, and he was grateful for the view. It was a wonderful scene. Roy and his pals looked as innocent as stuffed animals. The old gang wore their old clothes—dungarees, white T-shirts, and canvas sneakers. Roy removed his cap and revealed a crew cut, flat and bristly. Nicky fondly remembered the crew cut. It was Roy's trademark hairdo before he let his hair grow over his forehead, over his eyes, down his neck, the moppish hairstyle that boiled Dad's blood. Nicky was comforted to see Roy's old crew cut, thin layer of Brylcreem glistening in the sunshine.

Nicky watched Roy play stickball. He watched Roy swing the bat for a solid hit. He watched Roy take first base. He watched Roy lean his hands on his knees, just like the big leaguers. He watched Roy move smoothly off the base—his trademark little bounce and hop. Roy dancing in the sunshine. Nicky wondered, "I'm crazy? Who wouldn't want to see this?"

Nicky withdrew his head from the kitchen window and said to Mom, "Guess what?"

"Oww," Mom said sharply. She had clipped a finger with the knife.

"Know what I'm going to do this summer?"

"Right on the knuckle, as always."

"I'm gonna play stickball this summer."

Mom carried her bloody finger to the faucet and said, "Don't be crazy. Nobody plays stickball around here anymore."

6

Hypnotizing Icky

This happened two weeks later.

Nicky sipped Kool-Aid, sunshine on his face, and kept watch out the kitchen window. On the kitchen table were Roy's old baseball mitt, Roy's old Spaldeen, and Roy's old yellow stickball bat. In a previous life, the bat was a mop handle. Nicky surveyed the PS 19 schoolyard, looking for something old, hoping for something new. He stared at the PS 19 playground until his eyeballs ached. All he got for his trouble was a pain in the eyeballs. Down on the asphalt, a pigeon waddled, a paper cup tumbled end-over-end. There was nothing from the old days. No Roy. No stickball. The sweet visions hadn't returned since the morning Roy shipped out.

"I've lost my powers," Nicky moaned. "Another change, for the worse."

Mr. Misener, the grouchy superintendent of Eggplant Alley, dragged a garbage can down the back stairs of Building B. He sang one of the old love songs, warbling over the racket of the banging metal can. It was the kind of beautiful, soft spring day that made crabby men sing. The kind of day that shrieked for stickball.

Nicky stared harder. He wrinkled his brow, adjusting his forehead the way Dad adjusted the rabbit-ears antenna on the television.

Nothing old.

Nothing new.

In the late afternoon, the sun put a yellow glow into the tenement windows. Cool shadows crept across the stoops. Nicky watched the bricks change from red to orange to purple in the fading light. But he didn't see the beauty of the sun and light. Instead of enjoying what was there, Nicky pined for what was missing.

In the far corner of the PS 19 schoolyard, a basketball thunked and a metal backboard twanged. Two black kids from the Groton Avenue tenements were shooting hoops. Nicky's stomach grumbled. He thought, "If they can play their game, why can't we play ours?"

Nicky let his eyes sweep the schoolyard, one last time. Mom would come around the kitchen soon and begin to build sandwiches for supper, a Martini family tradition on Sunday nights. Then Nicky wouldn't be allowed to leave the apartment, no matter if the Yankees themselves showed up at the playground, shouting at Nicky to grab a glove and come down.

And out of the long shadows of Building B appeared the redheaded Icky Rossilli. One of Roy's old gang.

Icky walked briskly toward the short wall on the schoolyard's edge. He walked as if the wall were a train that might pull out of the station. He couldn't wait to get to that wall. Icky hurried and tossed glances over his shoulder, keeping watch on the black boys playing basketball. Icky slumped onto the wall, sighed deeply, fired up a cigarette. He examined the concrete between his sneakers. His head swiveled to check on the black boys on the basketball court. Nicky remembered that Icky was a pitcher.

Nicky squeezed the Spaldeen ball as the elevator rattled toward the lobby. He had found the ball stuck in Roy's mitt in the back of their closet. The ball must have plopped into the mitt during that last stickball game. The ball sat in the mitt in the closet for four years. Nicky looked at the ball, once pink, now darkened to the color of rotten meat. He thought about the ball hiding in the dark closet for the past four years. "Sounds good to me," Nicky thought.

Icky's head snapped up when he heard Nicky's footsteps. Icky was on guard out here. "Hey. What do you know, little Nicky Martini," Icky said without enthusiasm.

Icky wasn't Nicky's first choice to find on the PS 19 schoolyard this afternoon. Icky was a hard case. Nicky thought Icky was not the type to get enthusiastic about playing stickball, even for old times' sake.

Icky was not a boy to get enthusiastic about anything, except maybe a six-pack and a girlie magazine. He was the first of Roy's friends to swear, the first to smoke, the first to get a girlfriend, the first to dump his girlfriend, the first to get a job, the first to get fired from a job. Icky was barrel-chested and tough, and he tried to act tougher. Icky talked a lot about joining the marines and killing commies, but he never got around to it. Icky also said he would cheerfully go to Vietnam if drafted. He made the boast after he was sure he would never get the call. Icky was among the luckiest in Nixon's new draft lottery. The Ping-Pong balls had tumbled his way. His birthday had come up 351st—no chance of getting drafted. In this same lottery, Roy's birthday came up number one—guaranteed to be drafted. "The only lottery a Martini ever won," Dad joked.

"Hear anything from Roy?" Icky said, yawning.

Nicky told Icky about the postcard from Roy. The card was passed out to the troops upon arrival in Vietnam. The card was pre-printed with the message that BLANK—and Roy wrote in his name here—had arrived in the Republic of Vietnam and was awaiting assignment. Mom taped this postcard to the refrigerator.

"Good," said Icky. "If you write him, tell him I want a souvenir. Like a silk smoking jacket or one of them necklaces made out of gook ears."

"Yeah, I'd like one of them myself," Nicky said, feeling stupid, because the last thing he wanted was jewelry, especially jewelry made from body parts.

"Is he still going with that hippie chick? The one with the screwy name?"

"Search me."

Margalo was the last topic Nicky wanted to talk about. The light was fading on the schoolyard.

Nicky held the Spaldeen to Icky's face.

"Hey, look what I found," Nicky said, as if the squishy ball had appeared by pure magic.

"Whazzat?" Icky said. He squinted at cigarette smoke curling into his eyes. "Lemme see."

Nicky handed it over. Icky squeezed the ball. He examined it and turned it, like a chimp regarding a coconut. Icky bounced the ball hard into the cement between his feet. A spongy thud. The old sweet sound. He smiled with the cigarette in his mouth. Icky's eyes cleared. His face freshened. His red hair brightened.

"We used to have some games," Icky said. "You never played, right? You was too young."

"I missed them."

"We used to have some games." Icky snapped his wrist with the ball in his hand. "Drop pitch. Nobody could hit mine. Roy couldn't."

Nicky said, "Lookit. I got a stick."

"What for? You couldn't hit me."

Nicky shrugged. He watched Icky's face. He screamed at Icky in his head, "Come on, come on. Let's just play!" Icky's eyes went somewhere far away. He stood. He took the cigarette out of his mouth, dropped it, and stepped on it.

Nicky thought, "The first step."

Icky made a P-U face and said, "Nah." He flipped the ball to Nicky. He grimaced. "Nobody plays stickball around here anymore. You can't do nothing around here anymore. Because of them." Icky cocked his head toward the basketball court, where the black kids were playing. "You should know that better than anybody, right?"

Nicky thought, "Come on, you dope. Forget about them. Let's just play. Come on, come on, come on." Nicky bounced the ball, hoping the magical spongy thud would hypnotize Icky.

Icky stretched, yawned, belched, and said lazily, "Nobody plays stickball around here no more."

Icky folded himself onto the wall, shook a Lucky Strike loose from the pack, plucked out the cigarette with his lips, and reached for his silver lighter. Icky and Nicky sensed movement, and Fishbone Callahan appeared out of the shadows of Eggplant Alley. Another from the old gang. Tall and thin. Nicky remembered Fishbone was an infielder.

Fishbone was about forty feet away. Forty feet was the old stickball distance from the pitcher to the batter. And it's a fact that anyone who has thrown a ball, summer after summer, sometime in his life, can't resist the urge to throw it again, no matter when the opportunity arises.

Icky dropped the lighter and the fresh cigarette, snatched the ball from Nicky, and whipped the ball at Fishbone.

"Think quick!"

The ball reached Fishbone on one bounce.

"You never could throw."

"You never hit me."

"In your dreams."

"You wish."

Fishbone nodded at Nicky, asked about Roy. Nicky told him about the postcard, but Fishbone wasn't listening.

"I guess you forget the one I hit off that front stoop over there," Fishbone gloated. He pointed at a tenement on the other side of Groton. "If somebody was sitting there, the impact woulda killed them."

"Bullshit."

The swear word made Nicky tense.

Fishbone said, "Really? The kid's got a bat. Wanna try? The squirt can chase the ball after I clobber your little-girl pitches."

Fishbone continued, "In fact, know what? I saw Mumbles and

Little Sam on the front steps just now. The other day, we were hashing over the old stickball games. Just the other day. Let's go get them."

Nicky cheered in his head, "Come on, come on, come on."

"I dunno," Icky said. But he was standing and moving away from the wall. Icky and Fishbone walked onto the schoolyard, into the sunlight, onto the old stickball field. Nicky followed. A slight breeze swept the playground and touched Nicky's cheek, like the tickle of a clean sheet. Nicky thought the old concrete diamond was pulling at them, the way the tide pulls you at the beach.

"Look. The old baselines," Fishbone said. He scraped his sneaker along the faded white lines painted onto the cement. "Let's go get the guys. We can get a quick game in before dark."

Icky shrugged. "I don't care."

Nicky silently rejoiced.

A loud yelp echoed from the far end of the schoolyard. The sound came from where the black kids played basketball. Icky, Fishbone, and Nicky swiveled their heads. The basketball backboard quivered crazily. Someone had shot and missed badly, and the basketball was bounding away on the concrete, bouncing straight for Icky, Fishbone, and Nicky.

The black kids ran a few steps, then gave up the chase when they saw the basketball headed toward the white boys on the stickball diamond.

"I got it," Icky said.

Icky ran toward the basketball like a kickball player. He met the basketball with a mighty boot. Maybe he really intended to kick the ball back to the black kids. Nicky would never know.

Icky kicked the basketball and it sailed high and hooked sharply to the left. The ball cleared the wall near the long concrete staircase that led down to Summit Avenue. The ball made a hollow ring as it bounded down the steps. Theoretically, with a few fateful bounces, the ball could have rolled all the way down to the Hudson River.

Two of the black boys swore loudly and sprinted across the schoolyard. They ran, sneakers slapping, down the steps. Nicky pictured a long night of looking for that ball. A third black boy sauntered toward the steps, shaking his head, swearing bitterly. He hollered, "Dumb-ass. What's your problem?"

Icky boomed back, "I ain't got no problem. What's your problem?" Then he added, "Jigaboo."

"I ain't got no problem, white trash. What's your problem?"

"I'll give you a problem."

"Oh, yeah?"

"Yeah."

And so forth.

The black boy hissed, "I oughta whip your ass," and took off down the steps.

"Let's beat it," Icky said to Fishbone. Then to Nicky, "You better get out of here before they come back with a bazooka."

Icky and Fishbone loped into the shadow of Eggplant Alley. Nicky followed them across the concrete diamond, toward Building B. He thought, "What a lousy day. Nothing new. Nothing old. Nothing, nothing."

The Creature from the Second Floor

7

"So this is the historic first Earth Day," Nicky thought, crunching cornflakes, listening to the radio news. The radio announcer declared Earth Day would "raise John Q. Citizen's consciousness to the ills of polluted air, dirty water, the chemicals and poisons in all things, from the meat we eat, to the milk we drink."

Nicky eyed the grinning cow on the milk carton.

He examined his bowl of milk-sodden cornflakes.

He pushed the bowl away.

"Another turn for the worse," he thought. "Some holiday. We don't even get a day off."

The historic first Earth Day was a major topic at St. Peter's Elementary. Students drew posters about the smelly Hudson River. They read a story, and the moral of the story was: Littering is bad. They recited poems about the American Indians and clean air. Nicky's social studies teacher, Mr. McSwiggin, as usual, went a step farther. He took the class out of school, on a mission to clean up the empty lot next to Tony's Auto Body.

Mr. McSwiggin was fresh out of Fordham. He had arrived in the autumn with a full beard, which the principal, Sister Teresa, instructed him to shave back to a droopy mustache. Even then,

Nicky was unhappy to have a teacher with a cool mustache. Another break with tradition. A teacher with facial hair. It was a first, unless you counted Mrs. Hamm.

Nicky didn't like this Mr. McSwiggin, who wore a mustache but wanted a beard. Nicky suspected the energetic little man was a hippie. One of Them. Now and then Mr. McSwiggin spoke of rock 'n' roll music that he favored. This, from a teacher. Hippie stuff. Nicky already had a bellyful of hippies in his life, starting and ending with Roy's horrid hippie girlfriend Margalo.

And here was Mr. McSwiggin, leading the class down the block in this very hippie-style endeavor.

"Today we will clean this little space," Mr. McSwiggin said. "Tomorrow the world."

"Pinko," Nicky muttered.

They marched out of school with bags and rakes and did a job on an empty lot, which didn't even belong to St. Peter's. The students at St. Peter's had not made the mess, but here they were cleaning it up. The seventh-graders picked up dirty bottles, crushed cartons, bashed cans, yellowed newspapers, wadded wrappers, smashed cigarette packs, shredded cigarette butts. The girls performed most of the actual cleaning. They worked earnestly, with a solemn goodness in their eyes. The boys mostly threw things, wandered aimlessly, and searched for oddball treasures. Vinnie Slezak found a container of glop that smelled like airplane glue. Tim Gemelli produced a knob from a car radio.

Nicky went all-out to find bottles. He dug into thick weeds. He crawled under a splintered wooden fence. He turned over rusted sheets of tin. He did this in order to impress the yellow-haired

Becky Hubbard, who carted around the bottle bag. He scrounged up four bottles, and made sure Becky Hubbard was alone when he dropped them, clanking, into the bottle bag. She said nothing. Nicky thought, "She's shy."

Nicky was a mess when he got home from school. His hands were black to the wrists. The knees of his good school pants were caked with mud. He had a cut above his eye, from the trip under the fence. His cheek was smeared with oily grime.

"What happened? Were you in a fight? Were you mugged?" Mom wanted to know.

He told her about the Earth Day activities.

"Great, we're sending you to school to learn how to be a garbage picker," Mom said. "Look at you. At least the vacant lot is nice and clean, right?"

She glanced over the other piece of Mr. McSwiggin's Earth Day lesson. Nicky had produced a Crayola rendition of our planet, continents and oceans and all. The masterpiece was captioned in block letters, as instructed by Mr. McSwiggin: THE EARTH IS YOUR MOTHER.

"Oh, yeah?" Mom said. "Next time you need to puke at three in the morning, have the Earth bring you a bucket. What baloney. What's going on at that school?"

Nicky shrugged. Another sign of the general downhill slide.

Mom went on, "And since when does anybody clean up after their mother? What baloney. Go wash up. Change your clothes. But go get the mail first, will you?"

That was the real source of Mom's touchy mood. The mail. There wasn't a single piece of it from Roy, not since the pre-printed postcard.

"Unless his fingers got cut off, he should write," Mom said quietly, sadly.

Nicky was happy to travel to the lobby for the mail. The chore once belonged to Roy. Young Nicky was awed in the old days when his big brother ventured alone to the lobby and returned with the day's mail. In Nicky's young eyes, Roy was a dashing explorer, a regular Lewis or Clark.

Mom told Nicky, "Remember, don't take the stairs, don't talk to strangers, don't linger down there. For crying out loud, if Mr. Feeley gets on the elevator, you get off at the very next floor. Did I tell you not to take the stairs?"

"A million times," Nicky said. "Why not? Roy always took the stairs."

"Times have changed," Mom said.

"Oh, yeah," Nicky thought. "How could I forget?"

Nicky pressed for the elevator. The elevator shaft came alive with the growly hum of heavy machinery. The elevator thumped and stopped on the fifth floor. The door shuddered, crunched, and slid open and Nicky's nostrils were filled with a sharp stench. Someone had gone to the bathroom in the elevator again. Most residents suspected black kids from Groton Avenue, but Nicky had a hunch it was the Rosatto brothers. Once he spotted Ernie and Sabby Rosatto zipping up as they stepped off the elevator.

Nicky took the stairs. He passed along floor by floor and read the apartment numbers. He barely knew the tenants behind those numbered doors anymore. He was well aware of who used to live there. Friends who went bye-bye. Nicky forgot their names (except for Andrea Abbananzo, formerly of 2-C). Now there wasn't a single kid near Nicky's age in all of Building B. Apparently, nobody with kids wanted to live in Eggplant Alley anymore. Not if they could help it.

Nicky passed 3-B and the door was ajar. A kid named Bobby-something used to live there. Nicky didn't know the current tenant. As he walked by, Nicky stole a peek into 3-B—an umbrella stand, an oval rug, brown shoes. And the door slammed shut, a lock snapped, a bolt clanked. Nowadays, footsteps in the hall were a signal alarm—*Close up fast!* To walk through Eggplant Alley nowadays was to hear doors slam and chains rattle, as fast as the fingers could work.

Nicky moved along the second floor, sighed deeply at the sight of 2-C, and started down the final flight of stairs to the lobby.

Behind him, out of sight on the second floor, an apartment door squeaked open.

Feet shuffled.

A door banged shut.

Slow footsteps sounded along the second-floor hall tile. Grown-up shoes that made a clicking, scraping noise.

Click-scrape. Click-scrape. Click-scrape.

"I'm being followed," Nicky concluded.

He did not stop, wait, and look to see who was there. In most places, in most times, that would be the natural reaction: "Who is that? Hey, hi, hello!" In Eggplant Alley, the reaction was: "Just keep walking." In Eggplant Alley, you never looked back. Somebody might be gaining on you.

Click-scrape. Click-scrape. Click. Click.

Somebody was gaining on Nicky.

Nicky bounded down the stairs to the lobby. He halted and stood, still as a statue. He clenched his teeth and listened hard.

Click-click. Click-click.

Slow, careful, creeping footsteps descended the stairs from the second floor.

Click.

The footsteps stopped.

Someone was standing on the landing, out of sight, waiting. Nicky felt like the antelope in a *Wild Kingdom* special, stalked by the cheetah.

Nicky quietly unlocked the mailbox. He plucked out the envelopes.

He gasped.

Big mistake. Exactly what the stalker wanted. The mail—that's what afternoon muggers craved. Envelopes stuffed with checks and cash. They wait for you to unlock the box, smash you over the head, leave you on the tile in a puddle of blood, make off with your mail. The lunatic was probably on the landing right now, grinning evilly, dripping saliva, rubbing his grimy hands.

Nicky considered his options. Go back up the stairs?

No way.

Run out into the courtyard and scream for help?

Maybe.

Hop on the elevator and make a break for home?

Go for it.

Nicky hit the button to summon the elevator. Heavy machinery clunked and the elevator shaft hummed.

The shoes scraped on the landing. The lunatic was up there, listening, waiting, breathing through his mouth.

Nicky smacked the button again and again and again. He banged it with his fist, over and over, as if a solid punch would hurry the elevator down to rescue him. He thought, "Why didn't I listen to Mom?" She warned against taking the steps. She was right, once more. Nicky thought, "When they find pieces of my dismembered corpse scattered throughout the Bronx, that ought to be a consolation to Mom."

The elevator shuddered down the shaft, slower than ever. Nicky whispered, "Come on, come on, come on." Sweat dripped down his back. His socks were hot and sweaty. The cut on his face stung.

The elevator thumped on the ground floor.

Click-click click-click click-click.

Footsteps cascaded down the stairs, coming for Nicky.

The elevator door grumbled open. Nicky squeezed through when the opening was barely wide enough. He smacked his palm on the CLOSE DOOR button.

Click-click click-click click-click.

The footsteps hit the last of the stairs. The odd thought occurred to Nicky: I am being stalked by a tap-dancer.

He leaned into the CLOSE DOOR button.

The door grumbled and slid across. Like everything else in Eggplant Alley, the elevator door had seen better days. It shuddered, moaned. The door stopped closing.

Clickety-click. Clickety-click. CLICKETY-CLICK.

Frantic footsteps sounded on the lobby tile, nearby to the elevator.

"Close, door, close!" Nicky begged.

The door shuddered, crunched. The door slid, closing.

Click-CLICK.

A face flashed in the narrowing space of the elevator door. The face was contorted, thick-lipped, grotesque and yellow-red in the shadows thrown by the elevator light. Nicky saw eyes bulge behind black-rimmed eyeglasses. The lunatic creature emitted a raspy panting sound. Nicky was horrified when he saw tiny fingers claw around the sliding elevator door. The fingers scratched and hissed on the metal.

Nicky opted for surrender. He would hand over the mail.

"I'll let you have it," Nicky howled.

The small fingers snapped away from the elevator door.

And the door clonked shut.

"Close shave," Nicky said, breathing heavily. He felt the sweet lift of the elevator in his belly.

Nicky squeezed out of the elevator on the fifth floor. He thrust his key into the lock of 5-C and zipped through the door in record time. He slammed the door, turned the lock, and hooked the security chain, as fast as his trembling fingers could work.

8

File Clerk

Nicky huffed and puffed into the kitchen. The envelopes clattered in his shaking hands. Mom was seated at the kitchen table and did not look up from her beadwork. Beadwork involved stringing exactly 467 orange plastic beads onto an twelve-inch length of elastic to produce a cheap necklace. A friend of Uncle Dominic's from Brooklyn would send over big spools of elastic and huge cardboard boxes filled with thousands and thousands of beads. The guy paid Mom two cents for every necklace she put together. Beadwork was part of the effort to get money to move away from Eggplant Alley.

Nicky panted, "Mom! This guy, this creature, came after me in the lobby."

"I've made two dollars today," Mom said without a trace of pride. "That will make a nice down payment on a house, right? I never want to see an orange bead for the rest of my life."

"He chased me from the second floor to the lobby. I think he was after the mail."

"Anything in the mail?" Mom said over her shoulder.

Nicky shuffled the envelopes in his moist hand. Second from the top was an envelope with a red, white, and blue border. The envelope had a military postmark. The script writing on the envelope was Roy's.

"Yeah," Nicky said. "This."

Mom dropped a string of beads, and forty-five minutes' work unraveled onto the table. Mom grabbed the envelope. She took a seat, carefully peeled open the envelope flap, and extracted the letter. The letter was written on a slice of thin paper, which folded over Mom's hands like a tissue. Mom chewed her lower lip as she read.

"Okay, okay. Good," Mom said, nodding. She handed the letter to Nicky. "You want to see?"

"No, tell me what it says."

Mom read off the main points. The weather was really hot in Vietnam. The place stank like the back alley of the Chinese Palace restaurant on Broadway. Roy was assigned as a file clerk at a huge base called Long Binh. Roy and some of his fellow soldiers at the base were thinking of playing stickball. Half the day he worked in an air-conditioned office.

"Look here," Mom said, running her index finger to the last line of the letter. Roy had scribbled big: "I'm nice and safe!"

"That's really, really good," Mom said.

Nicky shrugged.

At five thirty, the door thunked open and the security chain jangled taut.

"What the hell is going on here? Let me in!" Dad boomed.

Nicky ran to the door, unhooked the chain.

"Dad! A creature, a fiend, came after me in the lobby," Nicky said.

"There's a letter from Roy," Mom called from the kitchen.

Nicky said, "He looked like a real killer."

Dad said, "Lemme see that letter."

Dad was already reading as he felt behind him for a chair at the kitchen table.

"An air-conditioned office," Dad said approvingly. "Maybe I ought to join up this summer. Not like when I was in the service. Jesus. An air-conditioned office. How do you like that? Somebody get me a beer."

And that night, thanks to Roy's letter, there was a change in the air. For the better.

Mom went to work on a meat loaf—just one meat loaf. Mom was back to normal.

Dad settled into his chair in the living room and unfolded his *Daily News*. Nicky went into the living room and got the television going. He turned the dial from channel to channel until he found what he was searching for: there was a musical on Channel 5. Two guys in sailor suits tap-danced on the fake deck of a fake ship.

Dad crumpled his newspaper in his lap. "Hey Nicky, for crying out loud. Switch that, will you? You know I can't stand that stuff."

Dad was back to normal.

Nicky was not normal. He was sad, disappointed, shocked, and ashamed. He had his own thoughts on the subject of Roy's letter.

They were very private thoughts, the kind Nicky would never reveal to anyone, ever, not even to a best friend, if he had one. Nicky would not reveal these thoughts even to an imaginary friend. These thoughts were like dynamite, even more dangerous than Nicky's imaginings of Becky Hubbard in a swimsuit. If Dad, just a few feet away, sipping a Ballantine behind the *Daily News,* could read Nicky's mind, there would be big trouble.

No one would get it. No one would understand. Mom and Dad wouldn't like this.

The truth was, Nicky hated Roy's letter. That was supposed to be great news? That Roy was cooling off in a safe office, doing sissy work in the middle of a war? In Nicky's way of thinking, if you go to war, you might as well do something besides file reports and shuffle papers. Going to war and doing paperwork was like joining the Yankees and refusing to play. Like going to Paris and skipping the Eiffel Tower. Like going to Disney Land and passing on the rides. What was the point?

Nicky knew something of war. He faithfully read the comic books *Sergeant Nick* and *Battle Aces.* He never missed an episode of the television show *Combat!* Once, he read a whole book on war, *God Is My Co-Pilot.* Nicky knew the horrors of war, and he thought they made great reading and terrific TV. Nicky wondered what sort of book Roy would produce about his war exploits: *Paper Clips Are My Co-Pilot.* Some joke. Nicky wanted Roy to come home with vivid accounts of stormed pillboxes and heroic stands and close calls. He wanted Roy to come home and speak gravely of the whine of bullets, the smell of gunpowder, the roar of artillery. Of flags snapping overhead. Of victory and glory.

Nicky recalled the night before Roy shipped out. Dad's shouts. Roy's yells. Mom's sobs. The stupid porcelain monkey.

"All that," Nicky muttered, his mind dropping into the past, to that terrible night. "To become a file clerk."

Late in the afternoon on the day before Roy left for Vietnam, Nicky secretly peeked at the army orders on Roy's bureau. They were right out in the open, next to Roy's Yankee bobblehead doll. Nicky was excited and nervous to think that the official, no-nonsense United States Army wording was directed at his big brother: "Will proceed . . . report no later than 0800 . . . for civilian air transport to MACV . . ." Nicky also snuck a look at the plane tickets that would ship Roy from New York to Chicago to San Francisco to Tan Son Nhut AFB in the Republic of Vietnam.

Nicky thought, "Wow." No one in the family had ever flown in an airplane.

Nicky ran his fingertips along the green wool and brass buttons of Roy's army uniform, stiff on a hanger behind the bedroom door. Nicky touched the area above the left pocket. "That's where the medals go," he thought.

Later, as the sun set behind the aspirin factory, Mom happily put together Roy's going-away meal (everyone was careful to not call it a last meal). As Mom cooked, Nicky read the Sunday comics on the floor and Dad watched the Yankee game. In these final moments of peace, the apartment smelled of frying eggplant.

Roy marched into the living room, cleared his throat, and asked Dad if he had a minute. Nicky looked up from the comics. Nicky was still startled by Roy's army-regulation haircut. The buzz cut made him resemble Roy from the old days. It was like going back in time, and Nicky was comforted by the sensation.

"What is it?" Dad said, looking away from a bases-loaded rally by the Yankees.

"I ain't going."

"Ain't going where?"

"You know."

"No, I don't know."

"To Vietnam."

"Some joke."

Roy said, in a tone of voice straight out of big moments in black-and-white movies, "This is no joke."

Dad slid forward in his easy chair. He nearly slid off the cushion.

"What is this? A gag? So where do you think you're going?"

"To Canada. I have it all planned out."

Dad said, "Planned?"

Roy said he had given the matter a lot of thought. He said the war was clearly a big stupid mistake. He said he had no desire to get shot, blown up, burned alive, dismembered, disemboweled, or beheaded for a big stupid mistake.

Dad said, "They didn't ASK your opinion. They TOLD you to go."

"This is an unjust war."

"Don't give me that crap. What do you know of war?"

"Plenty," Roy said. "I know it's rotten."

"Oh. An expert."

"I took a walk through the VA hospital the other day. You should see."

"The VA hospital?"

"Yeah. A friend. She knows a doctor there."

"Oh. Oh-HO. I smell Margalo in this. I should have known."

"What does that matter?" Roy said. "I ain't going. And you can't make me." He sounded like Roy at age nine, a boy refusing to eat beets.

Dad said, "Sit down. Listen to me."

"No."

"Sit."

"No. I'll stand."

"Sit down."

"No."

Dad stood. Roy sat on the couch.

Dad sat in his chair.

Roy stood.

Dad stood.

Roy sat.

Mom entered the room with a wooden spoon, dripping tomato sauce onto the rug.

"What in God's name is going on?"

Dad said, "Roy and me need to have a discussion. But we're doing a jack-in-the-box thing instead."

"Nicky," Mom said. She crooked her forefinger. "Come with me. Roy. You sit and talk with your father."

Nicky and Mom listened from the kitchen table as Dad and Roy conducted their discussion. The discussion raged into nightfall.

"You will do your duty."

"I have an obligation to NOT go."

"Are you afraid? Is that it? Listen, we were afraid. We went."

"You can't even run your own life, I'll be damned if you'll run mine."

"It's that hippie girlfriend of yours, isn't it? Am I right? That's it, right?"

"This is my decision."

"You will have to live with this the rest of your life."

"At least I'll have a rest of my life."

"Don't you want to be a man?"

"That's just stupid."

"I'm stupid? You're the stupid one."

And so forth.

Nicky sat at the kitchen table and listened to the voices rise and fall in the living room. Mom switched on the plastic radio. She turned off the burner under the pot of bubbling tomato sauce and turned off the burner under the skillet of sizzling eggplant. The tomato sauce ceased to bubble, went flat, and developed a hard skim. The eggplant slivers cooled, and the olive oil congealed. Nicky felt a wave of grief as he watched a promising happy hot meal turn cold and die.

Mom and Nicky jumped when Dad shouted loudly, "I WILL STUFF YOU ONTO THE PLANE MYSELF IF I HAVE TO."

They giggled when the tenants downstairs banged on their ceiling with a broomstick, the apartment house signal for "Shut the hell up!"

"I don't know who they are," Mom said. "New people."

Mom fixed coffee—instant. Brewed coffee was for happy occasions.

In the living room, a fist pounded the coffee table.

Followed by murmurs.

Then a thump against the footstool.

And silence.

Followed by the sound of a Sunday newspaper tossed high and fluttering.

"Only a fool would go over there. A total fool."

"Was your mother's brother a fool to go? To give his life for his country? Is that what you are saying?"

"That was a different war."

"Oh, an expert. Listen, kiddo—war is war."

"What if they gave a war and nobody showed up?"

"You got to be kidding. I think I'm gonna puke."

Mom sat at the table and held on to her coffee with two hands, as if the cup might fly away. Nicky doodled on scrap paper. He drew tanks and airplanes and soldiers storming beachheads, the sort of doodles Roy once favored.

At last, Dad came into the kitchen. He smelled of hot sweat. Dad breathed like a man who had just run up five flights of stairs. His eyes were wide and watery and frightened.

"I don't know what to do with that kid."

"Where is he now?"

"In their room."

Nicky pushed back his chair. He said he was going to the bathroom.

He went to the bedroom.

Roy lay on his bed, smoking a cigarette. With the military buzz cut, he looked precisely like Roy from the good old days. The Roy who gobbled up *Sgt. Rock* comics, the Roy who was glued to John

Wayne movies, the Roy who wanted to be a fighter pilot when he grew up.

"Roy?"

"Forget it. I ain't going," Roy said quietly.

"I know."

Nicky's eyes were drawn to the plastic model ships on his bureau. Nicky picked up the USS *Sullivans,* a destroyer named after the five Sullivan brothers who went down on the same ship during World War II. Nicky had heard that story a million times. He had heard that story from Roy.

"Remember this, Roy? The *Sullivans*?"

"I don't want a ship named after me, thanks. We already have a drink named after us."

Nicky replaced the model on his bureau. Roy looked like his old self, from the old days. But he did not sound like him.

Nicky stretched out on his bed. The room was dark except for the light from the hallway. Roy finished his cigarette, stubbed it out in the ashtray balanced on his belly, and lit another one. Nicky heard the lighter scrape. He saw Roy's face in the glow.

Roy said out of nowhere, "I ain't going."

The apartment door slammed. Moments later, familiar shoe steps rang on the courtyard walkway five stories below. Nicky raised up on one elbow and peeked through the curtain.

"Dad's going somewhere."

"Probably getting the cops to arrest me for desertion."

"You don't want to go to jail."

"I ain't going," Roy said quietly.

They lay in the dark and neither of them said a word for a long while.

The apartment door slammed again. Dad appeared in the bedroom doorway. He balanced a pizza box in one hand. The smell of hot tomato sauce was soothing. Tucked under Dad's arm was a porcelain statue of a monkey.

Nicky said, "Dad, what's the . . ."

Dad said, "Roy. Come on out and have some pie."

Roy sighed, put out his cigarette. He rolled off the bed.

"My last meal," he grunted.

Nicky hopped happily out of bed to join the party. He was hungry for food. He wanted pizza pie. And he was hungry for fun and manly fellowship—tall tales, risqué jokes, and worldly secrets. He wanted the inside stories, the stories that the grown-ups must be telling when he walks into the room and they cease talking. He desperately wanted the story behind that monkey. He could barely wait . . .

Dad said, "Nicky, stay here. Roy and me need to have a talk."

Nicky fell asleep without his supper. He thought, as he drifted off, "And I didn't even do anything wrong."

And the next day, in the beautiful spring morning, Roy loaded his duffel bag into a cab and was on his way to Vietnam, increasing the list of things that ruined Nicky's childhood to five.

9

Nicky's Fortune

This happened on a rainy Saturday morning, three weeks after Roy's chicken-flavored, safe-and-sound letter.

Mom went to work cleaning out the refrigerator, which had been wheezing and rattling worse than usual. The noise kept Mom awake at night. The ancient Kenmore was crying for help. The freezer was overloaded with tinfoil packages of eggplant, ravioli, soup, cheesecake, stuffed peppers, chicken cutlets—leftovers from Mom's cooking spree on the day Roy shipped out. The old white fridge could not take the strain.

"It's a sin to throw out all this food," Mom said. "Take these down to Mrs. Furbish. I'm sure the poor old woman needs food."

"She scares me," Nicky said. "Give it to Checkers."

Checkers painfully lifted himself to his feet under the table. He panted. This was the dog's breakfast he had been dreaming about his whole life.

"Get going," Mom said.

Nicky rode the elevator, which was not stinky this morning. The Rosatto brothers had not paid a visit. Nicky shivered from the rock-hard frozen packages stacked in his bare arms.

Mrs. Harriet Furbish lived on the second floor. She was an Eggplant Alley legend. No one knew how old she was, but she didn't look a day under 112. Mrs. Furbish was from the South. Nobody knew how she'd ended up in the Bronx. If you listened to whisper and rumor, she had been a witch, a nurse, a vampire, a seamstress, a professional bowler, a waitress, a gypsy, a sword swallower, a lion tamer, a swimmer of the English Channel, a genie from a bottle, and a onetime girlfriend of President Chester A. Arthur. When Nicky was four years old, Roy informed him that Mrs. Furbish was a cannibal, with a special taste for tender little boys.

Mrs. Furbish especially gave Nicky the creeps because of another rumor. She was reputed to be a crackerjack fortune-teller. One look in your eyes, and Mrs. Furbish knew all about your past, all about your future. Nicky's stomach pretzeled at the very idea. He wasn't worried about a scandalous past. To his regret, he didn't have one. But he was stone-cold terrified of the future.

Nicky stood on Mrs. Furbish's worn-thin welcome mat and knocked on 2-E. A television was going across the hall. Nicky looked over his shoulder. He worried about the Creature from the Second Floor. Nicky imagined the horrid little weasel behind one of the doors, squinting those bug eyes at him through the peephole. Nicky wished Mrs. Furbish would hurry.

From inside 2-E came a slow, muffled noise. Squeak . . . squeak . . . squeak. That was Mrs. Furbish, hurrying. Nicky recognized the sound of her wheelchair, a battered wicker porch seat fitted with bicycle tires.

A bolt unlatched, a lock turned, a chain jangled, and the door opened. Mrs. Furbish half looked at Nicky with watery eyes and said, "What you want?"

"My mom sent down some food."

Mrs. Furbish scrunched up her prune face.

"Might as well bring it in. Put the eats in the kitchen."

The tiny apartment was dark in the rainy morning. A tired grandfather clock tick-tocked sharply. Nicky looked. The clock had no hands.

He pulled open the freezer. Mrs. Furbish scowled from her wheelchair in the doorway and said, "Jest put 'em on the table. I didn't say put 'em in the icebox. Now come and sit."

Nicky took a seat on a purple velvet couch that smelled of sweet powder. Mrs. Furbish wheeled in. She stared at the floor. Nicky felt like he was in a coffin with a corpse. He listened to the rain against the windows. Cars hushed along the wet pavement of Summit Avenue. Nicky was unsure how to talk to any woman, other than Mom. He was at a real loss for words with a 112-year-old woman.

"How you like Titus?" Mrs. Furbish said, staring at the floor.

Nicky had no clue about the identity of Titus. So he said, "Oh, fine. I like him fine."

"You don't know who I'm speaking of, do you?" She lifted a shaky finger, indicating beyond Nicky's shoulder. "I'm speaking of the bird, dummy."

A large black-and-green parrot was perched atop the bookshelf, just a few feet away from Nicky. He had not noticed the ratty bird, which was perfectly still. This bird was as big as Nicky's arm. Its beak was cracked. Nicky was sure the bird was dead and stuffed, until he saw one eye slowly close and slowly open.

"That's Titus. Was my big brother's. Till he got took in the army and didn't come back. Say he fell at Gettysburg."

Nicky stared at the bird. The bird did not look at him.

"Name of Jeb."

"Hi, Jeb," Nicky called to the bird.

"My brother 'twas Jeb, dummy. Bird's name is Titus. Titus used to talk. But he don't much no more. He over a hunnert twenty years old, so can't say as I blame him. He could whistle Dixie one time. Few bars, least."

Nicky was impressed. He nervously chattered, "Wow. A hundred and twenty years old. Imagine. He lived through the Civil War. I wonder what that was like?"

Mrs. Furbish looked directly at Nicky. "What was that like?" she said. "That what you wanna know?" She looked straight into his face. Her expression softened. Her eyes cleared and sparkled blue. The old fortune-teller smiled and arched her scabby eyebrows.

"Civil War?" she said, "Boy, you'll find out."

10

Us and Them

Three days later, on a beautiful May morning, Mr. McSwiggin conducted social studies class outside. Nicky thought this must be something Mr. McSwiggin picked up in college. Class outdoors. Nicky could not imagine a nun teacher from the good old days condoning such hippie-dippie nonsense.

So they sat on the hot, scratchy asphalt of the St. Peter's playground. Nicky had to admit, the sun felt good, and the air smelled fresher than in the classroom. By the first week of May, the classroom stank of old bag lunches percolating in the heat—ancient salami, sour milk, long-forgotten tuna, banana skins.

Mr. McSwiggin sat cross-legged and faced the class. Just like a hippie at a sit-in. The topic was the Vietnam War. It was hotter news than ever. American troops had jumped from Vietnam into Cambodia. This set off a frenzy of protests, riots, and demonstrations all over the country. There was extra-big trouble on college campuses.

During a protest over the weekend at a college in Ohio, four students were shot and killed by National Guardsmen. A photograph of one of the dead students, facedown, blood trickling from under the corpse, was splashed across the front page of the Sunday

Daily News. After church Nicky stared at the black-and-white picture and thought, "Roy is safer in Vietnam than this guy was in Ohio." But Nicky preferred to tune out this brand of disturbing development. He flipped over the *Daily News* and read about the Yankees versus the Senators.

And while Mr. McSwiggin conducted his outdoor discussion on the topic of the Vietnam War, Nicky concentrated on the puffy white clouds scudding by. Nicky thought one of them looked like Donald Duck. Nicky looked at the cloud and remembered that Donald Duck and his sputtery grouchiness always made him tense.

Meanwhile, his classmates said the usual.

"We have never lost a war, and I don't think we should lose one now."

"We have no right to be there. It's a civil war."

"If we don't stop them there, one thing will lead to another. I think it's better we fight the communists in Vietnam than having to fight them in California."

"If a neighbor's house was on fire, and they asked you to help put it out, you'd help put out the fire, right?"

"Don't you people understand? We're the bad guys in this war." This from Noreen Connolly, who wore a POW bracelet. The bracelets were all the rage that spring: silver-colored, each inscribed with the name of an actual prisoner of war.

Several boys in the class groaned when Noreen Connolly declared we were the bad guys.

Mr. McSwiggin jumped in. "For what it's worth, I happen to think Noreen has a point." He mentioned the My Lai massacre. It had been revealed in the news that a few years back, American troops had slaughtered an entire Vietnamese village of men, women, and children.

"Well, that's really bad," said Vinnie Bonura.

Nicky thought about the Yankees, then about stickball, then very deeply about Becky Hubbard. She sat a few feet from him. Her legs were folded neatly beneath her, her plaid uniform skirt just so, her knees pure white in the sunshine. Becky Hubbard's eyes were lowered as she toyed with a lone dandelion that sprouted through a crack in the asphalt. Nicky noticed she had blond eyelashes. He watched Becky Hubbard's delicate fingers touch the dandelion petals. He wished he could marry Becky Hubbard on the spot. He imagined her dressed in lacy, frilly white, clutching a bridal bouquet of dandelions. He wondered what she looked like in shorts.

During lunchtime, Nicky picked a seat by himself. This was his custom. He had no real friends at this school. He had transferred to St. Peter's just the year before, after a boy was stabbed in the eye with a protractor at PS 19. After that, Mom and Dad agreed the public schools were unsafe, and somehow they scraped up the $100 tuition for parochial school. In his first year at St. Peter's, Nicky had buddied around with another transfer, a quiet kid named George. George had not returned to St. Peter's for seventh grade. Nicky didn't care, because George liked the Mets and Eugene McCarthy. George was definitely not best-friend material. Now Nicky didn't mix with the other kids, and that seemed to be fine with them. "A lone wolf," Mom said, and Nicky liked that because it sounded way better than "a loser."

Nicky ate lunch and eagerly returned to the daydream about Becky Hubbard. He gazed at the tooth marks in his salami sandwich and imagined what she might look like when she ran a brush along that yellow hair. He built an image of her blond eyelashes, her white knees. He wondered how she might appear at the beach.

The sound of a chair scraping made him look up.

Becky Hubbard stood at Nicky's table, balancing her hot lunch tray. Nicky took this as a gift from God. Becky Hubbard appeared before him, at the precise moment he pictured her in a yellow polka-dot bikini.

Becky Hubbard cased the room. The only empty seat in view was the one across from Nicky. Becky Hubbard set down her tray. She sat. She smoothed a paper napkin onto her lap. She dug a stainless-steel fork into the cafeteria meat loaf.

Becky Hubbard chewed and gazed with great boredom to the left.

She chewed and gazed with greater boredom to the right.

Nicky peeked at Becky Hubbard over his salami sandwich. He prayed those spearmint eyes would focus straight ahead, at him, just for an instant. He watched her pick at the cafeteria meat loaf and thought she was a portrait of shyness and daintiness and incredible beauty.

When Becky Hubbard reached for her milk carton, her eyes flickered briefly across Nicky's face.

Nicky was transformed. He forgot about everything. He gulped the hunk of salami in his mouth and said, "That was a real nice thing, having class outside."

"What?" said Becky Hubbard. She speared a green bean and examined it.

"A real nice day," Nicky said.

"What is this?" Becky Hubbard said, making a face at the oddly shaped green bean.

Nicky sweated. This was his longest conversation ever with a girl. A historic record breaker.

He said, "I noticed you like dandelions."

"What?"

"They are weeds, you know."

"Really," Becky Hubbard said flatly.

Her eyes—such a color!—began to focus at something over his shoulder, on a point way across the cafeteria.

Nicky said, "That was an interesting discussion about the war today."

"Yeah," Becky Hubbard said. She looked into her meat loaf. "I really like Mr. McSwiggin."

This was a sign, a warning, a flashing light—and Nicky didn't see it. She was one of Them. Becky Hubbard said she liked Mr. McSwiggin. Mr. McSwiggin, the hippie. Looking back, Nicky missed many signs. Becky Hubbard had worn a STOP THE WAR button on her winter coat. During the class photo, she was one of the girls who flashed the peace sign. Nicky should have known. Not one of Us. But he missed the warnings. He was over his head, bobbing in the warm waters of a real-life conversation with the great Becky Hubbard. Nicky drank in the spearmint eyes, the yellow hair, the tender lips. He felt his chest fill with something glorious, and he ceased thinking altogether.

Nicky tried to come up with a grand quotation, something big and dramatic, old movie stuff, profound words that would sweep

Becky Hubbard off her feet. All he could produce on short notice was, "My brother is over there, you know. In the war right now. We're quite proud of him."

And Becky Hubbard fixed her spearmint eyes on him and said, "Oh, your brother is a baby killer. How nice. You must be proud. I wonder how many babies he killed today?"

After school, Mom took Nicky to Dr. Rosenbaum, the dentist. Nicky needed a molar pulled. It was that kind of day for Nicky.

During the bus ride to the dentist's office and in the unbearable tension of the waiting room, Nicky worked to forget all about the Becky Hubbard incident. He wondered how many days, how many years, had to pass before he would no longer see the disgust in her eyes or hear the slashing hate in her voice. He was too young to know he could awake in the middle of the night thirty years later, wincing, seeing her and hearing her.

Nicky vowed to be careful, starting right then and there. The world was divided into Us and Them. Nicky should have known Becky Hubbard was one of Them. He would not get fooled again.

As he tasted Dr. Rosenbaum's fingers in his mouth, Nicky wondered where this dentist stood. With Us or with Them?

And the nurse who handed over those frightful silver pliers. Us? Them?

When Mom paid the bill, Dr. Rosenbaum's receptionist advised them to avoid Columbus Circle if they were walking.

"There's a major demonstration going on over there now and traffic isn't moving at all," the receptionist said. She was young and pretty. Her hair was long and straight and blond. She wore blue eye shadow and a bright yellow dress with a crazy geometric pattern.

Nicky guessed, "Them."

Gums throbbing, Nicky studied the old, shaky man in the waiting room. The man had a fedora in his lap. Nicky thought, "For sure, one of Us."

Mom and Nicky walked toward the bus down quiet back streets. Mom looped her arm across Nicky's shoulder.

"I hate to see you in pain," Mom said.

Nicky thought, "And you only know about the yanked tooth."

Mom and Nicky passed three construction workers pouring concrete for a new stretch of sidewalk. Nicky was nuts about fresh concrete. It reminded him of cake batter. As they walked by, he watched the creamy stuff ripple out and he didn't feel a thing. Oozing concrete had lost its charm on this day. Nicky blamed Becky Hubbard for stealing his innocence.

Nicky turned away from the fresh concrete and saw two young men walking in their direction. The boys were about Roy's age. They made a lot of noise. Mom tightened her grip on Nicky's shoulder.

One of the boys was tall and slim, with bushy muttonchop sideburns. The latest hippie style. He was neatly dressed in a buttondown shirt, clean jeans, and white sneakers. He carried a sign attached to a two-by-four. A peace symbol the size of a large pizza was spray-painted, in a fuzzy purple design, onto the sign. The boy leaned the sign on his shoulder like a rifle as he walked.

The other boy was short and skinny. His wild mane of hair hung past his shoulders. This boy wore a sloppy red bandanna around his forehead, a tie-dyed T-shirt, tattered blue jeans, and leather sandals. The two young men bounced along, grinning, talking loudly, gesturing with their hands. They acted like two boys on their way to a party.

"Them," Nicky thought with disgust.

The young men reached Mom and Nicky. Mom clutched Nicky tighter.

The tall, neat boy waved his sign at them. The short, sloppy boy pumped his fist at them. The two boys chanted in harmony, "One, two, three, four—we don't want your goddamn war!"

"My, God," Mom said as the boys laughed and hooted and slapped hands. Bubbling with energy, they continued on their way.

"Don't look at them," Mom said, hurrying Nicky along.

Tools clattered, husky voices swore, and Nicky and Mom turned toward the commotion. The construction workers had seen the whole thing, and they dropped their shovels and hoes and were headed toward the two young men. The construction men, known around New York in those days as hard hats, did not look friendly.

"HEY! Hey, Tiny Tim!" one of the hard hats hollered.

The tall boy and the short boy heard the noises, saw what was happening, and tried to get going, walking faster and faster, just short of running. The hard hats swarmed down on them like linebackers.

"What do you want?" the short boy said, trying to be challenging. But the boys knew they were in trouble. You could see it in their eyes. The construction workers were twice their age. But they were thick, muscled men who labored all day outdoors, lifting heavy things. And these muscular hard hats were ticked off.

They went straight to work, "You got some goddamn fresh mouth," one of the construction men said. Another said, "You need to learn some respect," and he slapped the tall boy's peace sign to the sidewalk.

The boy did not think before he blurted, "Asshole."

The construction man leered and skillfully feinted with his right fist; the boy flinched; the construction man's left fist jabbed squarely into the boy's lips. The punch was just like in the movies, except for the wet, meaty sound of the blow, the cracking of teeth, the spurt of blood, the wail of the tall young man as he crumpled to his knees, the construction worker shaking his cut knuckles.

"Let's get out of here," Mom said. "This is terrible."

"Yeah," said Nicky, who in truth desperately wanted to stay and watch the two hippies get beaten by the hard hats—Them pummeled by Us.

"Mom, please walk slow. Because of my tooth."

Two other hard hats surrounded the short, long-haired boy. The boy blubbered, "Wait, now wait . . ."

One construction man said, "So, get him, Bill."

Bill clasped a large hand around the short boy's skinny throat. A sandal slipped off. The boy's long hair swung wildly. Bill growled through clenched teeth, "Hey, Tiny Tim, what do you call this? What's this supposed to mean?"

Nicky saw what was eating the hard hats. It was the boy's jeans. Sewn onto the seat of the jeans was an American flag. The flag was affixed squarely in the center of the boy's bony butt. As if the implication of this weren't enough, the American flag was upside down.

"I fought under this flag. I saw good buddies die for this flag," Bill said in a low, angry voice.

Bill folded the boy onto the pavement. He tried to tear the flag from the pants, but the flag was sewn on tight. It didn't budge. Bill yanked hard on the flag. This merely lifted the short boy, flag still attached to his pants, off the pavement. Bill tried to shake the flag loose. His construction hat fell off and clattered on the street.

Before Mom led him around the corner, Nicky looked back. Bill had a boot planted on the boy's back and was pulling on the flag with two hands. Nicky heard a ripping sound.

"Mom," Nicky said as they walked toward the bus. "Mrs. Furbish really scares me."

A Big Sneeze

11

Nicky awoke with a premonition, or maybe it was a lingering dream. Something big was coming today. He just knew it. It was more than a hunch. It was a certainty. You know the tickle you get in your nose just before a big sneeze? Nicky woke up with that kind of tickle in his soul. He sensed it.

Something big.

A change.

For the better.

"So this is what it's like to be Mrs. Furbish," Nicky thought, dropping out of bed to face this historic Saturday.

The idea stuck in his brain like a catchy tune. At breakfast Nicky pestered Mom to turn on the radio news. She had switched off the news for good after Roy went away. Nicky thought the major development might make the radio. Maybe North Vietnam surrendered. Maybe the boiler at St. Peter's Elementary exploded and blew the place sky-high. Maybe the Yankees traded for Willie Mays.

Mom turned on the radio to the all-news station. Typewriters clacked in the background while a man read the latest bulletins. Nicky was fairly sure the typewriter noise came from a sound effects tape. The radio guy told a story about a pig that thwarted a bank robbery in Missouri. Then came the story of an actress with a new husband, her eighth. Then came the tally of the week's Vietnam War casualties. The numbers were 217 Americans killed, 1,271 wounded, and Mom shivered in the warm kitchen. It was like hearing of a plane crash, when your loved one is up in a plane. Nicky knew Mom was thinking of 217 Roys and 217 mothers. That's the kind of person Mom was.

Mom cracked five eggs into the frying pan when she needed two. The announcer went on to say that the North Vietnamese and Vietcong dead totaled 1,566.

Nicky said, "Hey, Mom, not bad, right? We won, fifteen hundred and sixty-six to two hundred seventeen. I wish the Yankees would win like that."

Mom switched off the radio.

"Mom, don't worry," Nicky said. "He's a file clerk."

Nicky gobbled two of the eggs and mashed up the other three. He was happy. He had a promise to carry into the day. A sweet little treasure in the back pocket of his brain. Something to look forward to. It was like having a Yum-E-Cakes cream pie tucked into your lunch bag, only better.

Dad walked into the kitchen, wearing his nylon jacket, jangling his keys, on his way to make Saturday deliveries.

"Got enough eggs there?" Dad said to Nicky. Then to Mom, "I'll be back around two." He walked across the linoleum, then stopped and turned, as if an idea had popped into his head, out of nowhere.

Dad said, "Hey. Nicola—you want to come with me?"

"Who?" Nicky said, eyes wide. "Me?"

"Is there anybody else here named Nicola?"

"I'll get my coat," Nicky said, bolting from the chair.

Nicky was going with Dad on a delivery run. This was a major development. Roy used to go with Dad in the good old days, and when Roy lost interest, Dad was hurt by the loss, and the subject of ride-alongs with Dad never came up again. Until today.

To tell the truth, as far as Nicky was concerned, this was better than Willie Mays joining the Yankees.

Nicky sat high, legs dangling, on the saggy passenger seat as Dad expertly steered the Yum-E-Cakes van through the narrow streets. Dad weaved around double-parked cars, dodged a jaywalking pigeon, sped up in order to catch a green light, and coasted nicely through a yellow light. Nicky proudly thought Dad would have made a fine fighter pilot, if given the chance.

"Slide open the door for some air," Dad suggested.

"Are you sure?" Nicky said. "I might fall out."

"Don't worry about it. Roy never fell out."

Nicky grunted as he slid back the rusting door and was hit by a rushing blast of warm air, exhaust fumes, and the sounds of passing car radios. The sensation was thrilling.

Their first stop was the DeSerpico Bros. distribution warehouse in the South Bronx. When they passed the bright white hulk of Yankee Stadium, Nicky gawked and felt a surge of longing and excitement.

"Dad, think we could go to a game this year?"

"Maybe," Dad said without enthusiasm. "Or maybe next year, when Roy is back. The three of us. Like the old days, huh?"

Now they were rolling along narrow, potholed streets bordered by junkyards, barbed-wire fences, weedy lots, and abandoned factories with punched-out windows. Nicky was enthralled by a magnificent mountain of crushed cars, tailfins glittery in the sun. Nicky's teeth chattered and he was nearly bucked out of his seat when the van rattled over a stretch of broken railroad tracks. He grinned wildly and held on tight as the van rocked along the muddy dirt road leading to the DeSerpico warehouse, hard by the banks of the green, smelly Harlem River.

Dad braked sharply, toppling an empty coffee cup from the dashboard.

"How was that, squirt?" Dad said.

"Better than a ride at Playland."

"I'll be right back."

Dad yanked a dolly from the rear of the truck. Nicky watched his father in the side-view mirror. A man stacking boxes on a loading dock called, "Hey, Sal, howzit going?"

"Hardly working. I mean, working hard," Dad said.

"Yuh," the man said, grinning.

Nicky wondered if he would ever grow up to be as witty and quick as Dad.

Dad and Nicky worked their way north, delivering Yum-E-Cakes on a route that ran through the Bronx and looped into Yonkers. Dad told inside stories about each stop. Adolph of Adolph's Luncheonette once appeared on the television prank show *Candid Camera*. He was victimized by a talking mailbox. They bleeped out his swear words. Bob Hope once dropped into O'Brien's Sundries for an egg cream. "They had the best egg creams in the Bronx while O'Brien was alive," Dad noted. "Now—not so good."

Dad said Moe's Deli used a rigged scale. Ching's Grocery had a rat problem. Scungilli's Meats did a thriving business illegally selling pig intestines.

And so forth. Nicky ate up every morsel of juicy, inside information, because it made him feel in-the-know, grown-up, savvy, and best of all he felt like a confidant of Dad's. The way Roy used to be.

Dad double-parked in front of J&M Variety in Yonkers and said, "After this, what do you say we swing over to the Nathan's and get a couple hot dogs? How does that sound?"

"That's sounds great," Nicky said, amazed that this great day kept getting better and better.

"Keep your eyes open out here," Dad said over his shoulder. "This ain't the best neighborhood anymore."

Nicky kept his eyes open. The street was quiet, except for a handful of black teenage boys up the block, one boy sitting on the hood of a car, two standing in the street. Nicky wasn't sure, but he thought one of the boys gestured toward the Yum-E-Cakes van. He wished Dad had not turned on the van's blinkers, which surely drew attention. Nicky wished Dad would hurry up.

Dad stumbled out of J&M Variety, doubled over, clutching his stomach, holding on to the door. At once, Nicky knew what must have happened—Dad had interrupted a holdup and was shot or stabbed. Nicky opened his mouth to shout, but the scene was too horrible, too unbelievable for his brain to grasp. The words stuck in his throat.

Still doubled over, Dad leaned against the truck and worked his way to the driver's side. With great effort he climbed behind the wheel.

Nicky said in a small, terrified voice, "Dad, were you shot? Knifed?"

"Worse," Dad said numbly, staring at the windshield. "Nicky . . ."

He turned his face toward Nicky. Dad's skin was gray.

"There was a message in there. From Mom. It's Roy."

"What about Roy?"

"He's . . . gone. He's gone."

"Daddy . . ."

"He's gone. I don't know what happened. He's a clerk. I don't know. Oh, God."

Dad started the van and roared away from the curb.

"Oh, God. What did I do?" Dad said in a small tight voice as he careened down the streets. "What did I do? What did I do?"

Nicky and Dad said nothing on the drive home. The only sound inside the van was the squeaking of Dad's hands as he twisted them on the steering wheel. Dad wordlessly drove like a madman, speeding, weaving, cutting off cars, narrowly missing pedestrians.

Nicky's mind worked on what to do next, with Roy gone. He came up blank. All he could think about was the day Roy took him to Popop's variety store and bought him a set of plastic dinosaurs. Then Roy took him home and helped him fashion a dinosaur park on the coffee table out of paper plates and plastic forks.

At a stoplight, Nicky caught the festive, happy smell of french fries on the warm air, and the odor made him sick to his stomach.

When Dad careened off Lockdale and roared down Groton,

straight toward Eggplant Alley, Nicky picked out their kitchen window. As the van rumbled down the ramp into the underground garage, he caught a glimpse of Mom's face at the window. Her face was twisted into a horrible mask of grief. Even from five stories down, from a speeding delivery truck, Nicky could tell Mom had been sobbing. So it was true after all.

Nicky followed his father in a mad dash up the stairs thinking, "Our lives will never ever be normal again." And as they reached the fifth floor, "I'm sorry I ever ever complained about anything, because now I really have something to be sad about."

Dad's back heaved as he worked his key into the door. He pushed the door open. Something made the door push back at him, and Dad straight-armed the door so that it swung open with a bang, the way cops burst into an apartment on a raid.

Mom appeared in the hallway, and the sight of her unglued Dad. His hands were shaking. Dad pulled at his fingers like a little boy and whimpered, "What have I done? What have I done?"

Mom said, "Salvatore? What's the matter with you? Are you drunk? Take it easy. Don't get so upset. You'll give yourself a heart attack. Salvatore?"

"Don't get upset? You just said I shouldn't get upset. Is that what you said? So this is just a nightmare, right? I wanna wake up."

Dad rocked from foot to foot. He whispered, begging, "Come on! Wake me up then!"

Mom slowly reached for Dad's shoulder. She put her hand on him carefully, as if he might shatter. She called to him, as if talking to a person on a bad phone connection. "SALVATORE? Sal? Sal? Can you hear me? Take it easy. I'm sad Checkers is dead, but he was an old dog. Count your blessings. Thank God it wasn't me or the kids. Can you hear me in there? Did you take too much cough syrup again? Pull yourself together."

Dad stared blankly at Mom.

"Checkers?"

Mom made a motion with her head, indicating behind the door. Dad and Nicky looked at the remains of Checkers, stiff on the tile. Nicky gasped. He had never seen a dead creature bigger than a rat. Checkers lay on his side. Checkers was like a rock. Nicky had never seen anything so completely still. The dog's black nose was tucked under the door. The last movement of his life was one final sniff of hallway air, to see if Roy was coming home.

Dad said, bewildered, "Not Roy?"

Mom exploded, "Roy? Whaddya mean, Roy? Bite your tongue. What's the matter with you? Who said anything about Roy? How could you say that?"

"Malena," Dad said, suddenly calm. "Take it easy. I need to sit down."

Mom and Dad sorted out the mess. They put it all together at the kitchen table. How on this particular afternoon, once again, one thing had led to another.

Mom had found Checkers dead by the door long after Dad and Nicky left. After a hearty cry in the living room, she faced a dilemma: Checkers's body blocked the door. There was no way she could bring herself to move him. She didn't know what kind of horrible things might ensue when you moved a dead dog, and she didn't want to find out.

As the hot morning dragged on, Mom grew nervous about the heat. Checkers might start to smell. Then what? She was trapped. Mom considered climbing down the fire escape, but in the end she was more terrified of heights than of bad smells. She considered packing Checkers with ice cubes, but there were only two ice trays in the freezer.

She called Uncle Dominic at the butcher shop, but he would not close his business to move a dead dog.

Mom said, "Then who? The superintendent? He took three days to fix a faucet. The cops? They don't come if you're getting strangled. The fire department?" Mom kept the fire department in reserve.

She got the idea to call J&M Variety in Yonkers. She knew Dad's route. Mom tried J&M and got old lady Ottaviano on the line and filled her in about Checkers. Mom asked her to tell Salvatore Martini, the Yum-E-Cakes guy, to swing by the apartment as soon as possible.

Old lady Ottaviano needed to leave J&M Variety for a doctor's appointment. She wrote on a paper bag, "Wife called. Come home right away. Dog is dead." She ordered the girl who worked the register part-time to pass along the message on the bag.

"You give this to the Yum-E-Cakes delivery man. You make sure," she said.

Dad arrived at J&M Variety, stocked the shelves with Yum-E-Cakes, and wheeled his dolly toward the door. The register girl said, "Oh, yeah, I almost forgot. You're the Yum-E-Cakes guy, right? I got a message for you." She handed Dad the paper bag.

Old lady Ottaviano's handwriting was poor, and her mastery of

English was shaky. Her pencil was dull. Dad's worried imagination was sharp. And the word *dog* could easily be scribbled poorly, the letters not closed properly. *Dog* could be scribbled to read very much like the word *Roy*. That was the case here, at least. Dad thought the pencil writing on the brown bag broke the news: "Roy is dead."

Now Dad wobbled out of the kitchen to the embrace of his living room chair. Nicky followed and plopped onto the sofa. His legs ached as if he had walked twenty miles. There was still the matter of Checkers at the door, and Dad would do his duty and deal with that. But first he had to pull himself together. Dad's hands were still shaking.

It was an hour before Dad said, "I'll take care of the dog." He lifted himself out of the chair. "I wish there was some way to call Roy in Vietnam, just to make sure that this wasn't one of them premonitions or anything."

"There's no such thing as premonitions," Nicky said scientifically, glumly.

"Smart guy, huh?" Dad grunted. "Poor Checkers. I'll bet it was from eating that Blue Castle hamburger."

Nicky didn't want to know Dad's plans for Checkers. What can you do with a dead dog in the Bronx? They didn't even own a shovel.

Dad passed through the living room carrying an old sheet, the one traditionally spread under the Christmas tree. Nicky heard Dad grunt and swear, the jangle of Checkers's dog license, the door open, and the door slam shut.

"No more dogs," Mom said from the kitchen. "They just die."

Nicky sat on the gritty front steps of Eggplant Alley and watched the sun sink behind the aspirin factory. He shook his head at the memory of the morning, when he tingled with the sureness that something good was on its way, like a special delivery package.

"And what happens?" Nicky muttered. "What happens? I get the crap scared out of me. And Checkers kicks the bucket. And now Dad is out there, tossing my dog in some dump."

He flung a bottle cap off the steps.

"I am a numbskull, for ever tingling about anything."

And the thought would never occur to him: If Checkers had not died that morning, Nicky would not be seated, at that very moment, on the front steps. And he would have missed, forever and ever, what happened next.

Lester Allnuts

12

Nicky sat on the front steps in the dusk, hunched over, lost in his own little miserable world. He was not alert. He was tuned out, thinking, thinking, thinking. He didn't hear the footsteps behind him until the feet were very close. A shoe clicked sharply on concrete nearby and Nicky jumped. He turned quickly and stared up at the thick glasses and evil scowl of the Creature from the Second Floor.

The Creature from the Second Floor was actually a young boy, about Nicky's age and not quite Nicky's height. Which meant the Creature was pretty short. He had wiry, rust-colored hair. His glasses were in fact thick. The Creature had an odd, full mouth. Maybe he would need braces. But the scowl wasn't all that evil and maybe not a scowl at all. It might have passed for a nervous grimace.

"Do you live here?" the Creature said, in a flat accent that came from somewhere far beyond the borders of the Bronx.

"Who wants to know?" Nicky said.

"Me. I live here," the Creature said. "My name is Lester Allnuts."

Nicky snorted.

Lester Allnuts frowned at the ground and said, "That's what everybody does when I tell them that."

"Oh," Nicky said. He had too much practice at "good-bye," not enough practice at "hello."

"I'm Nick Martini."

Lester said nothing.

"Like the drink."

Lester said nothing.

"I live on the fifth floor."

Lester said nothing. He didn't move. Nicky thought, "What does this kid want, an engraved invitation?"

Nicky said, "Sit down, if you want."

Lester examined the step and took a seat next to Nicky. He said he was from a small town upstate. He told Nicky the name of the town, and Nicky immediately forgot it. Something-ville. Nicky heard "upstate" and imagined cows in the road, men wearing straw hats and overalls, pigs in the living room. Lester said he and his mother moved to the Bronx to be near his grandmother, who lived in Washington Heights.

"My daddy thought it was a good idea, to be around family and whatnot. He's away," Lester said.

"Oh, yeah?"

"On business."

Under normal circumstances, Nicky would have allowed the conversation to die right there. It was getting dark. Supper would be ready. Television shows beckoned. And Nicky was not fond of talking to strangers. He was usually as talkative as a mummy. But because Checkers died that morning, Nicky was in no hurry to go upstairs to the apartment, now an apartment with plenty of gloom and without a dog. One thing led to another. So at this moment in time on the steps, Nicky was a regular chatterbox.

Nicky said, “My brother is away, too.”

“Very interesting.”

“He’s at college.”

Nicky was not happy about lying, but he had learned his lesson about the truth. The truth can hurt—him. He had no inkling whether this odd-looking duck was one of Us or one of Them.

He couldn’t think of anything else to say, so Nicky said, “Did you notice how the elevator stinks?”

“Yes. Like a barn.”

“That’s Eggplant Alley for you,” Nicky said.

“What is?”

“A stinky elevator. That’s Eggplant Alley.”

“Where is Eggplant Alley?”

“You’re sitting in it, pal. You live in it.” Nicky liked calling the country boy “pal,” to show him how jaunty city kids talked.

Lester twisted around and looked up at the archway over the steps that led to the courtyard. Soot-streaked gold-colored lettering spelled out:

HUDS N VIEW G RDENS

Lester said, “I thought this was Hudson View Gardens.”

“Nobody calls it that. If you called the cops and told them to come quick to Hudson View Gardens, they wouldn’t come here.”

“Very interesting.”

Nicky said, “There’s a lot to know about living in these parts.”

“Yes. Very interesting.”

Nicky said, “It’s different down here in the city, you know.”

"It surely is different in the city."

"Yeah, and getting worse every day," Nicky said, sounding weary, old, and wizened. "You got to be careful around here. This is becoming a rough neighborhood. Lots of crime. Keep your doors locked. Don't ever let anybody into your apartment. Don't talk to strangers. If you see a guy named Mr. Feeley—run, don't walk. Don't trust anybody. Keep an eye out for shady characters."

"Oh, that one I already know," Lester said. "I know that. Right after we moved in, something happened when I was practicing riding the elevator."

"You practiced riding the elevator?"

"Yes. I wanted to work on summoning the elevator to the lobby. So I went down to the lobby and just as I got to the lobby I saw the elevator door was closing. I reached in to stop the door with my hand."

"Never do that."

"Yes. My mama told already told me. At any rate, just as I reached in, I caught sight of a smelly filthy character in the elevator. His clothes were ripped and his face was smeared with dirt. And he threatened me."

Nicky said, "Threatened?"

"Yes. He sounded just like the gangsters in the movies. He said, 'I'll let ya have it.' Just like that."

"Would you know this guy if you saw him again?"

"Oh, certainly."

Nicky didn't know what to add to this. So he said, "Why donchya fill me in about the country."

Lester shrugged. "We lived in a house. With a lot of land. Not a lot of people. I had a tree house."

"You had a tree house?" Nicky said. He thought tree houses only existed in children's books. He had never met anyone who actually owned one.

"Oh yes. I miss it. It was my favorite place to go. It was a perfect place to think."

"About what?"

"About everything, I guess. About nothing. You know."

"Yeah," Nicky said, knowing.

"It's so crowded here. It's no wonder city people are jumpy. You can't hear yourself think. My mama says it's like cramming a bunch a rats into a small cage, the city is."

"Jumpy? New Yorkers?" Nicky said, his voice in a higher pitch. "You must have us mixed up with somebody else. We're cool as cucumbers. Like rats, huh? Just because we don't live in trees like country people."

"We don't live in trees."

"Well, we ain't rats."

They sat in silence for a moment. A police car roared up Summit, siren screaming, throttle wide open. Its tires whinnied as it careened around the curve, down Mayflower.

"Pardon?" Lester said. "I missed what you said."

"I said, in fact, we have plenty of peace and quiet around here."

"I'm sure you do."

"Yeah. As a matter of fact, I know a place better than any tree house. Peaceful as a baby's crib."

"That would be something. I'd like to see it."

"So, let's go," Nicky said, standing.

Lester blinked at him.

Nicky said, "Come on, whaddya need, an engraved invitation?"

Lester stood and the two boys walked into the courtyard. Lester's shoes clicked on the pavement.

"I gotta know something. What's with the tap shoes?" Nicky said.

"I used to tap-dance," Lester said.

Nicky made a face.

Lester said, "I stopped."

Nicky and Lester climbed the stairs to the second floor. Lester needed to drop by his apartment before visiting the roof. He said he was required to tell his mother where he would be, at all times. Lester turned the doorknob to 2-C and the door clunked without opening.

"Locked," Lester said.

"Well, that's good. You're not upstate anymore."

A tall, thin woman with green eyes and red hair opened the door. She smelled of bread dough. Lester introduced his mother.

"This is Nicky, my friend," Lester told her.

Nicky thought, "Friend? Not so fast, bub."

"How do you do, Nicky," Mrs. Allnuts said, also in the flat accent.

Lester said, "Why don't you come on in for a visit?"

"Well, we'd better get going if I'm going to show you the roof."

Mrs. Allnuts said, "The roof?"

"It's safe," Nicky said. "It's not the kind of roof you fall off. It's not a country roof."

"Mama, Nicky says it's better than a tree house."

The boys rode the elevator and got off at nine, the top floor.

"This way," Nicky said. He felt grown-up and important to be the leader, for once. He would have to show this hick how things were done.

They climbed single-file up a narrow, dark stairway. Nicky pushed open a heavy iron door, which made a scraping sound. They stepped onto the spongy tar of the roof, into the breezy air and fading daylight.

"Whoa," said Lester. "We're high."

"Ten stories," Nicky said proudly, as if he had built each story personally. "Of course, I've been on plenty taller."

"Ever been to the top of the Empire State Building?"

"Are you kidding? That's for tourists."

Nicky let the country boy take in the grandeur of the city rooftop. It was a magnificent place. The air was fresh and reviving, like the air at the beach. It was quiet but not silent. There was the faraway hum of city noise, which Nicky thought way more soothing than silence. Silence allows the imagination to stir up unpleasant thoughts.

From somewhere below, a woman hollered and a kid cried. Somewhere else, a radio was going. Mr. Storch pinged his xylophone. Out on Summit, a truck crunched its gears. High in the purple sky, a small propeller plane throbbed. Far away, a police siren howled. The sounds mixed gently.

"Take a look around," Nicky said. "Don't worry, there's a wall. I told you, you can't fall off."

The rooftop itself was an alien landscape. An apartment building shows its loose ends in the basement and on the roof. And up here there were odd brick walls; chunky, chimney-like outcroppings; pipes out of nowhere; a rat's nest of spindly television antennae; swirling, globe-shaped vents; rows of clotheslines, empty tonight except for a wide girdle dancing in the wind.

Lester walked the edge, riding his hand along the top of the wall. The sunset conspired to impress Nicky's guest, splashing orange and red behind the hulk of the aspirin factory. The streetlamps came on and traced dotted lines along Summit.

On the Summit side of Eggplant Alley were small homes with teeny yards. Nicky and Lester looked down on the black rooftops. They could make out the dark greenery and elaborately angled rooftop of the big Victorian house on Mayflower Avenue, known as the Only House With Trees. A touch of pink and lime green sputtered from Broadway—the neon sign of Rosner's appliance store. Neon was ugly close up, but as exciting as Christmas lights when viewed from far away. Nicky pointed out the wide towers of the new apartment buildings over by the parkway, windows lighted in a checkerboard pattern.

"Look there," Nicky said. He nodded to a string of bluish white pearls, far off and hazy. "No—there. The George Washington Bridge."

"Holy smokes," Lester said. "Wow. I guess I see what you mean about this place. Do you come up here a lot?"

"All the time," Nicky said, lying.

Nicky had not visited the roof for years. Roy took him to the roof often in the good old days, and it was always a special treat. It was a place without adult supervision, perfect for big-brother mischief. On the rooftop, Roy would smoke cigarettes; drop marbles into the air vents; toss water balloons at cars on Groton; ignite rotten-egg stink bombs under the drying laundry. Nicky viewed the naughtiness with horror and glee and in total awe of Roy.

On the roof Roy dispensed fabulous tales and forbidden facts, a big-brother specialty. No adults eavesdropped and censored, so Nicky learned about the not-shy stewardess across the courtyard; about Mrs. Binzetti's three previous husbands; about the mind-boggling uses of the X-Ray Specs.

"I really ought to come up here more often," Nicky said.

Lester checked his watch. Nicky took note that it was a Mickey Mouse watch, a very cool accessory that spring, way too cool for a kid with thick nerd glasses. Nicky thought, "Maybe looks can be deceiving."

Lester said, "I have to go."

"Okay." Nicky was disappointed, dreading the apartment without Checkers but with plenty of memories of Checkers.

Lester said, "Is that the door to the stairs?"

"The gray one."

Lester walked, shoes scraping the roof tar, and tugged on the door.

"Those shoes," Nicky said. "No offense, but they've gotta go."

"Go?"

"Yeah. When they click. That will make it easier for muggers to stalk you."

"Oh," Lester said, examining the shoes. "I guess I have a lot to learn about city life."

Nicky said, "Hey. If you want, I could meet you up here Monday after school. I could fill you in on the ropes. On the neighborhood and stuff. There's a lot you oughta know."

"I'll ask my mama. But I'm sure it will be all right. She wants me to make friends."

"Yeah, I can fill you in at least," Nicky said, shrugging.

After three tugs, Lester yanked the door open and picked his way down the steps. His clicking shoes slowly faded down the stairwell.

Nicky planned to stay on the roof by himself for another hour or so. He had forgotten how much he loved the roof. But it was no good. He left after five minutes. Nicky discovered he did not want to be up there alone, after all.

13 The Second Thing That Ruined Nicky's Childhood

Nicky could not stay asleep. It was after midnight, and he wondered if this was the night when he finally stayed awake all the way till dawn.

Roy's bed, empty and smooth, the bedspread chalky white, pulled at Nicky's eyes. Nicky stared until his eyeballs hurt. And Roy appeared in the dim light. On his back, hands behind his head, staring at the ceiling. His old lecturing position, from which he explained about the giant alligators living in the sewer system; why you never loan your baseball mitt to anyone; the secret ingredient in Coney Island hot dogs; and much more inside information about the world and life.

Nicky stared back at the ceiling. So many questions. Was that a long-dead bug on the ceiling or a new, live bug? What about this Lester? Now, past midnight, Nicky was sorry he talked to the kid, gone to the roof with the kid, arranged another meeting with the kid. Nicky knew what would happen, sooner or later. Nicky knew that Lester would disappear, just like Andrea Abbananzo, Bobby What's-his-name, Checkers. And here in the dark, he had to admit this to himself: He was sure Lester would disappear, just like the only real friend Nicky ever had. He was sure Lester would disappear just like Roy.

In the good old days, Nicky tagged along after Roy all the time, everywhere. When Dad took the boys to Cherry Street for crew cuts, they would push through the door, and Barella the Barber would look up from snipping and say, "Hey, here comes Roy Martini and his shadow."

Roy was Nicky's pal, his buddy, his chum. Until the Great Blackout of 1965. The night that changed everything, for the worse.

That autumn, Roy steadily built a vendetta against Popop, the nasty old man who ran the dirty, cramped variety store six blocks from Eggplant Alley. Popop was a caricature of the mean candy store owner—every New York neighborhood seemed to have one. Popop was from somewhere in Eastern Europe. He was short and wide, with a head shaped like an Idaho potato. His eyes were cold, blue, and mean. "Like a sniper's eyes," Roy said.

Popop assumed that every customer was a shoplifter, or at least a thief at heart. This led to an incident that stirred the boiling bad blood between Roy and Popop.

One day Nicky tagged along with Roy to the store. Nicky was on a mission to buy a set of wax lips for Halloween. He thought wax lips were the funniest gag he had ever seen. That day in school, all Nicky could think about was wax lips. So Roy flipped through the comic books, which always enraged Popop, while Nicky picked through the wax lips, searching for the perfect pair. Nicky's right hand was buried in his pocket. To Popop's prison guard mind, the hand in the pocket was sinister. Popop hustled around the cash register and snared Nicky's right arm. Popop shook Nicky and dug his pudgy fingers into Nicky's pockets.

"You are stealing, I know you are doing," Popop said.

Roy was not afraid of Popop, or anything else. (Nicky thought so, in those days at least.) Roy pushed himself between Popop and little Nicky. Roy put a finger close to Popop's crooked nose and growled breathlessly, "If you EVER lay a hand on my little brother again, I will KILL you. You got that? You lousy fink. You got that?"

"Pretty smart mouth you are having there," Popop said, tilting back the potato head.

Nicky howled and clutched Roy by the arm. Nicky tugged his big brother toward the door.

"I'm going because HE wants me to," Roy shouted, voice straining, pointing down to Nicky's head. "Not because YOU want me to, got it?"

"You better be beating it out of here before I teach you some lesson you are never forgetting."

"I'll be back," Roy said. "You can count on it, you old fink. You crumb. I'll be back."

It took Roy ten whole days to come back. Revenge required careful planning, down to the last detail, from devising the perfect alibi to choosing the right weapon.

On the afternoon before the big night of vengeance, Roy showed Nicky a lumpy handkerchief under his mattress.

"If you don't want Mom to find something, hide it under your mattress," Roy advised. "She would never think to look there."

Roy placed the bundle on his bed, and with one eye on the doorway he slowly unfolded the handkerchief. Inside the handkerchief was a slingshot. Not the toyish kind of slingshot favored by Dennis the Menace and other lovable scamps. This was an aluminum killer, featuring industrial strength, yellow rubber tubing, and a leather ammo pouch. If the Marine Corps issued slingshots, this would be the model.

"Isn't it a beauty?" Roy said. "I borrowed it from Mumbles. I'll bet you could stop a Buick with this beauty."

"We're going to shoot a Buick?"

"Numbskull. We're going to punish Popop." He reached under the mattress and produced a jangling Band-Aid box. Roy opened the box and let Nicky see the colorful array of marbles.

Just before supper, Roy gave Mom the cover story, the one he had dreamed up during history class.

"Ma, we gotta go to the store."

"What for at this hour?"

"Glue."

"We have glue."

"Special glue."

Nicky and Roy hurried down Summit in the gathering autumn night. The streetlamps were coming on. House windows glowed warmly orange. They walked briskly, two boys on a righteous mission. Nicky could see Roy's breath in the cooling night air as he spelled out the big plan.

"We're going to hit the old buzzard's neon sign," Roy said. "Stupid sign. Know how it says POPOP's, right? I'm going to punch out that middle P. The old buzzard's sign, it'll say P-O space O-P'S. Get it? POOP'S! Ha ha ha ha. Am I a genius or what?"

Nicky felt queasy. He wished he were behind one of those orange windows, sitting down to a comforting plate of piping-hot meat loaf. He didn't like this caper. Nicky imagined the reform schools were crammed with kids who lied to their parents and went out at night and broke things with slingshots.

Nicky and Roy walked on, sneakers flapping on the sidewalk. They crossed Summit and started down Radford Street, a crummy stretch of cracked sidewalks, empty lots, and row after row of four-story tenements. One of the many neighborhoods going bad. Nicky had never walked along Radford at night. He felt as if he were strolling into a dark forest.

The red neon sign of Popop's variety came into view, and Roy nudged Nicky across the street into Ludlow Park, a weedy patch of broken benches and piles of litter. Roy grabbed Nicky by the sleeve and led him into the tall bushes that bordered the park. They moved along, branches brushing their faces and jackets, bottles clinking at their feet, until they were positioned directly across from Popop's.

Popop's neon sign hummed. Behind the dirty front window of the store, a smaller neon sign burned green, advertising Ballantine beer. A dim light shone inside the store, and a potato head moved back and forth in front of the light.

Roy coolly, quickly, methodically got down to business. He locked his wrist into the slingshot. He selected a marble from the Band-Aid box. He pulled back on the tubing. Nicky eyed the taut, quivery rubber and got goose bumps from the sight of such deliciously pent-up destructive power.

Roy let go. The slingshot made a snapping sound.

There was silence.

Then a sharp knock—the sound of a marble striking wood, like a baseball hitting a bat.

"Shucks," Roy said.

Roy loaded. He aimed.

He fired.

Nicky saw the marble blur into the darkness.

There was a whining sound—the sound of a marble ricocheting against concrete.

Followed by a click—a marble skipping along asphalt.

Then from far down the block came a clank—the marble against automobile hubcap.

"Darn," Roy muttered.

Roy reloaded. He aimed.

He fired.

The marble flashed against the red neon and this time Nicky knew for sure, he could feel in his belly . . .

The first P in Popop's sign disintegrated in a shower of delicate glass. The P fizzled as the glass tinkled gently to the sidewalk.

And the second P sputtered electrically and went dark.

For a second, the sign flashed:

O OP'S.

Then the entire sign went dark.

And the Ballantine sign went dark.

The lamp in the window went dark.

The lights of the apartment towers went dark.

The red light atop the water tower went dark.

The halo glow from Broadway went dark.

Two cars careened through the intersection at the end of the block, horns shrieking. The traffic light was dark.

Nicky and Roy swiveled their heads. There wasn't a light burning anywhere. Somehow, Roy had turned off every light in the Bronx.

Windows scraped open. Voices called in the darkness.

"Hey, anybody got power?"

"Who turned off the lights?"

"I think the whole block is out."

Nicky clutched Roy's sleeve. He feared he would lose his big brother in the blackness.

"Take it easy, numbskull," Roy said. "The lights will come back on in a minute."

They waited in the bushes. They waited a minute.

They waited ten minutes. The lights did not come back on.

"Oops," Roy said.

Nicky and Roy ran home. They barely recognized Eggplant Alley. The buildings appeared dead, like three giant burned-out lightbulbs.

Nicky clasped Roy's jacket as they climbed the dark stairway in Building B. On the second floor, Mr. Bartolo stood outside his apartment. He swung a camping lantern. Mr. Bartolo was a former marine, always well prepared for emergencies. A transistor radio was going inside his apartment.

"Mr. Bartolo, are the lights out all over New York?" Roy said.

"The radio said the lights are out all up and down the eastern seaboard. From Washington, DC, to Canada."

"That's quite extensive," Roy said casually.

"I wanna go home," Nicky said.

Mom was waiting for them at the doorway of 5-C. She had jammed a fistful of birthday candles into the supper meat loaf. She held the flickering, glowing slab of meat shoulder-high, like a torch. Mom looked like the Statue of Liberty, if the Statue of Liberty moonlighted as a waitress. For the rest of his life, Nicky could not see meat loaf without remembering this sight.

The Martinis passed the night of the Great Blackout around the transistor radio. They ate cornflakes and Yum-E-Cakes by candlelight. They played poker. The radio batteries ran down. The last snatches of news they heard reported that the blackout was the largest in history, and the cause was unknown, and the FBI was on the case to investigate reports of sabotage.

Nicky and Roy lay in bed in the darkest, quietest night in the history of Eggplant Alley.

Nicky whispered, "Roy, maybe we ought to go on the lam."

"Don't be a numbskull. We don't know for sure if we did this. Besides, nobody's got proof."

"I think we ought to tell Mom and Dad."

Bedsprings cheeped with startling shrillness and suddenly Roy's face was inches from Nicky's nose, close enough for Nicky to smell mint toothpaste on his big brother's breath.

"Not a word of this, to anyone," Roy said. "You and me are in this together. This is real trouble."

Roy sat on Nicky's bed. Roy slipped his hands under his pajama collar and lifted his silver chain and St. Christopher medallion over his head. He felt for Nicky's hand in the dark, and let the chain slither into Nicky's palm.

"I haven't taken this off since I made First Communion," Roy said.

"I know." Nicky said. He could not remember his brother without the silver chain.

"I'm giving it to you. It's a symbol of our loyalty, courage, and all that junk. It's you and me, for good. We're a team. Like Roosevelt and Churchill, Abbott and Costello. Like Sacco and Vanzetti."

Nicky slipped the chain over his head and tucked the medallion inside his pajama top. The metal felt cold against his chest.

Long after midnight, Nicky was awakened by a bright light shining directly into his eyes.

FBI agents with flashlights!

Coming to take him to reform school!

"It was ROY!" Nicky mumbled, and then he realized the light in his face was the bulb from the dresser lamp. The lamp was switched on when the lights went out. The power was back.

The kitchen radio was going at breakfast. The latest news report said Governor Rockefeller thought the blackout was "unbelievable," and that President Johnson thought it was "an outrage with grave implications." The cause was still under investigation.

The news announcer added, in a solemn tone that Nicky considered ominous, "Nothing has been ruled out."

Nicky pushed away his Cocoa Puffs.

Late that afternoon, Nicky moped into the kitchen. Mom looked up grimly from the potatoes she was mashing.

"What's wrong?" Nicky cried. "Why are you looking at me?"

"Nothing is wrong," Mom said. "Why so nervous?"

"I am not nervous," Nicky said, nervously.

Mom shook her head sadly.

"What is it?" Nicky said, jumping.

Mom said, "I was just on the phone with Mrs. Moscowitz and she told me some very disturbing news."

"She saw us?"

"She said that when the power went back on, the elevator started up and went down to the lobby. You know, I don't think I should tell you this. Never mind."

"What? What? What?"

Roy strolled into the kitchen and said, "The doors opened in the lobby and out plopped Mr. Van Der Woort."

"So?" Nicky said.

Roy said, "He was stiff as a board."

"Roy!" Mom barked, shaking the wooden spoon, flipping bits of mashed potato onto the floor. "Show some respect."

"Colder than a mackerel," Roy said, leaving the room.

On Saturday morning, Nicky sat on the rug in front of the television and stared at Bugs Bunny cartoons. Mom stood three feet away, ironing. Dad and Roy were down on Cherry Street, buying lard bread.

Nicky had the creepy sensation he was being watched. He glanced up. Mom was watching him.

Mom ironed and stared. Nicky blinked at Mom. He was nervous. He knew the woman had radar.

Mom said, "It's written all over your face, you know." And

Nicky cracked, right there on the living room rug, as the television showed Bugs blowing up Daffy Duck.

Nicky cried. He spilled his guts. He sang like a canary. He told Mom everything.

In the fiery aftermath, while Dad foamed and Mom lectured, Roy shot a look at Nicky and said, "I am through with you."

The next time Nicky walked into Popop's, Popop called him "the little anarchist" and asked, "Where is your brother the big Bolshevik?"

Nicky could only shrug.

Roy was many places, but no longer at Nicky's side.

No longer on Nicky's side.

No matter what Mom threatened, Roy refused to talk to Nicky. He refused to watch television with Nicky. He refused to pass the peas to Nicky. He refused to buy a Christmas present for Nicky. He refused to apologize when he stepped on and crushed Nicky's brand-new Gemini space capsule.

On New Year's Day, Nicky found Roy at the kitchen table. Roy was drinking hot chocolate topped with whipped cream and reading a comic book.

Nicky sat at the table with Roy.

Roy looked up. Nicky smiled.

Roy grabbed his mug by the handle, closed his comic book, pushed back his chair, and strolled out of the kitchen.

Nicky placed his face onto the tabletop. He pressed his cheek to the warm circle left by Roy's mug.

"Hey."

Roy was calling from the doorway. In the seconds it took his big brother to pad across the linoleum, Nicky's mind eagerly worked. Maybe Roy was going to shake his hand. Let bygones be bygones. Whip up a hot chocolate. Tell a naughty joke he heard in high school. Nicky longed for the day when the big boys finally let him hear the naughty jokes.

"The medal," Roy said flatly. "Gimme back my medal."

Roy walked out of the room, St. Christopher medal in his fist, and Nicky thought about a day at the beach years earlier. Nicky was about three. He was left on the beach blanket under the charge of Grandma Martini. One of the Scalopini cousins had borrowed his favorite beach pail, his beloved Mr. Peanut beach pail, and left it at the water's edge. Nicky was too scared of the sand and ocean to retrieve the pail. He sat under the umbrella on the blanket and watched the waves roll in. The waves lifted his pail and carried it toward Europe. Grandma Martini refused to leave Nicky to get it. She waved a hand and said, "Don't worry, Nicola. One thing leads to another. It come back sooner or later."

Nicky remembered the total heartbreak of watching Mr. Peanut's dimpled face drift away, receding to a colorful speck on the gray waves, leaving him forever. Because he had the same feeling when Roy, his big brother and only friend, grasped the St. Christopher medal and walked away from the table, out of the kitchen.

Nicky listed this, in the black composition notebook under his mattress, as the second thing that ruined his childhood. In the night, he remembered this and fell asleep reminding himself to not make friends with this goofy Lester Allnuts. Dogs just die, friends just disappear.

14

The Ropes

Nicky rapped softly on the door to 2-C. He was passing by the apartment on his way home from school. He figured he might as well stop by and ask Lester about going to the roof. Not that Nicky cared one way or the other. He merely wanted to map out his afternoon. Set the agenda for this bright Monday. If Lester wasn't going with him to the roof, Nicky planned to brush up on his yo-yo skills.

Lester opened the door, eyes bugging out happily behind his thick glasses.

"Roof today?" Nicky said, motioning toward the ceiling with his thumb.

"Yes, my mama gave me permission. I'm looking forward to it." Lester stepped back from the doorway. "Would you like to come in?"

"Nah, thanks." Nicky hefted his book bag. "I gotta get home. See you up there at four?"

"Yes. You can teach me the city ropes."

Nicky reclined in the sun on the warm roof tar. Lester pushed through the gray door at four o'clock sharp, just as the bells of St. Peter's clonged over on Ludlow Street.

"Take a load off," Nicky said, indicating a place near him on the tar.

Lester examined the gritty tar and sat.

"All right," Nicky said. He took a deep breath. "Here's what you have to know about Eggplant Alley."

"I have a question," Lester said, raising his hand.

"Already?"

"Yes. Why is it called Eggplant Alley?"

Nicky scratched the side of his face.

"I dunno," he said. "Doesn't matter. Now, do you wanna hear what I have to say or not?"

"Surely."

"Okay," Nicky said. He took a deep breath. "First thing to know, if a ball goes in the sewer, don't stick your hand in after it."

"Okay."

"Because there are alligators living in the sewer system. They'll chomp off your hand. People bring baby alligators as souvenirs from Florida. The 'gators start growing. People flush them down the toilet. They live off sewage and grow to be like six hundred pounds."

"Very interesting," Lester said.

Nicky continued, "Okay. Now. Did I tell you about never letting anyone into your apartment? Not even if they have some sob story about needing to use the phone."

"Very interesting. Got it."

"All right. If you see the Moon Man down on Broadway, do NOT make eye contact. He's the guy who bangs on a coffee can. If he sees you look at him, he'll pick up his coffee can and follow you for blocks. Banging and yelling."

"Yelling what exactly?"

"Gibberish."

"Very interesting."

"Somebody keeps going to the bathroom in the elevator. It stinks. So a lot of the time, you gotta take the stairs."

"Very interesting."

"Except sometimes it isn't safe to take the stairs. If somebody unscrews the lightbulb, the stairwells are dark. You'd never see somebody lurking."

"Lurking. Very interesting."

"If you come home and find a burglar in your apartment, run out the door."

"Run where?"

"Go bang on somebody's door and have them call the cops. Not that the cops will come before next Christmas."

"Very interesting."

"Except you can't go around banging on doors here because you don't know what kind of people are moving in. You might bang on a door and get a machete stuck in your belly."

"I have a question," Lester said, raising his hand.

"What?"

"Is there anything good you can tell me about living around here?"

Nicky thought for a few seconds. "Nope."

Lester grimaced. "Very interesting," he said. "Very unfortunate."

Nicky shrugged. "That's just the way the ball bounces. Nobody wants to live here anymore. You should have seen this place in the good old days."

Lester said, "I was hoping for a better outlook. We were thinking of relocating here permanently. When my daddy returns. He said the city might be a more suitable place for us. He said we might stay here. From what you tell me, I don't know how that will happen. I don't think Daddy will like this. Daddy will probably pack us off back to Bradleyville."

"When is your dad coming back?"

"Next April."

"April? Wow. April? Where is he again?"

"Traveling. On business."

Nicky whistled. "April."

"Yes. Well, maybe the situation around here will improve by then."

Nicky said, "I wouldn't hold my breath."

The sound of a basketball thumping came up from the PS 19 schoolyard. A chain net jangled, boys shouted. Lester stood and walked to the wall and poked his head over the edge.

"I see basketball is popular around here," Lester said. A breeze mussed his wiry hair.

"Among some people."

Lester sighed into the wind.

"I fear a long boring summer is ahead. No wonder people in the city are so grouchy."

Nicky stood and joined Lester at the wall.

"Who's grouchy?" Nicky said. "We have our fun, you know. What do you folks do for kicks in the country? Chase chickens?"

"Not usually," Lester said. "We have all varieties of outdoor activity. We hunt frogs. I had a hammock. There is the tree house.

Swimming at Hadley Pond. Fishing for snappies over in Dorn Creek."

"Golly gee whiz," Nicky said with a smirk. "I don't think my heart could take that much excitement."

Lester shrugged. "I guess it's not that exciting. Mostly, once school is out, we played baseball. That's the thing to do, where I come from."

Nicky didn't say anything.

Lester sighed.

"I guess I have been running off at the mouth."

Nicky shrugged.

Lester said, "Is there any baseball playing around here?"

"Not really."

"Too bad," Lester said. He sighed again. "Those games in the meadow. You don't know what you're missing."

Nicky imagined the baseball games in the country meadow. He often daydreamed of playing real baseball, on emerald grass and red clay. Nicky wondered what life was like for a country kid. Ball games in the shadow of a picturesque barn. Off to the swimming hole for a dip. Onto the porch swing in the night air, soft as a newborn kitten, while Grandma squeezed lemonade and Ma and Sis baked berry pies. Quiet. Peaceful. Heaven on earth.

But he said to Lester, "Baseball in a meadow? Sheesh. You can have it. Who needs to play ball in a bunch of cow poop? Hick stuff. Now, around here, we had a game. We used to play it from morning till supper, right down there. Stickball. Now, there was a game."

"I guess I don't know it."

"I guess you wouldn't. It's just like baseball, except with a broomstick for a bat. The ball—a Spaldeen. That's a pink rubber ball. Ever see one? I guess not. You can get them at the five-and-dime."

"Very interesting. Where did you play? Down where?"

Nicky said, "There. On the schoolyard. You can still see the white lines. See them?" He continued in poetic tones, "Stickball was the best thing about summer around here. End of discussion. It was better than lemon ices from Lombardo's. Better than falling asleep listening to the electric fans around the courtyard in the summer. Better than Jones Beach and the Good Humor man."

"Very interesting." Lester adjusted his black-rimmed glasses on his nose and said, "Sounds like something I'd like to take a crack at."

Nicky chuckled. "Sure. Except nobody plays stickball around here anymore."

"No?"

"Nope."

"Why not?"

"You'd know if you grew up around here."

"Very interesting. But I have to tell you, there is no sense to what you say. If stickball was so terrifically great, stickball should be played."

Nicky stared down at the PS 19 playground. He was surprised the old painted baselines were still there.

Lester said, "Come summertime, I'm going to miss those baseball games in the Simmons meadow. It was the first thing I thought of when Mama and Daddy told me we were moving down here."

Nicky said quietly, "I never stopped missing those stickball games. It ruined the whole neighborhood when stickball stopped. It was the final nail in the coffin for this neighborhood. The last straw for Eggplant Alley. It's a very interesting story. Know what's funny? That day was a long time ago. Four whole years. I can remember everything, how everything looked, what everybody said."

Lester said, "Look at all those pigeons on the roof there. I've never seen so many pigeons. Are city pigeons dangerous?"

Nicky said, "You asked why nobody plays stickball around here anymore. Do you want to hear the story or not?"

"I'm all ears," Lester said, taking a seat on the roof tar. "It's good for me to be versed on local lore."

15

The Third Thing That Ruined Nicky's Childhood

So Nicky told his story.

Everything good was in place that April morning, four whole years earlier. Birds cheeped crazily in the shadows of PS 19. The sun glinted off the windows of Eggplant Alley. Bases and foul lines were freshly painted onto the asphalt. The strike zone was freshly painted onto the brick wall. Paulie Phillips had supplied the paint, which he found outside an apartment on the fourth floor. The painters inside the apartment were unaware of the donation.

For Nicky, at age nine years, it was a historic morning. A change was riding on the spring breeze.

A change for the better.

This stickball season, for the first time, Roy said Nicky could tag along as batboy. Nicky was welcomed to join the fun on the PS 19 playground. Mom was probably behind this concession, likely forced out of Roy under threat from a wooden mixing spoon. Nicky didn't know, and he didn't care, because he felt a lightness in the chest. No question about it. The evil gloom between him and his brother, in place since the Great Blackout, was finally fading. The dark cloud was lifting, lifting.

Nicky walked in the sun and was totally thrilled to be out of the kitchen window and onto the schoolyard. Now he would be one of the gang. It was a miracle. Roy promised Nicky could serve as batboy for the entire summer. Nicky was moving up in the world, stepping out with the big boys. He wondered if some little kid was watching wide-eyed from a kitchen window in Eggplant Alley. He hoped so.

A full roster of Roy's friends was on the concrete diamond. The boys wore T-shirts and dungarees with rolled cuffs. They all had crew cuts. (Within a year, only the geekiest of geeks would be caught dead with a crew cut.) They pushed and shoved and teased. They were full of excitement, too. Who wouldn't be?

Nicky sniffed the air, which smelled clean, like freshly washed bedsheets. Nicky watched Roy mix with his pals. Roy said, "Numbskull here will be our bat boy. My mother is making me. Don't worry, he'll stay outta the way."

Life was changing for the better, with one thing leading to another. Nicky looked forward to stickball with Roy, which would lead to Monopoly with Roy, which would lead to tossing water balloons off the roof with Roy, which would lead to getting the sacred medal back from Roy. Nicky was thinking this when the skinny black kid showed up.

This kid had his hands jammed into his pant pockets as he strolled across the asphalt, straight into the huddle of Roy's friends. He walked up like he was a lifelong chum, just one of the old gang. This black kid said, "Looks like you could use another."

Roy and his friends blinked at one another, shrugged, and exchanged glances that said, "Beats me." No one knew what to say. This was a shocking development. It was an unwritten rule. The white kids of Eggplant Alley and the black kids of Groton Avenue did not mix.

Lester interrupted the story. "Very interesting. Why didn't we mix in those days?"

"We still don't mix. I already told you. That's not the way it works around here."

"How come?"

Nicky sighed and said, "Are there any black folks where you come from?"

Lester studied the roof tar. He said, "Not too many."

"Then you don't know about it. It's like cats and dogs. Cats don't play with dogs. Why? I dunno. They just don't."

Nicky went on with the stickball story.

Mikey Loughran spoke up first. He asked the skinny black boy, "What's your name?"

The skinny black boy said, "Jackie."

Mikey Loughran didn't see Icky's angry glare, and continued "Are you from around here?"

Jackie said, "Yeah, sure. Right over there. Second from the end. Number Ten." He pointed to a yellow brick building across Groton Avenue. The building had saggy wooden front steps. A window on the second floor was cracked and repaired with a length of black tape.

Icky snorted, "What a dump."

Jackie made a face and said, "Yeah, well, it's home." He rubbed his hands together and said, "Okay, whaddya say, sports fans? Let's play."

Icky said solemnly, "Geez, you know what? We don't need no more players. Too bad. Maybe some other time."

Jackie lifted his chin and moved his lips as he tallied up the players. "Sure you need players. Come on, man. I can PITCH. Let me see the ball."

Mikey Loughran numbly handed over the ball.

"Loughran, what are you doing?" Icky snapped.

Jackie windmilled his arm and pretended to throw. "I got a heat ball you won't even see. It's got wings."

Icky said, "Wings? That's nice. But you know what? We got plenty pitchers. We got pitchers coming out our ears."

Jackie rolled the ball in his hand. He bounced it on the asphalt a couple of times. He flexed his wrist—the curveball motion. He looked fresh, young, and happy as he handled the Spaldeen. Jackie itched to play. You could see it in his eyes. He couldn't resist the spring warmth, the watercolor blue sky, the excitement of the freshly painted white lines. When Jackie set foot onto his wobbly steps and saw the white kids gather across the street with gloves and sticks and balls, he probably had no choice. He was lured off the steps to the schoolyard, like a thirsty man to a water fountain. He was just like the boys from Eggplant Alley.

"I'll strike you all out, one at a time. My pitches have wings."

Icky said, "Maybe. But not today."

Jackie took a step toward the mound and said, "Batter up, sports fans. I'm pitching."

Icky's face shaded pink and his red crew cut seemed to bend

forward, like the hair on a dog's back. Icky inhaled deeply, signaling that enough was enough.

"Now, hear this. I already told you, we don't need no players. We . . . don't . . . need . . . no . . . players."

No one said anything. Icky went on, "So go play your games and let us play ours."

Jackie said, "But . . ."

"We don't need players."

"But . . ."

"We don't need players."

"But . . ."

"We don't need players. I don't want to have to tell you again. What can't you unnerstand? Jesus Christmas, you people really are stupid."

Jackie stopped bouncing the ball. He squeezed the Spaldeen in his hand.

"What was that?"

"You heard me. Get the wax out of your ears."

"Man, what is your problem?"

"I ain't got a problem. And don't you look at me that way. You wanna start something with me?"

"I ain't looking for a fight."

Icky pushed Jackie's shoulder and said, "Well, maybe you found one."

Jackie stepped back and said with disgust, "I ain't trying to start nothing."

Icky said, "Who do you think you're starting with? I guess you want to start something with me."

Jackie looked into the white faces. The white faces stared backed with expressions that said, "What did you expect?" And Jackie gave up. He seemed to fold. He examined the ground. He studied his sneakers.

Icky maintained his fighting stance, hands clenched, feet planted, body coiled. Icky's eyes were blinking fast. He wrinkled his nose and said, "If you wanna start with me, let's get started. Otherwise—take a powder."

Jackie flipped the ball to Mikey Loughran. Jackie blew air out through his lips.

"Cool your jets, sports fan. I'm going. I don't need your stupid damn game."

Jackie jammed his hands in his pockets and strolled away casually, as if he would simply move on to something else on that sweet April morning. He bobbed out through the playground gate and onto Groton. There was a loud, metallic twang. The sound of a fist banging against a NO PARKING sign.

"Listen to him, breaking things, as usual," Icky said.

Mikey mumbled, "Maybe we shoulda just let him play."

"Yuh," Icky snapped. "And maybe we oughta let him take your sister to the prom."

"Drop dead," Mikey said.

"Maybe you want the beating?" Icky said.

Roy said, "Cut it out. We wasted enough time. Let's get started."

They played, and Icky must have been dying to hit something, because he walloped the first pitch as hard as anyone can hit a Spaldeen. He swung and grunted, "HA!" The ball sailed high over the chain-link fence. It became a pink speck in the blue sky. It looked like something hit by Mickey Mantle.

The ball dropped into the middle of Groton Avenue. It bounced once, high enough to be seen from the schoolyard, then squirreled away on the other side of the street.

Icky started his home run trot and snapped, "Go get it, batboy."

"Get what?" Nicky said.

"The ball, brainless. That's what bat boys do. Hurry. We only got two."

"I dunno where it went," Nicky said with a shrug.

"LOOK for it."

From center field, Roy shouted, "Hey, numbskull. Get the ball before it goes down the sewer."

Nicky looked both ways and scampered across Groton. He looked up at the tenements. Nicky's eyes were drawn to the dusty windows. He imagined black faces watching, stalking, ready to pounce on him, a helpless white morsel. The sweet sounds of the stickball game seemed far off, miles away, in another land.

"Whatcha looking for?" a voice said close behind him. Nicky jumped as if an ice cube had dribbled down his shirt.

It was Jackie. The kid who wanted to play stickball. The kid that Icky had shoved and pushed and humiliated. Now it was just Jackie and Nicky, alone on the sidewalk. Jackie stood between Nicky and the street. He had Nicky blocked.

"Well, hello there!" Nicky chirped, as if seeing a long-lost pal.

"Looking for this?" Jackie said, not at all chirpy. He showed the ball.

Nicky said, "Hey! Great!" He reached for the ball.

Jackie stashed the ball behind his back. "Not so fast, sports fan," he said. "Now it's mine. Finders keepers, losers weepers."

Jackie had Nicky there. As far as Nicky was concerned, that was that. Case closed. He turned and started to walk away.

Jackie pulled him back by his sleeve.

"Whoa. Hold on. Don't you want the ball?"

Nicky once watched a cat toy with a cockroach in the bread aisle at Popop's variety. The cockroach ran. The cat calmly reached out a claw and dragged back the jittering bug. The cockroach skittered away. The cat scraped him back. Now Nicky knew what it was like to be the cockroach.

"You want it, it'll cost you a nickel."

"I ain't got a nickel," Nicky said.

"Then you ain't got a ball."

Nicky shrugged. Case closed again.

Nicky took a step. Jackie reached for his sleeve.

Nicky darted past him, toward the street.

Jackie barked, "Don't run." His fingers fluttered off Nicky's shirt.

Nicky leapt off the curb, and felt his stomach rocket into his throat as his right foot plunged between the grates of the sewer. He heard a crack like a broomstick snapping, and the roadway flew up and smacked him in the face and he felt sick in his stomach.

Roy, Icky, and the rest of the gang swarmed out the playground and around the parked cars on the other side of the street. Here is what they saw:

1. Nicky wailing in the gutter, his right foot flopped at a new angle, blood making a spiderweb pattern down his face. The dripping blood showed brilliantly on his white T-shirt.
2. Jackie standing over Nicky's bloody body, tugging on Nicky's stretched-out shirt collar.

Maybe Jackie was trying to help Nicky up, maybe he wasn't. No one would never know.

Nicky felt Jackie release his grip. He heard huffs, puffs, and curses. A herd of sneakers slapped on the sidewalk. Nicky saw a redheaded blur—Icky leading the chase down Groton.

And one thing led to another.

Nicky got the story later. Icky and the gang caught up with Jackie three blocks over on Poplar Street. Jackie clung to the post of a parking meter while Icky, Skipper, and Rocco Doyle kicked him, punched him, and pulled on his legs. Icky and the gang stretched Jackie like a Gumby doll.

Three black kids from Groton Avenue happened to be walking by. Two of them pushed and swung on Skipper and Rocco. The third found a garbage can lid and clanged Icky on the head.

Two police cars rolled up, red lights rotating, and the four cops broke it up. The police pushed the white brawlers in one direction. They shoved the black brawlers in another direction. The cops shouted and held their nightsticks in the air and told everyone to beat it, get lost, scram before they pinched the lot of them.

Nicky spent the summer with a broken ankle encased in a sweaty, itchy, smelly cast. The residents of Eggplant Alley saw him hobbling through the courtyard with the cast and shook their heads. What was the neighborhood coming to?

And one thing led to another. A permanent gloom settled over the neighborhood. Fun, play, lightness, and joy were replaced by tension, suspicion, fear, and anger.

The battle lines were drawn. Us against Them.

Mr. Cabrini from the first floor was pushed to the pavement late one July night. Mr. Cabrini did not see his assailants, but there was no doubt who did it.

Them.

On a sweltering August day, the black kids from Groton Avenue opened up the hydrant and danced under the cool spout of water. The police came and shut down the hydrant and there was no doubt who had phoned the cops.

Us.

Dad began to carry a baseball bat when he walked Checkers at night.

Because of Them.

On Labor Day, five cars parked in front of the tenements had their tires slashed. The black people who owned the cars stood on the sidewalk near the tattered tires and squinted at Eggplant Alley.

Angry at Us.

The great exodus picked up steam. A cloud of panic set into Eggplant Alley. No one wanted to live there anymore, just as nobody wanted to stay on the *Titanic* after the iceberg. That fall, the DiGiulios, the Sullivans, and the Cabrinis found new homes to the north.

"Last one out, turn off the lights," Roy said as the overloaded Sullivan station wagon rolled away down Groton.

One crispy Saturday afternoon in November, Dad and Mom took the Yum-E-Cakes van up to Westchester. They were on a scouting mission, to look at houses. For three sweet hours Nicky imagined clean safe streets and wide-open yards and tire swings and the Good Humor man and peaceful summer afternoons of stickball.

Mom and Dad returned at dusk, sweaty and tired. Dad said, "Those houses are just too much dough."

Mom said, "Maybe I should talk to Dominic about doing beadwork."

"We're not that desperate," Dad said.

Spring came around and the stickball diamond remained empty. Stickball was finished, once and for all. No one from Eggplant Alley dared to play on the PS 19 schoolyard again. There was no use trying. It was impossible. Stickball cannot be played while looking over your shoulder, while keeping an eye on front doors, while memorizing escape routes.

Roy's Spaldeen went into his glove and the glove went into the back of the closet. The sticks were rolled under a bed, and except for Roy's yellow favorite they were tossed out in a spring cleanup. The white lines faded in the sun, under the snow, and under the sun again, season after season after season.

"Very interesting," Lester said.

"The end of stickball was the last straw for Eggplant Alley," Nicky said. He did not mention this was third on the list, in the composition notebook, under his mattress.

Lester got up, stretched, and walked to the wall. He was deep in thought as he gazed out onto Groton Avenue.

"I have much to learn. So all the black people live over there?"

"Yeah, so stay away from there," said Nicky, standing. "Come here."

They walked to the Summit Avenue side of the roof, overlooking the small homes, tiny yards, and the swaying greenery of the Only House With Trees.

Nicky said, "And all the white people live down there. The only thing standing between the coloreds on Groton Avenue and the whites on Summit is us—Eggplant Alley. Eggplant Alley is like the Alamo." On this very same patch of roof, Roy had explained these matters to Nicky. Still quoting Roy, he said, "We're the only thing that stands in their way. We're holding back the tide."

"Very interesting. No black people live in Eggplant Alley?"

"Noooooo," Nicky said. He chuckled. "That would be the end of us."

Lester returned to the side of the roof that overlooked PS 19, the playground, the tenements of Groton Avenue.

"Hey," Nicky said. "How come black kids can't play in the sandbox?"

"They can't?"

"Dummy, it's a joke. Black kids can't play in the sandbox because cats will come along and try to cover them up."

Lester didn't say anything.

"Get it? Because they look like turds."

"Okay," Lester said. Then, "We should do something about this."

"About what?"

"The decline of this neighborhood."

"Oh, sure," Nicky scoffed. Then, "What did you have in mind?"

"Bring back stickball. When we have time. Maybe when school is out."

Nicky said, "Nooooo."

"Yes. Why not?"

"Nah."

"Yes."

"I don't think so."

"I think so," said Lester.

"If you wanna. I really don't care," Nicky said, shrugging, caring.

16

Close, But No Cigar

"This is a really stupid idea," Nicky said, talking to himself as he rode the elevator down to the second floor. "Sure hope it works."

It was morning on the first day of summer vacation—a great moment in time, the farthest calendar point from the next day of school. Nicky carried Roy's Spaldeen, Roy's baseball mitt, and a roll of black electrical tape.

Lester answered the door. His eyes bugged out behind his glasses.

"I thought I was going to meet you downstairs," Lester said.

"So sue me. I thought I'd come by on my way down. You got the broomstick?"

Lester stepped barefoot out onto the hallway tile and closed the door to 2-C behind him. Nicky thought this was curious, this barefoot walk onto the filthy hallway tile.

"What are you doing? Where's the broomstick?" Nicky said. He took a step toward the closed door, reached toward the knob. "Come on. I'll show you how to tape the stick."

"I'll get the stick and meet you downstairs," Lester said.

"Let's go get it now. We can tape it in your apartment."

"We can't."

Lester paused. He said, "My mama isn't home. She says I'm not allowed to let anyone enter the apartment when she isn't home. Her rule. No exceptions."

Nicky shrugged. Mrs. Allnuts, new tenant from upstate, was scared spitless by the big, bad urban jungle. Nicky found this pleasing and said, "Have it your way."

Lester said, "I'll be down in a moment."

Then Lester did something else peculiar. He didn't move. He stood and watched Nicky walk toward the stairway. He acted like a cop who tells someone to move along, then stands and watches, to make sure the person actually moves along. Not until Nicky was out of sight, partway down the stairs, was there the sound of Lester's feet on the tile, and the door to 2-C opening and abruptly closing.

"I guess everybody in Eggplant Alley is out of their tree," Nicky said out loud, with a shrug.

Lester arrived in the lobby in no time. He held out a black broomstick, freshly sawed from the broom.

"Perfect," Nicky said.

"My mama cut it for me just now."

"You said your mom wasn't home."

"She just got home."

Nicky and Lester stepped out of the cool darkness of the lobby and into the warm sunshine of the courtyard. Spread along the stairs on Summit Avenue was a generous sample of the old gang: Icky, Fishbone, Mumbles, Little Sam, Skippy, and Skipper. Nicky had seen them from his window. He breathlessly telephoned Lester with the report, and told Lester they must hurry, because these older boys, these potential stickball players, might wander off.

Nicky and Lester arrived on the scene just in time. The older boys were still draped along the steps, but there were signs of flight. The older boys were restless. They were not the sunbathing type. They could not stay draped for long. They tossed pebbles. They smoked cigarettes. They stood up, sat down. They sighed. They swore. They belched. Skippy was telling a long story about a short skirt on a woman riding the No. 6 bus three days ago.

"I swear, she wasn't. I could see," Skippy said.

"Get out," Skipper said.

"I'm telling you, she wasn't."

As a way of joining the crowd and showing Lester his close association with the older boys, Nicky said, "She wasn't what?"

Skippy blew smoke rings and said, "Never you mind, kid. We'll tell you when you're older." And the older boys all laughed.

Nicky shrugged, and he and Lester sat on the stairs. They did this casually, as if the stairs merely happened to be the nearest place to plop down. Nicky placed the stick across his thighs and unraveled a length of electrical tape. He began to spiral the tape onto the stick.

"The tape is a grip, for when you swing the bat," Nicky said. "Otherwise the stick'll fly out of your hands and kill somebody."

Lester adjusted his glasses and watched closely. "Very interesting," he said. He didn't know this was Nicky's first attempt at taping a stickball bat. The job was a Roy specialty in the good old days.

"You're doing it all wrong," Fishbone called out.

Nicky looked up at Fishbone, who was perched on the stairs, knees wiggling with excess energy.

"Lemme see," Fishbone said. He arose and ambled over, weary and wise. He took charge of the stick and the tape, and went to work. He pushed his long black hair out of his eyes as he taped. It all came back to Fishbone. He taped the grip onto the stickball bat, in a perfect crisscross spiral pattern. A masterpiece.

"There," Fishbone said. He swung the bat. It made a satisfying whip sound.

"Hey," said Little Sam, who was busy tossing pebbles aimlessly. Little Sam tossed a pebble at Fishbone and Fishbone clocked it with the bat, producing a neat little line drive. The pebble plunked metallically off the roof of a parked Plymouth.

"Lemme see the ball," Little Sam said, and the forces of nature took over. The older boys were hypnotized. No one could resist. Not even these wise guy Bronx boys, world-weary, a year or two out of high school. Not even these self-proclaimed tough guys, too grown-up and too cool to dabble in childhood games—except this game. You never grow too old for stickball, not any more than you get too old for eating or sleeping or watching pretty girls ride the No. 6 bus.

The gang rose from the steps, a couple at a time, then all at once, like birds from a telephone wire. The boys drifted into the courtyard of Eggplant Alley. They were lured there.

Nicky and Lester followed the pack. Nicky gazed around the courtyard and wondered why they didn't play stickball here in the good old days. There was even a stretch of grass in the middle, long ago cleared of trees. Who needed a meadow?

Little shouts came up from the older boys. A game was forming. The signs were unmistakable, like the first twisty winds of a tornado. Little Sam tossed the ball and Fishbone took a swipe and missed and yelped again. The swing and miss made Fishbone crazily eager for a next swing. The other boys were waltzing onto the walkway and onto the grass, on the verge of choosing up sides.

Fishbone connected on a toss from Little Sam. The Spaldeen darted straight into the ground. Icky gathered up the ball and elbowed Little Sam out of the way.

"Lemme show you," Icky said. He reared back and threw.

Icky's drop pitch, rusty after all the years, didn't drop.

Fishbone connected, right on the button. The ball sailed and thumped on Building B, against a fourth-floor window.

"Get the ball. Get the ball," Icky said. "That was plain dumb luck."

Icky took charge and harangued the boys into picking teams. He surveyed the group and noticed Lester for the first time.

"Who the hell is this?" Icky said.

"This is my pal. Just moved in. Say hi to Lester," Nicky said, remembering to leave off *Allnuts*.

"Sure," Icky said, not giving Lester a second thought.

The teams were chosen: Icky, Little Sam, Skippy, and Nicky versus Fishbone, Mumbles, Skipper, and Lester.

Lester was picked last, because he was a new kid, because he wore glasses, and because he was smallest, even smaller than Nicky.

"We're up first," Icky said.

"I wanna go up and get my glove," Fishbone said.

"You don't need a glove," Icky said.

"I know, but it's more fun with gloves."

"Next game," Icky said.

Nicky silently rejoiced: Next game!

He angled near Lester, who was on his way to the field.

"Didya hear that?" Nicky said. "Next game. Who said nobody plays stickball around here anymore?"

Nicky and Lester exchanged smiles as wide as their skulls.

Mr. Misener the superintendent strutted from Building A. The crabbed, wiry little man had a shovel in his hand. He squinted in the bright sunlight and said, "What do you think you're doing out here? You know there ain't no ballplaying allowed in here."

"It's just a Spaldeen, it won't hurt anything," Icky said.

"I don't care if it's a cream puff. There ain't no ballplaying allowed in here. Now get the hell out of here."

Mr. Misener held more authority in Eggplant Alley than the police.

"Punks. Go get work instead of hanging around here," Mr. Misener muttered, glaring hard at the boys.

The boys grumbled and griped and took their sweet time moving out of the courtyard while Mr. Misener stared, on guard, rusty shovel in his red hands.

"Wanna play on the street?" Skipper said.

"Too many cars," Icky said. "Just forget it."

"Let's go to Glen Island, like I wanted to."

"It's too late. The bus takes forever."

There was silence. Fishbone looked at the Spaldeen in his hand. Icky swung the stickball bat. Stickball held hypnotic allure. Men from Mars could not resist playing stickball. The tug to play was as strong as the urge to eat. But even the Yankees would be stuck, plain out of luck, scratching their heads and cooling their heels, if they didn't have a playing field.

Nicky heard voices, young and faraway. And the whop of bat on ball. And perhaps the clatter of a bat. Sweet sounds from the PS 19 schoolyard, dripping down the alleyway from up the hill.

"Let's go up to the schoolyard," Nicky said.

"Screw that," said Icky.

"Yeah, I ain't in no mood to fool with the mulignane today," Skippy said. "They're all over the schoolyard."

"Yeah. Who needs the aggravation."

Instantly, the life went out of the stickball idea. It was a dead issue. And the sweet sounds from Groton Avenue no longer sang in Nicky's ears.

Icky handed the bat to Nicky. Fishbone handed the ball to Lester.

The old gang dropped themselves onto the stairs like sandbags. They went straight back to lounging and sighing and belching. Without enthusiasm, Icky began to tell the boys a long pointless tale about a female shopper, a girl in a tiny T-shirt, for whom he sliced baloney at the deli counter.

"I'm pretty sure she wasn't," Icky concluded.

Nicky said glumly to Lester, "We came so close."

"But no cigar," Lester said.

Nicky jerked his head at Lester. "Let's beat it."

They walked through the courtyard toward Building B.

"Why don't we go over to the schoolyard?" Lester said.

"They didn't wanna."

"Then we should go. They'll follow."

"No, they're right. You heard Skippy. Too many mulignane."

"Huh?"

"Mulignane. That's what we call the blacks. The colored. Too many of them over there. We'd get eaten alive, just the two of us."

Lester sighed. He shook his head. He sighed again.

"Very interesting," Lester said, sounding weary. He took a deep breath. Lester said slowly, "Mull-yarn. MOOL-ing—oh, I just can't say that word."

"Mulignane," Nicky said. "You'll learn."

They walked into the lobby of Building B and Nicky added, "Just so you know, it's not a nice word. I would never say it to their face, if I were you."

17

Mysteries

Nicky was bored, and ashamed of his boredom. In the smelly classrooms of May and June, he had daydreamed about the lazy days of summer. Now it was only July 1, and he didn't know what to do with himself.

"Bored?" Mom said. "Count your blessings. When I was your age, it was the Depression. I had to work in the summer."

"I thought there were no jobs during the Depression."

"We didn't fresh-mouth our parents, either," Mom said. "Why don't you go get the mail, if you're looking for something to do. Maybe there's something from your brother."

Nicky took the stairs to the lobby, which was dark and cool. He unlocked the mailbox and pulled out four envelopes: three bills, plus one airmail envelope, red, white, and blue trim around the border. A letter from Roy.

"Mom has radar, I swear," Nicky said.

Nicky climbed the stairway, and his ears picked up the faint thwock of a Spaldeen and the clatter of a stickball bat on pavement. The sounds were coming from the PS 19 schoolyard. The old sweet sounds swirled softly against the red-brick nooks and crannies of Eggplant Alley and curled into the open window on the second-floor landing. Nicky heard the chain-link fence jangle. "Home run," Nicky whispered.

Nicky rapped on 2-C. He glanced at the mail, at the envelope from Roy, with the glaring airmail border and military postmark. He shuffled Roy's letter out of sight into the pack.

Nicky heard footsteps inside the apartment. Slippers shuffled on the floor on the other side of the door. He heard breathing and the gentle brush of a face against the peephole. And the door did not open.

"Hey, Lester," Nicky called.

Nothing.

Nicky imagined Lester inside the apartment, freezing in place, perfectly still, now not even breathing.

"Lester, what's the matter? Open up. I know you're in there. I can hear you."

Nicky squatted and peeked under the door.

"I can see your slippers, even. Open up."

Nothing.

Nicky stood. He sighed.

"Come on up if you wanna play Monopoly. I was also thinking maybe, you know. About stickball."

Nicky's mind worked as he walked upstairs. Like all New Yorkers, he was proud of his native-born knack for quickly flushing out the story behind the story. Dad always called it "the inside dope." It came with the territory—that is, from growing up in the capital of the world, the center of the universe. Nicky put two and two together and he thought, "Lester can't fool me. He has something to hide."

Nicky couldn't stop thinking. His mind churned. He had recently checked out of the school library a book titled *Reds Under the Beds,* a mildewy volume about communist agents honeycombing America. They were everywhere. By the time he reached the apartment, Nicky had formed several theories about the Mystery of 2-C, all of them centered on the theory that Lester's apartment was a den of enemy espionage. This made Nicky sad, because Lester was becoming a friend, and this made Nicky happy, because the notion of Red agents in Eggplant Alley was grand adventure.

Nicky pushed through the door and announced, "Mom! I think there are commie spies in our building."

Mom came around the corner and said, grabbing, "What's that? A letter from Roy?"

She tore open the letter and walked to the kitchen table, reading. She felt for the chair, reading. She sat at the table, reading. She bit her bottom lip, reading. The letter was several tissue pages long.

"I have to go food shopping," Mom said.

"Mom, I think there may be a Russian spy ring operating in the building," Nicky said.

Mom said, "You can read the letter if you want." She grabbed her purse. On her way out the door, she said, "I'll be at the butcher's, the fish store, the A and P, Lombardo's, and whachamacallit's, the place over on Tilton that sells pig intestines."

Nicky read the letter from Roy.

Dear Gang,

Sorry that I have not written to much of late. I am real busy. They have us work from 6:45 in the morning to 5 PM. Than we come back for 6–8. You can't believe how much paperwork goes with a war.

It is like living in a small city here. Except for the helicopters all day and the artillery all night and the OH-2 observation plane that is based here you would not know there was a war. (I really want to grab a ride on that OH-2 before I go.) This is a big bore. I work, watch TV, listen to the radio. The highlight of my week was going to the Italian restaurant on post and it was lousy. I miss your eggplant Parmesan, Ma! The only real fun we have is playing stickball. Yesterday I hit a home run off a guy named Joe Bell. He's a New York guy, too, from Harlem. You do not know how much fun it is to play that again. Even the country guys who never heard of stickball are into it. Hey Nicky—when I get back I have to show you my curveball. Except for the stickball games, it is all very boring.

It is so boring that the Sp.4 I work with told me he volunteered to do three months in the bush. He saw some action and now he is happy to do paperwork. He did this before I got hear. He did it and now he will have something to tell his children when they ask what he did in the war. He did his part and I am starting to think I should do something a little more. If I stay here and push papers someone else has to go out in the bush and fight. Right, Dad? All

I see about the war is what I read in the paper and see on the TV, same as you. I feel skeevy about that.

That is all for now. See you in 40 weeks!

Love,
Your son,
Roy

PS—I have sent a slew of letters to Margalo but have not received any from her. I wonder if she moved. Could you call her, Ma? The number is GH3-8806.

Nicky shrugged. So Roy was bored. At least he got to play stickball.

Nicky lounged in his room, on his bed, mulling over and over the Mystery of Apartment 2-C. The commie spy theory made sense. Roy once said there were communists everywhere in New York. He said they caught a slew of commie spies in New York before Nicky was born. In fact, the top man in the Communist Party of the United States of America lived in a nice house up in Yonkers. Nicky knew this because years before Roy and some of the gang rode bikes up to the house in Yonkers, a long ride, and rang the man's doorbell and ran away. Roy often bragged about this tiny but satisfying victory in the Cold War.

Mom came home, lugging brown paper bags, and five minutes after she pushed through the door, Nicky heard the crash of pots and pans. He shuffled to the kitchen and said, "Ma, I really, really think there are commies in the building."

Mom was greasing pans. A thin layer of flour already powdered the radio. A fresh sack of sugar stood on the counter like a tombstone. The table was piled with bananas. Nicky counted them. There were ten bunches.

"Ma? Why did you buy ten bunches of bananas?" Nicky said.

"That's all they had. Now leave me alone. I have to cook."

Tired and sweaty, Dad came through the door at five thirty. Nicky said, "Dad, have you seen anybody who looks like Castro in the building?"

Dad unfolded his *Daily News* and said, "Yeah, he was smoking a stogie in the lobby. A guy with a beard."

Mom shouted from the kitchen, "There's a letter from Roy on the coffee table."

Dad caught the edge in Mom's voice and said, "What's the matter with it?"

"Read it yourself."

Dad dropped his newspaper and bolted for the letter. He read as he shuffled backward and felt for his easy chair. He finished reading and sat in his chair, the thin slice of paper in his lap. He did not pick up the *Daily News*. He did not turn on the television. He just sat, pulling a grim face. He glanced at the letter again and again, as if he hoped the words would change.

Nicky took a seat at the kitchen table. He watched Mom work. She was sweating and mumbling. "If he thinks I'm calling that floosie, he's bananas. What he ever saw in her is a mystery to me."

"Mom, I got a question for you. Why would somebody not want somebody they knew, a friend, to come into their apartment?"

"Is this a riddle? I'm not in the mood for a riddle."

"No," Nicky sighed. "It's just a mystery."

"Somebody won't let you into their apartment? They're a friend? Is it that Lester?" Mom said. Mom shrugged. "No mystery. There's only one thing to do."

"What? Tell me."

"Mind your own business."

Nicky thought that was sound advice, especially for this time and this place. He thought they should engrave those words in stone, at the entrance to Eggplant Alley.

For supper that night, Mom served pig intestines, with fresh banana bread for dessert. Seven loaves of banana bread were scattered on surfaces around the apartment. The loaves cooled and scented the air.

After dinner, Dad sat at the table and stirred instant coffee. He spoke his first words since reading Roy's letter.

"What's the matter with that kid, anyhow? Why would he say something stupid like he wants to get into combat? It's a mystery. Did he say he's bored? Bored? He should just do his job."

Nicky thought, "Sure, Dad. Do as you say, not as you did, right?" Nicky had heard the stories from the war. He knew about Dad's strong urge to fly B-17 bombers. He knew Dad looked wild-eyed at the leather-jacketed pilots on the recruiting posters and quit high school and volunteered for the Army Air Corps. Dad wanted to be in the thick of the war, in the middle of the action, in flak-covered skies, in lumbering crates battling sleek Nazi fighter planes. Dad was turned down because of a bum eardrum and no college attendance. Dad told Nicky that story. Dad told Roy that story. A million times. Why didn't Dad remember that story?

Mom passed the night wrapping banana bread in double layers of tinfoil. She tried to fit seven loaves into a box only big enough for six and muttered, "If I called her, I'd call her to tell her what I think of her. Call her. Sheesh. Margalo the magnificent. The girl who keeps her sister locked up in the house."

Dad sat with the television going. The Yankee game was on, but Dad wasn't watching. Nicky knew this, because a Yankee struck out with the bases loaded and Dad didn't flinch. Usually Dad would holler at the screen, sputter about the bums of modern-day baseball, and grumble reverently of the Great DiMaggio. Now Dad's eyes weren't even aimed at the television. Not even close. Dad's eyes were focused on the coffee table, at a spot near the metal Holiday Inn ashtray, squarely on the letter from Roy.

18

The Horrid Hippie Margalo

Nicky gazed the *TV Guide,* the latest edition, the one with the actress Ann-Margret on the glossy cover, and felt a strange airiness in his chest. The only other time he had felt this was at first light on Christmas morning.

Ann-Margret, pictured from the waist up, wore a wispy dress that was so low-cut, Nicky thought it could be a nightgown. Her magnificent red hair cascaded onto her bare shoulders and her face was turned to one side but her eyes looked directly at Nicky as he stared back at her. He had come across the *TV Guide* two days earlier, and ever since he could not pass by the magazine rack next to Dad's easy chair without rummaging for a look at Ann-Margret. He studied her face with same sensation he had when he first saw the top-of-the-line Rawlings B-4000 baseball mitt in the glass display case at Gimbels.

Ann-Margret's lips were the color of Bazooka bubblegum. And those eyes. Nicky could not tell if they were green or blue. This time he locked onto them and decided they were blue. On the spot, he decided he preferred women with blue eyes. He searched his memory. Noreen Connolly had blue eyes. She sat in front of him in social studies and he recalled looking into her eyes as she swiveled in her desk to pass back test papers. Mrs. Murray might have blue eyes. There was also an alley cat with blue eyes that frequented the garbage cans outside Popop's. Nicky gazed at Ann-Margret with a sad and pleasant longing and then he remembered another woman with blue eyes and he felt something drop inside him.

"Margalo," Nicky said, spitting out the name like a sip of curdled milk. He pushed the *TV Guide* back into the rack and decided the lovely Ann-Margret must have green eyes after all.

No one in the family knew exactly when Roy and the horrid hippie Margalo started going out. The best guess was they hooked up during the long, hot summer of 1967. Mom and Dad, and even young Nicky, first sensed her presence around then.

"I don't know what's wrong with that kid," Mom would say, before they all found out the answer—the horrid hippie Margalo.

Roy was not his old self. He was turning into someone else. He completely lost interest in the old things. No more Monopoly, water balloons, smoke bombs. No more trips to the roof, walks to Popop's for baseball cards, throwing the squeaky toy for Checkers. The only old game that seemed to interest Roy was stickball—he still spoke wistfully about that, at least—and stickball was extinct.

By the end of that summer, Roy's Roger Maris–style crew cut had disappeared for good. His head became overgrown, like an untended garden. Before long he had a mop-top, in the style of the early Beatles. Dad no longer said "Hi, kid," to Roy. His standard greeting to Roy became, "Get a haircut."

Dad and Roy fought endlessly over Roy's hair. When Roy's

sideburns started to creep south of his earlobes, they fought over those, too. During one battle, Dad compared his haircut to that of Moe of the Three Stooges. Roy yelled at Dad and called him a dinosaur. They shouted in each other's faces. Roy was eating a banana during the yelling and shouting. Roy gestured wildly with his hands, and a hunk of banana broke off and found its way down the front of Dad's favorite sports shirt. Dad and Roy didn't speak for two weeks after the Banana Incident.

During this silent, cold snap, Roy came home one early evening and emptied a large brown bag of brand-new 45-rpm records onto the coffee table. Dad was reading the *Daily News* in his easy chair and did not look up. Previously, Roy had purchased exactly one record in his life—"The Ballad of the Green Berets." But today he had gone on a record-buying spree. There were at least twenty records spread on the coffee table. They cost at least 79 cents each. The old Roy would never blow that much cash in one place.

Nicky wandered to the coffee table.

"Whatcha got, Roy?"

"What does it look like? Don't put your greasy fingers all over them."

Nicky read the record labels out loud.

" 'Peppermint and Polka-Dots,' by the Ajax Dream Factory.

" 'Bullfrog Betty Gotta Jam,' by the Funkadelic Limited.

" 'Baby, Baby, Baby, Baby,' by Flysie and the Gnomes."

From behind his *Daily News,* Dad made a growling sound.

Roy clicked on the old hi-fi, a 1950s model, the turntable and single speaker encased in a fake mahogany cabinet. He threw back the lid, slid one of the new records out of the sleeve, and placed the record on the turntable. The aging hi-fi popped and hissed and Roy's song came on, and right away the Eisenhower-era needle skipped.

"They call me mell . . . BIP . . . they call me mell . . . BIP . . . they call me mell . . ."

Dad crumpled the newspaper into his lap.

"What the heck is THAT?" he said. "And why is it up so loud? Lower it."

Roy bumped the hi-fi with his knee to unstick the needle and said, "It's a record. My record. "

The needle skipped again. "That's right slick . . . that's right slick . . . that's right slick . . ."

"Stupid crappy hi-fi," Roy said.

Dad bounded from his chair and reached into the hi-fi cabinet. He grabbed at the record and there was the horrible screech of needle across vinyl.

"Your record," Dad said with a smile. "My hi-fi."

Roy bellowed, "You ruined my record!"

"That record was ruined the day they made it," Dad said.

Roy slammed the apartment door on his way out.

"What's gotten into that kid?" Dad said, because this was before everyone knew the answer—the horrid hippie Margalo.

Another day, Nicky was alone in the apartment when Roy came home and walked into the kitchen, giggling. He was giggling like a little girl who was handed an oversized lollipop. Nicky had never seen his big brother giggle.

"What's so funny?" Nicky said, eager for a good joke. Roy always heard the best jokes.

"Don't you see it? The linoleum. It . . . is . . . so . . . cool," Roy said, his voice throaty. This was followed by more giggling.

"What do you mean?" Nicky said. He looked at the linoleum, which was a faded black-and-red checkerboard pattern. It had been in place since before Nicky was born.

"So . . . cool," Roy said, looking down with Nicky. "I like floors. Way better than ceilings, you know?"

"What's that smell?" Nicky said, sniffing, trying to identify the odor that was a mixture of Old Spice and wet grass and heavy perfume.

"Do we have any cream soda? I had three cans of cream soda and I want another. Have you ever noticed the girl on the White Rock label? I mean, really noticed her?" And then Roy slowly walked from the room, giggling and trailing the strange scent. Nicky wondered what on earth was wrong with him, because this was before anyone could guess—the horrid hippie Margalo.

Mom was the first to get a look at her. Mom was walking up Mayflower on a bright fall afternoon. Walking down Mayflower on the opposite sidewalk were Roy and a girl.

"Hanging on to each other like chimps at the zoo," Mom reported.

"What did she look like?" Dad wanted to know.

Mom shrugged. "Her hair looked a little messy."

Like the Japanese at Pearl Harbor, Mom struck early in the morning, at breakfast, when Roy was sleepy and off-guard.

"So who's the dame?" Mom said, stirring coffee, clanging the spoon.

"Huh? What dame?" Roy said through a froggy throat.

"The one you were glued to, over on Mayflower Avenue yesterday afternoon."

Roy's face reddened. The muscles in his jaw clenched. But he coolly went on eating Frosted Flakes. And he clammed up like a Mob witness. The only information Mom could extract was that the girl was named Margalo and she was from "around here."

For Mom, that was something to go on. At least now she could place a name on the foreign presence that had invaded their lives, lengthening their son's hair, twisting his taste in music, poisoning him against the old ways.

One day Mom came into the kitchen as Roy was eating a hoagie. The sandwich had unfamiliar wrappings.

"Where did you get that?" she demanded.

"The May-Po Luncheonette. On the other side of Radford Street."

"All the way over there? For a sandwich? What's wrong with Lombardo's?"

Mom paused.

"Ohhh, is that where your friend Mangalo told you to get your sandwiches?"

Another day, Mom was sorting laundry and while emptying Roy's pockets, she discovered a book of matches from a place called Louie's Italian Restaurant in south Yonkers.

"You have to go all the way up there to eat? Where is this Mango going to lead you next, Timbuktu?" Roy did not stop wandering far from home, but he was more careful about matchbooks.

By the winter, Roy had developed an oddball habit. By way of greeting, he no longer said the standard "hello." Instead, he said, "Hey-lo."

"Hey-lo, everybody," Roy said, passing through the living room.

"Hey-what? What's with that crap?" Dad said, scowling around the corner of the *Daily News*.

"Three guesses," Mom said from the ironing board.

Mom and Dad and Nicky wondered what Roy would pull next.

Then came the Blue Castle hamburger incident.

Dad hated Blue Castle hamburgers, and he had brought up his sons to hate them, too. No one knew what grudge Dad held against the bite-sized burgers. It was probably another instance of Dad reading a horror story in the newspaper, probably about some kid who ate a Blue Castle hamburger and dropped dead. That kind of story stuck with Dad forever. After reading a story like that, Dad was more likely to eat a hand grenade than a Blue Castle hamburger.

And on this particular winter evening, Roy came through the apartment door, dripping rainwater, a half-eaten Blue Castle burger in one hand, a Super Max sack of Blue Castle hamburgers in the other hand.

"Hey-lo," Roy called with his mouth full.

Dad said, "What the? Jee-sus. Get those out of here!"

"Why?" Roy shrugged. "You don't have to eat them."

"What, are you trying to kill yourself?"

"You're nuts. You should try one yourself. They're quite tasty."

"Tasty?" Dad said, bewildered, staggered by one thing after another. No one in the family ever uttered the word *tasty*.

"Three guesses where he got that," Mom noted with a smirk.

Roy tossed a hunk of Blue Castle burger to Checkers. Dad exclaimed, "Now he's trying to kill the dog!"

It was clear Margalo was not going to fade away like Roy's other fleeting passions (roller skates, the harmonica, painting-by-numbers). So Mom needed a closer look at her, and she demanded one. For months, Mom pestered Roy to bring the girl home.

She nagged Roy.

She badgered Roy.

Roy cracked. Out of total exhaustion, he threw up his hands and waved the white flag. He surrendered, and the deal was struck. Margalo would meet the family at Easter dinner.

All that week, Roy had a severe case of the jitters. He jumped at the sound of loud noises. He talked in his sleep—fearful mumbling. He complained of a nervous stomach and unleashed unusually long, anguished farts from his bed at night. On the morning of the big day, he grimly left the apartment to fetch Margalo and he looked like a boy on his way to the gas chamber.

The apartment was spruced, primped, and buffed for the special occasion. The rugs were crisscrossed with fresh vacuum tracks. The tables smelled of oil. The plastic slipcover was off the couch.

Dad set up the "dining table" in the living room. The dining table consisted of a sheet of plywood placed across Roy's old Junior Play-Town Ping-Pong table. The contraption was then covered by a tablecloth. Dad was the mastermind behind this arrangement. Each time he put it together, he set his hands on his hips and marveled, "Now, that's using your noggin."

Dad was transferring wine from a screwtop jug to a glass decanter and Mom was arranging pink mints in a serving dish.

Mom instructed Nicky to get the fancy napkins she had picked up at Walgreens. "They're in the kitchen," she said. Nicky went to the kitchen and rummaged in a paper bag on the floor and found a box of Kotex brand sanitary napkins. He opened the box and was impressed. He figured it didn't get any fancier than individually wrapped napkins. He was placing them near each plate on the table when keys jangled in the lock.

The door opened and an unfamiliar female voice sounded softly from the hallway. Roy and Margalo walked into the living room.

"Hey-lo, everyone," Margalo said with a small wave.

Margalo had blue eyes and chestnut hair, straight and parted in the middle. Her hair ended in a pert flip at the shoulders. She was slightly shorter than Mom. The top of her head only reached to Roy's chin. She wore an orange-and-lime-green blouse of a swirly design, and a teensy, pure white mini skirt.

Roy mumbled introductions. Margalo smiled brightly, and the corners of her mouth slipped under her hair.

Dad gazed at Margalo and kept pouring until wine glubbed up the neck of the glass decanter and overflowed onto the coffee table and cascaded onto the rug.

Mom squawked. Dad said, "Sonavabitch!"

"I'll show you the rest of the apartment," Roy said, heavy with despair. "It won't take long."

Mom worked a rag into the wine stain and hissed, "Did you see that skirt?"

"What skirt?" Dad said.

"She doesn't look so evil to me," Nicky said vacantly.

Mom said, "Looks can be deceiving."

Mom and Margalo were unlikely to get chummy, but a stroke of fate made the idea out of the question. It was just bad luck that Mom was banging pots and pans in the kitchen while she inquired about Margalo's family.

Margalo said, "It's just me, my father, my brother Eugene . . ."

And Mom clanged a skillet onto the stovetop as Margalo continued, "plus my setter, Martha. She's three."

Later events suggested Mom mistakenly heard, "plus my sister, Martha. She's three."

"And what is your family doing for Easter?" Mom said, stirring gravy.

"Father and Eugene are going to the movies," Margalo said.

"Uh-huh," Mom said. "What about Martha?"

"She's home."

"Alone?"

"Yes."

"You could have brought her," Mom said, wrinkling her forehead. "We have plenty of food."

"Oh, no," Margalo said. She chuckled daintily. "My goodness, she'd be a total nuisance. Running around, knocking things over. Drooling, scratching, begging for food."

Margalo shook her head at the thought. "Martha can be a total pest," she said, and she giggled. Mom stared, bewildered, not at all pleased with this coldhearted girl, standing in her kitchen, giggling, wearing a mini skirt.

Nicky, who was planted near the kitchen table, stared at Margalo, his lower lip hanging open, and he didn't hear a word said by anyone.

The other dinner guests, Aunt Serafina and Uncle Dominic, arrived and kissed and hugged everyone including Margalo. Within minutes they all sat around the makeshift dining table.

"What are these?" Aunt Serafina said, letting an unwrapped sanitary napkin dangle from her thumb and index finger.

"Nicky, Jesus Christ, are you brain-damaged?" Mom said. "Give me those."

"Very nice touch," said Uncle Dominic.

"I'm sorry," Roy said to Margalo, and Mom gave him a hard look.

They all got started on the food. They dug in and steadily ate, course after course. They ate through the cold cuts and cheeses and roasted peppers and black olives and marinated artichokes and fresh bread from Orzo. They ate through the ravioli. They ate through the lasagna. Mom was the only one who moved from the table, relaying dishes and platters back and forth to the kitchen. By the time the ham hit the table, all eyes were glassy and every forehead was sweaty.

The meal slowed down. The jug wine quickened. Actual conversations began to form. Uncle Dominic used his fingers to pick pineapple from the ham and said, "So, Roy. One more year of high school, right? What's the plan?"

"I dunno," Roy shrugged. "College, I guess."

"Unless Uncle Sam got other ideas for you, right?"

"Oh, I hope not," Mom said.

"Hey, if you gotta go, you gotta go."

Dad said, "Unless you're one of those peace creeps. Then you burn your draft card and let somebody else go in your place."

"Disgusting," Aunt Serafina said.

"Bunch of chickens," Uncle Dominic said. "Nobody wants to go to war. But we went. We couldn't wait to go. Right, Sal? We couldn't wait. The war. That was our college."

Uncle Dominic speared a slice of ham.

"I'll just pick," he said. "Yuh, the army made men out of us. It was good for us. Going to war never killed anybody."

Dad poured more wine for Dominic. Nobody said anything until Dominic belched and muttered, "Bunch of chickens."

And Margalo joined the discussion.

"I suppose it does take a measure of physical courage to fight in a war," she said. She spoke politely and calmly. "But I have to say, it also takes a great deal of courage to stand up and say no. I will not go. I refuse to take part in your war."

Margalo flickered her eyes around the table and grimaced shyly. She said, "I don't mean to make anyone uncomfortable."

"Oh, we're not uncomfortable," Uncle Dominic said. "But lemme ask you something. All right? Let's say Roy here gets drafted. And he don't go, God forbid. Let's say he runs off to Canada. You think that will make them call the war off?"

Roy said, "Let's talk about something else."

Margalo looped her hair behind her ears and said, "Well, yes, I do think that one person can make a difference. Look at Gandhi."

"Yeah. I guess one person can make a difference," Uncle Dominic snorted. "Lookit Hitler."

Mom removed the ham from the table and said, "Sal, put out the figs."

"Oh, yeah," Dad said, brightening.

Dad glowed when he placed the gigantic holiday box of Sun-Spot California Candied Figs in the center of the table. The figs had arrived on Thursday. The parcel post had left them on the Martini doorstep by mistake. Dad hated figs, but he was overjoyed by these figs because they had been dropped into his lap by lucky accident. In his whole life, not much had been dropped into Dad's lap by lucky accident.

"Feast your eyes at those beauties," Dad said.

"They are nice, Mr. Martini," Margalo said pleasantly.

Dad said slyly, "A little gift."

Nicky said, "Uncle Dommie, how was your Easter display this year?"

Uncle Dominic's home in Brooklyn was well known for its elaborate holiday displays. He put out strings of lights and plastic figurines for every occasion. He marked every single holiday, large or small, even Washington's Birthday. He placed a plastic cherry tree, illuminated by a ten-watt bulb, on his tiny lawn for that.

"Ahhhh, I didn't put 'em up," Uncle Dominic said.

"You didn't put them up?" Mom said.

"Nah, we didn't do nothing. Not after what happened on St. Patrick's."

Mom said, "Nobody told me. What happened?"

"Nothing. Just some animals busted a bunch of my green lights and walked off with my Lucky the Leprechaun."

"Animals?" Margalo said. "You think raccoons? Squirrels?"

"No," Uncle Dominic said. He snorted. "Not them kind of animals. The other kind. The coloreds."

"Dominic," Aunt Serafina said.

"Oh, I'm sorry—the Negroes. Whatever you call them now. All I know is, they're ruining my neighborhood. From what I hear, they're doing a nice job on this neighborhood, too."

"We're trying to get out," Mom said.

"It's a damn shame," said Aunt Serafina.

Margalo touched her mouth with a napkin and said, "I'm sorry, but I can't allow myself to sit here and not say anything. I don't mean to make anyone uncomfortable. But I think you are forgetting that anger and despair, and hunger drive people to steal."

"We were poor, but we never took anything that didn't belong to us," Dad said, biting a fig.

"Let's talk about something else," Roy said.

"It's a free country. Let her talk," Dominic said, rubbing his round belly. "I think you're right, missy. I think they stole my Lucky the Leprechaun so's they could eat him."

Mom stood and said, "Who wants pie?"

Roy touched Margalo on the arm. Roy looked into her eyes. Margalo nodded. Nicky thought they were exchanging a secret signal.

"We gotta go," Roy said, getting up.

Mom said, "Whaaaaat? With no dessert?"

Margalo said, "Thank you for a tasty meal. But I really have to get back home. I have homework. I have to let Martha out. It really was a wonderful meal."

Mom gave it one more try. "Well, how about I wrap up a nice piece of apple pie for Martha?"

"No, thank you, Mrs. Martini," Margalo said sweetly. "I never give her that kind of food. It would make her sick."

Mom dropped into her chair. She gulped wine from Aunt Serafina's glass. "I give up. Good-bye."

Roy slammed the apartment door on the way out.

"Nice girl," Uncle Dominic said. He belched. "A little mixed up, but a nice girl."

Roy came into the bedroom after midnight. Nicky was awakened by the creak of floorboards. Roy smelled of cigarette smoke. Coins hit the dresser top, bedsprings cheeped. There was a big sigh. Roy's breathing became slow and regular. He could always fall asleep in an instant.

Nicky was wide awake. His big brother was just a few feet away in the next bed, but Nicky felt Roy was a million miles away. Farther away than ever. His brother was becoming someone else, and Nicky knew why.

"Margalo, oh, Margalo," Roy murmured in his sleep.

"Margalo," Nicky said, retrieving the *TV Guide* from the magazine rack, looking at Ann-Margret, whom he decided definitely had green eyes, and remembering the fourth thing that ruined his childhood, stomach cramping at the memory.

"Now your horrid sweetie doesn't even return your letters," Nicky thought savagely. "So there."

19

Goombahs on the Beach

Dad and his brother, Uncle Angelo, were in the front seat and Mom, Nicky, and Aunt Amelia were in the backseat, watching the sun climb as Uncle Angelo's Buick inched across the Whitestone Bridge in a line of sizzling traffic. As far back as Nicky could remember, the annual Goombah Picnic was held the first Sunday in July. Dad's relatives and old neighborhood pals would gather at Jones Beach, the magnificent, vast shoreline way out on Long Island. It was one of the few surviving summer treats. The only good excuse for not being there was if you were in jail, in the army, or dead.

Nicky was in the backseat wedged between the women, but he wanted to be in the front seat between the men. Aunt Amelia's perfume smelled sweet and hot in the stuffy rear seat. Mom fanned herself with the church bulletin. Nicky leaned forward and rested his chin on the front seat.

"Sit back," Mom commanded.

Nicky sat back. Roy would ride in he front seat with the men on these trips to the beach. Roy was away, so now there was an opening. He wanted to be with Dad and Uncle Angelo. He watched the backs of their heads as they spoke over the car radio, which was tuned to the all-news station. Dad mentioned the Yankees. Uncle Angelo nodded solemnly. Uncle Angelo pointed out a nearby car. Dad shrugged and said he had heard bad things about the engine block on that particular model.

The men talked about movies, mentioning the war picture about General Patton and a gangster movie and then Dad's voice dropped and Nicky heard him say "that one with Stella Stevens."

Nicky leaned forward and rested his chin on the front seat.

"Sit back," Mom said.

"Sit back," Dad said over his shoulder.

Nicky sat back.

Two hours later, Mom, Dad, Uncle Angelo, Aunt Amelia, and Nicky traipsed across the broiling-hot sand, sweating, lugging coolers and beach chairs and blankets and umbrellas.

"There they are, at last," Orzo the Baker said. "We thought you got captured."

"Muddun, the bridge," said Uncle Angelo.

Dad and Uncle Angelo planted chairs alongside the boys from the old neighborhood. They were handed sweaty bottles of Ballantine beer, cold from the cooler.

"We got lasagna if you want," Orzo said.

The beach was packed. Nicky imagined he could walk from blanket to blanket for miles without touching sand, and the thought appealed to him. Nicky hated the sand. He also hated the water, because he was secretly afraid of slimy sea creatures. He hated the hot sun, too, because he tended to burn crispy red.

But he loved the beach, because he loved the sensations of the beach. The smell of salt water and coconut tanning lotion. The sound of waves thudding and seagulls squawking and hundreds of tiny radios squeaking out Top 40 hits and baseball games. And starting last year, he enjoyed staring with telescoping bug eyes at the young girls, hundreds of them, some in yellow polka-dot bikinis.

The women and children of the Goombah Picnic migrated to the water. They moved as a unit. The men stayed behind, serene in their chairs low to the sand. Bottles of Ballantine were plucked steadily from the cooler. Nicky stayed behind with the men. This was a first.

"Hey, Nicky-boy, that's some scar you got there."

Orzo was calling. Orzo pointed the neck of his green beer bottle toward the ripply red zigzag on Nicky's right ankle. "You got that when the jigs broke it, huh? I never noticed."

Nicky shrugged and slid the ankle under the blanket.

Orzo saw Nicky hide the ankle and said, "Well, no matter. It ain't no big deal."

Orzo belched loudly. He said, "I mean, that's nothing. Barely notice it. It's nothing." Ballantine cooking in his brain, Orzo didn't know when to stop. "I mean, lookit this. Take a look."

Orzo settled his bottle into the sand. He twisted his right shoulder blade into view and cocked his head, indicating "Take a lookit this." The skin was pocked with dozens of holes, as if someone had poked a pencil into the skin, a quarter inch deep, over and over.

"German grenade," Orzo said. He sat back and smiled proudly. "Looks like the goddamn moon, don't it?"

Tommy Two-Shoes said, "That's nothing."

"Christ, Tommy, don't," Franky the Angel said.

"Don't look, if you don't wanna see," Tommy Two-Shoes said. He sipped his beer and smiled a big Ballantine grin. He kicked off his powder-blue loafers. He held his feet out toward Nicky at eye level.

"Oh, for crying out loud," Franky the Angel said.

Nicky stared at the feet. He looked at Tommy. He looked back at the feet. Nicky jerked his head side-to-side, showing that he didn't get it.

"Well?" Tommy said. "Geez, kid, what school do you go to? The toes. Count 'em. Hey, Sal, what school you sending this kid to?"

Nicky counted. One, two, three, four, five, six, seven . . .

Seven.

"Oh," Nicky said.

"Yeah," Tommy Two-Shoes said, grinning. "I got frostbit at the Battle of the Bulge. I was lucky. Some of the guys, their whole feet got chopped off."

"My turn," said Tizino, another from the old neighborhood.

"Here we go," said Franky the Angel.

"This guy, he's gonna get us thrown in jail," Tommy Two-Shoes said cheerfully, working back into his loafers.

"Nicky, you gotta see this," Tizino said.

Tizino stood, swayed, steadied himself. He lowered one side of his baggy bathing trunks and uncovered his left buttock, a handful of flesh missing.

"Can you believe this guy?" Franky the Angel said.

"Our tin can went down off Guadalcanal," Tizino said, off-balance, swaying. "Jap sub got us. I was in the water three days.

Guess some shark was inna mood for Italian food, 'cause he took a chomp out my rear end."

"Okay, put it away, Tizzy," Angelo said.

"Hey, just because you got away without a scratch," Tizino said. "I had my close calls."

"We all did," Tommy Two-Shoes said. "Muddun, we all did. Right, Sal? Hey, Nicky, ask your father about the monkey statue. He ever tell you about that? Jesus H. Christ. Saved by the monkey."

"Okay, enough," Dad said.

"Tell me about the monkey," Nicky said.

"Go for a swim, why don't you."

"Come on, Pop."

"I'm not in the mood for stories," Dad said.

"Yeah, enough with ancient history," said Tommy Two-Shoes.

"Yeah," said Angelo, rattling the ice as he fished into the cooler. "Who needs a brew?"

Green bottles were passed out up and down the line. Dad put his fresh beer down in the sand and headed toward the water.

"The men's room is the third wave on the left," Tommy Two-Shoes said, and they all laughed. Dad gave the A-OK sign over his shoulder as he walked.

"Hey, Nicky-boy, how's Roy doing? You hear from him much?" Tizino said.

Nicky shrugged.

"What's he doing? Is he seeing much action?"

"Not too much yet. I don't know."

"Well, the important thing is, he's there. He answered the call.

Not like the rest of them goddamn peace creeps. I swear, they make me sick. You seen them on TV?"

"Someday they're gonna have to answer for not doing their duty," Uncle Angelo said.

"That's right," said Franky the Angel. "What the hell they gonna say when their kids ask what they did in the war? 'Well, son, I ran to Canada like a scared bunny.' "

The men shook their heads, disgusted.

"Yuh, 'I did my part by growing a beard and skipping baths,' " Uncle Angelo said.

The men grunted and shook their heads.

"Old Roy will be able to hold his head high. For the rest of his life," Tommy Two-Shoes said.

"You gotta live with what you do, what you don't do, and what happens because of what you do and don't do," Tizino said.

"And that's the straight doo-doo," Frankie the Angel said solemnly.

Nicky peered through the hot haze to pick out Dad. He was waist-deep, getting shoved by the rolling waves. Dad was shading his eyes with his hands, looking up. He walked farther into the surf, deeper under water, and a wave rolled hard into his chest, staggering him. A small plane, glittery in the bright sun, engine throbbing, flew out to sea. Dad kept walking, looking up at the plane. He watched the plane until it was a small buzzing speck on the horizon.

The Porcelain Monkey

20

That night a loud boom jolted Nicky from a deep sleep. Nicky wondered if he had dreamed the noise or if the noise really happened. Either way, he was awake.

Nicky hated feeling alone in the dark. He tried to go back to sleep. He wondered if the boom was an atomic blast. It's the kind of thought that makes perfect sense in the first hours past midnight. He was sure an atomic bomb would hit New York one of these days. Atomic bombs always hit New York or Washington in the movies, so it added up. Every day at noon, the air raid siren went off. They tested it seven days a week. It was a sickening sound. A howl of terror. Now in the dark Nicky wondered what would happen if the Russians happened to attack at noon. Every citizen would think it was just a test, and go on eating their Velveeta sandwiches as enemy bombers closed in. Nicky wondered if anybody besides him thought about this.

Only small sounds came from the courtyard. Cutlery hit a plate softly; someone home from the night shift, snacking. The fans were humming. A child coughed. Probably one of the hard-luck Sweeney boys.

From the kitchen came a raspy belch. One of Dad's. His signature burp. What was Dad doing awake? Now what? A heart attack? A burglar? A fire? Atomic bombs tumbling toward Eggplant Alley?

There was no good reason for Dad to be awake at this hour. Nicky hit the floor with bare feet, gritty with Jones Beach sand, and hurried to the kitchen.

Dad jumped when he saw Nicky. Dad said, "What is it? What's the matter?"

Nicky said, "Nothing. What is it? What's the matter?"

"Nothing. My stomach. I think there was something bad with Orzo's lasagna. I wish I could burp. Go to bed."

On the kitchen table were a glass of fizzy water, a pen, a pad of paper, and the monkey statue. It was a porcelain rendition of a leering chimp. The monkey wore a blue suit, a green shirt, a red tie, and a beret at a jaunty angle. In the corner of the monkey's mouth was a tidy hole the diameter of a cigarette.

Nicky slid into a kitchen chair and lifted the porcelain monkey.

"Don't touch the monkey," Dad said.

Nicky carefully placed the monkey on the table. He noticed writing on the paper in front of Dad.

"What are you writing?" Nicky said.

"My Christmas list. Go to bed, Nicky. Don't touch the monkey. Don't give me any more agita."

Dad was not the kind to scribble on a notepad. He didn't write much. Mom handled absence notes to school; lists for the milkman; letters to Roy; Christmas cards.

"Are you writing a letter?"

"What, are you writing a book? Nicky, do me a favor, go back to sleep, will you please? Don't be a scooch. I wish I could burp."

"You're not having a heart attack or anything, are you?"

"You're gonna give me one, I swear. Go to bed."

Nicky placed his fingertips on the porcelain monkey.

"Don't touch the monkey," Dad said.

"I want you to tell me the story."

"Ain't you a little old for bedtime stories?"

"I want you to tell me the story about this monkey. I'm sick of being the only one who doesn't know the stories."

"Not now, Nicky. Geez, can't I get any peace, even in the middle of the night?"

"Why won't you tell me the story?"

"Not now."

"Please?"

"Not now."

"Please?"

"Not now."

"Please. Please. Please."

Dad dropped the pen onto the pad and rubbed his fingers into his temples. He sighed.

Dad said, "If I tell you the story, will you go to bed?"

"I swear."

"Get me a beer. It will help my stomach."

Nicky pulled a can of Ballantine from the refrigerator. He punched two holes in the can with an opener and handed the can to Dad.

"Thanks, pal," Dad said, taking a sip. "That's good coffee. So you wanna hear the big story? Okay."

And Nicky and Dad had the longest talk they would ever have.

"You know I was in Europe during the war, right?" Dad said. "Of course you know. I was in the Third Army. Patton's army. I was with the Hundred and Fiftieth Ordnance Battalion. Bomb disposal squadron. You know what that means? When they found a bomb that didn't blow up, it was our job to disarm it. Take it apart. Make it safe. We were good. The best. Tough work, lemme tell you. The kind of job for the young and stupid."

Nicky had heard all this before.

Dad sipped and continued. "Because when you're young, you think you're gonna live forever. You get old, you know better. Anyway, we were in this town in Czechoslovakia. This was after the war. The war was all over. But they were still coming across bombs that didn't go off. We had plenty of jobs.

"One day, my squad was on duty. One squad would be on, the other squad off. We took turns. Just sitting around. We would go days without nothing. Just sat around.

"On this day we were sitting around. We were going to pull out of the town that night. Got it? There was this little shop down the block. It had this porcelain monkey in the window. There was this girl back home. I guess you could say I was sweet on her. A Cherry Street girl. This was before I knew your mother. This girl's name was Gina. She was crazy about monkeys. Don't ask me why, because I don't know. But I wanna get her this monkey. Bring it home as a present. So I asked the lieutenant if he minds if I go down to the shop and buy this monkey. Because I don't want the shop to close and then we move out and I can't buy it. I mean, Gina. She was a real doll. You following this?"

Nicky nodded eagerly.

"Anyhow, the lieutenant says sure. Just hurry up, he says. Go ahead. There's nothing going on. So I go.

"I'm gone maybe fifteen minutes. It took a little longer, because I haggled about the price. I get back—my squad is gone. I ask the other guys where did they go? They got a goddamn job. A thousand-pound bomb in a basement. They took off without me. But they needed a fuse man, because I wasn't there. So my pal Grabowski, the fuse man from the other squad, he goes in my place. Grabowski goes on the job. He was a ballplayer. From Cleveland."

Dad stopped and took a long gulp of beer. He licked his lips.

Dad said, "And so."

"So what?" Nicky said.

Dad took a deep breath and said, "So something went wrong." He shrugged.

"Wrong?"

"Yeah. The bomb went off and everybody got hurt and one guy gets killed. And of course that guy was Grabowski, the fella who went in my place."

Dad shrugged.

Nicky didn't say anything.

"Everyone says I was lucky because I didn't go on the day something went wrong. The other guys, they even started to call me Mr. Lucky. My new nickname. Mr. Lucky. Except I didn't feel so lucky."

Dad drained his beer. He belched. He put his hand on the porcelain monkey. He tilted the statue and examined it. He shook his head and smiled a sad smile.

"Roy Nicholas Grabowski. Two days don't go by when I don't think about him. I didn't go. He went and got killed. That kind of stuff stays with you for the rest of your days."

Nicky didn't say anything.

"And that's that," Dad said with a shrug. He picked up the pen. "That's the story. Glad we had this talk, kiddo. Now go to bed."

Nicky slid off the kitchen chair.

He said, "I'm happy you didn't get killed, Dad."

"Hey, me too."

21

True Confessions

Nicky woke up after sleeping late. He shuffled, head fuzzy, eyes gummy, from room to room. The apartment was empty. No Dad. He was working. No Mom. She was probably shopping. No Checkers. He was dead. Nicky was not accustomed to life without a dog. He still dropped food on the floor and left it there, because he expected Checkers to click-clack to the scene and clean up the mess. Nicky wondered: "How long before I stop missing Checkers?"

Nicky sat on a sticky vinyl kitchen chair. He grabbed handfuls of Lucky Charms, straight from the box. He thought about Ann-Margret on the cover of *TV Guide,* then noticed a neatly folded sheet of paper near the sugar bowl. A note from Mom?

Nicky unfolded the paper and looked at the unfamiliar handwriting. It was a rare sight—Dad's handwriting. So this is what Dad wrote in the middle of last night. Nicky unfolded the paper and read.

Dear Roy—

It was nice to get your last letter. We all enjoy hearing from you. We would like to hear from you more often. We know you are busy. We are all well. Although Checkers has been ill lately. We will have to keep an eye on him.

I have something to say about your letter. You said you were so bored you would prefer combat. Roy, don't be stupid. I know what I am talking about. The army has given you a job, they know what is best and what they need to win the war. Just do your job and come home safe. You need to be smart. No combat, no joyrides on airplanes, no monkey business at all. You are at a war, not at Palisades Amusement Park. I know that at your age you think you are invincible. I used to think that, too. Stay in the office and do your work.

Be seeing you in the spring.

—Dad

Dad's penmanship was perfect. But Nicky saw nothing else to admire about this letter. He fought the urge to crumple the paper into a tight ball and pitch it out the window, onto Groton Avenue.

What was Dad thinking?

He was telling Roy to stay safe and sound in the air-conditioned office. To hide like a frightened bunny. Cower like a trembling bird. Skulk like a jittery little mouse. Stay in the office.

Not exactly John Wayne stuff.

In his private thoughts, Nicky thought: Dad was telling Roy to act like a coward. And Nicky in his most private thoughts thought Roy didn't need encouragement along those lines.

Nicky imagined Roy on Jones Beach in thirty years, showing off scars from the war—"Lookit this. From a paper cut, back in nineteen seventy."

"The world has gone nuts," Nicky muttered, refolding the loathsome letter. "Whatever happened to heroes?"

Around noontime, Mom returned from her shopping trip. She had a Val-U-Pack bag of new white socks. "Half for you," Mom said. "Half for Roy when he comes home."

She squinted at Nicky.

"What's with the long face?" Mom said. "You need to get out of the house. Use your imagination. Find something to do. Go to the library."

"I'd rather go to the store."

It was a sound idea. Nicky had not purchased a pack of baseball cards in over a year. Baseball cards cheered him up every time.

"Before you go, wait a minute," Mom said. She fished a stamp from her purse, licked it, made a face. She stuck the stamp on an envelope and handed the envelope to Nicky.

"Drop this in the mailbox, will you? Be careful. Don't take shortcuts. Come right back. Don't talk to strangers."

Nicky examined the envelope. It was addressed to Roy in Vietnam. Dad's letter, filled with the advice on how to play it safe, safe as a scared fuzzy bunny.

"Oh, this," he thought.

Nicky banged on the door to 2-C. He heard footsteps. He saw a shadow on the threshold.

"Lester, open up," Nicky said. "It's me. I've got something cool for us to do."

Inside the apartment, there was the shuffle of slippers; a grunt;

a click, the creak of a closet door; the jangle of coat hangers; a closet door closing.

The door to 2-C swung open. Lester stood before Nicky. Lester was sweating, adjusting his glasses, grimacing nervously.

"Whatsamatter?" Nicky said.

"Gas pains."

"You want to go to the store with me?" Nicky said. "I'm going to Popop's to get baseball cards."

"Yes, surely. It sounds very interesting."

"Get some dough and let's go."

"Um, wait right here and I'll tell my mama. Right here, okay? I'd invite you in, but my mama just waxed the floors."

Nicky stood in the hallway in front of the open apartment door. Nicky poked his head around the doorway. He saw a closet door. A set of keys on a small table. A white wall. An umbrella stand. A floor that was not freshly waxed. Standard stuff. Nothing out of the ordinary.

"Some pal," Nicky thought. "Won't let me in his apartment."

Of course, Nicky could never allow Lester into the Martini apartment. Under the same circumstances, Nicky would have to leave Lester in the doorway with some lame excuse, such as freshly waxed floors. "I'd say the toilet was overflowing," he thought. "Much better excuse." Allow Lester into Nicky's apartment? Nicky cringed at the idea. Not with that framed photograph of Roy, in his army uniform, right there on the living room table. Not with Mom liable to let it slip, at any second, that Roy was in Vietnam. Lester would know Nicky lied about college. That would be the end of this particular friendship.

Nicky remembered one of Grandma Martini's favorite expressions: "Lying is like eating the garlic."

And he remembered the one time he asked Grandma Martini, "How come?"

"Because just like garlic, the lie keeps coming back up you gullet. Even when you no more inna mood for lying."

Lester reappeared and without pause marched straight out of the apartment and into the hallway. He looked like a boy in a big hurry to get out of there. He gave the door a hard tug and the door slammed behind him. He nearly clipped Nicky's sneaker in the slamming.

Lester said, "I have a quarter. What is this Popop's like?"

"A dirty little place with a grouch for an owner," Nicky said. "But it's the only store around here you can get baseball cards."

"Very interesting."

As they reached the stairwell, a commotion sounded inside 2-C. Mrs. Allnuts could be heard exclaiming, "Who on earth put this in here?"

"Let's get going," Lester said.

Halfway through the lobby Nicky remembered the envelope in his hand. A letter addressed to his big brother in Vietnam. He didn't want Lester to see this envelope. Nicky casually slipped the envelope to the back pocket of his jeans. He was smooth. He was nonchalant.

"I'm a regular James Bond," Nicky thought.

He dropped the letter. The envelope looped-the-loop and skidded gently onto the tile, at Lester's feet.

Address-side up.

"What's this?" Lester said. He bent down to pick up the envelope. "Hey, isn't this your brother's name? Private Roy Martini. This is an APO."

"Lemme have it."

"Private? APO? I thought you said he was in college."

"He is. He's at APO College in a private room."

"No, he's not. I know what APO is. APO means Army Post Office."

Lester handed the envelope to Nicky.

"Is your brother in the army?"

Nicky didn't say anything. His face was aflame with shame and fear.

Lester said, "He is not in college."

"Maybe."

"What does that mean?"

Nicky shrugged. He sighed. He said, "Let's go up to the roof."

The boys sat on the hot roof tar. A set of bedsheets swayed limply on a clothesline, scenting the warm air with chlorine bleach. Nicky tossed small pebbles at the retaining wall as he made a full confession. He told Lester that Roy was not actually in college. He told Lester that Roy was actually in the army, actually serving in Vietnam.

"But he's not in combat or anything," Nicky said. "He doesn't hurt anybody. He's just a file clerk. He really didn't want to go. In fact, you know what? My father practically had to drag him to the airport."

This was Nicky's way of saying, "In case you are wondering, my brother is not a baby killer." Nicky thought he should make that clear, just in case. Lester did not look like Becky Hubbard or Margalo or any other hippie. But looks could be deceiving. Nicky didn't know if Lester was one of Us. Or one of Them.

"Very interesting," Lester said.

Lester gazed at the puffy clouds. He fiddled with his eyeglasses. He licked his lips. He smirked at Nicky.

"I didn't mean to make up stories," Nicky said.

"Very interesting."

"It's just that people get weird sometimes when they find out."

"Very interesting."

"It's hard to have your brother in Vietnam with the ways things are. You don't know."

Lester said, "I know."

"No, you don't. It's really crazy."

"I know. It is crazy."

"You don't know. You don't have a brother in Vietnam."

"No," Lester said. "But I have a daddy in Vietnam."

Nicky blinked rapidly. His bottom lip stuck out. He said, "Very interesting."

Lester said his father was a master sergeant serving in the air cavalry. A combat soldier. He had fought in Korea. He left the service and took a job selling insurance upstate in Something-ville. Mr. Allnuts worked all day selling insurance and came home every night and watched the Vietnam War on TV. And he just couldn't sit in his recliner and watch any longer. He wanted to do his part. He was needed over there. He said he knew a lot about staying alive in combat. He could help. He could save lives. So Mr. Allnuts re-enlisted and volunteered for Vietnam.

"He's proud of what he's doing," Lester said. "We're proud. But my daddy got spit on and swore at the last time he walked through the airport in his uniform. So he told us it would be a better idea to lay low. Not advertise where he was and what he was doing. He didn't want to worry about Mama and me back here. He has enough to worry about. You understand?"

"Sure I understand," Nicky said. He recalled the look of cold hate in Becky Hubbard's spearmint eyes. The memory made him shiver. "I've seen more than my share of peace creeps."

"You know what my daddy calls the peace symbol? The footprint of the American chicken."

Nicky chuckled. He felt his whole body, head to toe to fingers, relax completely. "That's a good one."

A breeze swept across the hot rooftop. Nicky felt refreshed. He felt relieved. The truth was out.

Nicky said, "Is that why you never let me in your apartment? Lemme guess—you've got a picture of your father in his army uniform right out in the open."

"Good guess," Lester said. "And my mother has loose lips."

"Oh-ho. I know what that's like."

More progress. The Mystery of Apartment 2-C, solved.

Case closed.

Nicky was glad Lester was not a communist spy. He was extra glad Lester, son of a Vietnam combat soldier, was most definitely one of Us. He was more than one of Us. He was a close chum, confidant, real pal. Practically a brother.

"Hey, wanna hear a joke?" Nicky said.

"Of course."

"Okay, so this colored guy is walking down the beach," Nicky said.

"I see."

"And he comes across this genie's lamp. So he rubs it and the genie comes out and grants him three wishes."

Lester didn't say anything.

"The black guy says, 'Make me a white man.' So—poof—the genie turns him white."

Lester's eyes were on the sidewalk as they walked.

"Then the colored guy goes, 'I want me a Cadillac.' So—poof—the genie gives him a Cadillac. Are you listening?"

"Yes."

"Then the colored guy goes, 'I never want to work another day in my life.' And so—poof—the genie turns him back into a colored guy!"

Lester didn't say anything.

"Get it?" Nicky said. He backhanded Lester's arm as they walked. "Never worked a day in his life. Get it? Pretty funny, huh?"

"Sure," Lester said. "Say, how far is it to this store?"

"Getting tired?"

"Very," Lester said

The two boys strolled down Summit in the sunshine. Nicky's steps were fresh and springy, as if he were walking in brand-new sneakers.

"Do you think your father knows Roy?" Nicky said.

"I doubt it. Did you say your brother was a clerk or something?"

"For now. I think he's going to transfer to the infantry soon."

"My daddy is in the air cavalry. They don't sit around offices much."

Nicky didn't say anything.

Lester added, "But I have to tell you, I wish my daddy was a clerk. You've got it good. You don't have to worry. I wish my mama and I didn't have to worry about Daddy."

"I can't believe your father asked for combat duty."

Lester adjusted his glasses on his nose. He said softly, "A lot of men do. That's the kind of man my daddy is. He is a good man."

At Popop's, they each bought two packs of baseball cards. Popop was nasty and impatient. A rat slept on the bread display. And the store smelled of damp cardboard. "Perfect," Nicky thought. He wanted Lester, the new kid, to sample the full ambience of the place.

Nicky and Lester agreed to each open a pack of baseball cards right away and save the second pack for the front steps of Eggplant Alley. This would stretch out the pleasure and excitement of the baseball cards.

"Washington Senators," Nicky said. "How come I always get six Washington Senators in every pack of baseball cards? I'll bet there's a kid down in Washington who gets nothing but Yankees and is sick about it."

"We still have the other packs to open," Lester offered.

With something to look forward to, the walk home was pleasant. Lester remarked that some of the homes on Summit looked pretty nice.

"For now," Nicky said.

They reached the corner of Summit and Mayflower, where they

could look down the hill at the Only House With Trees. Lester said, "Look, that one down there even has some fine maples and elms."

"For now," Nicky said.

Nicky and Lester sat on the front steps of Eggplant Alley and opened the second packs of baseball cards. They chewed the stiff gum and compared their accumulated treasure. A hot breeze scattered the wrappings, and Nicky gathered them before they could blow away.

"I'll toss 'em," Nicky said.

Nicky went to the gutter to stuff the baseball card wrappers down the sewer. He looked over his shoulder. Lester's eyes bulged behind his glasses and he chewed madly on his gum as he studied the backs of his cards.

"Did you know Zeke Samuelson collects classic automobiles?" Lester said through a gum bubble.

"No fooling," Nicky said. He reached into his back pocket. He made sure Lester was not looking. This was something he did not want anyone to see. This was something no one could ever know, ever suspect. This was worth a bolt of lightning from the sky, a plague of locusts, seven years of bad luck.

"This is bad," Nicky thought, as he dropped the baseball card wrappers and Dad's letter to Roy down the sewer.

22

Dominoes

Nicky's life changed. For the better.

The truth was out, and he was a free boy. He was unleashed from the worry and work of protecting a lie from his best friend (and there was no use denying it, Lester had become his best friend, at least till Roy came home). Nicky no longer had anything to hide.

That photo of Roy, with a shaved head, in his army uniform, the one in the gold frame, extravagantly displayed on the living room table?

"Can't hurt me anymore," Nicky thought, heart soaring.

Mom and Dad's loose lips, liable to spill the secret of Roy's true whereabouts?

"Let them sing like canaries," Nicky thought, head swooning.

He was safe. Nicky enjoyed the truth like a new toy. He was eager to play with it.

"Hey, Mom, can Lester come over for supper tonight?"

"Sure, why not? Let's feed the whole neighborhood while we're at it." Mom was beading the cheap plastic necklaces in the humid afternoon. The sweat stung her eyes and made the plastic beads slippery as she worked six hours to earn seven dollars.

Mom sighed.

"I don't mean to be crabby," she said. "It's the lousy heat. Of course your friend can come up. I'm glad you finally made a friend of your own."

Nicky banged on the door to 2-C, heard footsteps, a bump, a thump, a closet door creak, hangers jangle. "Maybe he sits in the closet all day," Nicky thought.

The door opened.

"You should call," Lester said, cheeks pink and sweaty.

"Next time. Wanna come up for supper tonight?"

Lester glanced over his shoulder.

"I'll go ask Mama. You wait . . ."

"I know, right here."

"Yes. My mama just shampooed the rugs."

Lester disappeared into the hot apartment. Nicky heard murmuring. He sniffed the air. He did not smell rug shampoo.

Lester returned. "Yes, thank you. I may come up for dinner."

Mrs. Allnuts called from inside the apartment, "Lester? Is your friend out in the hallway? Goodness. Why don't you invite that boy in?"

"He's got to go, Mother," Lester called. His cheeks were heating up, from pink to red.

Nicky nodded and said, "I do gotta go. I'll see you later. Come up at four."

Lester closed the door. Nicky walked to the staircase, but he stopped on the bottom step. He cocked his head in the direction of 2-C and closed his eyes and listened. He heard muffled talking, and then Mrs. Allnuts shouted, "Lester, goodness gracious. What's the matter with you? Why do you keep putting this in the closet?"

Lester showed up at four o'clock on the button. Mom had the big fan going in the kitchen window and the little fan going in the living room, but the fans didn't help. It was a stifling humid night. The kind of night when Roy would say, every time, "This feels like the inside of a used gym sock."

The moist linoleum sucked softly at Lester's sneaker bottoms as he walked into the kitchen.

"Nice to meet you," Mom said. She shifted in the vinyl kitchen chair, which adhered to her thighs.

"Yes, ma'am," Lester said. His wiry hair was neatly parted and combed for the visit, but cowlicks were already unspringing and curling in the moist air.

"Well, aren't you a nice clean-cut young man? It's nice to see these days."

"Yes, ma'am."

"It's too hot to cook. So Mr. Martini is getting a pizza pie from Lombardo's. That sound okay?"

"Yes, ma'am."

"So polite!" Mom said. "Nicky, I hope you're this polite when you visit Lester's apartment."

"Me, too," Nicky said.

Lester examined the linoleum.

Nicky said, "Hey, Mom, is it okay if me and Lester go up to the roof and catch a breeze until Dad gets back with the pie?"

Mom scowled. "Nicky, why don't you . . . All right, if you want to. I wish you wouldn't. I don't care. But if there's anybody else up there, you come right down. Don't talk to anybody. Be careful your friend doesn't fall off in the dark. He doesn't know the roof like you do."

Nicky said he had to use the bathroom, putting his delicious, evil plan into motion. He carefully closed and silently locked the bathroom door and filled two ancient party balloons at the faucet. He filled them just the way Roy taught him: not too much or they burst in your hand, not too little or they split meekly on impact, producing a thud with no splash. Nicky tucked the balloons under his shirt and cradled them, and the cold water against his belly startled him.

Nicky rushed past the kitchen and called, "Okay, let's go."

Mom said, "Come down right away if you see lightning."

In the hallway, Nicky showed Lester the two quivering, plump beauties.

"Ever throw a water balloon at anybody?" Nicky said.

"Of course."

"Ever throw a water balloon at anybody from ten stories?"

Lester's eyes widened with bad-boy delight. He adjusted his glasses. "No. Really? Very interesting. Won't it hurt somebody? Really? Oh, boy."

On this night, even on the roof, there was no breeze. Lester and Nicky picked their way along the retaining wall and looked out. The streets and buildings seemed closer in the humid night. Rosner's pink neon sign, sputtering down on Broadway; the dark squares of the rooftops on Summit Avenue; the hazy lights of the apartment buildings by the parkway; the purple hulk of the aspirin factory, dark now because the second shift was laid off last December—all nice and cozy together under the same wet blanket. The sounds were intimate, too. Every window was thrown open. Hundreds of fans whirred; television laugh tracks erupted; ice chuckled in a tumbler; a toilet flushed; a man belched; a telephone rang and the boys could clearly hear a woman say, "Hello. Yeah. What? He ain't home. Who the hell is this?"

Nicky led Lester to the Groton Avenue side of the roof. They peeked over the wall. The residents had spilled out of the steamy tenements and onto the stoops, curbstones, and car hoods. They fanned themselves with folded newspapers. They tugged at their soggy clothes. Two shirtless young men leaned against a streetlamp and smoked cigarettes in the cone of hazy light. An old man, shriveled into a white T-shirt, lounged on a stoop and lifted a beer can to his mouth. Someone had a radio going, tuned to the Yankees game. The Orioles were beating them. Only two small girls found the energy for movement. They played hopscotch in the lamplight on the sidewalk. Nicky and Lester could hear the stone click on the pavement as they played. Nicky and Lester could hear and see it all, and no one could see them. The excitement was almost unbearable.

"No target in range—yet," Nicky whispered. "We'll wait. One of them will wander close enough."

Lester adjusted his glasses. He looked at the yellow water balloon shimmying in his hand.

"I have an idea. Why not drop them on somebody walking through the courtyard? There's always someone walking through the courtyard. Then we don't have to wait."

"What? Do you have to catch a bus? We'll wait."

"But the courtyard . . ."

"I don't wanna drop it on somebody in the courtyard. I wanna hit one of them."

"All right." Lester shrugged. He pulled his lips together into a pout.

"Don't you want to?"

"I don't care," Lester shrugged. "I just don't want to start a riot or anything."

"Oh, there won't be any riot," Nicky scoffed. "You afraid of them? Give it to me. I'll throw then both if you don't want to. Are you chicken or something?"

"I am not chicken. I want to. I just don't want to start trouble. Why start something with them?"

Nicky slumped down. He sat with his back to the wall. Lester sat against the wall, imitating him.

"Why? Because it feels good," Nicky said. "You want to know why? You haven't lived around here long. You don't know. I'll tell you why. Because of them, no one wants to live in Eggplant Alley anymore. All my friends moved away because of them. And there's no more stickball around here because of them. And you can't walk down Groton Avenue at night because of them. My mother does beadwork so maybe we can save up enough money to get out of here. Because of them. And the Good Humor man doesn't come here anymore. Because of them."

Lester didn't say anything.

"Yeah. I'll give them a nice bath."

Nicky knelt and peeked over the wall. Lester peeked over with him. They watched in silence.

One of the young black men under the streetlight dropped his cigarette. He stepped on the glowing butt and strolled off the sidewalk between two parked cars.

"Here we go," Nicky whispered.

The young man walked casually in the street, straight toward Eggplant Alley.

"Coming our way," Nicky said.

The young man put his hands in his pockets and walked toward the apartment building. He looked down at the pavement as he walked. Nicky and Lester crouched lower and lower as the young man moved closer and closer. Then the young man was directly below them, ten stories straight down. The boys ducked.

Nicky felt his heart hammering. He said, "Hold on. Listen."

There was silence.

Lester said, "What's he . . ."

"Quiet."

The iron gate that led into Eggplant Alley creaked.

"He just went through the back gate," Nicky said. "That's right below—" He jabbed a finger at a section of wall four feet away. "There. It's right below there. Throw. Now!"

Nicky smoothly heaved his water balloon. He tossed it over the section of wall precisely where he had pointed. Lester flung his, too. He threw it wildly, as if the balloon were something he just wanted to be rid off.

Then came the sweet moment of tantalizing suspense, the tingling seconds between when water balloons are thrown and when they hit.

Pause.

Splish.

Pause.

Thunk-clunk-splish.

And an enraged, garbled voice howled from below: "Whuh the . . . ! Son of a blumpin' crack! No good! Hey! Son of a . . . ! Bam glibbing cashew bluppers!"

Nicky and Lester clutched each other by the shoulders. Their cheeks puffed out with suppressed laughter. Their heads quivered with smothered giggles. This was funny, and even funnier because they could not laugh.

Then from Groton Avenue: "They came from up the roof. I saw 'em. They came from up the damn roof."

Nicky said, "We better get out of here."

Now they were the hunted.

Even better.

Nicky and Lester pounded across the tar to the roof door and piled down the steps to the ninth floor and pressed the elevator button. They were breathless with fear and joy. They listened. Somewhere in the lower floors of the building, feet shuffled angrily. Swear words echoed up the stairwell. Were enraged citizens running up the steps? Coming for them? Nicky and Lester were wild with excitement. Nicky pressed the button madly. They needed to get in the elevator. Once they were on the elevator, they were safe. Just two kids riding the elevator.

Roof? We weren't on the roof.

The elevator arrived, the door trundled open, and they jumped in. They leaned forward, hands on their thighs, to collect themselves. They were laughing and sweating and talking between gulps of air.

"I wonder what that . . . second one hit?" Nicky said. "It sounded like it . . . bounced off something hollow. Maybe that guy's head!"

"I have to . . . admit . . . this was very interesting," Lester said.

"Did you see me time it just . . . right? Am I the best . . . or what? Roy taught me that. All you have to do . . . is memorize landmarks. I'll show you. Next time, we'll toss some . . . eggs. You should hear an egg hit a car . . . windshield from ten stories. Crunch! Splat!"

"Ha ha ha! Very interesting."

The elevator shuddered to a stop on five.

"We better settle down," Nicky said, choking down a last laugh. "My mom will know we were up to no good. She has radar, I swear."

The boys breathed in short gasps when they entered the apartment.

"You look hot. Go wash up," Mom said. "Your father should be here any minute."

Nicky and Lester were in the bathroom when, over the rush of the faucet, they heard the apartment door slam open followed by hollering. They hurried out, hands dripping. Dad stood in the entryway, shaking and swearing. In his trembling hand he balanced a pizza box, bashed, folded into a V-shape, oozing water laced with tomato sauce. A tatter of yellow balloon hung limply in the crease of the box.

"What happened?" Mom said.

"What happened? I was coming in the back way and some colored mutts hit me with a goddamn water balloon, that's what happened!"

"You know you shouldn't take the shortcut at night," Mom said.

"No-good stinking rotten colored sons of bitches. What's it mean? What's it mean when a man can't even walk home with a pizza pie without getting attacked?"

"Did you see them?"

"No, but I heard them. They were yelling something at me after they hit me. I saw one guy near the building, but it wasn't him. He almost got hit himself."

"Maybe he was their lookout," Mom offered.

Mom took the battered pizza box from Dad. She opened the lid. It was like opening a book with a huge wad of chewing gum pressed between the pages. A gooey spiderweb of mozzarella stretched between the cardboard.

"I'll see what I can save from this mess. Boys, did you ever eat pizza with a spoon before?"

The boys played board games after dinner. Mom ironed. Dad watched the Yankees game. Then the boys begged and Mom telephoned Mrs. Allnuts to make the arrangements for Lester to sleep over. Mom did not need to be begged hard. It was clear she enjoyed having two boys underfoot again.

Nicky lay in his bed. Lester was in Roy's bed.

"That was the first game of Monopoly I ever won in my whole life," Nicky said.

"Very interesting," Lester said. "I have never won one."

"You will."

Lester went on, "Does this ever happen to you? The teacher

always calls on me when I don't know the answer. Never calls on me when I do know the answer. Never."

"Alla time," Nicky said.

"Very interesting."

A damp breeze lifted the curtains and swept across the beds. Neither of the boys said anything for a long while.

"So what do you think is going to happen when your dad comes back?" Nicky said. "Do you think you're going to move away?"

"I really don't know," Lester said carefully. "I guess a lot depends on what happens around here."

"What happens around here?"

"If the atmosphere improves."

"Oh."

"You've said it a million times. Nobody wants to live in Eggplant Alley anymore. But who knows? Maybe that will change."

Nicky said, "Well, don't hold your breath. This place is going downhill. Like my grandmother used to say, one thing leads to another."

The springs of Roy's bed cheeped. Nicky clenched his eyes at the sound. He was glad Lester could not see him in the dark.

"My grandmother had a saying, too," Lester said. "She used to say, 'Dominoes can fall in either direction.' "

"Very interesting," Nicky said.

"Yes, it is. So you know what I think we should do, first thing tomorrow? No matter what?"

"I dunno? What?"

"Play stickball."

"Nobody plays . . ."

Lester said, “You’ve said that a million times, too.”

Nicky said nothing for a while. Then, “I guess we could give it a try.”

“So we try? No matter what?”

“Okay. Sure. No matter what.”

“So we push the dominoes in the other direction. No matter what.”

“All right, already.” Nicky shrugged in the dark. “No matter what.”

The springs of Roy’s bed cheeped as Lester fidgeted into sleeping position.

Cheep-cheep.

The sound was like a lullaby.

Shoes

23

The next morning, Nicky and Lester stood in the Building B vestibule and watched the rain pour into the courtyard of Eggplant Alley. The drops hit the pavement so hard, they appeared to bounce. Water chuckled in the drainpipes. Spattering pools formed on the courtyard walkways. The boys looked up at the rain. They looked down at the two baseball mitts, the two Spaldeens, the broomstick. They looked up at the rain again. They felt foolish, like two boys carrying surfboards in a snowstorm.

"Maybe it will stop," Lester offered.

"Yeah, sometime the next century. Dirty rotten rain," Nicky said.

"I think it's letting up some," Lester said.

It was not letting up.

The boys made themselves small in the doorway to keep from getting wet. Nicky took a seat in the threshold and folded his legs out of the rain. He took a big, sad sigh. Lester sat next to Nicky and imitated him, exactly, down to the big sigh.

"Guess we're not playing stickball," Nicky said.

"Maybe it will stop."

"Even if it stops. Maybe we oughta face it. Nobody plays stickball around here anymore," Nicky said, realizing for the first time in his life that ideas hatched with enthusiasm late in the night usually seem silly the next morning.

Lester didn't say anything.

Nicky said, "I wouldn't blame you for moving back to the country." He was surrendering to the gloomy weather.

Lester made a grim face. "The country wasn't so hot."

"Whaddya mean? With those baseball games in the meadows. And all those kids?"

Lester shrugged.

"There were a lot of kids. But I didn't really play with them much." Lester spoke slowly and sadly, in the tone of a confessor. Nicky thought he saw a terrible, private hurt behind the thick glasses.

"I was always kind of the outsider," Lester said, and he stopped there. Lester had the look of someone locking away wounds, the kind that cruel children inflict through breathtaking viciousness and stone-cold neglect.

"I know how you feel," Nicky said. "I been in those shoes."

"I don't think so. You seem like the popular type."

"Me? Popular? Yeah, sure. You think it's been easy around here?"

Lester shrugged. He was sinking into a deep well of gloom. Nicky didn't like this—Lester was the optimistic one. If he turned grim, all would be lost.

Nicky said. "With all the kids moving out of here? Even my imaginary friend moved away."

"Very interesting," Lester said as the rain quickened. And the corners of Lester's mouth turned up. Officially, a smile.

"Mom's great idea was for me to play with kids my own age,"

Nicky said. "Great idea—play with kids my own age. All the kids my age moved out of here. Then I switched schools. And, you know what? All those kids at school already knew one another. It's hard being the odd kid out."

"I am aware of that," Lester said.

"Why would I wanna play with kids my own age? No kid my age knew Willie Mays's lifetime batting average or how to pull the wings off a fly without killing it. Roy told me that stuff. No kid my age knew where to buy cherry bombs and how to put pennies on the railroad tracks and how to make crank phone calls and who commanded the Third Army during World War Two and . . ."

"General George S. Patton," Lester said.

"Correct," Nicky said. He nodded. "Pretty good. You're a regular Encyclopedia Brown."

Lester's eyes were looking past Nicky toward Summit Avenue. Nicky turned to see a black boy huddled under the archway to Eggplant Alley. The boy wore a yellow rain slicker and stared out at the gray curtain of rain.

"What's HE want?" Nicky said sharply.

"Probably to get out of the rain," Lester offered.

"What's he doing over here to begin with?" Nicky knew that each black face on Summit Avenue was a threat, an omen, a terrible warning that slowly, surely the residents of Eggplant Alley were being surrounded.

The door to Building C groaned open and Mr. Misener stepped out, shovel in hand. He stalked across the pathway in the rain toward Building A. The black boy under the archway caught his eye.

"Hey, fella!" Mr. Misener called out. He tugged down his blue cap to keep the rain off his face. "Hey, fella! There's no loitering allowed here."

The black boy said, "Oh, yeah? Who are you?"

"Never mind who I am. I'm the superintendent of this building, that's who I am. And there's no loitering allowed here." Mr. Misener's shirt was splotching dark in the heavy rain.

The black boy made a face and stepped out from under the archway and clomped wetly down the steps. He walked out of sight onto Summit.

"Good!" Nicky declared.

Lester said quietly, "Oh, come on. Put yourself in that kid's shoes."

"Excuse me? Mr. Expert? Put yourself in our shoes," Nicky said. "You haven't lived here long enough to know. But you'll find out. Besides, you know what? I have been in that kid's shoes."

"You have not."

"Have too."

"What are you talking about? You haven't."

Nicky grinned. "All right, Encyclopedia Brown. Wanna hear another story? This is a good one."

"I'm all ears," Lester said. "Unless the rain stops. Then we play."

So Nicky told his story.

When Nicky was five years old, he acquired an odd habit. He began to pick a word or phrase and say it over and over again, just to hear the sound. He liked the way certain words struck a chord. Words such as *sausage links; leotard; whirling dervish; chicken delight; ham*. Nicky would lock on to a word and sing it out, over and over, like a new hit song.

Mom said it was an inherited habit, from her side of the family. There was a Scalopini family story about a great-uncle Paolo who liked to repeat words, just for the sound. He was a riveter who worked on the Empire State Building. On the day he died, in a fall from a seventy-fifth-floor construction beam, he had been saying "Smoot-Hawley" on the job for over a month. His family presumed he was pushed.

Nicky also made a real nuisance of himself. He nearly drove everyone in the family over the edge. Dad would go "shopping" for six hours on Saturday afternoons just to get away from him. Roy threatened to murder him as he slept. Mom would turn up the kitchen radio to drown him out.

One night Nicky woke up frightened, and wanted to wake Roy for the company. Roy was mumbling in his sleep about Marilyn Monroe, so he would have been grouchy if disturbed even for a good reason.

Nicky said, "Hey, Roy. Roy. Pssst. Roy."

"Whazzat?"

"Smelts. Smelts. Smelts. Smmmmelts."

Roy bolted upright. He stared at his little brother through bleary eyes.

"Lulla-by . . . and good smelts . . . ," Nicky sang cheerfully, giggling.

"Hey, Nicky-boy. You know what?"

"Smelts?"

Roy propped himself on one elbow, making the bedsprings

cheep, and said, "I guess it's time someone told you this. Mom and Dad are not your real parents."

Nicky giggled. He said, "Aw, stop smelting. Smelts. Smelts."

And Roy skillfully went to work, his words low and soft and sincere in the dark. He summoned every drop of his considerable big-brother rat fink powers. Roy explained that Big Nick, the black man who worked part-time as janitor at Eggplant Alley, was Nick's real father. "And whoever his wife is, she's your real mother."

Nicky didn't say anything. The words seeped into his sleepy head. Could it be true? His name was the same as Big Nick's. That was true.

Roy continued. He explained that Big Nick and his wife already had twelve children when Nicky was born. They didn't see how they could feed and clothe a thirteenth child on a janitor's paycheck. So they asked Mom and Dad to look after Nicky for a few years, to take him in as one of their own.

"It was awfully nice of Mom and Dad to do it," Roy said. He lay on his back again, bedsprings cheeping, hands behind his head. "Awfully nice."

"You're lying," Nicky said, but his pink brain was infected by the crazy idea. Could it be true? Dad was extra friendly with Big Nick. That was true. Whenever Dad saw the janitor, he'd say, "Hey, Big Nick, how's business?" And Big Nick would smile and say, "Oh, just great. I'm cleaning up." It was their little joke. Now Nicky wondered: Why was Dad so friendly with a black fellow who pushed a broom? Why? Why?

"Wait a minute," Nicky said. "I'm white." He held up his arm into the dim light from the courtyard. "Big Nick is colored. I'm white. You lie like a rug. I ain't stupid."

Roy chuckled softly and said, "You don't know anything, do you? Of course you're white NOW. All kids are born white. Colored kids don't turn black until they're about six or seven. You didn't know that? It's like a Dalmatian getting its spots."

Nicky wrinkled his brow. Could it be true? He was confused. The awful notion wormed into his head. It was the kind of far-fetched idea that could take hold in the middle of the night and become rock-solid truth.

"Wait," Nicky said. "You lie. I'm telling Mom. I've seen black babies on the bus. Little babies. You're lying."

"Well, they must have been born in Africa," Roy said calmly. "American black babies don't turn dark until they're six or seven. It has something to do with less sunshine here. You don't know nothing, do you? Say, how old are you anyhow?"

"Five years and three months."

"Oh, in that case, don't worry about it. You still have another year before Mom and Dad have to give you back. That was the deal. As soon as you turn, you're going back to Big Nick and Mrs. Big Nick. No blacks live in Eggplant Alley, after all."

"You're lying. I'm telling."

"Mom and Dad will deny it," Roy said, yawning for effect. "Of course. They don't wanna scare you. Well, anyway, just thought you should know. Now go to sleep. Good night."

"You're lying."

"Good night, Nick Junior."

"You're lying."

Roy didn't answer.

And in the quiet and dark, Nicky reached the awful conclusion that his big brother spoke the truth. Nicky believed every word. It swept over him like a revelation, like the moment he finally nailed down the alphabet. The story made sense. Nicky didn't want to believe it, but the more he fought believing it, the more he believed it. He had no choice.

He had to face facts. It was true. He was a little black boy.

He would miss Mom and Dad and Roy. He wondered if he would be allowed to visit them. Probably not. He imagined walking through Eggplant Alley, and everyone staring at his black face, slamming their doors, clutching their purses close to their coats, hurrying their children along, fleeing the pint-sized black-faced invader.

Nicky passed the next day moping around the apartment. He hoped to forget the entire Nick Junior story. He hoped the whole matter would simply slip his mind. And naturally the more he hoped to forget, the more he remembered.

When Mom took him grocery shopping after noon, Nicky thought Mrs. Capicola shot him a queer look on the elevator. Nicky thought, "She probably noticed my dark arms."

And at the store, Mrs. Lombardo followed him, aisle-to-aisle, watching with squinty eyes. Nicky imagined he must be turning black, fast, the process quickened by stress. He angled his face to catch his reflection in the chrome edging of the meat counter. No doubt about it. He was much blacker. Mr. Misener would probably order him out of Eggplant Alley, tomorrow if not sooner.

Nicky thought, "What if I refuse to go?"

Nicky imagined torch-carrying mobs coming for him.

Late that afternoon, Roy and his friends played their daily game of stickball. Nicky sat at the kitchen window and watched the big boys play. He listened to their happy shouts and the thwock of the ball and the clatter of the bat.

"Why the long face?" Mom said.

Nicky shrugged.

"Because they won't let you play? You'll play in a few years. When you're old enough."

"No! I'll NEVER play! NEVER! NEVER! And you know it! I know you know it!" Nicky howled.

Mom took his temperature. Normal.

Mom studied Nicky's face.

"I know what's going on," she said. "You might as well talk to me about it."

Nicky sniffed, "Okay." Through a fit of hiccups, the kind that follow a hard cry, he related the Nick Junior story, as told by Roy.

"What's the matter with you?" she said. "How could you believe that?"

Nicky shrugged.

Mom patted his head and moved around the table to the kitchen window. Mom leaned out and bellowed operatically: "Roy MAR-TIN-EEE! Roy MARTIN-EEE! Get UP here!"

In a minute, Roy clomped through the door, sweating and grumbling.

"Ma, I was in the middle of a game."

Then Roy saw the wooden mixing spoon, Mom's favored weapon for special punishments, which she handled like an expert.

"Tell Nicky the truth," Mom said, shaking the spoon. "Make sure he believes it."

Roy admitted in a bored monotone that the Nick Junior story was a hoax. Roy promised he was telling the truth.

"May lightning strike me," Roy said

"I don't believe you."

"May lightning strike Checkers."

Nicky believed him.

"Very interesting," Lester said, giggling so that his shoulders trembled. He buried his face in his arms. He looked with disbelief at Nicky and bit his lip. He slowly shook his head. "How could you have been so . . . stupid?"

Nicky shrugged. "But I was right, wasn't I? I know what it's like to be black in Eggplant Alley. Sort of."

"I guess you do," Lester said. "So tell me, Nick Junior, how did it feel? Creepy and scary?"

"Plenty."

Lester smirked. "I can only imagine."

"Hey, you keep sitting in the sun and darkening up, and you'll know," Nicky said.

Lester looked at his arms. They were nicely tanned. "My mama burns in the sun. I get this from my daddy," Lester said. "He's half Italian. My grammy was a Campanella."

"Italian? No fooling? You never said that before."

Lester shrugged. "I didn't think it mattered."

24

Cockroaches

It was still raining hard the next morning when Nicky and Lester returned to the doorway. They cradled the stickball bat and the gloves and the Spaldeens. The rain quickened. Mr. Cradewlewksi squeezed past them and made the usual joke about building an ark.

Nicky and Lester camped on the damp step until the air raid siren sounded at noon. They went upstairs to Nicky's apartment for peanut butter and jelly sandwiches, prepared by Mom.

"You boys plan to stare at the rain all day?" Mom said.

"The rain will stop after lunch," Lester said, cheeks puffed by sandwich.

"It has to stop sometime," Nicky said, sipping Kool-Aid.

The rain strummed against the kitchen window. Mom said, "Wait up here until it clears. Why sit down there and watch it rain?"

Nicky said, "It makes us feel like we're doing something about it."

After lunch, Nicky and Lester returned to the doorway. They looked out at the courtyard. They tried to make rings with their breath in the damp air. The rain continued. Mr. Misener came along and eyed the bats and gloves. He reminded the boys that ballplaying was prohibited in the courtyard.

"Not that it's ever gonna stop raining enough for fun and games," Mr. Misener said, squinting at the black sky.

"The rain will stop," Nicky said.

"It will," Lester said.

Mr. Misener growled, "I think we're gonna hafta build an ark."

Nicky and Lester gave up at four thirty.

The boys shuffled, defeated and damp, into the lobby. They waited for the elevator. They were two downtrodden boys. They silently boarded the smelly elevator. The door was closing when a black lacquered cane clacked into the opening. The door stopped, shuddered, crackled, and reversed course. Into the elevator stepped old Professor Smith.

The Professor was tall, thin, and white-haired. He wore a suit and bow tie. Professor Smith lived on the sixth floor. He was widely known around Eggplant Alley as a retired professor of philosophy from New York University and a world traveler.

The elevator shuddered and lifted. The Professor's watery eyes regarded Lester and Nicky. He said loftily, "Good evening, gentleman. Quite the rain out there. But we can use it. Did you know that our average precipitation is down twenty-six percent over the last decade?" The Professor was a talker, whether you talked back or not.

"I didn't know that," Nicky mumbled.

"Very interesting," Lester said.

The elevator made a screeching noise. It shuddered, jerked, moaned. The elevator stopped dead between the first and second floors.

"A malfunction," the Professor declared. "We'll be under way in a trice."

The Professor squinted down his nose at Lester.

"You're one of the new ones, aren't you?" he said.

"Yes, sir. I moved here in the spring."

"One of the newer new ones. Smith is my moniker. Welcome to Hudson View Gardens."

"Thank you," Lester said. Then to Nicky, "I thought nobody called it that anymore."

The Professor said, "The old breed called it that, and I'm the last of the old breed. Do you know how the name *Eggplant Alley* originated?"

"Is this thing ever going to start going?" Nicky said.

"I'll be glad to tell you," the Professor continued. "After the war, the new people began to move in. Fresh faces. Shiny faces! The Capicolas, the McCarthys, the O'Haras, the Moscowitzes, and the like. The old breed moved out. The Van Slykes, the Grants, the Browns. They packed up and ran like the flood was coming."

The Professor laughed heartily, showing crooked teeth. He went on, "At any rate, it was about that time when the vegetable cart started making the rounds around back. On Groton Avenue."

"I hope somebody calls the fire department," Nicky said.

"No need," said the Professor, waving the cane. "The vegetable cart was operated by an old Italian gentleman with an old nag of a horse. The horse would come clip-clopping down Groton Avenue in the morning. Pulling this vegetable cart. And that lovely old Italian gentleman would sing out his specialties of the day."

In the tiny box of the elevator car, the Professor bellowed, "STRAW-berries! STRAW-berries. PEACH-es. PEACH-es. EGG-A-plant. EGG-A-plant."

Nicky and Lester cringed.

"Now, old man Davidson, who lived right here on the second floor, he liked to take his tea in his kitchen every morning. His table overlooked Groton. Which was once a fine tree-lined avenue, by the way. Any-who, to be frank, Davidson didn't care for the new people. He was suspicious of them. Around that time, our milk bottles began to disappear from our doorsteps. The milkman refused to come here for a time, did you know that?

"Any-who, old Davidson called a meeting of the Hudson View Gardens Residents Association. He demanded the vegetable man be banned from making his rounds on Groton Avenue. Well, of course, we could do no such thing! We had no jurisdiction over commerce on Groton Avenue. We made that clear to old man Davidson. I told Davidson, 'We can't do it, sir. Besides, put yourself in their shoes, man. They need their eggplant!' "

Professor Smith smiled at the memory. He continued, "Davidson, who did not share my populist bent, jumped to his feet and he declared, 'Well, then I will be moving from here as soon as I can make arrangements. I for one don't wish to live in Eggplant Alley.' Lo and behold, the name stuck. And Eggplant Alley soldiered forth, frothing with fresh blood. Frothing—my, I like that word."

All this while Nicky toed the elevator floor and Lester stared, eyes bugging out behind his glasses, at the Professor.

"Very interesting," Lester said.

The elevator thumped and lurched. From the shaft came a screech, a hum, a disturbing clunk. The elevator shuddered and resumed climbing.

The Professor said, "Say. Look." He nodded toward the floor near Lester's sneakers, where a cockroach crawled with purpose.

"Ewww," Lester said, and stepped back.

The cockroach stopped, tested the air with quivery antennae, and moved steadily onward.

"Oh, they're harmless. *Blatella germanica*. This area was infested by them after they opened the reservoir. Fascinating creatures."

Nicky stepped out of the cockroach's path. Bronx cockroaches were known to crawl up pant legs.

"Resilient. We poison them, trap them, starve them. If there's no food, they'll eat paper, leather, anything. Have you seen these new contraptions, the Roach Motels? The bugs will always triumph. They survive, ad infinitum. They'll likely be the only ones left after the atomic attack. Imagine."

The cockroach made a left turn toward Nicky, attracted to his soppy sneakers. Nicky stomped the cockroach, hard enough to sway the elevator.

"Careful, boy. You'll send us plummeting to the basement," the Professor said. "Of course, your cockroach friend would survive the fall. We would not."

Nicky lifted his foot. Out from under his sneaker limped the cockroach, wrinkled and missing an antenna.

"See! Exactly my point. Resilient!" the Professor said.

The elevator stopped, jerking hard, on five.

Nicky and Lester stepped off the elevator.

"We could learn a lot from these little creatures," the Professor declared, waving the cane as the door closed and the elevator carried him away.

"What a bag of wind. I'll bet he's still talking in there," Nicky said. "Makes you wonder why anybody would pay good money to go to college."

Lester said, "I thought he had some very interesting points."

Nicky shrugged.

Lester said, "Know what we're going to do tomorrow?"

"Whazzat?" Nicky said, unlocking the door.

Lester said, "Play stickball."

"If it ever stops raining."

"It will."

Nicky said, "It just has to."

"Look."

From under the elevator door crawled the cockroach, antenna missing, body crumpled. The bug hobbled across the hallway tile, toward the smell of simmering stew in 5-A.

"He doesn't give up," Lester said.

"Yeah," Nicky said. "What a numbskull."

25
The Moon and the Stars

The next morning, Nicky opened his eyes and listened. He heard no rain. He darted to the window. He saw no puddles, no clouds. The weather had changed. For the better.

The sky was summery blue. A feast for the eyes. Nicky pulled on a T-shirt and dungarees, skipped breakfast (who could eat?), and made straight for Lester's apartment, taking the steps down two at a time.

"Today we will play stickball," Nicky thought, but then he ceased this hopeful thinking. He knew if you thought about something too hard, expected something too much, it would never happen.

Lester's mother, wearing a terry-cloth bathrobe, her red hair stored in a tight bun, answered the door to 2-C.

"He's outside. I think he's on the playground organizing that ball game," she said.

"Yeah. Stickball," Nicky said. "Thanks a lot."

Nicky turned to go.

"Wait for a minute, Nick," Lester's mother said. She stepped into the hallway. "I hope you accept my dinner invitation one of these nights. I'm not that terrible a cook, you know. I make a very nice corned beef."

"Okay," Nicky said, confused. What dinner invitations?

"Good, then," Lester's mother said. "Enjoy the stick game."

The sun was bright on the schoolyard. Nicky blinked against the light and focused on what appeared to be a crowd of older boys. A large sampling of the old gang was hobnobbing on the sun-washed concrete. Icky, Fishbone, Freddie, Mumbles, Joe Z., Bob (who somehow never acquired a nickname), Little Sam, Skippy, Cuddles, Duke, and Skipper—all present and accounted for. It was like a reunion. Except for the shaggy hair and side-burns, except for the bell-bottom jeans, the scene was straight out of 1965, an Instamatic print from the good old days.

"Hey, here he is, little Nicky all grown up," someone said.

The voice belonged to a skinny kid, with bushy brown hair covering his ears. The kid wore gold-rimmed glasses. Nicky tried hard to place this skinny kid, then all at once he understood. This was Paulie the Mick, now taller, now without the crew cut, now without the nerdy black horn-rimmed specs.

Paulie the Mick was here, and that was all the evidence Nicky needed. He was convinced the sweet hand of fate was pushing events along this morning, arranging this, setting up that, making sure nothing went wrong, not this time. Paulie the Mick's family had moved away three years earlier. And here he was on the playground. The morning shaped up to be something truly mystical and amazing. Like a dream. One for Ripley's.

Paulie said, "Whaddya hear from Roy?"

"He's good," Nicky said. "What are you . . . Did you move back here?"

"No, I ain't crazy. I just came down to see this jerk," Paulie said.

He pointed at Little Sam, his old best pal, his shadow from the good old days.

"I'll jerk ya," Skipper said. He grinned and swung the stickball bat with gusto.

Paulie the Mick shrugged. "I just got it in my head to drop in on the old neighborhood. Funny thing, I don't know why. And just the other day, I was telling the guys at the shop about stickball. It was like I had a preposition or something."

Lester appeared at Nicky's side. He wore a San Francisco Giants cap, pulled a little too far down on his head. The cap made his ears stick out.

"Where did you find all these guys?" Nicky said.

"It was very interesting," Lester said. "They found me. I came out with my glove and the bat and the ball. I sat on the wall over there. I was waiting for you. Next I knew, they were swarming around me. They were around me like bees on a Popsicle."

"That's very poetical," Skipper said, eavesdropping.

Icky's voice boomed from the crowd. "All right, let's cut the crud. Are we gonna get this game going? Let's pick sides. Mumbles and me are captains."

Sides were chosen. Nicky was picked second-last, again. Lester was picked dead last, again.

Icky put his hands on his hips and surveyed the playground and Groton Avenue. "Listen up. I don't think we're gonna have any trouble with the colored folks today. I don't see any around."

The gang of boys swiveled their heads. The tenement stoops were empty. The sidewalks were empty. There were no faces and elbows perched in the tenement windows. It was eerie, as if the residents of Groton Avenue had simply moved away overnight. Nicky thought, "This is fate, destiny." He thought the moon and the stars were lined up just right, creating this perfect moment, this sweet spot in time to play stickball. Everything was clicking. The sky was clear. The old gang was on hand and somehow, as if by magic, they were filled with little-kid enthusiasm. The black people were out of sight. The universe was snapping into place.

Icky continued, "And if we do have any trouble, there are plenty of us here. We don't have to worry about nothing. If anybody tries to crash the game, just tell them to take a long walk off a short pier. That simple."

Lester cleared his throat and said, "Pardon. Excuse me, please. I'd like to mention something."

"What?" Icky snapped.

"I was only thinking. We should consider this."

"What?"

"If anybody else wants to join in, I propose we merely let them." Lester shrugged. "That way, we are guaranteed to avoid trouble."

"Oh, thanks for the advice—stupid advice. Anything else?"

"Please, if I may, we could use an extra player or two. Imagine playing with full teams? That would be great, don't you think?"

"What's with the soft sell?" Paulie the Mick said. "Who is this kid?"

"New kid," another voice said.

"I already said NO," Icky said. "No mulignane crashes the game. It'll only lead to trouble. Okay? If I want any more advice from you, I'll beat it outta you."

Paulie the Mick said, "Hey, remember the time Ick tried to play basketball with 'em?"

"Forget that," Icky said.

Lester refused to let the matter go. He held on, like a terrier to a chew toy.

"Fellows, if I may . . ."

Nicky glared at his friend. Didn't he know the planets and the stars were lined up? What more did he want?

Lester looked away from Nicky's glare and went on, "It's just an idea. I have an idea. Why don't we take a vote?"

The boys moaned.

"Sheesh. Enough with the Boy Scout schtick," Icky said. He shook his head and simmered. His face developed a pinkish glow. "You're new here, and now you know better than us how to live here? You outsiders crack me up, you really do. Martini, where did you find this nigger-lover anyhow?"

Lester's head jerked back, as if he had been slapped hard in the face. Mumbles shook his head. Leave it to Icky to cross the line.

"Do we have to go through this crud now?" Mumbles whined. "Let's just play."

Paulie the Mick said, with a trace of embarrassment, "Okay, Icky made his point. Let's just play."

Icky pulled a battered, folded Yankees cap from his rear pocket and yanked it down onto his head. The tight cap made strands of his long red hair curl over his sideburns. He said, "Okay, let's play."

Lester, injury in his eyes, looked at Nicky.

Nicky looked down at the asphalt, as if searching for a dropped coin.

Nicky's team trotted onto the concrete diamond. The positions were sorted out. Mumbles at pitcher; Freddie, Little Sam, and Skipper in the infield; Paulie the Mick in center field; Cuddles in left field; Nicky in right field.

Right field was the traditional exile for the worst player. Nicky was not insulted by the assignment. He didn't feel bad about anything. Not even the ugliness between Icky and Lester—he planned to explain to Lester later that Icky was a totally nasty crude jerk. Icky was always talking loud and saying stupid things. Not even Icky could ruin this day.

They were about to play stickball.

"Anything hit to the outfield, I got it," Paulie the Mick said. He was called the Mick because he played the outfield like Mickey Mantle. Paulie was known as the second-best center fielder in Eggplant Alley. Roy was known as the best.

"Got it," Nicky said.

Nicky grew happier with each step into right field. The sunshine on his neck soothed him like a warm, tender hand. In the open space of the schoolyard, a delicate breeze rippled Nicky's T-shirt. Nicky felt as if he were walking into a concrete heaven, a place he had imagined, a place he had looked forward to, and a place he would look back on.

He reached his position and soaked up the scenery. He was moved deeply. His teammates swayed and shuffled as they awaited the first pitch. The boys with gloves flexed the leather, massaging away the awful deathly stiffness of summers without stickball.

Skippy, the first hitter, took practice swings, hitched up his jeans, and arranged himself into a batting stance. Eggplant Alley loomed over the players. The windows of Building B glinted and the red brick glowed in the morning light. The building seemed to smile.

Nicky wanted to pick out his kitchen window. He wanted to find the place where he once sat and mooned down on the stickball games, hoping and wishing and dreaming, day after day, summer after summer in the good old days. He wanted to recall the ache, now that the ache was gone.

Nicky counted windows from the bottom floor up.

". . . five," he said to himself, gazing up at the familiar kitchen curtains. He grinned, because he was down here at last, playing the game, finally playing stickball, and while he silently rejoiced, there was the thwock of bat on ball.

Nicky glanced away from Eggplant Alley. His eyes focused on a pink blur cutting through the air. The Spaldeen rocketed straight at him. Car accidents, narrow escapes, split-second sports plays—they actually do unfold in slow motion. Nicky was fascinated by the ball as it grew larger and larger. He meekly raised his arms at the last moment, almost in afterthought.

The ball whacked him in the forehead.

Nicky's forehead tingled. He was vaguely aware of jeers and yelps. He thought he had better look for the ball. Where was it? Down at his feet? In his glove? Where was it? He was moving, staggering, as if in a dream. A crummy dream.

Behind him were footfalls and a rummaging sound and a chain-link clatter. Paulie the Mick swore and kicked through the newspapers, wrappers, cans, and bottles accumulated like beach flotsam near the fence. Paulie fished out the ball, heaved it. The throw was far too late. Skippy was dancing across home plate, laughing.

Mumbles glared at Nicky.

Paulie the Mick barked, "Get your head out of your butt." He trotted back to center field, muttering.

"I wasn't ready . . . ," Nicky said.

From the other team, someone taunted. "Butterfingers in right field! Hit it to right!"

Nicky thought, "Butterfingers. They mean ME."

He wished Roy were there. He needed a friendly set of eyes. He picked out Lester, who toed at something on the asphalt, eyes down, arms folded.

"Look alive!" Mumbles shouted, and he squared his shoulders for the next batter.

Nicky's forehead was numb. His ears and face burned with embarrassment. He prayed the inning would pass without another ball coming his way. He did not want the ball hit to him.

"Not to me," he thought. "Please, not to me."

It was a desperate sensation, the worst feeling in the world for anyone wearing a baseball mitt, on a baseball diamond anywhere. Don't hit the ball to me—it was a plea of surrender and cowardice.

Fishbone popped out to Mumbles. Nicky exhaled with relief.

Joe Z. walked.

"Whew," Nicky said.

Bob struck out.

Nicky thought, "Good."

Icky walked. The bases were loaded.

"Not to me, not to me, not to me," Nicky chanted to himself.

Lester was up. Lester stepped uncertainly to bat. He adjusted his cap, further splaying out his ears. He pushed his glasses to the bridge of his nose and rested the stick on his shoulder. Nicky thought his friend looked terrified.

Now Nicky relaxed. Poor Lester. Easy out. No batter. He was more likely to fly to the moon than to get a hit.

Strike one. A pink blur smack in the middle of the painted square.

Strike two. A weak, feeble wave. Lester swung like Mrs. Furbish. Nicky thought Lester probably had his eyes closed.

Nicky turned his head to his right and stared at Paulie the Mick. Nicky stared until his eyeballs ached and then he saw Roy, from the old days, cap perfectly cocked, tall and graceful in center field. Roy walked and scratched and spit masterfully, exactly like the big leaguers on television. Roy pounded his fist into his glove and crouched, ready to sprint after a fly ball, the way he did all those days while Nicky watched from the fifth-floor kitchen window.

Thwock.

Lester had connected, proving that even a blind rat finds steak now and then. The ball skipped into right field. It bounded straight toward Nicky like a sprinting alley cat. The ball seemed to pick up speed along the concrete. Nicky put his glove down.

The ball scooted between his ankles.

Nicky looked into his empty glove and between his legs. He got a glimpse of the ball as it rolled all the way to the fence.

Two runners scored.

Lester, smiling big, was perched at second.

"Butterfingers!"

"You play like you're in another world," said Paulie the Mick.

A sandpapery voice shrilled out from Eggplant Alley, "Boy, oh, boy, criminy. That one stinks. Send him packing." Nicky's eyes swept Building B, mortified to be heckled. On the second floor, framed in the open window like a portrait, was Mrs. Furbish's ancient face. She scowled down on him in disgust.

"I am being razzed by a hundred-year-old woman," Nicky thought.

Skippy stepped to bat.

"Not to me, not to me," Nicky pleaded.

Skippy grounded out to Mumbles.

Inning over.

"Thank you, thank you, thank you," Nicky thought as he ran off the field as fast as he could—fleeing. He felt as if the school bell had rung before the teacher could call on him again.

Icky's team trotted onto the field. Lester ran awkwardly to right. "Let's see how HE does out there," Nicky thought bitterly.

"Listen up. We're down, three–zip," Mumbles said. "Let's do some cutting and slashing, boys. Some cutting and slashing."

Mumbles stepped to bat. Icky had his drop pitch working, just like in the good old days, and Mumbles struck out.

Paulie the Mick could hit the drop pitch, just like in the good old days. He singled.

Freddie, as patient as he was in the good old days, walked.

Little Sam whacked a lucky ground ball up the middle for a hit. He always was lucky.

Skipper walked.

Icky pounded his mitt and swore.

Cuddles stepped to bat. The bases were loaded. Nicky was glad no one could read his mind, because he was heartily rooting for Cuddles, his own teammate, to make an out. Nicky prayed to come to bat with the bases loaded, with a golden chance to be the big hero. He didn't want Cuddles to take his chance away.

Cuddles walloped the first pitch. It was a beautiful fly ball, a parabola out of the algebra textbook, to deep right, toward Lester.

Poor Lester turned one way, then another.

He stumbled.

He tripped.

He ran, glove extended limply, toward the chain-link fence. Lester moved like a boy who never saw a fly ball before in his life.

Lester's hat flew off.

He careened into the fence. The chain-link jangled.

And the ball plopped into Lester's glove, as if supernatural powers had ruled that this particular fly ball on this particular day was simply going to be caught.

"What a catch!" Icky hollered.

Lester's team cheered and screamed. There was a clacking sound from Eggplant Alley—Mrs. Furbish slapping her cane on the windowsill.

Nicky thought, "This stinks."

"Okay, okay. That's only two out," Mumbles said roughly. "Who's up? Who's up?"

Nicky raised his hand.

"Oh," Mumbles sighed.

The life went out of Mumbles's voice.

"Well, go get 'em, Martini. I guess."

Nicky picked up the dropped bat and stepped to the plate. And this was one of the reasons Nicky loved baseball, in all its forms. The game offered redemption. Nicky had made two boneheaded errors minutes before. But right before him, on a serving platter, was a chance to wash away the shame, clean the slate, make penance. In any other sport, the two stupid plays would have cooked him for good. In football and basketball or hockey, his teammates would never let him near the ball or puck again. He would have been banished, written off, forgotten. But this was stickball. And Nicky stepped up to bat with the bases loaded and two outs. A once-in-a-lifetime chance to be a hero, no matter how much his teammates wished someone else, anybody else, was hitting.

"This is my rendezvous with destiny," Nicky thought, tightening his jaw while his stomach fluttered crazily. Nicky heard his heart thump loudly. And for an instant he thought everyone else heard it, too, because Mumbles said, "Hey, what is that?"

Mumbles shielded his eyes to see deep right field. The other players looked toward right field, too. What they saw was Lester, by the gate, staring up at a big, muscular black man. The man was trim-waisted and broad-shouldered. The man had his arms folded and he looked down with amusement at Lester. The man's thick biceps pushed against the sleeves of his orange sport shirt. He wore wraparound shades. At the curb, another black man leaned against a red convertible. He had his arms folded and chomped on a toothpick. These were clearly two tough guys.

"They have Lester surrounded," Nicky thought.

The big black man reached out a big paw. He wiggled his fingers, as if to say, "Gimme the ball." Lester handed the ball over. The big man rolled it around, chuckled. He showed the ball to his friend with the toothpick.

"They're toying with him," Mumbles said.

The stickball players in the field edged away from Lester and the two big black men. The players took baby steps and put some distance between themselves and the disaster brewing in right field. They moved away, the way you would move away from an automobile engulfed in flames. Move, before the gas tank blows.

Lester threw glances toward his retreating teammates as he jabbered to the big black man. Lester's eyes were bugged out behind his glasses. Lester looked like a boy who needed rescue.

Nicky thought, "He's scared out of his skull."

But none of the players moved. Those two black man looming over little Lester were grown-ups, bad dudes, big and strong and mean. None of the Eggplant Alley boys wanted to mess with them.

Lester was on his own.

"Hey FELLAS . . . ," Lester sang out.

Lester's eyes bulged. His face shone with sweat. He pointed to the big man and gestured to the players. His hands flew in wild directions. His lips trembled. He squeaked out a silly giggle.

Lester was unraveling.

Icky snatched the bat from Nicky's hands. Icky's face was a maraschino cherry shade of red.

"Where did those guys come from?" Icky growled. He shouted an angry plea across the schoolyard, "JERKS! BUTTHEADS!

JUST LEAVE US ALONE!" His words echoed on the walls of PS 19 to Eggplant Alley and back again.

The big black man swiveled his head toward Icky. The man scowled. The players near Icky jumped at the sight of the scowling face, focusing on them. The man jerked a thumb toward Icky. The boys edged away from Icky.

Lester's mouth was going fast. His head bobbed as he jibbered.

"Hey! Fellas! Hey fellas!" Lester said.

Lester rocked on his feet, stepping away, stepping closer, blabbering and turning in an excited little dance. Lester didn't know if he was coming or going. He looked like a puppy, waiting for the big black man to throw the ball for him.

Nicky thought, "He's gonna make a break for it."

Lester's voice pitched high, into desperate octaves. "Hey fellas. FELL-ahhhhss! This is . . . he wants . . . he wants . . ."

Icky cleared his throat deeply, spit on the pavement savagely, swore bitterly. He slammed the stickball bat onto the pavement. The bat snapped in two.

Paulie barked, "Why did you do that for?"

Mumbles whined, "That was our only bat."

"So sue me," Icky said. He kicked the bat pieces and they spun along the asphalt. "So what? Game's over. Ruined again by you-know-what. Come on. We better get out of here."

"What about Lester?" Nicky said.

"That's your problem," Icky said. "He was mighty keen about playing with the coloreds. Let him play with that guy."

Icky and the gang shuffled away from the concrete diamond.

"BUTTHEADS!" Icky shouted, out of a need to make loud noise.

They moved like scraps of paper in the wind, drifting toward the steps to Summit Avenue. They looked over their shoulders as they walked, watching Lester, watching the black men, reluctant to go, but more reluctant to stay around.

Nicky watched his friend. The men were leading Lester away, out of the PS 19 playground, out on the sidewalk, farther from the stickball players and safety, into no-man's-land. Nicky imagined his friend was about to be slaughtered or, if he was lucky, only kidnapped. The two black men loomed over him and escorted him to the car. The man with the wraparound shades plucked the glove from Lester's hand, as if to say, "I'll be taking that now, sonny."

Nicky heard himself whimper. He was overwhelmed with a desire to help Lester. His heart pounded deeply and his head pulsed with heroic urges, whipped up in him by years of war movies and cop shows and comic books and adventure stories. He knew what he must do.

And he could not do it. Nicky could not make his feet move toward Lester and the two hulking black men on Groton Avenue. He wanted to go there, but he could not. His feet were like battleship anchors. It was like trying to run in a dream. He couldn't move. It was like trying to convince himself to walk off a cliff. His feet would not respond to the order. He was simply too scared.

Then the black men strolled away from Lester. Lester was left all alone on the sidewalk.

Two car doors slammed. The sporty red convertible backed up, engine screaming, all the way down Groton.

Lester waved as the car zoomed away. The car's thick tires squealed out into traffic on Lockdale Avenue.

"He waved to them?" Nicky said.

Icky and the gang stopped in their tracks. "Whaddya know, he's still alive," Mumbles said.

Lester scooted through the gate and ran, sneakers flapping, across the playground. Nicky noticed Lester still held his glove and the ball. It was a miracle.

Nicky said, "Are you hurt?"

Lester gasped for air and said, "Of course . . . I'm not hurt. Jeepers creepers . . . you fellas . . . Why didn't you come out there?"

Icky snapped, "Do we look like cops?"

Lester exhaled deeply. "Do you know who that was?"

"Your father?" Icky said.

"No. It was Willie Mays. Himself. Willie Mays. The great Willie Mays. The greatest center fielder in baseball history. And he wanted to play stickball with us. He wanted to play with us, fellas."

"You lie."

"I do not."

"Do too."

"You're full of baloney."

"Look," Lester said. He held open his glove. It was autographed in blue ballpoint ink: "To Lester, Nice catch! Best wishes, Willie Mays."

"He said they were making a commercial for coffee or something down on that big street. Broadway. He said he always likes to play stickball in the neighborhoods. When he comes back to New York. With the Giants."

Mumbles said, "Willie Mays. Holy smokes. Willie Mays wanted to play stickball with us. Icky chased him away."

"I didn't chase nobody away."

"The chance of a lifetime," Fishbone said.

"Come on. It's not like it was Mickey Mantle or something. Now, Mickey Mantle, he was something," Icky said lamely.

"Mickey Mantle don't even play anymore," Skipper said.

Icky and the gang shuffled their sneakers and shook their heads. Lester gazed, eyes moist, at the autographed treasure. His face was glowing.

Icky said, "Big deal. Just some writing on a glove. Ruined your glove, too." He started toward the steps to Summit Avenue. "I'm going to get some smokes."

"Wait up," said Fishbone.

Icky and the gang wandered away, toward the steps to Summit Avenue.

"You know, fellows," Lester piped up. "You know, there is a valuable lesson here for all of us."

Icky said, "Dink. I got your lesson right here . . ."

"No, the kid's right," Fishbone said. "The lesson is, forget about playing stickball around here."

Nicky watched as Icky and the gang walked away, taking summer with them. Their heads bobbed as they descended the stairs. Their baseball caps dipped behind the wall, sinking from view like setting moons and shooting stars.

26

Autumn

On the first day of eighth grade, Nicky sat in the fourth row, close to the window. He could feel the warm afternoon air, which reminded him of summer. He wore new dress shoes, new gray slacks, a white shirt fresh from the cellophane package, and last year's green clip-on tie. The tight collar, the stiff shoes, the scratchy pants reminded him that summer was gone, done, over.

Nicky consoled himself with this fact: "In the third semester of this very school year, Roy will be home." He opened his new notebook and flipped about three-quarters through, drew an X in ink on a page, and thought, "I will be taking notes on this page when Roy comes home. Or at least doodling on this page when Roy comes home."

After lunch, Mr. Sullivan passed out American history textbooks. They were brand new, hot from the presses, shiny, sleek smelling, crackly in the binding when opened. Nicky turned directly to the back pages to see how up-to-date this edition was. His previous American history text did not include the outcome of the Korean War. This edition went clear through to Kennedy. There was a portrait of the president and a news photo of Kennedy and Mrs. Kennedy bathed in bright sunlight, riding in the blue Lincoln Continental in which he was assassinated.

"By the time we are reading this in class, Roy will be home," Nicky thought.

Nicky sought out the single paragraph that recounted Kennedy's death. He felt odd, reading in a history book about events he clearly remembered.

"No mention of Dad's involvement in the shooting," Nicky thought. He shook his head, embarrassed by the memory. "How could I have been so stupid?" He smiled at his private joke, and at how foolish he was when he was a kid.

"I'll never be that stupid again," Nicky noted.

Nicky flipped back to the section on World War II. He loved reading about World War II. That war was over. We won. The troops were home, showered with gratitude, love, confetti, drinks on the house, and rousing documentaries such as *Victory at Sea.*

"Mr. Martini, what are you doing there?" It was Mr. Sullivan, another new teacher, addressing him from the front of the class.

"Nothing."

"You mean, 'Nothing, SIR.' You must be doing something."

"I was reading. Sir."

"Did I instruct the class to read?"

"No."

"You mean, 'No, sir.' "

"Yes, sir."

"Yes? I instructed the class to read?"

"No. I mean, no sir."

"Then do not read. Understood?"

The class tittered, and the fun was out of Nicky's game of flipping ahead and dreaming of spring.

When he got home from this first day of school, Nicky found Mom at the kitchen table, peeling apples. Four pie plates layered with floury crust were lined up on the countertop. Water bubbled furiously in a large pot. A pile of eggplants, stacked like cordwood, awaited peeling. A lineup of tomato cans, super-jumbo-sized, awaited opening.

"What's wrong?" Nicky said. "Why are you cooking like that?"

"Like what?" Mom said. "Nothing's wrong. Don't be such a worrywart."

She dropped a peeled apple into the bowl and selected another apple.

"There's a letter from your brother over there if you want to see it."

"What's wrong with Roy?"

"Nothing is wrong," Mom said. "Calm yourself." She let a ribbon of apple peel fall onto the nest of apple peels on the table. "Roy is fine. But your father is going to be beside himself when he reads it. Sometimes I don't know about Roy. What's the matter with that kid?"

Nicky dropped his book bag and plucked Roy's letter from the counter. The letter was written in tiny lettering on the front and back of a flimsy slice of tissue paper.

Dear Gang,

I guess I don't know how to say this so I just will. Last night I saw combat action. I am all right but it was quite a scare.

I guess I will start at the beginning. I was getting sick and tired of working day and night as an office clerk while others are out there in the bush risking their butts. I felt like a goof off.

One of the fellows in maintenance even volunteered to go out into the bush but his commo said no way. At least he pulls guard duty every two weeks and that is a bit more dangerous because you are out on the perimeter, on guard and so on. I don't even do that because my commo says our office is so fouled up it will take a year to get it back in order and so he made a deal and he doesn't let any of us do guard work because he needs us in the office 14 hours a day. I asked him once twice and three times to please let me do guard duty and he said no and then the fourth time he finally said, "Okay, Martini, if you are so anxious to get your buttocks blown up go ahead but just for one night."

They drove us out to our bunkers in the afternoon. The bunkers are sandbagged with little slits to look out of. There's also a cot. Boy did it stink. There are three men to a bunker and two are awake while one sleeps. It was a quiet night while I was on watch except for a few flares and the helicopters going by and our artillery going off every hour or so. I was asleep at 2:30 AM when there was a big WHOOSH and a loud explosion that shook the bunker. I fell out of the cot. That was my only wound, a scraped knee. (Do not worry, Mom, I washed it and put a band-aid on it. Ha ha.) The VC were firing 140MM rockets at us and at the base camp. They fired 14 rockets and we sat in the bunker sweating it out and I prayed a lot. Nobody knew if the bunker would take a direct hit and survive and to tell you the truth none of us wanted to find out. It was over in a few minutes but I was shaking the rest of the night.

Now here is the awful strange thing about war. Only one rocket landed in camp but it landed between my barracks hut and the bunker we use for shelter and it caught one of the guys from my barracks and killed him. He was Joey Carlisto, a nice kid from St. Louis. Remember I told you we were playing stickball here? Joey was our second baseman. I often walked with him from the mess hall. I might have been with him that night running for the shelter. He liked the Cardinals. We are all pretty sad and it was real creepy to look at his stuff and his bunk until an officer came and packed up all his things to ship home.

Do not worry, Mom, because you have as much chance to get hit by a rocket here as getting hit by lightning. Joey Carlisto was just unlucky. That's the way we look at it. Also, there will be no more guard duty for me. My commo said it will take two years to clear up the backed-up paperwork in the office and I am his best typist. So I will type away the rest of my tour, and now at least I know I have done my part even if it was just one night.

Love to all. Be home in 27 weeks.

—Roy

PS—How is Checkers?

Nicky placed the paper to his face, hoping for a whiff of Roy's aftershave.

"Don't rub that on your face. Who knows where it's been," Mom said. She waved the apple peeler. "So what do you think of that letter? What's with that kid? Your father specifically told him not to volunteer for dangerous duty. You knew that, right? Remember that letter you mailed for me? That was in the letter."

Nicky's tummy gurgled.

"He went out and did it anyhow," Mom said. She let the apple peeler fall onto the table. She took a deep, shuddering, tear-choking sigh. She clasped her hands over her eyes.

"Just thank God he's all right," Mom said from behind her hands. "I keep thinking of that Joey boy's mother. I won't relax until my baby comes home."

"I'm going out to sit on the steps for a while," Nicky said.

"Take a jacket. It'll get chilly. Be careful. Watch out for Mr. Feeley. Please Nicky, I don't want to have to worry about you, too."

Nicky rapped on the door to 2-C. He heard footsteps inside the apartment, saw a shadow under the door. But the door did not open.

"Lester, I can hear you," Nicky said testily. He was not in the mood for Lester's shenanigans.

"Present," Lester said from behind the door.

"So open up."

"I can't."

"Why not?"

"I just got out of the shower."

Nicky didn't say anything.

"I'm not wearing any clothes."

Nicky didn't want to know that.

"Whatever. I'll be down on the front steps. Don't forget your pants."

Nicky reclined on the front steps and watched the sun set behind the aspirin factory. Mom was right about the chill, as usual. Nicky pulled on his old red baseball jacket. He had not worn the jacket since way back in the spring. He noticed it was short in the sleeves.

"I'm growing?" he wondered.

Lester arrived. Nicky saw that his hair was not wet, and his fingernails were dirty. He did not look like a boy fresh from the shower.

Nicky told him the story of Roy's letter. He confessed about the letter from Dad, the one he threw down the sewer. As he spoke, Nicky was surprised he was telling anyone about the dirty, horrible deed.

Lester adjusted the glasses on his nose. He squinted and worked his jaw, as if chewing on something.

"This is the way I see it," Lester announced suddenly. "Because you threw your daddy's letter down the sewer, your brother volunteered for guard duty and might have been killed because of it."

"Yes," Nicky admitted woozily, eyes stinging.

Lester continued, "But because you threw your daddy's letter down the sewer, Roy volunteered for guard duty. And his life was probably saved because of it. Roy might have been caught between the barracks and the shelter by the rocket, just like his friend. If he had not volunteered for guard duty, which put him in the bunker that night instead. See?"

Nicky nodded. It was a blessing to have a best friend. Nicky was especially grateful to have a regular Encyclopedia Brown for a best friend.

Nicky said, "I guess nothing is simple these days." He planned to read ahead tonight in his history notebook, in the section on World War II. The section on World War II would be simple.

The boys stood and walked up the steps and into the courtyard of Eggplant Alley. There were orange lights behind some of the windows. Dishes clattered. Faucets rushed. Televisions blathered. Mr. Storch's xylophone rang out. The sounds surrounded the boys and gathered them in as they walked deeper into the horseshoe, toward Building B.

"Wasn't that pretty gutsy of Roy to do guard duty?" Nicky said.

"You bet. Say, anybody who is over there has plenty of guts. My daddy says there are a million ways to get killed in a war. He knew a fellow in Korea who was killed by a can of tomatoes thrown out of a passing airplane."

Nicky made a mental note to write to Roy, to warn against tomatoes and airplanes.

"Feel better?" Lester said.

"Plenty."

Nicky had an urge to buy a nice gift for this Lester, a present for nothing in particular, a present just because.

Lester shuddered in the brisk air and said, "Fall is coming. Then winter. Then the spring."

The spring. Nicky felt light-headed, dizzy, sick to his stomach. He thought about the spring, when Lester's father would come home from the war. He imagined Lester's father taking one look at Eggplant Alley and packing up his wife and kid and fleeing north, back to Hick-city. Nicky wondered what he would do without Lester. He shivered at the possibility of another good-bye in the spring. Not again, not another one.

"In the spring," Nicky said. "Know what? In the spring, we really oughta give stickball another shot. This time let's make it work. We can do it, if we really try. If there's a will, there's a way. Whatever it takes. Let's make a pact."

"Very interesting," Lester said. "I couldn't agree more."

"Promise?"

"Surely. It's a promise."

Nicky pulled open the door to Building B. He took a last sniff of courtyard air. He thought the air smelled of liver and onions, but also of autumn, of change, of promise.

27

Familiar Faces

Nicky could not concentrate on his homework. It was a brilliant, warm autumn afternoon, the kind of afternoon that screamed, "Last chance before a long, gray, cold winter!"

He sat at the kitchen table and twirled his pen and stared at the ceiling and chewed his fingernails. Sheets of undone math problems lay before him. Sister Martine had really loaded them up. But the sun was warm on his back and he heard noises from the schoolyard, the old sounds of stickball games.

"I give up," he said.

He grabbed the old Spaldeen and Roy's mitt from the closet and hurried out of the apartment and down the stairs, two at a time. He skidded to a stop at Lester's door and banged his fist on it. No sound. No movement. No one home, for real.

"Gotta do this alone," Nicky thought, shrugging.

He zipped down the last two flights and out the back door of Building B.

The schoolyard was empty. Groton Avenue was quiet. Nicky passed through the gate and walked across the concrete diamond toward PS 19. He felt grown up, a boy of action. The open air invigorated him and blew the cramps of math homework from his brain. Nicky watched the faded baselines pass beneath his feet, took a long look at the faded strike zone painted on the wall, and he knew he was saying good-bye to them till the spring. He already looked forward to spring.

"There will be great games next spring," Nicky thought, hoping and wishing and praying.

Nicky slipped his hand into Roy's mitt. He tapped the Spaldeen into the glove and positioned himself across from the schoolyard wall, in line with the strike zone box. Bouncing a ball against the wall would do a world of good. Breaking a sweat in the Indian summer sunshine would be just the thing. He planned to return upstairs in fifteen minutes, long before Mom could walk all the way to the A&P on Broadway and hike all the way back with an armload of paper bags.

Nicky wound up with a high leg-kick, just the way Jim Palmer of the Orioles had wound up that afternoon in the World Series against the Reds. Jim Palmer was tall and lean. Nicky was already lean. He wondered if he would ever be tall.

Nicky pitched. The ball hit the wall and bounced back neatly, on one hop. Nicky found this satisfying. He pitched and caught, pitched and caught. He didn't throw very hard. He didn't hit the strike zone often. But he held a fantasy about pitching in the spring. That would be something. Nicky on the mound, Roy behind him in center field, barking at him to "put it in there, old kid. No batter, no batter." Just the way Roy used to chatter at Icky and Mumbles, in the good old days.

Nicky heard the young men before he saw them. They made a racket, howling and shouting, as they climbed the steps from

Summit and spilled out onto the schoolyard. Nicky counted five of them, white kids that Nicky did not recognize. They all appeared to be about Roy's age. One of them had long, greasy hair and an arm swirled with tattoos. The tattooed boy scared Nicky. He didn't want to mess with anyone who had gone out of his way to be stuck by needles.

"Hey, looky here," said the tattooed boy, a short stocky kid. "What have we? It's a baseball player. Looky, looky. Hey, kid. You. Give it here."

Nicky did not look at the tattooed boy.

"Hey, mozzarella, can't you hear? I said lemme see the rock."

Nicky rolled the ball in his hand, not looking at the boy.

With astonishing quickness, the tattooed boy was in Nicky's face.

"Hey, mozzarella, what is your problem? I said gimme the ball, can't you hear good?"

Nicky numbly handed over the ball and the boy said, "Ha HA." He examined the ball closely. He rolled it up his arm to the elbow and back to his hand.

"Like magic, huh?" he said.

"C'mon man, let's GO!" said one of the other boys.

Nicky's heart pounded deeply. His throat was tight, his mouth dry. He was afraid the tattooed boy would ask for the glove next, and that would mean real trouble. This was Roy's glove. Roy's glove from the old days, and it was precious on many counts. There was no way Nicky could give it up. "There will be real trouble if he asks for the glove," Nicky thought. "Please don't let him try to steal the glove. He will have to kill me to get Roy's glove away from me."

The tattooed boy said, "Hey, lemme see the glove."

"I can't," Nicky said. He tightened his grip in the fingers of the mitt. "It ain't mine. It's my brother's."

"It ain't even yours, then. Lemme see it."

"I have to go," Nicky said weakly.

The tattooed boy reached for the glove. Nicky jerked the glove away. The boy locked his arm around Nicky's neck.

"Oh, man," someone said.

Nicky smelled sweat, beer, and sweet smoke on the boy. Nicky saw a skull tattoo on the forearm pressed against his chin. The boy swung Nicky around, twirling him, flinging him toward the asphalt. Nicky bent his knees and stayed on his feet. The boy leaned his weight onto Nicky. Nicky planted his sneakers and stayed on his feet. Then a leg swept into Nicky's ankles, knocking his feet from under him in the classic schoolyard takedown. Nicky felt a plummeting in his belly and he braced himself with his hands and landed hard on his rear, chattering his teeth and shaking his eyeballs. His right hand stung sharply.

Nicky sat on the gritty asphalt for a moment, dazed and utterly helpless. The tattooed boy was muttering and walking away, nodding his head as if he had accomplished some great triumph. Nicky's hand felt sticky and he turned his palm up. A ragged cherry-red gash seeped blood with the rhythm of his heartbeat. He had driven the hand into a lemon-slice-shaped shard of clear glass.

Nicky's eyes were wide with pain and astonishment. He absently wiped his hand on his T-shirt and left a bright red smear. He watched the boys walk casually toward the gate to Groton Avenue. One of the boys shook his head. He looked disgusted. The tattooed boy strutted. He glanced back and caught Nicky's eye.

"Hey, piss ant, whatcha looking at?" the tattooed boy shouted, enraged. "You want some more?" Nicky could not help glaring. He was scared, shaken, brimming with tears. He was also filled with an uncontrollable fury.

The tattooed boy stopped at the gate and looked in his hand. He seemed surprised to have the pink ball. He reared back, knuckles nearly touching the ground near his heel, and heaved the ball over Nicky's head. It bounced once then vaulted down the steps toward Summit Avenue.

Nicky watched the ball disappear. When he stared back toward Groton the boys were gone. Nicky hoped they had not walked into Eggplant Alley. He hoped they were not new tenants.

Nicky popped to his feet. He looked at Eggplant Alley, windows flat and colorless in the dusk. He thought the building looked down at him sadly. He examined his palm. A fresh glop of blood was forming. He wiped his hand on his shirt again. He wanted the hand to stop bleeding. He wanted the pain and fear to disappear. He wanted the terrible episode to just go away, with no lasting effects.

Nicky took stock. He had managed to hold on to Roy's glove, thank heavens. The hand. It would stop bleeding, any second. The ball. It was Roy's ball, the one that had been safe and snug at the back of the closet all those years. And now it was lost, rolling somewhere along Summit.

Nicky thought, "I must find that ball. To fix everything."

He hurried for the stairs and was surprised his right ankle ached. At the top of the stairs a breeze cooled the tears on his cheeks. He hurried down the steps, calculating the path of the ball.

Nicky searched under cars parked on Summit. He looked along the curb, down the sewer, along the chain-link fences in front of the two-story houses. He peered into the postage-stamp front yards.

"The ball has to be somewhere," Nicky thought, and he was reminded about how deeply he hated to look for lost things.

Summit was sloped and angled in such a way that a ball could bounce against a curb or car and roll toward Mayflower Avenue, the narrow street that plunged steeply all the way to Broadway. Nicky squatted painfully and looked under the cars parked at the top of Mayflower. He kicked at cans and bottles in the gutter. He sidestepped dog droppings and searched the length of hard-packed turf between the sidewalk and curb. He found himself in front of the Only House With Trees.

"This would have to happen," Nicky said angrily, not knowing that if the tattooed boy hadn't assaulted him, if the tattooed boy hadn't thrown the Spaldeen over the fence, Nicky would not be standing on Mayflower Avenue at that moment. And Nicky would have forever missed what happened next.

"Where is that stinking ball?" he whined.

He gazed down Mayflower. He saw a small figure, barely in sight, trudge up the hill. The figure climbed closer, and he saw it was a woman. A young woman, with long straight chestnut-brown hair that bounced and shimmered as she walked. Nicky stood and watched, baseball glove on his hip. The young woman must have seen the glove, because she held her right hand above her head. In her hand was the pink ball. Nicky smiled. She smiled back at him. Even from this distance, in the fading fall light, he could tell that the smile was something special.

Something familiar.

"Hey-lo, there," the young woman called out.

And slowly her face came into full focus, and Nicky placed the smile as that belonging to Roy's horrid hippie girlfriend, Margalo.

28

The Only House With Trees

The smile flickered from Margalo's face. She narrowed her eyes and wrinkled her forehead, like someone working on a math problem. She was trying to place this kid with the baseball mitt. Then she remembered. Her forehead relaxed. Her smile did not return.

"You're Margalo," Nicky said stupidly. "Do you remember me? I'm . . ."

"I know who you are," Margalo said softly. She took a deep breath. She locked her blue eyes on to Nicky's face. She held out the Spaldeen. Nicky opened the glove. Margalo dropped the ball into the glove.

Nicky thought Margalo was waiting for him to say something.

So he said, "Nice day, isn't it?"

She exhaled.

"I am a numbskull," he thought.

Margalo said, "I better be going."

Nicky didn't say anything.

Margalo said, "You should get back to your game."

"Game?"

Nicky followed her eyes as she lowered them to the baseball

mitt, which held the Spaldeen. He said, "Oh, yeah. There's no game. I was just playing with myself."

"Numbskull, numbskull, numbskull," he thought.

"Well, good-bye," Margalo said. She edged backward, half turned away, all the while locking her blue eyes on to Nicky's face.

She said, "Do you have any . . ." She blinked against the strands of hair in her eyes.

She pursed her lips.

"Good-bye," she said, nodding firmly.

Nicky wiped his right hand across his shirt, adding a bright red smear of blood to the maroon smears, and waved meekly.

"My Goddess, what have you done to your hand?" Margalo gasped. She stepped quickly to Nicky. She looped her hair behind her ears. She cradled his wounded hand.

"It's really bleeding. What did you do?"

"I fell," Nicky said. "Making a catch. A diving catch. Think I hit some glass or something. It's nothing." He was trying to come across tough and stoic, a regular John Wayne. "I broke my ankle once, you know."

"Dumb, dumb, dumb," he thought. Nicky could feel his IQ plummeting in the presence of this girl.

Margalo pressed her fingers to his palm. Nicky winced and sucked in air.

"I think there's glass in there," Margalo said gravely. "Come with me. That might need a stitch or two. It surely needs cleaning out."

Nicky withdrew his hand. "No, really, it's nothing."

"Don't be silly. Come with me." She moved toward the black

iron gate to the Only House With Trees, motioning for Nicky to follow.

"You live here?"

"Yes, I live here. You didn't know that?"

"Yeah, I knew that," Nicky lied. He shrugged. He examined his hand. "I think I'll just go home."

"Look. My father is a doctor," Margalo said, as if that settled that.

Nicky didn't say anything.

"Please come with me," Margalo said softly, sweetly, with a slight smile that gave a glimpse of perfect white teeth.

And that was that.

Nicky followed Margalo through the gate, past the tall, thick green hedges, onto a gray cobblestone path, into the grounds of the Only House With Trees. Nicky's head swiveled as he walked toward the sprawling, clapboarded house. He passed a sundial; a gazebo; a wrought-iron black bench; a cement fishpond, drained and collecting orange leaves. There was a statue, right out in the open—a stone cherub playing a small harp near some bushes. Nicky passed under the trees. Tall, old, healthy trees with thick, corrugated trunks. Nicky gawked up at the canopies of lime green and orange and red.

The path led to a magnificent wooden door, high and wide with a brass knocker the size of Nicky's head. The doorway was guarded on each side by stone lions as tall as Nicky. He looked at the stone lions. The lions looked back with suspicious eyes.

"We'll go around to the kitchen," Margalo said.

Margalo cut to the right. Nicky followed, sneakers crunching on a gravel path. He watched Margalo walk. Her hair was longer than last time he saw her—it reached halfway to her wide leather belt. A peace symbol was sewn onto the back pocket of her faded, flared jeans. He forced himself to look away from the peace symbol. He stared at the back of her head, at this young woman who smelled of green apple shampoo, the fourth thing that ruined his childhood.

They reached a short set of steps that led to a standard-sized door with a small, round window. Margalo pulled open the door. Nicky could not believe the door to this house in this neighborhood was left unlocked.

He followed Margalo through a darkened breezeway into an airy room. Margalo turned a switch and the room was bathed in soft, yellow light. It was a kitchen, roughly the size of the entire Martini apartment.

"Over here," Margalo said.

Margalo walked Nicky to one of the sinks and pushed up a stainless-steel lever to turn on the water, which came on with a mighty rush. (The water here did not have to climb five stories to reach the faucet.) She tested the temperature with two fingers and turned down the water pressure. Margalo gently held Nicky's slashed hand and guided it under the warm water. Nicky jumped at the sting, not wanting to jump. He watched the side of Margalo's face as she examined his cut. He inhaled the scent of green apple in her hair.

"I think I have all the glass out of this," she said. "I don't think it needs stitches."

Stitches—merely the sound of the word made Nicky queasy.

Margalo snapped a clean kitchen towel out of a drawer. She pressed the towel against Nicky's palm.

"Hold that there," she ordered. "I'm going to see if my father is home. He can take a look at this."

Margalo left the room, moving deeper into the grand home, turning on lights as she went along.

A stately red dog trotted loftily into the kitchen. The dog sniffed Nicky's ankles, nosed a water dish, and trotted out. The dog brushed past Margalo in the doorway.

"Martha," Nicky said out loud.

"You have a good memory," Margalo said. Now her hair was pulled into a ponytail. She said, "My father is not here."

Nicky shrugged. "Thank you," he said. He tried to think of something more to say. Something snappy and clever. But what? He and Margalo had one thing in common.

Nicky said, "Roy . . ."

"No," Margalo said. She held up both hands, like a basketball player on defense. She averted her eyes, shook her head from side to side, ponytail wagging. "No, no, no, no."

"No?" Nicky said.

"No."

Nicky said, "But Roy . . ."

"NO," Margalo said. She touched Nicky's forearm. Her eyes were shiny.

"No," she said, softly. "Please. No."

Nicky shrugged. "Okay."

"I can't hear about Roy. I can't hear how he is, what he is doing."

"You haven't heard from him?"

Margalo drew in her bottom lip. Her eyes went somewhere far away. "I have not. We have not communicated, not since he left."

"He hasn't written you?"

"We have not communicated."

"Oh," Nicky said. "Oh. Well, if you care, he's okay."

"Enough," Margalo said. She wiped the backs of her hands along both cheeks.

Nicky's bottom lip stuck out. He was bewildered, and his customary response to bewilderment was retreat. He said, "I guess I better get home," hoping she would beg him to stay.

"Yes, you had better," Margalo said.

She walked Nicky out of the kitchen, through the breezeway, to the outer door. He stepped out into the evening, onto the gravel path. Margalo stood in the half-closed door.

"So long," Nicky said.

Margalo said quietly, "Good-bye, Nicky."

Nicky walked along the path, now lit by unseen amber lights. Dead leaves crackled beneath his sneakers. The door hinge squeaked behind him.

"You have no idea how much I care," Margalo said softly, through the closing door.

Nicky hurried across Summit. He considered climbing the stairway to Groton Avenue, the shorter route home. But he felt the dull throb in his hand and thought better of it. The stairway lamplights were broken and the stairs were dark. Anybody could lurk there.

He was ten paces from Eggplant Alley when he heard a familiar truck engine and a familiar horn blast and a familiar voice that hollered, "Nicky, hey Nick-EE! Is that you? Thank God it's you."

Dad pulled alongside in the delivery van. He stopped in the middle of Summit, engine running. Dad crouched in the big doorway of the Yum-E-Cakes truck.

"Nicky, where in the name of Francis Albert Sinatra have you been? Are you trying to give us heart attacks? What's that on your shirt? Is it paint? It looks like blood. What's that on your hand? Are you all right? Don't we have enough to worry about with Roy without you disappearing on us?"

Nicky stuck with the story that he was bouncing a ball against the PS 19 wall (which was true). And he lost the ball down Summit (which was sort of true). And he had lost track of time looking for the ball (which was pretty much untrue). And he sliced his hand on glass (which was true) while looking for the ball in the gutter (which was a lie). There was no way he would mention the twin evils of the hooligan mugger and the hippie Margalo. That would cinch it. His parents would never allow him out of the apartment again.

Nicky lay in bed that night, his hand aching, the scent of green apples in his nostrils. That girl had unnerved him. As he fell asleep, Nicky made a promise to himself. He promised that if Margalo came walking down the street toward him ever again, he would simply run away, as fast as his feet could carry him.

29

Letters Unread

The next afternoon Nicky stood in the rain at the big front door of the Only House With Trees. Nicky banged the big brass knocker. He stared at the stone lions and the stone lions, dripping rainwater, stared back with surprised eyes.

Nicky dropped his book bag, heavy with textbooks, and knocked with wet knuckles. He had walked straight there from school. He had remembered during lunchtime, over baloney and milk, that Roy's glove and Spaldeen were left behind in the big house, lost in the shuffle of the sad, strange farewell the night before.

A lock turned and the big door swung open. A short, wiry black woman, dressed in white pants and a white blouse, looked down at Nicky. She said in a British accent, "Yes, how can I help you?"

"I'm here to see Margalo, please," Nicky said, water dripping off his nose.

"And your name is please?"

"Nick Martini."

"Martini?"

"Martini."

"Rick?"

"Nick."

"Wait, please."

The woman closed the door and latched it. Nicky moved closer to the house, under the shelter of the overhang, out of the rain.

The door was unlatched and it swung open and Margalo was saying over her shoulder, ". . . outside in the rain, for goodness' sakes." Then with a smile to Nicky, "Hey-lo, there. Come on in. You look like Oliver Twist out there in the rain."

Nicky stepped in, shivering in the dry warmth of the house. He wondered, "Who the heck is Oliver Twist?"

Nicky's school clothes and book bag dripped and made small pools on the thin rug. A grandfather clock slowly clunked. He said, "I hope it's okay. I came by to get my glove and ball. I left them here yesterday."

"Yes," Margalo said. "I'm glad you came by."

"Mad?"

"Glad. I am glad," Margalo said.

Nicky, dripping water, said, "I'm glad you're glad. Are you glad I'm glad that you're glad?"

Margalo sighed. "As silly as your brother." She looked in the direction of the kitchen. She looked back at Nicky. She looked up the stairs. She said, "Why don't we go up to my room? We can talk. We can't hang out in the kitchen. Maria is cooking. She blares her soap operas so loudly you can't hear yourself think. Come on."

Nicky followed Margalo up a wide, carpeted staircase. Nicky's shoes squished as he climbed.

"You were lucky to catch me," Margalo said as she reached the landing. "I was at the university all day and just returned."

She said over her shoulder, "Columbia."

On the second floor, they walked down a long corridor. They passed two closed doors. Margalo stopped at the third door. A poster was thumbtacked onto the door, advising in fantastic psychedelic lettering: WAR IS UNHEALTHY FOR CHILDREN AND OTHER LIVING BEINGS.

"Here's my humble sanctuary," Margalo said.

The bedroom was a dazzling array of clutter and color. Nicky's bottom lip hung open as he took it all in. The orange carpet and lime-green bedding. The aquamarine curtains. The bright blue beanbag chair. The cherry-red beanbag chair. The oversized, striped pillows strewn here and there on the floor. The yellow gooseneck lamp. The stacks of books, piled like toy blocks. The mounds of tossed blue jeans, belts, shiny boots, skirts, vests, dresses. A pair of pure white panties on the bed, which made Nicky struggle to keep his breathing normal. The albums and album covers everywhere, scattered like a dropped deck of cards. The posters of long-haired rock stars. A protest sign that wondered sweetly, WHAT IF THEY GAVE A WAR AND NOBODY CAME? The protest sign was propped in a corner, alongside a pair of skis.

Margalo swept a hand toward the beanbag chairs. "Your choice. Blue or red."

Nicky plopped onto the blue beanbag. There is no dignified way to sit in a beanbag chair. And in this case Nicky landed so that he was slightly tilted upward, his black school shoes in the air, pointed toward the ceiling. His white socks seemed to shine like headlamps.

Margalo struck a match and touched it to a small stick propped in a drinking glass. The stick looked exactly like a punk stick, the kind Roy used in the old days to light firecrackers. A gray curl of smoke rose from the glass and filled the room with a smell like that of roach spray.

"What's that?" Nicky said, worrying about illicit drugs.

"Incense," Margalo said. "Do you like it?"

"Sure," Nicky said, his head aching instantly from the stench.

Margalo clicked on her stereo and moved the phonograph arm onto an album. The room reverberated with the braying of an electric guitar. She lowered the volume.

Margalo sat cross-legged on the floor. She adjusted her long, flouncy skirt over her knees. She reached behind her neck and tugged away a rubber band and her hair fell around her shoulders, adding the scent of green apples to the incense stink. She twisted the rubber band onto her wrist.

"Comfy?" she said.

"Sure," Nicky said, shifting because his legs were tingly and falling asleep.

"I'm glad you came by."

Nicky didn't say anything.

"I didn't mean to blow your mind last night."

Nicky shrugged, making the beanbag squeak. "You didn't."

"About Roy."

"You didn't blow my mind," Nicky said.

"I didn't want you to go away thinking I didn't care. About whether Roy is all right." She took a massive breath. "He is all right, isn't he?"

"He's perfectly safe."

Margalo exhaled. She closed her eyes, as if she were allowing the words to settle into her tummy.

"Good." She ran both hands through her hair. Her blue eyes stared at a place on the carpet. "Good."

"I thought you knew," Nicky said. "I thought for sure that Roy was writing you. I guess."

Margalo didn't say anything.

"In fact, in one of his letters to us, he wrote that he wrote. To you. Letters."

Margalo didn't say anything.

Nicky shrugged. "Maybe they got lost in the mail or something."

Margalo said, "Go into that top drawer of my desk over there."

"Me?"

"Yes, over there," Margalo said, nodding toward a white rolltop desk, cluttered with books.

Nicky got out of the beanbag chair, which required rolling to the floor on his hands and knees. He went to the desk.

"This one?"

"Yes."

He pulled on the drawer, which slid open smoothly, revealing a stash of envelopes, all with red, white, and blue borders, all with the military return address. Letters from Roy, thrown in a drawer.

"He did write you. You said you didn't communicate."

"I haven't opened them. One person talking is not communicating," Margalo said.

Nicky blinked. He turned over one of the envelopes. The flap was unbroken.

Margalo said, "He called here once, too."

"He CALLED here? From Vietnam? You can't call here from Vietnam."

"You can, apparently. Maria answered."

"What did he say?"

"I didn't talk to him. I told Maria to tell him I wasn't here."

Nicky's mouth parted slightly, the bottom lip pulled down.

"I don't mean to blow your mind," Margalo said. She unfolded her legs and stood. She moved closer to Nicky. She locked her eyes on to Nicky's eyes.

"I love Roy with all my heart," Margalo said.

Nicky felt goose bumps rise on his arms.

"I told him not to go to that stupid war. I told him if he went, that I would cut him out of my life like a cancer."

She looped her hair behind her ears. The electric guitar music stopped. The phonograph arm rose, retracted, and clicked. Now the only sound in the room was Margalo's voice.

"I told him that if he wanted to go to war, fine. But he was not going to take me to war with him. Do you understand?"

Nicky shrugged.

"I don't want to know what he is doing and how he is. Do you understand?"

Nicky nodded. He did not want to talk about the war. Not now, not in this room, not with that green apple smell, not with this girl, not with those panties on the bed. Talking about the war made his stomach hurt. He wanted to change the subject.

He said, "I think I should go. I have a ton of homework." He made a P-U face and said, "Algebra."

"Yes," Margalo said densely. She spoke in a detached manner, like a peeved adult. "Yes. Algebra. Math used to drive Roy out of his mind, too. I'll walk you down to the kitchen. That's where the glove and ball are."

Nicky had forgotten about them.

Nicky preceded Margalo down the carpeted staircase, book bag bouncing against his knee. He couldn't see her face when she said, "I don't want this to sound harsh, but I don't think you should visit anymore. Is that too harsh?"

"No," Nicky said, feeling the harshness like a slap in the mouth.

"By seeing you, I'll know about Roy. It would be the same as staying in touch with Roy. Do you understand?"

"Yeah," Nicky said.

"I don't wish to be dragged to war."

"Yeah," Nicky said.

He stopped at the bottom of the stairs and faced her, waiting. He shrugged. "If I do happen to run into you, you know, by accident, or something, I could just make a deal. You know, promise not to say anything about Roy."

Margalo's hand dripped off the banister as she stepped down from the bottom stair. She faced Nicky. Those blue eyes drilled into him. He was glad, now more than ever, that he and Margalo were the same height.

"I would see it in your face," Margalo said softly. "I would know in an instant. So my answer has to be no."

They walked through the house, on thin carpets and gently groaning floorboards, past oil paintings illuminated by tiny brass lamps, past shelves crammed from ceiling to floor with clothbound books, through a small room with a giant black piano and a harp, through an elegant dining room with a long gleaming table, into the kitchen where the television was going full volume. Maria did not look up from the sink as they passed through to the breezeway.

Roy's glove, the Spaldeen in the pocket, was balanced atop a battered leather suitcase. Nicky picked up the glove. Margalo opened the door for him. Nicky stepped out into the rain.

"If you're really having trouble with algebra, I can help you with it," Margalo said.

"Help me with it?"

"Sure. I hate it, but I am very good at it. Why don't you come by tomorrow after school? If you want."

"Sure," Nicky said. "But what about, you know. My face . . ."

"You're starting to look like him more and more."

"Who?"

"Roy, silly. Same milk-chocolate eyes."

"Oh."

"Yes. You ought to let your hair grow."

"Yeah."

"Well, so long," Margalo said. She partially closed the door, showing only her face in the opening, drops of rain glistening on her cheekbones. "See you tomorrow."

"Yeah, tomorrow."

Nicky walked home, barely noticing the soaking rain, or the car that needed to brake suddenly to avoid striking him on Summit. He entered the courtyard to Eggplant Alley. He didn't hear Mr. Storch's xylophone dingling from Building A. He didn't smell the fish dinner cooking somewhere in Building C. Nicky's brain was scrambled. Margalo had done it. She had blown his mind.

30
A Friend of Margalo

Nicky visited the Only House With Trees the next afternoon, straight from school. Nicky knocked on the big door. He looked at the stone lions, and the lions looked back with smugness.

"Hey-lo," Margalo said. She locked her blue eyes on to his face. She studied. She smiled. "Come on in, I've got popcorn popping."

Together that afternoon they unlocked the mysteries of algebra. And Nicky tossed popcorn to the setter dog, Martha.

"How is your dog? Chuckles? Was that her name?"

"Checkers. He's a little under the weather," Nicky said, not wanting to get into the sad subject during this happy moment.

Nicky returned to the Only House With Trees the next day to solve the puzzling Periodic Table of Elements. And to listen to music. On some of the songs, Nicky could actually understand the words.

The next day was literature. Nicky was stumped by a long poem that was said to be written in Old English, but did not resemble any English he had heard or read in his lifetime.

Nicky visited the Only House With Trees steadily for two weeks.

"Your grades are really great," Mom said, perusing Nicky's

first-semester report card. "All these afternoons at the library are paying off."

"I am applying myself," Nicky said.

On a day when Nicky was not scheduled to visit the Only House With Trees, he just happened to stroll down Mayflower Avenue at the exact moment Margalo climbed the hill from Broadway. A chance meeting.

Margalo was happy to see him. "Hey-lo," she said. She ran her blue eyes across his face. She smiled. She invited him in.

Nicky was not in the mood to study and Margalo was not in the mood to tutor. So they ate potato chips from a tin—they were actually delivered to the house like milk from the milkman—in her room and drank cola, as much as they could hold. Nicky knocked off his third can of soda and went for a fourth. He could not get used to this house, a place with no adult supervision. Dr. Gildersleeves was always working. The divorced Mrs. Gildersleeves lived in Washington, DC.

"A little touch of heaven," Nicky thought, climbing the stairs with his drink.

Margalo played "Bridge Over Troubled Water" on the stereo. She played it loudly and the windows shuddered in their casements. Nicky had never listened to the great song at earsplitting decibels, and he was moved. And no one hollered at them to turn it down.

After four cans of cola, Nicky needed a toilet. He was embarrassed to ask Margalo for directions to the bathroom. She was too fine and too precious, not the kind of girl you ask about toilets. So he merely rolled from the blue beanbag chair and casually moved toward the door.

"Where are you going?' she said.

"Um, I'll be right back."

"Oh. My bathroom is the third door down on the right."

Nicky hurried along the carpeted hallway, wondering if every female on the planet had radar.

Lost in this deep thought, Nicky miscounted the doorways. He found himself at the end of the corridor, wandering through an open door, into a darkened room. The room smelled of sweaty clothes, sweet perfume, and something like mothballs. A bare mattress was flopped on the floor. A gleaming red electric guitar was leaned against a massive amplifier. On the wall was a flag—a yellow star on a red and blue background.

"Canada, maybe?" Nicky thought.

His eyes fell on a partially opened door to his right, and through the opening he saw a tile floor and at last, a toilet bowl. By now he could not be picky about which bathroom he used.

Nicky pushed open the bathroom door and entered. The room was hot and humid and glowed with a purplish fluorescent light. All around him—in the bathtub, along the floor, along the sink-top, in the sink—were plastic pots of black soil, out of which grew tall, leggy green plants with clusters of pointy leaves.

"Mint?" Nicky wondered, having seen mint plants portrayed on a package of mint candy.

Nicky flushed and found the sink, choked in a thick growth of this strange foliage. He turned out the light and walked out of the humid bathroom. He nearly bumped into a tall beefy boy with shoulder-length hair. Nicky noticed the hair was exactly the same chestnut brown as Margalo's.

The long-haired boy towered over Nicky. He said, "Who in the name of Janis Joplin are you?"

"Nick."

The long-haired boy wore tattered flared blue jeans, a loose-fitting, rough linen shirt, and sandals. A triangular patch of frizzy brown hair pointed from his chin. The long-haired boy stomped past Nicky and reached into the bathroom and turned on the lights.

"You turd! Turn off the lights, man, and you kill the GOODS," he said, not in a friendly tone.

"Sorry," Nicky said, startled to hear anger from a total stranger.

"Who did you say you were?"

"Nick Martini. I'm a friend of Margalo."

The boy smirked.

Nicky said, "I guess I better go. Nice to meet you."

"Hey, do me a favor. Don't come down this end of the house anymore."

Nicky returned to Margalo's room. She was stretched out on her bed, reading a magazine. Banging, whining electric guitar sounds pumped out of the speakers at a deafening volume. Nicky felt the bass in his belly.

"I guess I kind of got lost," Nicky said over the music.

"WHAT?"

"I SAID I GOT LOST."

"HOW COULD YOU GET LOST?" Margalo said. She sat up on the edge of the bed, stretched her arms over her head. She plucked an elastic from her wrist, and pulled her hair into a ponytail.

The door thumped open and the big long-haired boy stood in the doorway. He planted his hands on his hips. He shouted over the music, "HEY, MARGIE, IF YOU WANT TO HAVE BOY SCOUT MEETINGS HERE FINE, BUT KEEP YOUR LITTLE FRIENDS OUT OF MY END OF THE HOUSE."

Margalo continued to wrap the elastic into her hair. She rolled her eyes and said, "ALL RIGHT, Eugene." She shook her head at Nicky and said, exasperated, "THIS IS MY CHARMING BIG BROTHER. EUGENE."

"HELLO," Nicky said. He wished Margalo would turn down the music.

Eugene didn't say anything. He stared.

The record ended, and the room fell into a startling silence. Nicky's ears kept throbbing.

"This is Roy's little brother," Margalo said, leaning on her hands.

"Whose little brother?"

"You heard me—Roy's."

"Oh, yeah. Him. The guy who thought *Easy Rider* had a happy ending," Eugene said. "Whatever happened to him?"

Margalo rolled her eyes. "You know where Roy is, Eugene."

"Yeah," Eugene said. "Yeah. Now I remember. He's busy. Baby killing."

"Eu-gene," Margalo said.

"Just being real."

"Good-bye, Eugene," Margalo said. "Don't pay any attention to him, Nicky."

Nicky stared blankly at Eugene.

"Just being real," Eugene said evenly.

"Good-BYE, Eugene."

"I can take a hint."

"I wish. Good-bye, Eugene. Stop hassling us, Eugene," Margalo said in a singsong voice.

Eugene said, "Screw you," and rocked out of the room.

"Jerk," Margalo said. "Sorry."

"It's all right," Nicky said. His hands shook and his stomach cramped. "I guess I shouldn't of used his bathroom. I got lost."

"You went into his BATHROOM? No wonder he's freaking out on you," Margalo said.

She swung out her legs and rolled off the bed. She replaced the phonograph arm on the album, cranked up the volume, and the guitar music pounded out, bruising Nicky's ears again.

Margalo assumed a ballet position. "HE GETS JUMPY IF ANYBODY POKES AROUND HIS PRECIOUS MARIJUANA."

"WHAZZAT?"

"MARIJUANA. WEED. GRASS. MARY JANE."

"HE GROWS MARIJUANA?"

"WELL, DUH. YES," Margalo said. She twittered on tippytoes across the rug. "WHAT DO YOU THINK OF THIS? A ROCK 'N' ROLL BALLET."

"GREAT," Nicky said.

"YOU DIG HENDRIX?"

"SURE," Nicky lied.

Margalo pirouetted. "WHAT DID YOU THINK THOSE PLANTS WERE? BOSTON FERNS?"

"OH, I THOUGHT THEY MIGHT BE MARIJUANA," Nicky lied. He thought for a moment. "ISN'T THAT AGAINST, YOU KNOW, THE LAW?"

"NO, REALLY?" Margalo said, dancing. She glanced at Nicky. She smiled. "AND YOUR POINT IS? YOU'RE JUST LIKE ROY. SO UPTIGHT."

Margalo tugged Nicky's arm, yanking his hand from his sweaty palm. Her free arm swept up behind her. Her long delicate fingers fluttered gracefully. All this while the electric guitar howled and twanged. Nicky felt her fingertips slip from his palm, tickling him, and he didn't care to talk any longer about the bathroom plants.

"I NEVER SHOULD HAVE QUIT BALLET," Margalo said, puffing. She swept up her hair and piled it on top of her head. "IT ONLY SEEMED FOOLISH TO DANCE WHEN CHILDREN WERE GOING TO BED HUNGRY IN THE WORLD."

Nicky nodded. He watched as she let her hair slip from her fingers and fall mussily across her face and onto her shoulders.

Margalo shouted over the music, "I DON'T MEAN TO BLOW YOUR MIND."

Nicky walked up Mayflower Avenue, the bright foliage of the Only House With Trees receding behind him. His mind was blown. He tromped up the hill in the rapidly chilling November air. He came within sight of Eggplant Alley, shivering as he walked out of one world and into another.

It was almost five thirty, and dads were returning from work, tired and stinky and bored and utterly thankful to have jobs. Nicky reached the unshaded sidewalk of Summit Avenue, and the echo of the piercing electric guitar music faded in his head. Now he heard Mr. Storch's xylophone. He no longer smelled the heavenly scent of green apples. Now he smelled fish frying. He pushed aside thoughts of the evil Eugene when he saw Mr. Willis, machine-gunned in the leg fighting Japanese in World War II, limping home from the sugar factory. Officer O'Dell trotted down the steps onto Summit, heading to his night shift at the 11th Precinct. And on the front steps of Eggplant Alley, picking at the tangled string of a yo-yo, sat Lester.

"There you are!" Lester said brightly. "Hiya, stranger. It's been forever. Where have you been keeping yourself?"

"At the library, studying," Nicky said.

"Your mother told me," Lester said. "Very interesting. I should join you there next time." Lester held up the tangled yo-yo. "Say, do you know anything about these?"

Roy had tutored Nicky extensively on yo-yos. Nicky was an expert handler of yo-yos. Nicky said, "No. I don't know nothing about yo-yos."

"Oh," Lester said. With great force, he spat out a massive blue wad of gum. The gum landed on the sidewalk and glistened in the setting sun.

"Have you ever noticed how closely a chewed-up piece of gum resembles a brain?" Lester said.

"Not really."

A man wearing a plaid jacket hurried past. The man's footstep pressed directly onto the gum. He looked down, shook his foot, swore. The man left a lacy trail of gooey footprints on the sidewalk as he walked away, swearing.

"Did you see that? Did you see that?" Lester whispered, suppressing a cackle.

"No, I didn't," Nicky said, and Lester gave up. Anyone who looked at Lester's face could have seen a cloud gather on the boy's heart, because he was sure Nicky didn't like him anymore, for some reason, and Lester was terrified what the reason might be. Lester's scared, bug eyes revealed an imagination unleashed.

What did Nicky know? How did he know?

Anyone who looked at Lester's face would have seen the cold fear. But no one was looking at Lester's face, certainly not Nicky, a boy with a scrambled, jumbled, blown mind.

"Well, I'm going upstairs," Nicky said without enthusiasm.

"You have a lot of homework?"

"Plenty."

Lester followed Nicky up the steps and across the courtyard and into Building B. Neither said a word. Lester was thinking about Nicky. Nicky was thinking about Margalo. He was frightened and excited. He felt on the edge of something. His mind was sprinkled with a million glittery images and ideas. He thought of green apples and blue eyes and the beauty of the female form. He could not believe that his mind and heart were doing this. He loved these thoughts and he hated them, because they filled him with longing and hopelessness.

They climbed the staircase, and on the second floor Nicky said, "Lester, I have something to talk to you about."

"Very interesting," Lester said. He continued nervously, "Like what?"

"For one thing, do you think my hair is too short?"

Lester blinked, bewildered. He said, "No fooling?" He surveyed Nicky's head and said, "No. It's not too short." He joshed, "Are you planning to grow your hair long like one of those hippies?"

"Why would you say a stupid thing like that?" Nicky snapped as an image of Eugene Gildersleeves flashed in his skull.

Lester mumbled sadly, "Very interesting."

Nicky cleaned his ear with his pinkie. He pictured the evening, his mind a jumble, his skin jittery, at home with Mom and Dad. The idea did not appeal to him. Nicky looked at the door to 2-C. He blurted, "Let's go inside for a minute. I've got a story to tell you. I've got to tell someone, and you're the only one I can tell."

Lester licked his lips and took a step away from the door.

Lester said, "Even better, why don't we go on the roof?"

"What? I don't wanna go all the way up there. I can't sit on the roof in my school clothes. Mom will kill me."

"Let's go to your apartment then."

Nicky stared hard at Lester.

"You're not going to let me into your apartment, ever. Are you."

"It's not that."

"Guess what?" Nicky snapped. "I've had it with you."

Lester burbled, "No really. My mama just washed the floors."

"Forget it," Nicky said with disgust. He huffed toward the staircase. "There are places around here where I'm welcome. To come in and have sodas and potato chips. And listen to music."

Lester said, "Don't go."

"I'm going. Call me when you think I'm good enough to come into your precious apartment."

Nicky should have let it go at that, but he was not his old self. He stopped with one foot on the bottom stair and added, "And you can forget about playing stickball in the spring. Guess what? I don't wanna anymore. I ain't good enough for your apartment, you ain't good enough for stickball."

"Wait," Lester said weakly.

Nicky stomped up the staircase. He was acting like a two-year-old, and it felt delicious. Lester called up to him. Nicky kept walking, climbing, stomping, and with each harsh footstep, Lester's voice sounded smaller and sadder.

31

Barella the Barber

On the last Saturday before Thanksgiving, which was also Roy's twentieth birthday, Dad cornered Nicky in the kitchen. Dad announced they were going down to Barella's for holiday haircuts. Nicky tried to talk his way out of the trip. He complained of a brewing head cold, an awful lot of homework, a strange itch. Nicky promised to get a haircut first thing next week, no fooling, first thing.

"Grab your coat and hat," Dad said. "Don't you start, Nicky. I mean, come on. Look at this."

Dad clutched a handful of Nicky's bushy hair. "For crying out loud, if I had wanted a daughter, I would of had a girl. Don't you want to look well groomed for Thanksgiving?"

Nicky said, "Dad, come on. I don't wanna . . ."

"Enough," Dad said. "What, are you going to give me a hard time about your hair? Didn't I have enough of that with your brother?"

So Nicky walked alongside Dad, block after block down Summit. They were on their way to Barella the Barber on Cherry Street, where Dad grew up, but Nicky felt like a boy on his way to the dentist.

Cherry Street was also known as "the corner" and "the old neighborhood," and Nicky knew it was out of love and thrift that Dad did business there. Part of Dad's heart would always remain on those narrow streets, walking hand-in-hand with Grandma Martini; under the elevated subway tracks, where he played stickball; in those alleys, where he smoked pilfered cigars at age ten; on those fire escapes, where he slept on hot summer nights with his mutt dog, Benito. Dad loved going back to his old haunts. Plus, they got free haircuts from his second cousin Barella.

Nicky and Dad walked, and it was not a pleasant walk. The skies were mean and gray. A brittle wind cut into them and that made Nicky's nose dribble. The air felt cold enough for snow. And proceeding southwest on Summit was to move deeper and deeper into what Nicky understood to be a sinister neighborhood.

Nicky relaxed when he saw Barella's red-and-white-striped barber's pole. The barber shop was a safe haven. The place never changed, year after crazy year. Everything was still the same in that tiny sliver of the Bronx.

Dad and Nicky entered the sanctuary of Barella's, and the small bell on the door tinkled. Nicky beheld the two huge barber chairs of red vinyl and chrome, the canisters of combs soaking in green fluid, the wide black razor straps, the scent of masculine lotions and cheap cigars. Same as ever, same as the good old days.

Seated near the back wall was the same old gaggle of Cherry Street goombahs. Nicky was sure these characters were seated there on the day he came in for his first haircut at age two. He knew some of their names—Dickie Dee and Fat Freddie and Junior, who was in his nineties. The goombahs grunted and hitched up their baggy pants and chewed green cigars and guffawed and whispered racy punch lines and cleared their throats with terrible growls and spat into handkerchiefs. Long ago, Dad told Nicky to stay away from where the old guys sat, because "there are dirty magazines back there." Nicky didn't understand why they didn't just wash the magazines if they were dirty.

Nicky climbed into the barber's chair. Barella cranked up the seat. He snapped open a clean white cloth and draped the cloth over Nicky. Barella, shiny bald on top, a basketball-sized gut flopped over his belt, was in a grouchy mood, which was also a permanent feature of the shop.

Barella started snipping and said to Dad, "So, Fragole, how you doing?"

Leaning back in his seat, legs crossed, Dad seemed to relax in this familiar place, in his old neighborhood, getting addressed by his boyhood nickname. He fluttered his hand in disgust. He told Barella that when he parked his truck to make a delivery the day before, he came out to find half a dozen boxes of Yum-E-Cakes scattered and smashed on the street. Nicky had not heard about this incident until now.

"Where was this?" Barella demanded, snipping faster.

"East Street," Dad said.

"Sheesh, no wonder," Barella said with disgust. He hacked at Nicky's hair and considered the outrage. "That neighborhood has gone to the dogs. The coloreds got that neighborhood by the throat. You know your truck ain't safe there." He flailed his free hand toward the window, poking the scissors point into Nicky's scalp. He boomed, "For crying out loud, THIS neighborhood ain't even safe. Not no more."

"E vero," Dad said gravely. The only time Dad spoke Italian was on Cherry Street.

Barella muttered and told the same sad story he told the last time Nicky was there, and the three visits before that. So many black people were moving into the neighborhood and so many white people were moving out, he barely had enough customers to keep up business.

"I had to let go of Enzo," he said, thrusting the scissors toward the unused barber's chair, narrowly missing Nicky's ear with the thrust. "I couldn't cut the coloreds hair even if I wanted to. I can't cut that hair. It's like wool."

Barella snipped and muttered and exhaled and Nicky choked on the smells of coffee and salami on Barella's hot breath.

The door opened, the bell tinkled, and Frankie "The Pimento" Cabrone strutted into the shop.

"Hey, Frank-EE," Barella said, perking up. He rested his hands on Nicky's shoulders. The Pimento was the neighborhood bookmaker, and he used the pay phone in the rear room of Barella's to call in his illegal bets.

"Cheechi," the Pimento said to Barella. "I got some stuff you may be interested in. Watches."

"Bring 'em by," Barella grunted.

Barella poised his scissors and comb, ready to resume cutting. Emboldened by the pause, recalling the scent of green apples, Nicky said quietly, "Um, please leave it a little longer than usual on top."

"What?" Barella said, leaning his ear closer to Nicky. "What did you say? I didn't hear you."

"I was wondering if you could leave it a little longer than usual on top, so I could have a little something to, you know, comb."

Barella rested his hands on Nicky's shoulders again.

"Hey, Salvatore," he called to Dad. "What have we got here, another one who wants to wear the hair like a girl?"

"Eesh," Dad said, disgusted. "Another one to give me agita. He didn't even wanna come down here today. I had to drag him."

"What's the matter with you?" Barella barked in Nicky's ear. "Don't you want to look like a man? Why do you kids all want to have your hair looking like someone dropped a mop on your head?"

"I just thought . . ."

"You thought. Hey Salvatore, he thought. These kids. Muddun, these kids. Imagine if you told YOUR father you refused to get a haircut!" With each syllable, Barella slashed a piece out of Nicky's hair.

Dad sat back in his chair, rubbing his chin. Nicky wished Dad would spring to his defense. But Dad just sat, rubbing his chin. Nicky suspected Dad's mind was on something else. Nicky imagined Dad was thinking about this day, Roy's twentieth birthday, and remembering old days and the cake he brought home from Orzo's on Roy's first birthday; and the tin milk truck on Roy's fifth birthday; and the cowboy hat and cap gun on Roy's seventh birthday; and the Mercury Space Capsule model kit on Roy's eleventh birthday.

While Barella snipped with a vengeance, Nicky looked at the empty seat next to Dad, the one in which Roy would sit after his haircut. Roy always went first. Roy would fidget and watch Nicky's turn in the chair, making faces and blowing bubbles with the free gum Barella handed out to kid customers.

"Whatsamatta with these kids?" Barella muttered, swiveling Nicky's head forward and clipping with gusto. "No sense of responsibility. They dress like girls and grow beards and run around like crazy people. Kids today. Hanno un atteggiamento ostile."

"You bet," Dad said.

From the rear seats, Junior pointed a bony finger toward Barella and piped up, "My grandson. The other day. He throws a banana at my son when he tells him to get a job."

Barella started the electric clippers and went to work on the top of Nicky's head.

"Hey, tell me about it," Barella said, speaking up over the buzzing clippers. "What a world, huh? That's what I took a Kraut bullet in the foot for. So the coloreds can take over, our kids can throw bananas in our face and wear their hair like Ish Kabibble."

He threw up his hands, pinching Nicky's jawbone with the clippers.

"We slaved for them. What for? Huh? What for? What for? I'll tell you what for. So your kid can wear his hair like Ish Kabibble and my kid can buy a Japanese car. Did I tell you that? Anthony went out and bought one of them Jap cars. Like a Chevy ain't good enough for him."

Barella resumed work, grinding the electric clipper into Nicky's head.

"This is good, Nicola. You're gonna get a good old-fashioned haircut. Like a man," Barella said, calming down.

When Nicky and Dad got home, Mom examined Nicky's hair, which looked like it had been cut by a drunken monkey with garden shears.

"Heavens to Betsy, what did Barella do to you?" Mom gasped.

"He can wear a hat," Dad said.

A Taste of Blue Castle

32

After church on Sunday, Nicky lit a candle and prayed for miraculous hair growth. Record-breaking hair growth. Hair growth eligible for *Ripley's Believe It or Not*. He had only six days. Six days before his next visit to the Only House With Trees. Six days till the next afternoon with Margalo, the treasure of a girl who adored boys with long hair.

Like all bad haircuts, this haircut had staying power. Nicky read somewhere that hair grows faster while you sleep. So he went to bed directly from the supper table on Wednesday night. Mom suspected illness and awoke him to take his temperature.

On Thanksgiving, Nicky wondered if turkey promoted hair growth. He ate two helpings.

The Saturday after Thanksgiving arrived. It was the day of his visit with Margalo. That morning, Nicky ran straight from his bed to the bathroom mirror. His head was still a hacked-up mess. He hurried to the hall closet and dug out his wool winter cap. He would simply have to wear this wool cap with a snowflake pattern. Maybe Margalo would take it as some sort of hippie statement.

Wearing his hat, Nicky walked down Summit toward Mayflower. He sweated hard. Temperatures in New York that day were shattering records. The man on the radio said highs should reach the low seventies.

Nicky knocked on the massive door to the Only House With Trees. He looked at the stone lions and the stone lions looked back with amused eyes. Margalo opened the door.

"Hey-lo," she said. She studied Nicky's face. She smiled. "What's with the hat?"

Nicky shrugged.

"You're going to broil in that," she said, as they walked through the big house, across the thin rugs, past the musty books, to the big kitchen.

"I just feel like wearing it," Nicky said. It was the best he could come up with.

"That's cool," Margalo said. She lifted her chin and assessed the hat. She nodded. "Let your free spirit fly."

Nicky nodded dumbly.

"Let's do homework," Margalo said.

Nicky tried to concentrate on algebra, but he was hot in the hat. The wool itched his scalp. He was also strongly distracted by the smell of green apples from across the kitchen table. Margalo was tip-tapping a political science term paper on an orange portable typewriter. Nicky secretly watched her. He could not keep his eyes on his workbook. She stopped typing and sucked on her lower lip, deep in thought. She chewed on a pencil. He watched her teeth press into the soft, yellow wood. She nodded at the paper in the typewriter carriage, and tip-tapped faster. Nicky felt empty, deep in his stomach.

He tried to say something. "You are a great typist," he said. "You could be a professional secretary."

"Ugh. Perish the thought," Margalo said.

"Yes, perish it," Nicky agreed.

Late in the afternoon, purple clouds rolled in and the temperature plummeted. Nicky's head no longer itched.

"I'm famished," Margalo announced, tossing her pencil on the table. "What do you say we go pick up some hoagies?"

"I could eat a horse," Nicky said. He felt hungry and festive.

"We'll need coats."

From the breezeway, Margalo grabbed a man's corduroy jacket. She wore it over her blouse and flared blue jeans. For Nicky, she produced a worn army field jacket. The jacket was embroidered with a peace symbol; an upside-down American flag; another flag, with a yellow star, same as the flag tacked over Eugene's mattress; a button that recommended, STOP THE WAR NOW.

Nicky said, "Is this yours?"

"This is Eugene's," Margalo said.

"I don't think it'll fit me."

"Roll up the sleeves, it will fit."

"I don't need a coat."

"You wear a hat, but you don't need a coat. That makes sense. Put it on. There. It looks great on you."

"Maybe Eugene will need it."

"He's skiing in Vermont for the weekend. Let's go."

Margalo and Nicky walked down Mayflower toward Broadway in the cooling night. Nicky hunkered deep into the field coat, trying to stay warm, hoping to stay unrecognizable. What if Mom or Dad happened to see him, hippie girl at his side, hippie coat on his back? Nicky shuddered. He did not want to imagine that one.

"What flag is this?" Nicky said, examining the coat.

"I believe that is the flag of the National Liberation Front."

"Whazzat?"

"You know. The Vietcong."

Nicky didn't say anything. Now he calculated the chances of running into Mom and Dad, the way a swimmer calculates the chance of sharks.

When they hit Broadway, Nicky veered to the right toward Lombardo's. Margalo walked to left.

"Come with me," she said.

"Where?"

"The May-Po Luncheonette," she said proudly.

Nicky shrugged and followed her. They passed under a streetlamp, and the bulb burned out as they walked.

"Make a wish," Margalo said.

Nicky clenched his eyes shut. He concentrated, then relaxed. "There."

"What was your wish?"

"If I say, then it won't come true."

"That's only for birthday candle wishes. What did you wish? You can tell me."

Nicky could do nothing but tell the truth.

"I wished that Roy comes back in the spring and we play stickball together just like the old days." It was the first thing that popped into his head, so the words spilled from his mouth. But immediately he worried about Margalo's reaction. He would have preferred to say he wished for something more noble—peace on earth, goodwill toward men, mandatory recycling of bottles and paper.

"I know it's silly," he said, shrugging.

"No way. That was a sweet wish," Margalo said.

Nicky and Margalo passed a mailman, in uniform but without a mailbag. The mailman wore a crew cut straight out of the good old days. As he walked by, the mailman sucked on a cigarette and flickered his red eyeballs across Nicky's jacket, then glared at Nicky and Margalo with pure hate.

"Rotten creeps," the mailman muttered.

"Fascist pig," Margalo snapped.

Nicky wanted to call after him, "Mister! This is not my coat! I am NOT one of Them!"

They stopped at the curb to cross Radford. Nicky said, "Where is this place, Timbuktu?"

"It's worth the walk. They make the best hoagies," Margalo said.

They crossed Radford Street and continued to walk south. Nicky felt like he was strolling across the face of the moon. He was only six blocks from Eggplant Alley, but he had never walked this far south on Broadway before. This was his first time on foot past Radford. There was no reason to walk down here. It would be like going all the way to Shea Stadium to see the Mets when the Yanks were right here in your backyard. Why bother? Everything you needed was within four blocks of Eggplant Alley—Popop's, Lombardo's, Mary's Bakery, the A&P, the Paramount Movie

House, Tom Thumb Toys, Izzy's Used Autos. Now Nicky was strolling past an Ernie's Bakery, a Super Shop, an RKO theater, a Sam's Chevy. Strange places, with strange goods and services, with strange people on the sidewalks. And across the street, Nicky saw the periwinkle neon of the strangest place of all—the Blue Castle hamburger stand.

"Home of the killer hamburger," Nicky mused silently. "So that's where it is." Nicky shivered to imagine Roy actually walking in there, actually eating those hamburgers.

Nicky and Margalo reached the May-Po Luncheonette. The green awning was rolled up tight, the windows were dark, the neon sign advertising Kent cigarettes was switched off. A placard on the door informed, SORRY! CLOSED. COME AGAIN! Margalo tried the door anyhow, the way disappointed people do.

"Bummer," Margalo said. "They make the best hoagies."

"Lombardo's makes pretty good hoagies, too."

Margalo wrinkled her nose. "Yuck, Lombardo's. Grease," she said.

Nicky shrugged. "Yeah. Yuck."

They walked back the way they came. Margalo said, "I am starving." And Nicky could see the next development coming, like a runaway train, like a fly ball to the face, like the papers being passed around for an algebra test for which he did not study.

"Hey," Margalo said. The winking neon from the Blue Castle reflected in her eyes.

"Oh," Nicky said. "I dunno. I really don't like Blue Castle hamburgers."

"Have you ever tried them?"

"Well, sort of. No."

"Silly. Then how can you know? They're quite tasty. Come on, I'll buy you a bag. My treat."

"Nah. You know, I'm not hungry."

"You lie. You said you were starved."

"All this walking kinda killed my appetite."

Margalo placed her hands on her hips. She set her mouth. She locked her eyes onto Nicky's.

"What is it with you Martini boys?" she said. "I practically had to drag Roy into trying Blue Castle. You would have thought I was trying to get him to eat live slugs or rat poison or something. And then he LOVED them."

Nicky watched her lips as she spoke. He thought they resembled soft little red pillows. He smelled green apples on the cool air. He felt powerless. And he followed Margalo across Broadway, into the Blue Castle.

They stood on line. Nicky looked out through the glass at the street. He half expected Dad to burst through the door, yelling "Stop!"

Margalo ordered two sacks of the tiny, bite-sized burgers. One sack for her, one sack for Nicky. She insisted they eat the burgers on the spot, at the counter that rimmed the outer wall of the restaurant. "We don't want them to get cold," she said.

They sat at the window, where every passerby on Broadway could see. Nicky unwrapped a Blue Castle burger. He held it. He sniffed it. He eyed it.

"Honestly, just eat it," Margalo said. "You'll love it."

Nicky took a small nibble, then a bite. He waited for wrenching gut pains, twitches and spasms, death. He bit again. He chewed and he did not want to love it, he was appalled at the thought of loving it, but he could not fight the sensation. He loved it.

He said to Margalo, "Tasty."

Nicky and Margalo walked home by way of Radford. They passed Ludlow Park, shadowy and sinister in the night. Nicky was anxious to move along. He imagined dozens of muggers and drug fiends following them with beady eyes. His legs crawled with the urge to put some distance between them and the wretched evils of Ludlow Park. He knew if there were trouble, it would fall to him to defend Margalo, to the death.

But Margalo stopped walking. "Look," she said. "How sad."

At the edge of the park, on a battered wooden bench facing the sidewalk, under a cracked lamp light, an old black women huddled inside a frayed cloth coat. She held a purse tightly in her lap and a paper bag at her side. From inside the sack the woman produced a peanut, which she held out for a squirrel. The squirrel tittered on the dirt near her worn sneakers. The squirrel placed one claw on the woman's leg, and carefully plucked the peanut from the woman's hand.

"I didn't know squirrels came out at night," Nicky said, who was frightened by squirrels and their potential for rabies.

"This one does," said Margalo. "I see that poor old woman here whenever I pass by this time of night. Every night around six thirty, she's here. That squirrel is probably her only companion."

"It's sad," Nicky said.

"It's beautiful," Margalo said.

"It's beautiful," Nicky said.

"She has nothing. She has been denied all the dignities of life. Yet she finds the time and compassion to come here and feed that squirrel."

"It's beautiful," Nicky said.

"It's sad," Margalo said. "Look at the scene. The woman has such dignity. But we as a society can't match her dignity. We consume and discard. I was just writing about this today in my poly-sci paper. And because of our piggishness, we force her to sit in garbage. Look at that."

Margalo was right. Behind the bench where the woman sat, on the ground all around her, the hard-packed turf was littered by scores of bottles, cans, and newspapers. The debris stretched out far into the darkness. It was like a garbage dump. You could not take a step without tripping over a bottle or can.

"Look at that," Nicky said. "Somebody should do something about that."

"Somebody," Margalo said. "Always somebody."

Margalo stared straight into Nicky's face. His head itched again under the wool cap.

"Always somebody else," she said.

Nicky could see Margalo's breath in the cold air, a lovely delicate cloud in the night. He was startled by the blue of her eyes, even in the dim light. A breeze stirred. Nicky caught a whiff of green apples and Blue Castle burgers. His mind clicked and whirred wildly. Beautiful, heartbreaking notions began to form.

"One person can make a difference," Margalo said.

"So can two people," Nicky said, his throat dry. "Why not us?"

Margalo gently touched Nicky on the cheek and for an instant he felt dizzy, as if he had snorted cola directly up his nose. They continued to walk, and Nicky surrendered to his thoughts, all of them. He let them wash over his brain and seep in. He was gleeful to be walking along the sidewalk in the autumn night with Margalo at his side.

And so the next afternoon, on a chilly Sunday, Nicky and Margalo marched down Radford, wearing heavy sweaters against the gray cold. They cleaned up the mess around the old woman's park bench.

Margalo supplied two large leaf bags, and they filled both bags to the brim with bottles and cans and newspapers and lunch bags and candy wrappers. They cleaned spotless the area all around the park bench, all the way back to the paved path. Not a shred of garbage was left. The old woman had a clean place to feed her squirrel, thanks to Margalo and Nicky.

As they lugged the lumpy bags up Radford, Margalo huffed, "I wish I could see that woman's face when she comes here tonight."

"Me, too," said Nicky.

33

Hi-C in 2-C

Mom made the announcement, while preparing supper, that a big change was coming on December 16. Nicky waited for Mom's next sentence and thought, "Must be a change for the worse."

Mom said she took a job at the Gimbels department store up in Yonkers. She would be a salesclerk. Full-time. She was hired for the holiday season, with a very good chance for permanent work after New Year's.

"We could use the extra money for Christmas," Mom said, dicing potatoes. "We could use the money to get out of this place."

Mom glanced over her shoulder at Nicky.

"I don't want to see a long face," she said. "Count your blessings. Be thankful I can find work."

On the first morning of this new arrangement, Mom hustled around the apartment, getting ready for work while Nicky got ready for school. (Dad was already gone, an hour into his Yum-E-Cakes delivery circuit.) Nicky poured his own cereal and milk, remembered his own lunch money, found his own shoes. Mom could not help him. She rushed to catch a bus, which would take her to another bus, which would carry her to the shopping center in Yonkers.

When Nicky arrived home after school, he was unnerved by the empty apartment. The place was silent and still. The apartment felt cold and deserted and bleak. There were no signs of life. The apartment was exactly the way Nicky had left it. He forgot to return the milk bottle to the refrigerator after breakfast, and the bottle was still there, warm on the table. His clothes remained on the floor near his bed. The toilet paper roll was still empty in the bathroom.

Nicky plopped cross-legged on the living room rug. He thought about the *TV Guide* featuring Ann-Margret, which he had hidden at the bottom of Roy's sock drawer. He hadn't looked at the magazine for weeks. Now with Mom at work, with no chance of her coming through the door unexpectedly, Nicky could stare all he wanted at the dress that might be a nightgown.

"I wonder who Oliver Twist is?" he said, talking to himself.

Nicky's ears picked up a quiet rapping. He went to the door. He heard shoes shuffle on the welcome mat. He heard breathing. Nicky put an eye to the peephole. A thick pair of nerd glasses, in fish-eye focus, looked back at him.

Nicky opened up for Lester. Nicky was glad to see an actual person. He was extra glad the actual person was Lester. He had to admit that to himself, but he did not have to admit it to Lester.

"Yes?" Nicky said frostily.

"Hello," Lester said. "How are you?"

"Couldn't be better."

"Are you busy?"

"I got some homework."

"Yes. I am really loaded down myself. I was wondering something."

"Yeah?"

"If you'd like to come down and do your homework with me."

"Where?"

"In my apartment."

"Did you say, in your apartment? Your apartment? Now? Your apartment?"

Lester nodded eagerly. Nicky pursed his lips, as if mulling the offer, weighing his options, considering other invitations. He said, "Sure. Lemme get my stuff."

As he toted his book bag and followed Lester downstairs, Nicky felt a welling in his chest. Finally, he was headed for Lester's apartment. Another breakthrough.

Nicky held his breath as he entered the formerly forbidden turf of 2-C. Nicky gawked here, gaped there. He moved along, down the corridor, past the kitchen, into the living room, and his eager eyes beheld . . . absolutely nothing. There was not a blessed thing remarkable about the place.

Nothing.

There was no evidence of spies, pirates, communists, Nazis, counterfeiters, or gangsters. No shrunken head collection. No skeletal remains of kidnapped neighborhood pets. No sign of Amelia Earhart.

"Well, here we are," Lester said.

"Where's your ma?"

"Downtown. She won't be back till six."

"Cool."

"Want some Hi-C?"

"Definitely."

While Lester went to the kitchen, Nicky examined the living room. He wasn't snooping, but if he happened across a clue, he wouldn't have averted his eyes. Nice recliner. Okay television—a little old, with brass-colored rabbit ears. Standard table of framed photographs, just like the one in Nicky's living room. All the photos were black and white. A portrait shot of Lester's mother, at a younger age. A slew of baby pictures.

The boys opened their books on the living room rug and dived into their homework. Inspired by the Hi-C and a pressing need to snoop, Nicky went to the toilet. In the bathroom, Nicky took note of the fluoride toothpaste, a strange comb in the medicine cabinet, and bath towels that might have come from a hotel.

On his way back to the living room, he peeked into the master bedroom (two twin beds, night table in between, pink slippers on the floor). He peered into Lester's bedroom (one twin bed, an old school desk, way tidier than the room Nicky and Roy shared). The whole layout was identical to Nicky's apartment. Kitchen, living room, two bedrooms, a bath. Everything seemed in order. If there were secrets in 2-C, they were well hidden.

When the apartment darkened, Lester switched on a lamp. Nicky announced it was time to get home before his parents returned from their jobs.

"They would never think to look for me here," Nicky said.

"Your mama is working?"

"For now," Nicky shrugged.

"Very interesting," Lester said. "Say. I was wondering."

"What?" Nicky said, loading his book bag.

"Do you mean what you said about stickball? About not wanting to play?"

Nicky saw pain and fear in Lester's eyes. But he also felt a new power, and he decided to leave the pain and fear right where it was, at least a little longer.

"We'll see," Nicky said.

Nicky returned to his apartment, which was still empty, now dark. He hurried from room to room and turned on every light, even in the bathroom. Then he parked at the kitchen table and peered down Groton. He looked and waited like he did in the old days.

Cars zipped back and forth along Lockdale. A van slowed, but did not turn. Nicky heard muffled noises and voices from other apartments, which made his apartment seem more quiet, more empty, more lonely. Nicky hummed, just to make sound.

At last Dad's delivery van, orange directional flashing, swung off Lockdale and rattled down Groton. Nicky was relieved. One missing piece was on the premises.

Dad settled into his chair and read the *Daily News*. Nicky resumed his homework on the coffee table. Fifteen minutes before six, Mom came home. Her eyes were puffy. She shivered from the cold walk from the bus stop. Nicky exhaled. Two missing pieces were on the premises.

"What a day," Mom said. "I'm bushed. When I left, there was

still a line from the men's department all the way to cosmetics. They wanted me to stay. Overtime. Any mail from Roy?"

"Nothing," Dad said from behind the paper. "I don't want you working late. It ain't safe on the bus late. Look, right here in the paper. Some guy got stabbed on the bus in Newark."

From the kitchen, Mom called, "Who left the milk out? P-U—it's spoiled."

The traditional supper-hour racket built in the kitchen. Pots slammed. The refrigerator door thumped angrily and the bottles inside clinked.

"Hey, Mom, what's for supper?" Nicky called. He was glad life was close to normal—Mom and Dad and Nicky in place.

Mom marched into the living room. She plopped a colander filled with brown potatoes into Dad's lap, crushing his newspaper. She presented Dad with the peeler.

"Potatoes," she said. "They need to be peeled."

She tossed a paper bag of green beans and a paper towel onto the coffee table. "Green beans. They need to be snapped." She started for the kitchen. "I'll do the meat loaf."

Dad numbly peeled potatoes. Nicky numbly snapped beans.

As they peeled and snapped, Dad and Nicky exchanged disbelieving glances. Nicky's bottom lip stuck out. Before that moment, supper was something that appeared on the table, like magic.

"I feel like I'm back in the army," Dad grumbled.

Nicky sat on the plastic slipcover and snapped beans. It was the sort of work that left time to think. Nicky mulled over the Mystery of 2-C.

"Hey, Dad, what would you think if your best friend never let you into his apartment. For a long time. Then all of a sudden one day, he lets you into his apartment."

"And?"

Nicky shrugged. "And it was just a regular apartment. There's nothing strange there."

"I dunno," Dad said. "Is this some sort of riddle? If it is, I'm not in the mood."

"I just wanted your opinion," Nicky said.

"I guess I don't know," Dad said. "Maybe the strange thing wasn't there anymore."

Nicky snapped a bean and said, "I think maybe you're right."

34

Gifts

Nicky walked home from school by way of Broadway. The wide street was a bustling holiday scene. People lugged shopping bags and hurried along the sidewalk. Plastic Christmas trees were fastened to lamp poles. Multicolored Christmas lights blinked in the window of Lucky's Tavern.

At the apartment, all the usual Martini family Christmas things were in place. The battered, beloved cardboard box was out of the back hall closet. Year after year after year, the box yielded the pair of stuffed reindeer—one for Nicky, one for Roy; the plastic manger; the Santa Claus with a cotton ball beard, crafted by Roy in fourth grade; the old Santa Claus snow globe, liquid half evaporated; ancient boxes of tinsel; ornaments; a rat's nest of tree lights.

The tree, undecorated, was already in the stand in the living room. Dad brought home the tree from Butch's Sunoco. It was a family tradition for Dad and Roy and Nicky, all three of them, to take the delivery truck down to Butch's and pick out a tree. They selected a tree together every year. But with Roy absent, Dad chucked tradition. Picking out a Christmas tree was just another chore. He grabbed a tree by himself one day on the way home from work.

Mom was baking sheet after sheet of Christmas cookies in the kitchen. The kitchen was hot and the windows were fogged by the oven. Nicky pestered Mom and she finally broke off from baking to scrounge a small box and wrapping paper from one of the off-limit nooks in her bedroom. Nicky asked Mom not to come into his room for a while. He said he would be wrapping gifts and he did not want Mom to walk in on him and ruin the surprise.

Nicky wrapped Mom's present, a silver crucifix purchased at the St. Peter's school Christmas fair. He wrapped Dad's present, a pen-and-pencil set from Walgreens.

He went to the doorway of his room.

"Hey, Mom. MOM. Remember. Don't come in here, all right?"

Eyes darting to the bedroom doorway, Nicky carefully placed the six scented candles in the box. He thought, "Margalo will love these." He nestled them, handling them like baby birds, on tissue paper. He admired the arrangement. He dropped his nose to the box, and the mixed smells of cinnamon, boysenberry, orange, lemon, and green apple made him swoon. He wrapped the box, taped a ribbon to it, and slid the present for Margalo deep under his bed. The presents for Mom and Dad went into the closet.

Nicky informed Mom that he had a quick errand to run to Popop's.

"What? It's almost dark. What do you have to go to Popop's for?"

"I can't tell you. It's a Christmas thing."

"Don't bother," Mom said. "Whatever it is, we don't need it. Stay here." She picked up a dust mop. "You can help me clean."

"I have to go to Popop's."

"What for?"

"I can't say. It's a surprise."

Mom sighed. "Well, if you have to go, hurry up. Look at it out there. It's dark. Honestly, I wish you'd just stay here. Go out tomorrow. Don't give me that look. All right, go. Just go. But hurry."

Nicky rushed to the bathroom and brushed his teeth, flushing the toilet to cover the sound of the brushing. He emerged minty-mouthed from the bathroom.

Mom stood before him with the dust mop in one hand and the present for Margalo in the other. Mom was truly amazing.

She said, "What's this?"

"A present."

"For who?"

Nicky shrugged.

Mom said, "Who's it for?"

"I dunno."

"What do you mean you don't know? Who's it for?"

"Dad."

"Oh," Mom said. She turned the box every which way. "I'll put a tag on it for you. I'll put it out by the tree, with the others. Now get going if you're going to go to Popop's. It's started snowing."

A steady snow fell from the black sky as Nicky reached the Only House With Trees. He pressed the bell alongside the massive door and watched snow gather in the crevices of the house. He caught snowflakes on his tongue. Cones of snow had formed on the heads of the stone lions. The stone lions looked back with merriment.

Margalo pulled open the heavy door. "Hey-lo," she said. She studied Nicky's face. She smiled.

"I was beginning to think you weren't going to make it," she said cheerfully. "Come on in. You look like Oliver Twist out there in the snow."

Margalo wore a bulky sweater and black slacks. Her chestnut hair, shiny in the hall light, was draped along her shoulders. Nicky took in the sight of Margalo and his stomach rumbled.

"We have to get going if we're going to beat this snow," Margalo said. The Gildersleeveses were driving to Vermont for the holiday. Suitcases, boxes, boots, and skis were heaped at the foot of the staircase.

Eugene careened down the steps, two stairs at a time, sandals clicking. His ponytail flopped against his back as he came down the stairs. He glanced at Nicky and grunted and moved along heavily.

"I can't stay long, either," Nicky said. "I have—" He fished the checkbook-sized, gift-wrapped box from his coat.

"Here."

"What's this? For me?" Margalo said. She shook the box near her ear, jingling her bracelets, and she smiled. "What could it be? Go in the sitting room for a sec. I'll be right there. Go on. Right through there."

Nicky walked across the thin, elegant rugs. The floorboards under the rugs groaned with dignity as he moved. He entered a warm room decorated with delicate furnishings, the kind of furniture that made Nicky nervous. To him, this kind of furniture seemed brittle, on the verge of snapping. He lowered himself carefully onto a velvet-covered sofa.

"Merry Christmas," Margalo said, sweeping into the room. She handed Nicky a gift-wrapped box the size of a toaster. She sat next to him on the sofa, close enough for Nicky to smell green apples. She cradled the gift-wrapped box from Nicky in her lap.

"You first," she said.

Nicky ripped off the paper. It was a baseball mitt. It was the Rawlings B-4000, stunning in its display box, clean and stiff and brand new behind the cellophane. Nicky had asked Mom and Dad for a mitt for Christmas, and like every kid he had admired the B-4000 in the sporting goods department at Gimbels. But he refused to even dream of getting a B-4000. How could he? They sold for a whopping $55. He had asked Mom and Dad for the D-250, and even then felt a twinge of guilt at the $17.95 price tag.

"You can use it in your stickball games in the spring," Margalo said.

Nicky felt dry in the throat.

"You'll need a mitt in the spring," Margalo said.

"Yes," Nicky said.

"You said you wanted to play stickball this spring. You said that the night we went to the Blue Castle."

"Yeah, I did."

"Now you'll have a brand-new mitt for the occasion."

Nicky said, "I will."

"Is it an okay mitt?"

"It's a great mitt."

"Now, mine," Margalo said. She flipped the hair off her shoulders and unpeeled the paper. Nicky thought Margalo in this moment looked like a little girl, bouncy and excited over a Christmas gift. Margalo placed aside the wrapping paper and admired the slender, imitation-leather box. She gently opened the hinged lid. She grinned and nodded in appreciation of the gold pen and pencil. Nicky saw that he had neglected to remove the Walgreens price tag.

"I can't wait to write with these," Margalo said. "Thank you Nicky." She leaned toward Nicky, and her movement depressed the couch cushion and tilted Nicky toward her. He felt her sweater against his arm and her breath on his face and then he felt Margalo's lips, sticky with frosty lipstick, touch his cheek, a sweet moist brush on his skin. It happened before Nicky could think.

When Nicky got home, he walked zombie-like past the kitchen. His mind was blown, delightfully. He had removed the glove from its box and ditched the box in a basement trash can. He had the new glove stuffed under his winter coat, near his heart.

"Where have you been?" Mom called. "Did you get what you wanted?"

"Yes," Nicky said quietly.

Nicky was examining his cheek in the bedroom mirror when Mom appeared at the doorway.

"What are you doing? What's that on your cheek?"

"Frosting. I had a cupcake at Popop's."

"Cupcake? You know I made cookies. What's the matter with you?"

35

A Christmas Story

On Christmas Eve, Mom put a Bing Crosby album on the hi-fi. The old songs were comforting, soothing and sweet, when the needle didn't skip.

Dad strung the lights. Nicky hung the ornaments. Mom took a break from cooking clam sticks and balanced on a chair to attach the star to the top of the tree.

Roy had always been in charge of the finishing touch—hanging the tinsel. The tinsel was right there on the coffee table. Two new boxes of it, on sale from Woolworths. But nobody touched the tinsel. The tree was just going to have to go without tinsel this year.

On Christmas Day, Nicky slept straight through till eight thirty. This was a Christmas morning record. Even on the Christmas when he was delirious with the Hong Kong flu, Nicky had leapt out of bed and dived under the tree, close on Roy's heels, at 6 AM sharp. But on this Christmas morning, Nicky swung his feet to the floor and absently gazed out the window, a boy not really looking forward to the day. The snow had turned to a slushy rain. His eyes were drawn to Roy's empty bed.

Nicky yawned and slithered off his bed. He found his slippers. He shuffled to the toilet. Then he went out to the tree. Mom and

Dad followed the same route, from the bathroom to the tree. No one bothered to turn on the tree lights.

They opened presents.

Nicky received the three top gifts he had requested. A blue turtleneck shirt, which he picked out of the Gimbels catalog. Five new books in the Hardy Boys mystery series. And the main present, the baseball mitt. Nicky gasped when he opened that one. His parents had sprung for the expensive B-4000.

"Do you like it?" Mom said. "Now that I'm working . . ."

"It's the best," Nicky said.

"We figured we'd get you the best," Dad said. "Although, it beats me what you need a mitt for."

"Salvatore, don't ruin it," Mom said.

"For stickball," Nicky said, admiring the mitt.

"Nobody plays stickball around here anymore," Dad mumbled.

Nicky said, "Mom, Dad. Open yours."

Mom adored her crucifix. Dad was puzzled by the scented candles. He removed them from the box one at a time. He sniffed them carefully. He wrinkled his forehead.

"Am I supposed to eat these?" he said.

And it was over before they knew it. The present opening passed in a flash, which only made sense. Roy wasn't here—the gift total was reduced by one-third.

Mom, Dad, and Nicky sat on the rug and fiddled with their gifts. They didn't know what to do with themselves. No one could look away from the presents that were tagged for Roy.

"I guess we'll have another Christmas in the spring," Dad said through a yawn.

"It's too quiet," Mom said. "Put on Bing Crosby."

Mom went to the kitchen to start breakfast. Dad pulled on his galoshes and headed out to buy the newspaper. Nicky thought they acted like two people who couldn't wait to get out of that living room.

For the first time in Nicky's lifetime, they did not visit Aunt Serafina and Uncle Dominic for Christmas dinner. Dad said the roads were too slippery for a drive. Nicky looked down the length of Groton. He saw traffic whoosh with ease through the skim of slush on Lockdale. He shrugged. He didn't feel like going anyhow.

Nicky read his new Hardy Boys books on his bed. He tried to pace himself. He didn't want to burn through them all at once.

Mom listened to the radio in her bedroom. Nicky heard her spin the dial when a news broadcast came on.

Dad camped out in the kitchen. He said the kitchen was the warmest room in the house, today at least. He drank coffee and ate Christmas cookies. He read the *Daily News* and sniffed his new candles. Dad seemed partial to the boysenberry.

By the late afternoon, Nicky had finished every one of the Hardy Boys books. He looked out his bedroom window. Christmas lights blinked colorfully around the courtyard. A man and a woman, bundled in heavy coats, strolled the walkway, their arms loaded with gifts. Suddenly Nicky's bedroom seemed suffocating. The apartment felt hot. Nicky's legs crawled.

"I'm going out for a walk," he told Mom.

"On Christmas?" Mom said from her bed.

"I wanna look at the lights."

As he passed the kitchen, he told Dad, "I'm going out for a walk."

"The boysenberry is nice," Dad said. "But this orange. It's starting to grow on me."

Nicky huddled against the cold and kicked at the slush as he walked though the courtyard. He strolled down Summit and rated the Christmas displays on the tiny lawns. One house was lit up brightly enough to be seen from New Jersey.

Nicky doubled back and headed down Mayflower. He gazed at the Only House With Trees. He looked through the bare branches at the large, dark house. He thought about the delicate sofa in the warm room. For the first time all day, he felt a Christmasy tingle in his gut.

He walked all the way down Mayflower. He turned left and walked along Broadway. It looked like a scene from one of those horror movies where Martians invade and the cities are evacuated and the streets are abandoned. There wasn't a soul or a car in sight. Even the crazy, dirty Moon Man was not at his beggar's post on the sidewalk. Nicky imagined the Moon Man at home, carving up a large turkey, surrounded by happy family and friends. Even the Moon Man was having a better Christmas than Nicky.

He started the climb up Radford. Popop's neon sputtered. Popop's was open. "It figures," Nicky said.

Across the street in Ludlow Park, the old black woman sat on her park bench, paper bag of peanuts at her side, and Nicky felt a warm glow in his chest. The woman stared at Nicky as he walked into the park and strolled straight to her bench. Nicky said, "Merry Christmas." The woman nodded.

Nicky sat on the bench.

The woman scooted farther down the bench away from him.

Nicky was happy. He surveyed the ground that he and Margalo had cleaned of bottles and cans. The grass was slushy. A small amount of trash had accumulated. But only a tiny amount. Nicky counted only six bottles and two cans. Thanks to Margalo and Nicky, on this Christmas, this old woman did not have to sit amid a pile of garbage to feed her squirrel.

"A beautiful night," Nicky said. He wanted to start a conversation with this woman and work his way onto the subject of the cleaned-up garbage. He wanted to bathe in the woman's happy reaction and torrent of thanks. He wanted this, as another Christmas gift to bring to Margalo.

The woman didn't say anything. She clutched her bag of peanuts closer to her lap.

"Say, isn't it great that this part of the park was finally cleaned up?" Nicky said, twisting to look over the ground with admiration.

The woman didn't say anything.

"Yup," Nicky said. "It took a lot of work for us to clean that junk up. But it sure was worth it."

"You?" the woman said, suddenly enlivened. "You're the one who took away those bottles and cans?"

"Well, yeah," Nicky said modestly. He shrugged. "No big deal."

"You cleaned this place up?"

Nicky nodded proudly.

"Well, I guess I owe you a heap of thanks," the woman said.

"No need . . ."

"For this," the woman said.

She removed her wool hat. A section of her hair was shaved clean. On the bare patch was a six-inch-long set of ugly black sutures.

"Do you know who put those bottles and cans there?" the woman said, her voice rising.

Nicky shook his head.

"I put them there," the woman said, not in a friendly tone. "I put them there so if any fool tried to sneak up on me in the dark, I'd hear him making a racket, creeping through all that garbage."

Nicky didn't say anything.

"A couple times, I heard them creeping up, way far down by those bushes. I just got up and got out of here with plenty of warning."

Nicky didn't say anything.

"But you cleaned them up. Well, thank you mightily. First night with them bottles gone, I don't hear a thing when that fool snuck up and conked me on the head with that pipe. He snuck up quieter than a cat. Grabbed my purse. AND my peanuts."

Nicky didn't say anything.

"I just got out of the hospital last week."

Nicky didn't say anything.

"I'd appreciate if you would bring them bottles back, so I can feed my squirrel and be safe."

Nicky didn't say anything.

"Although I haven't seen him. My squirrel friend. Without me to feed him for a month, I bet he up and died."

Nicky said glumly, "Listen, lady, I thought we were doing you a favor."

The woman glared at Nicky. She looked at the sack at her side. She gritted her teeth and simmered.

"You thought," she grumbled.

Nicky shrugged stupidly.

"You thought."

Nicky wished he were somewhere far away from this park bench.

"You thought WRONG," the woman barked. She flung the sack of peanuts at Nicky. The bag hit him in the chest and split open, showering Nicky with peanuts.

Nicky stood up.

"Next time, mind your own business," the woman said bitterly. "Do me a favor, son—don't do me any more favors."

Nicky started to walk away.

The woman shouted, "MIND YOUR OWN BUSINESS."

Nicky broke into a run. He ran out of the park. He felt a peanut trickle out of his hair. He heard it click on the sidewalk as he ran. He sprinted up Radford. His breath made clouds in the cold air. He thought, "I don't think I'll mention this to Margalo."

36

Promises

Nicky pushed the tiny button alongside the big door to the Only House With Trees. He looked at the stone lions and the stone lions looked back with bright eyes. It was morning on New Year's Day, clear and painfully cold. As usual, the start of a new year made Nicky ask the traditional dreaded question, "What will happen next?"

Margalo answered the door.

"Hey-lo," she said. She studied Nicky's face. She smiled. "Come on in, you look like Oliver Twist out there in the cold," Margalo said.

She wore red flannel pajamas. Her chestnut hair was delightfully mussed. A fire crackled and popped in the kitchen fireplace. It was the first actual fire in a fireplace Nicky had even seen. Every Christmas Eve, Nicky watched the Channel 11 broadcast of the burning Yule log. It was nothing more than a film of a fire in a fireplace, but it was perfect for city dwellers without the real thing. In the good old days, Roy would make a big show out of warming his hands by this roaring fire pictured on Channel 11.

Margalo prepared two mugs of hot chocolate. She topped off Nicky's mug with a mountainous splutter of whipped cream.

"How do you like the glove?" she said.

"The B-4000 is a great mitt," Nicky said.

"Do you think it will be cool for stickball?"

Nicky nodded while sipping the hot liquid through the cold whipped cream.

"It will be time for stickball before you know it," she said.

"I suppose you are right," Nicky said. "If we have enough players."

"You have whipped cream on your lip. You need players?"

"Sometimes not enough people want to play. Sometimes too many people want to play. If you know what I mean."

"I have no idea what you mean," Margalo said. "Think of this." Margalo tossed her head, flipping her hair off her shoulders. "Maybe I can play."

Nicky laughed. Margalo, not laughing, not smiling, fixed her blue eyes on him.

She said, "What's funny?"

Nicky didn't say anything.

She said, "Jesus, why are you putting me down? I can play."

"I wasn't. I didn't think . . ."

"I guess you didn't," Margalo said icily.

Margalo clunked her mug on the table. She pushed back her chair and stood. Nicky felt a sudden knot in the bottom of his stomach. So this is what it was like to have a girl throw you out of her house.

Margalo yanked open the door to the breezeway. Nicky felt a coldness on his shins, and on his heart.

"On second thought . . . ," Nicky said.

"Just be quiet," Margalo snapped. Nicky stared deep into his hot chocolate. He wished he were tiny enough to dive into the cup and disappear under the whipped cream. His throat was too tight to sip.

Margalo rummaged around the breezeway, tossing items heavily, muttering. At last she produced a tennis ball and a baseball glove.

"Come on," she said. She tossed the glove at Nicky. It smacked him hard in the chest. "You catch. I pitch."

After the sofa and a chair were shoved aside, the kitchen in the Only House With Trees was big enough for a real catch. Margalo stood by the table. Nicky remembered the distance from pitcher to batter on the PS 19 schoolyard—forty paces. Nicky counted forty steps from Margalo, moving far into the sitting room. He squatted like a catcher.

Margalo pinwheeled her arm.

"Ready," she said.

Nicky nodded.

Margalo threw fastballs, straight and speedy and true. She threw hard enough to make the tennis ball pop in Nicky's mitt. She threw a slithery curveball, a tough trick with a tennis ball. She broke off a tantalizing drop pitch, every bit as mesmerizing as the famous drop pitch thrown in the good old days by Icky Rossilli. She threw and threw. Nicky noticed she made a small grunting sound with each pitch.

"What do you think?" Margalo said. She was building a sweat, playing ball in flannel pajamas in the dry heat thrown off by the fireplace. Strands of moist chestnut hair were stuck to her cheeks.

"Do you think I can play with you boys in the spring? When the sky is powder blue and the sun yellow and the pear tree showers us with a blizzard of white blossoms?"

"Oh, yes," Nicky murmured.

"You want to play with me?"

Nicky nodded dumbly.

"Promise?"

Nicky nodded. He didn't trust his mouth to work. Because he was thinking some very private thoughts. He knew he shouldn't think this way. He knew these thoughts were silly and wrong, worse than all the other forbidden thoughts combined. But he saw Margalo, a girl who could pitch, her moist cheekbones delightful in the firelight, and he ceased thinking altogether. Nicky whispered in his head, "Oh, I love you. I do love you."

"You should see the expression on your face," Margalo said. "You didn't think a girl could pitch, did you? I'll show you in the spring. Wait till the spring. I'll show you I can play your freaking game. Why the face? Sorry. I don't mean to blow your mind."

Nicky strolled to the refrigerator on the morning of February 1 and ripped January off the calendar. He carefully folded the page into a paper airplane, just the way Roy had taught him. Nicky lifted open the kitchen window and the blast of icy air pinched his nostrils. He flicked the paper airplane out the window and watched it wobble on the gusts over Groton Avenue.

"What are you doing?" Mom said. "Do you own stock in Con Edison? Close the window."

"Look, Ma," Nicky said, pointing at the paper airplane. "Time is flying."

"Cute," Mom said. "Where are my boots?"

Nicky inhaled deeply and sang out, "February first. Spring is in the air!"

"Did you eat Sucrets for breakfast again?" Mom said.

"Yankees start spring training in eleven days," Nicky said smartly.

"That's in FLORIDA," Mom said. "You used to love winter. I have to go to work. Love it or hate it, either way, there's a lot of winter left."

The next morning, Nicky awoke to a blizzard raging.

"She has weather radar, too," Nicky muttered, as sleety snow hissed against the windowpane.

Nicky moped into the kitchen.

"Hey-lo," he grumbled to Mom.

"What was that?"

"I said, 'OH, no.' Because school is closed."

"Since when do you dislike snow days?" Mom said. "Did you want to go to school? Did you hit your head or something?"

"It's just all this SNOW," Nicky said. He wiped the fogged kitchen window with his hand and looked out at the PS 19 playground. The asphalt, the baselines, the bases were buried under huge, sugary mounds. Blowing snow was plastered against the schoolyard wall, whiting out the strike zone. Drifts of snow reached to the top of the chain-link fence.

"It's never gonna go away," Nicky whined.

"Count your blessings," Mom said. "It's just snow. Some people have to put up with earthquakes and tornadoes."

Nicky was oiling and flexing a new B-4000 baseball mitt when Lester rapped on the door.

"Come on in," Nicky said gloomily.

"Want to play Monopoly?" Lester suggested.

"Nope," Nicky said, working his fingertips into the mitt in endless circular motions.

"Want to watch television?"

"Nope."

"How about a spirited game of checkers?"

"Nope."

"What do you want to do?"

Nicky looked up and said, "Play stickball."

Lester swiveled his head to the window. Snow was falling harder than ever. He adjusted his glasses. He stared at Nicky, as if Nicky had cockroaches crawling out of his ears.

"I know it's snowing." Nicky shrugged. "But that's all I really wanna do. I just can't wait until spring."

Lester held up his hand. "Hold the phone. It's definite then? You want to play this spring? After all? No fooling?"

"Why do you think I was oiling the glove? For my health?"

"Very interesting," Lester said. "Very, very interesting." His eyes bulged behind his glasses. He slapped his hands together. It was the first and only time Nicky saw Lester clap his hands in glee.

Lester said, "No fooling. You mean it?"

"I ain't fooling."

"Promise?"

"Promise."

Lester moved to the window to take a good long gaze at the snow, heavy and swirling. Nicky put down his greasy glove and stood next to him. The wind shook the windows in their casements. In a heavy snow like this, the tenements of Groton Avenue actually looked beautiful. It was a winter wonderland.

"I hate this lousy snow," Lester said. "I sure wish this snow would go away and spring would get here."

"You took the words right out of my mouth," Nicky said.

The snow did not let up. The day dragged. The boy had their minds on only one subject. Nothing else would do. The Ringling Bros. circus could burst through the door, and they would not be interested.

They oiled the mitts. They swung the old yellow stickball bat in the living room, careful of the lamps. They gripped the old Spaldeen. All they cared about was stickball.

They watched the snow and longed mightily for tender breezes and baby-blue skies and bright sunshine on asphalt.

"We have to do something," Nicky said. "I'm jumping out of my skin."

"Me, too," Lester said, fidgeting.

Obsession is the mother of invention. Nicky and Lester improvised. They did what restless boys have done since the invention of indoors. They played ball in the house.

"Are we allowed to do this?" Lester said, popping his fist into Roy's old mitt.

"No," Nicky said, pushing aside the coffee table. "Let's get started."

"Very interesting. Have you ever played catch inside before?"

"Plenty," Nicky said.

Lester's first throw sailed past Nicky and knocked the rabbit ears off the television. Nicky threw back and Lester muffed the catch. The ball bounced off Lester's shoulder and plopped into a flowerpot, spraying black soil onto the floor.

"Kick the dirt under the table," Nicky advised.

Lester's second throw hit the ceiling and ricocheted solidly against the windowpane. The boys held their breath, awaiting the sickening crash of heavy glass.

The window did not break.

"Close but no cigar," Nicky said. "I guess this room is too small." He dropped onto the plastic slipcover on the couch. "Guess I'll just oil my mitt some more."

"What will I do?"

"Go get your mitt and oil it."

"I don't wanna get oil on Willie Mays's autograph."

Nicky shrugged.

"I have got an idea," Lester said. "I read about this in a magazine."

Lester told Nicky the story about a baseball player in the minor leagues. This player prepared for each season by eating the baseball cards of star players.

"He's nuts," Nicky said.

"Maybe," Lester said. "This fellow said if he eats the baseball card of a player, it gives him the skill of that player."

Nicky shrugged. Snow pelted the window. "Why not?" Nicky said. "We haven't got anything else to do."

Nicky toted the worn shopping bag of baseball cards into the living room. Lester wanted to improve his hitting. From the bag he selected a Frank Robinson card, a Willie McCovey card, and a Hank Aaron card. He placed them side by side on the coffee table. Nicky was interested in pitching. He selected a Mel Stottlemyre, a Sam McDowell, and a Jim Palmer. Nicky placed the cards on the coffee table.

The boys looked at the cardboard cards. The faces of Robinson and McCovey and Aaron and Stottlemyre and Palmer and McDowell, smiling in various action poses, stared back.

"I don't think I'm going to be able to do this," Lester said with a grimace.

"Me, neither," Nicky said. He thought for a moment. He snapped his fingers and jumped to his feet. He raced to the kitchen and returned with a jar of Skippy. "Peanut butter. Roy always said anything tastes good with peanut butter on it."

Nicky applied a layer of Skippy to Jim Palmer. Lester spread a swirly coat onto Hank Aaron. Covered by peanut butter, the baseball cards appeared exactly like crackers.

The boys dug in. They ripped and chewed and giggled. They bit some more and chewed some more. The cards still held a hint of bubblegum, which combined interestingly with the taste of cardboard and peanut butter.

"Water," Lester croaked.

"Yeah," Nicky gagged, bolting for the kitchen tap.

The boys gulped their water and licked the peanut butter from their teeth. They smacked their lips and grinned.

"I may be crazy," Nicky said. "But my right arm. It feels really strong."

"Very interesting," Lester said. "I think I know what you mean." He examined his hands. His eyes bugged behind his thick glasses. "My hands. My wrists. They feel powerful."

"Do you think it's possible?"

Lester shrugged and said, "You have to have faith. My grammy always said to believe in the power of faith."

"I believe it when I see it," Nicky said. He flexed his shoulder. His arm felt rippled, as if mighty steel bands were coiled tightly in his biceps. "I don't think I can wait for spring to see it."

"Me neither," Lester said, examining his wrists.

Nicky and Lester rode the elevator down and tried not to laugh. They wore heavy wool hats, winter coats, galoshes, and scarves. And they carried baseball mitts, the yellow stickball bat, and a Spaldeen.

"They're going to put us in the nuthouse," Nicky said.

"We ate baseball cards," Lester said. "Perhaps we belong in a nuthouse."

The boys stepped off the elevator in the lobby and waddled in their heavy getups toward the rear door. Professor Smith was passing through the lobby. There was snow on the shoulders of his overcoat and snow in the rim of his derby hat. His cheeks and nose were red. The Professor eyed the Spaldeen and the bat and the gloves.

"That's the spirit, gentlemen!" he said.

Nicky and Lester slogged through the blizzard, toward the PS 19 playground. Snow stung their faces. The wind took their breath away and their knees ached against the deep drifts.

The boys trekked across the playground. They giggled as they struggled, crunching the snow, marveling at the intimate hush of a raging snowstorm. Lester guessed the location of home plate on the wall and assumed his batting stance. Nicky counted off forty paces. He could barely see Lester through the snow. He took a pitcher's stance.

Nicky wound up and threw the Spaldeen through the falling snow. His pitch was straight and powerful and true, faster than any pitch he had ever thrown. It was faster in fact than any pitch he had ever seen. It was a pitch worthy of Jim Palmer.

And Lester, with the Hank Aaron baseball card bubbling in his belly amid peanut butter and tap water, locked his eyes on the ball as it sizzled through the snowflakes. He swung the bat with ease and power, a mighty, crisp swipe. He connected, right on the button. He walloped the ball high and deep. The ball took off in the direction of Groton Avenue and disappeared in the gauze of falling snow.

"If I hadn't seen it, I would not believe it," Nicky shouted into the wind.

"I saw it and I don't believe it," Lester said, making a face at his icy wrists, as if they belonged to someone else.

They searched for the Spaldeen in the snowdrifts near the chain-link fence. There was no sign of it. The Spaldeen had been swallowed up by the swiftly falling snow.

"That was Roy's ball," Nicky said, ice on his eyebrows.

"Don't worry, we'll find it," Lester said, eyeglasses fogging. He placed a frigid hand on Nicky's winter coat. "As soon as the snow melts."

"Yeah. In the spring," Nicky said, brightening at the promise.

37

One Thing Leads to Another

Now Nicky could look ahead to the spring and see promise and relief, which is to say he saw stickball and Roy. And because of this he felt a gladness creep into his heart and snuggle there.

He hopped out of bed each morning, rushed to the refrigerator, and drew a hearty X through another date on the calendar. And for the rest of the day, he lived light and happy. He felt like a traveler, motoring to a favorite place, making good time, heading in the right direction. He walked through his days smiling. People being what they are, they would ask him, "What are you smiling about?" And Nicky could not explain it to them. He didn't want to explain. Nicky would just shrug, and smile wider.

At school, Nicky suddenly got the hang of algebra. He merely looked at problems involving triangles and intersecting lines and immediately saw the course of action needed to solve them. This mathematical aptitude came out of nowhere.

In gym class, in his first crack ever at volleyball, Nicky scored the winning point. He slapped the ball into the face of Ricky McFarlane, the class tough guy. Nicky saw the red welt rise on Ricky McFarlane's cheek and marveled at the new strength in his pulsing right arm.

"Thank you, Jim Palmer," Nicky said.

One day during lunch, Nicky glanced up from his baloney sandwich and gazed without fear or shame at Becky Hubbard. She was seated two tables over, taking dainty nibbles from a sandwich. Her spearmint eyes caught him looking. And when she looked back, she might have smirked, but there was also a chance she had smiled. Nicky guessed that the odds were 70:30 in favor of a smile. Best of all, he didn't really care, either way. Becky Hubbard didn't seem so pretty anymore. Ann-Margret was prettier. Margalo was way prettier.

One sunny February morning, when there was a tiny trace of warmth in the air, Nicky passed Mr. Misener in the courtyard and said, "Hey-lo, Mr. Misener. Almost feels like spring, doesn't it?"

The old grouch grunted and moved on, but not long after that, the first-floor windows in Building B were suddenly repaired. These were the windows broken in the fall of 1963 and left unfixed since, and now the punched out panes were removed and replaced by shiny new glass.

The elevator smelled better, too. The Rosatto brothers moved to New Jersey, without saying good-bye. Right afterward, the elevator assumed the pine scent of cleaning fluid, and retained this new, pleasant odor. A young family from Cuba took the Rosattos' old apartment. And one day Mom came home from work and said, "I just rode the elevator with that new woman who moved into 3-D. The Cuban. She said she would be happy if I stopped by sometime for Cuban black coffee. She says it's stronger than espresso, if you can believe it." Mom thought over this development and concluded, "I think maybe I will. She doesn't seem so bad."

On Valentine's Day, the weatherman on the radio said the temperature was seventy-two degrees in St. Petersburg, Florida, where the New York Yankees huffed and puffed through the early days of spring training. Nicky removed his sweater in the kitchen upon hearing that news. The sports announcer on the radio said the Yankees were expected to field their best team in years, and they had a real crack at the World Series. Nicky daydreamed about taking in a Yankee game with Dad and Roy in the summer. And he wondered if Dad might somehow score World Series tickets from the big shots at Yum-E-Cakes Inc.

Late that afternoon, Mom came through the door from work and Nicky was in the living room, doing homework. In the kitchen, Mom sniffled and stifled a sob. Nicky heard the sounds of sorrow and his stomach turned.

"Nicky," she gasped. "Please come in here."

His heart thudded. He was afraid to walk to the kitchen. He had to force his feet to move. He reached the doorway to the kitchen. He held his breath and examined Mom's face. His eyes darted to her hands. She held an envelope, with a red, white, and blue border, and an unfolded piece of paper. But the handwriting on the envelope was not Roy's. The paper was the thin, tissue-like stationery used by Roy. But the handwriting on the paper was not Roy's.

Someone, not Roy, had sent them a letter from Vietnam. That kind of letter never brought good news.

But Mom was smiling. She licked her lips and closed her eyes. She was smiling. Nicky looked carefully. He was not mistaken—

she was smiling. Mom blinked through tears and presented the fluttering sheet to Nicky.

"It's from Roy," she said.

"Is he all right?"

"He's great," Mom sniffed. "Read it. He's coming home on March twenty-first."

"Next month?"

"The first day of spring."

Nicky took a deep breath. Now his hand trembled. He saw Mom stare at the hand. Nicky smiled weakly and said, "You scared me."

"Why do you always expect the worst?" Mom said.

"I don't," he said. "Not anymore."

Nicky read:

> Dear Gang,
>
> I am dictating this letter to my friend Sgt. Manuel Rivers. I will explain that in a moment.
>
> Sorry I have not written for so long. We have been straight out busy. I had to even work on Christmas Eve. (Manny says I should quit whining.) You would not believe the paperwork that goes into fighting a war. But I had a good Christmas. First me and some of the fellows went into Saigon during the truce. The place was really festive. It was my first chance to get to meet real Vietnamese people besides the girls who come in here and do our laundry. Anyway, it was a very busy and noisy place. It reminded me of Chinatown. Then we celebrated Christmas Day here at the base. Someone scrounged up a real tree. We decorated it. Then

we opened our presents and someone had a case of Schlitz. Then get this—we played with our toys! Man, it was like the old days when we were kids. Remember them? Some guy got a race car set and we set it up and took turns racing. Another of the fellows from my unit got water balloons. He was running around soaking everyone. Plus get this—Manny (he says to put in he is from Mount Vernon) got a Spaldeen from his mother. We got a broomstick and we played stickball all Christmas afternoon, drinking Schlitz. Hey Nicky, look out, I have developed a pretty good sinker pitch here and if you want to play stickball this spring you had better be ready to be struck out.

Oh, Ma, also, the Christmas cookies were a big hit.

This brings me to the good news and the bad news. I have been hurt. But not too badly. During a stickball game two days ago, my pal Sgt. Rivers stepped on my right hand. He is a big lummox (am not!). I was going for a ball and he was going for a ball, I slipped, he walked on my hand. This is what they call "a non-combat-related injury." The doc says my tendon is messed up and three fingers are broke. The hand is infected. Ma—I needed you to wash it and put a band-ade on it. The good news is, I can't type with a busted hand. By the time it heals, it will be time for me to come home. My commo said all I have to do is train my replacement and I can catch the bird home. I feel crummy, like I am not doing my duty. But the big man insists. So Gang, I am coming home early! My DEROS is now March 21. Circle that on your calendar.

I guess I should make plans, huh, Dad? I'm thinking about college for real, which I should have done before. Now I can use the GI Bill for it. I guess I will just be happy to see you all, and eat some of Ma's eggplant, and yes even to see you, Nicky. I guess your pretty big now, but not too big for your big brother to beat your brains in if I have to.

I have to run. See you all in 40 days.

Love,

Roy

PS—How is Checkers?

A squeaking sound made Nicky look up from the letter. Mom was using a black permanent marker to draw a thick black circle around March 21 on the kitchen calendar.

"It sounds like he had more fun on Christmas than we did," Nicky said.

"Oh, don't complain," Mom said. "Count your blessings."

Dad came home from work, and Mom met him at the door. She handed him the letter, as if it were a report card with straight A's. As he read, Dad stood with the door open, pine-scented elevator air puffing in from the hallway, *Daily News* folded under his arm.

"Where's the black marker?" Dad said.

"I already did it," Mom said.

"Okay, someone get me a beer."

Dad drank his Ballantine in loud happy slurps and stared at the date circled on the calendar. He was beaming. "Know what?" he said. He belched happily. "Know what? I'm gonna stop by Orzo's tomorrow. I'm gonna order up one of those big sheet cakes. Like the one we got him for graduation. I'll have Orzo write on it. WELCOME HOME ROY. How does that sound?"

Dad gazed at the circle on the calendar. He said, "Seeing that, now it seems real."

Dad took a seat at the kitchen table.

"It feels warm in here. Hey, Nicky-boy," he said. "Whaddya say the three of us take in a Yankees game in the spring? Like the good old days?"

"Promise?" Nicky said.

"Sure."

"Can Lester come?"

"Sure."

"Promise?"

"I just said so," Dad said.

Nicky rapped on the door to 2-C. He heard feet shuffle, a brushing against the peephole. Then a clunk, a squeak of a closet door, the jangle of coat hangers, a door click shut.

Lester opened 2-C.

"We just heard from Roy," Nicky said. "He's coming home March twenty-first."

"Very interesting," Lester said, eyes cloudy behind his thick glasses.

"Isn't that great? Maybe your dad will be home by then, too."

Lester shrugged.

"When is your dad coming home?"

Lester shrugged. "He doesn't write to us as often as your brother does," he said flatly. "He always said combat is twenty-four-hour work. I don't know. When we don't hear from him for a while, I worry that something's happened to him. Then I hope maybe he isn't writing because he's on his way home, and he will just show up at the door. That's how my daddy is."

"You'll hear from him," said Nicky, resisting the gloom that emanated from Lester like a bad odor.

Lester stood in the doorway to 2-C and shrugged.

Nicky said, "Gotta run. I gotta go to the library. Why don't you come over after school tomorrow?"

"Surely," Lester said.

"Bring your mitt. I'm sure it could use a good oiling."

"I don't want to ruin the Willie Mays autograph, remember?" Lester said.

"Maybe I can find a spare B-4000 for you to borrow," Nicky said.

"It will probably be too big for my hand."

Nicky gave up. "Listen. I gotta get to the library. I'm sure everything will be cool. I'll see you later."

Nicky strolled down Mayflower Avenue and patted the rear pocket of his flared blue jeans, brand new from Gimbels. He had a Valentine in that pocket, and he did not want it to fall out onto the sidewalk. On the front of the card was an outlandish cartoon drawing of a small dog. The inside of the card read, "They call it puppy love." Nicky had picked out the card at Walgreens, bought the card, filled out the card to Margalo, and carried the card in his book bag for three days. But he was unsure about this card. He pressed the small button next to the large door at the Only House With Trees, and looked at the stone lions while the stone lions looked back with sly eyes, and Nicky didn't know if he would actually deliver the card to Margalo.

Margalo pulled open the door. “Hey-lo,” she said. She wore a blue sweater and faded jeans and she was barefoot. Her hair was ponytailed. She said, “Why don’t you start coming around to the kitchen?” Then, as if remembering a chore, she studied Nicky’s face.

She smiled. She smiled extra big.

“You have brought me something,” she said.

“Maybe.”

“You have brought me some good news.”

Nicky shrugged. He thought, “They all have radar.”

Margalo pulled two kitchen chairs across the floor so they faced. She sat in one chair. She directed Nicky to the other. Their knees touched. Margalo leaned close and drilled her blue eyes into Nicky’s face. He could smell green apples in her hair.

She said, “What’s the good news?”

Nicky told her about the letter from Roy. He told her that Roy was all right and that he was coming home early. On March 21.

Margalo took hold of Nicky’s hands. “The first day of spring,” she said quietly.

She sighed.

“Oh, my,” she said.

Nicky said, “So what are you going to do? I mean, when he comes back?”

“Do? About what?”

Nicky said carefully, “About . . . anything.”

“About us?”

Nicky’s ears felt hot.

“I guess first thing I’ll do is read all his letters,” Margalo said.

She released one hand from Nicky's, touched her hair, and gripped Nicky's hand again. "Then I guess I'll see him. I'll kiss him. I'll marry him. I'll leave him forever." She laughed. She tossed back her head. "I don't know. How can I know? I don't mean to blow your mind."

Nicky didn't say anything.

Margalo continued in a low, solemn tone, "The most important thing is that he's done with that evil, immoral war."

Nicky didn't say anything.

She said, "He should have never gone. Never. I'm going to have to process that. I'm going to have to work to forgive him for that."

She flickered her eyes at Nicky.

"I don't mean to blow your mind."

"You didn't," Nicky said. He took a deep breath and said, "I want you to know something. I'm proud of Roy. He doesn't need to be forgiven. He needs to be thanked. He served. He did his part. He will always have that. And I want you to know something else. That when the time comes, I hope that I'm as brave as Roy. I hope I do my duty."

There was a long silence in the kitchen.

"I didn't mean to blow your mind," Nicky said.

"Well," Margalo said, smiling thinly. "What's gotten into you?"

Nicky shrugged.

Margalo gently released Nicky's hands and leaned back into her chair. Her blue eyes seemed to examine every pore on his face. Nicky stared back into her eyes. He saw something new in those eyes. He concentrated hard, telling himself, "Don't blink. Don't look away." He would hold his ground on this one. He saw tiny specks of green in the blue. He saw her pupils dilate, a hot black, then shrink again.

Margalo leaned forward. Her nose was just a few inches from Nicky's face. He could strongly smell green apples in her hair. It was like taking a big bite of green apple. She sucked in her bottom lip. She looked like a person weighing options. She looked a little like Roy, just before he tossed a water balloon.

Margalo spoke quietly, nearly in a whisper, as if to a co-conspirator. "How old are you going to be this year?" she said.

"What do you mean?"

"How old are you going to be this year?"

"Fourteen."

Margalo examined a place on the tile floor, then shifted her eyes back to Nicky. He felt the hair on his neck tingle.

She said quietly, "It would seem to me that you're old enough."

"Don't say anything," Nicky ordered himself. He heard a steady, rhythmic, sloppy panting. He panicked. "Is that me?" Then he saw the dog. The panting sound came from Martha the Irish setter, passing through the kitchen.

"I want you to come here tomorrow. At six sharp. There's something I have been thinking of doing with you. You may be a little young. But something tells me that you're not. I think you can handle this."

Nicky's throat felt tight. He said, "I think what how is . . ."

Margalo reached her fingertips to Nicky's mouth. He felt her trimmed nails brush his lips.

"You'll see," she said. "Can you drop by at six o'clock?"

Nicky walked home, up Mayflower onto Summit and into

Eggplant Alley, and he felt as if he were walking in a dream. His thoughts were hopelessly tangled, like last year's string of Christmas lights There was no way to sort them out. Nicky patted his back pocket. He had forgotten all about the Valentine card for Margalo. Nicky thought, "Tomorrow's another day. I'll give it to her tomorrow."

38

Six O'Clock Sharp

All day at school, Nicky had a goofy look on his face, like a boy who sat in mashed potatoes. If a teacher, any teacher, had shot him a question in any class, only one answer would have popped from Nicky's mouth: "Six o'clock sharp." On this day, that was the lone fact that mattered. Nicky didn't care about yesterday or today or tomorrow. He only cared about tonight at six. Six o'clock sharp.

When he got home, Nicky dashed straight to the bedroom and fished out his turtleneck. The blue one from Christmas. That was the only piece of clothing he was sure of. He had thought all day about his wardrobe for the evening. All he came up with was the turtleneck. How could he know what to wear? He didn't know where he was going or why. He only knew he was on his way.

A knock at the door made Nicky blurt, "Dammit!" His first swear ever uttered out of reflex instead of calculation. The way grown-ups swear. One thing was leading to another.

Nicky squinted through the peephole. He saw the distorted image of Lester's nerd glasses. He had forgotten all about the invitation to Lester.

Nicky opened the door and said, "Hey-lo." He examined Lester's face.

"You look glum," Nicky said. They walked aimlessly into the living room. "I guess you haven't heard from your father."

"Not a word," Lester said. "I have to admit I am worried. I wasn't truly worried until you told me you heard from your brother. I haven't been able to stop thinking about it."

Nicky didn't say anything.

"I have a bad feeling about this," Lester said. "Every time I hear the elevator stop on our floor, I hold my breath. I expect an officer and a chaplain to be knocking on our door."

"Is that how they do it?"'

"That's how they do it," Lester said. His eyes were moist and red behind his thick glasses. Nicky was at a loss. He didn't know what to do or what to say. Six o'clock sharp crowded all other thoughts from his cranium.

"You know what I'd like to do?" Lester said, suddenly perking up. He chattered now with enthusiasm, "I'd like to make a DEROS calendar. For your brother. Know what that is? Date Estimated Return from Overseas. I want to make a calendar with all the days between now and March twenty-first. That's what you said, right? March twenty-first. Then every morning, first thing in the morning, you can cross off a day until your brother comes home."

Nicky thought the idea sounded like a project for a kindergartner. He was about to say so when Lester said quietly, "That's what I plan to do the minute I find out about my daddy's DEROS."

Nicky rummaged through his closet and pulled out the Crayolas, colored markers, school-grade mucilage, and construction paper. In no time, the boys were cutting and drawing and collaging on the coffee table. Nicky had to admit, it was pleasing to make this calendar. The project would have been more pleasing with a wide-open afternoon and a free evening ahead of him. But he had something big and historic to do—and he could only guess what—at six o'clock sharp. The looming appointment with destiny made it difficult to handle safety scissors.

Still, Nicky happily colored and marked and drew, and he loved the sound of scissors slashing through construction paper. It was a sound of innocence, sweetness, and happiness. The sound of childhood. Nicky wondered when was the last time he cut up construction paper, and the thought never occurred to him that this might be the last time.

The living room smelled sharply of magic marker. Lester hummed as he worked a purple marker around the border of a sheet of paper labeled MARCH. The marker squeaked shrilly then stopped squeaking. Lester shook the purple marker like a thermometer.

"This is out of ink," he said.

"Use another color," Nicky said, wondering what time it was.

"That will look silly," Lester said. "I have a purple marker downstairs. I'll get it. I shall return."

As soon as the apartment door slammed, Nicky was on his feet, rushing to the kitchen clock. It was ten minutes past four.

Nicky scurried to the bedroom. While working on the calendar, he had formulated his ensemble: blue turtleneck, flared denim jeans, his super-wide leather belt with the big shiny buckle. He was undecided about socks and footwear.

"Maybe a pair of Roy's black dress socks," Nicky thought. "As long as I remember to put them back before he gets home."

There was a knock at the door. Nicky said, "Dammit." His second swear ever uttered out of reflex instead of calculation. Lester had made record time traveling round trip to the second floor. Nicky reached for the doorknob, but before he opened up, he felt his sinuses swoon. He thought he smelled Roy's aftershave. He sniffed. No doubt about it. From the other side of the door—it was Old Spice.

It was Roy's aftershave. It was a miracle.

Nicky slapped his face against the peephole, and unbelievably, amazingly, wonderfully, the viewfinder was filled with the olive-green uniform issued by the United States Army.

Nicky's heart thumped happily and he yanked open the door and looking down at him was a tall stranger wearing an officer's cap and alongside him was a priest.

Nicky gasped and said, "Are you here for Lester Allnuts? Oh, no. Is it his father? He'll be right back."

The man in the army uniform said with a gentle, syrupy southern accent, "Son, we're looking for a Mr. or Mrs. Salvatore Martini. Are either of them at home?"

Nicky led the two men into the living room. He felt as if he were floating.

"What happened? What is it? What happened? I'm his brother.

Tell me what happened." Nicky's voice was pitched high, like the yelp of a person falling.

The army officer and the priest stood near the couch. The officer held his cap in his hand. He said, "Son, how old are you?"

"I'm thirteen. Why would you want to know that? Too young to be drafted yet, if that's it. Tell me what happened."

"Son, I'm sorry, but per regulations we cannot release information to minor relatives."

The officer looked at the priest. The officer looked back at Nicky. Nicky noticed this man had baggy, sad eyes, like the eyes of a basset hound.

"What time do you expect your parents to come home, son?"

"My mother is home at around five thirty."

"Is there any way to contact either your mother or father right now?"

"No," Nicky said. He assumed Mom was already on her way to the bus. Dad was driving somewhere in the Bronx.

The officer pulled back his cuff and looked at his watch. He made a face.

Nicky whimpered, "Please, mister. This is torture."

The officer looked at the priest then back at Nicky. The officer licked his lips and said, "I can tell you this. It's not the worst news, son. That's all I can tell you. And I'm out on a limb by telling you that much."

Nicky relaxed. He took that to mean Roy was not dead. That was something.

"May we sit?" the officer said.

"Yeah. Yes," Nicky said. The officer removed his overcoat. He and the priest sat on the couch. The plastic slipcover groaned as they settled in.

Nicky sat in Dad's chair across from them. His stomach made a gurgling, moaning sound. They all just sat there. Nicky examined the officer's uniform. He looked at the colorful ribbons, the shiny buttons, the silver pins, the gold symbols. At the place for medals, there were no medals. Nicky looked at the black enamel name tag. It read: O'TOOLE. Whenever he saw or heard that name for the rest of his life, Nicky would think of this moment in the living room.

"You said five thirty, is that right, son?" the officer said.

Nicky nodded. His mind was working. He sorted through the horrible possibilities. Roy was wounded. Burns, bullets, bombs, land mines, punji sticks, bayonets, rockets. Maybe just slightly. Maybe very badly. Nicky wondered which parts of his brother might be torn, shredded, or missing altogether. Arms, fingers, nose, ears, jaw, belly, legs, feet, eyes. He went through the whole inventory.

"Will he be able to play stickball?" Nicky said.

"Pardon?"

"No matter," Nicky mumbled. "Nobody plays stickball around here anymore."

Nicky wondered which part of his brother was missing, and whatever happened to Lester.

Of all nights, on this night, Mom and Dad ran late. Nicky, O'Toole, the priest—none of them said another word for another hour and twenty minutes.

The army officer named O'Toole and the priest jumped to their feet when they heard keys in the door at six o'clock on the nose. The door opened and Mom sang out, "Nicky! Sorry I'm late. The bus . . ." Mom, clomping in her winter boots, entered the living room. Mom looked at the two men, and the two men looked back at her. She flinched, as if someone had smacked her on the back, between the shoulder blades.

Mom said vacantly, "Can I help you?"

O'Toole introduced himself and the priest. He removed a piece of paper and an eyeglass case from his overcoat. Mom lowered herself onto the couch. O'Toole put on half-glasses, coughed softly, and read aloud:

"Mr. and Mrs. Salvatore Martini. The secretary of the army has asked me to express his deep regret that your son Private Roy S. Martini has been missing in Vietnam since February thirteenth, nineteen seventy-one." Mom farted loudly into the plastic slipcover as O'Toole continued, "He was a passenger aboard a military aircraft. The plane did not return at its scheduled time of four fifteen PM on February thirteenth. Search efforts have been delayed because of bad weather. A representative of the commanding general of US Third Army will contact you personally to offer assistance. Signed, Floyd Devins, major general, United States Army, the adjutant general."

O'Toole took off his glasses. He handed the paper to Mom. She looked at the paper as if it were something vulgar.

"What was he doing in an airplane?" Mom mumbled.

"I'm sorry, ma'am. That's all the information we have. As soon as additional information is available, you will be contacted."

"Would you like me to stay?" the priest said. It was the first time Nicky heard him speak.

"No," Mom mumbled. "No. Thank you. If I were you, both of you, I could not wait to get out of here."

Dad returned home five minutes after O'Toole and the priest left. He whistled as he came through the door and approached the living room, then stopped whistling. Mom was on the couch, still wearing her heavy coat and boots. A puddle had formed on the rug around the boots. She opened her mouth, but said nothing. She handed up the slip of paper to Dad. He read it and as he read, the *Daily News* slipped from under his arm and splayed on the living room rug.

Dad sat next to Mom on the couch. It was a long time before he said anything. When he spoke at last, he said, in a small whisper, "What was he doing in an airplane? I told him . . . I told him . . ."

Nicky walked down Summit Avenue, crossed the street, and started down Mayflower in the dark. He had left Mom and Dad on the sofa. He wondered if Mom and Dad would ever be able to lift themselves off that couch. Nicky told his parents he needed to get out of the apartment, which was true. He told them he was going to visit Lester, which was not true.

Nicky pressed the tiny doorbell next to the big door of the Only House With Trees. He looked at the stone lions and the stone lions looked back with sad eyes. The door was pulled open and Margalo sang out cheerfully, "Hey-lo! You're late, you're late, for a very important date. If we hurry to the bus we can . . ."

She studied Nicky's face. She threw her hands over her eyes.

"No," Margalo said. "No." She uncovered her eyes and stepped backward, away from Nicky. She bent over at the waist, as if gripped by a terrible agony in the gut. "No. Go away. Don't say a word. I am begging you. Please, please, please. No."

Nicky said, "It's . . ."

"NO!" Margalo cried. The sound came from somewhere near her heart. She crept backward, putting distance between herself and Nicky, as if he were something dangerous.

Nicky stepped into the house, onto the thin rug, toward Margalo.

"Go away," Margalo said. She was red-faced and sweaty. Her voice was hoarse, throaty. "I mean it. Don't take another step. Don't say another word. Go away."

Nicky stepped toward her. "Lemme . . ."

Margalo turned and ran. She ran like a little girl playing tag on a schoolyard. She hit the staircase and climbed the steps two at a time. From the top of the stairs, she howled, "GO AWAY."

Nicky heard a door slam.

He clomped up the staircase, also two steps at a time. He ran down the hallway and leaned his cheek against the peace poster on Margalo's bedroom door.

"Margalo . . ."

From inside came a piercing scream, a wail from somewhere desperate.

The sound of heavy footsteps made Nicky look to his left. Eugene was stalking down the hall.

"What in the name of Janis Joplin is going on here?" Eugene said.

From inside the room came a plea, muffled words spoken by a face buried in a pillow: "Make him go away."

Eugene glowered at Nicky.

"You, what did you do to her?"

"I didn't . . . It's my brother."

"Oh," Eugene said. He glanced at his sandals for a moment, then looked up into Nicky's face, and shrugged, "Well, he went."

Desperate, mournful sobbing sounded from the bedroom.

Eugene opened the door slightly. He slid through the opening and said, "Margie, it's me."

The door closed gently in Nicky's face. From inside the room he heard Margalo's voice, retching and choking and gasping for air: "I wish . . . I had never . . . met him. I wish . . . I had never . . . laid eyes . . . on him."

Nicky walked softly down the hallway. He passed the staircase, without descending. He picked up speed and marched straight into Eugene's room. He stepped onto the mattress and pulled down the Vietcong flag from the wall. He flung open the bathroom door. He jammed the flag into the toilet and flushed it. He waited and flushed again. Water gurgled and backed up somewhere in the pipes. The pipes thunked in distress.

He was breathing hard and sweating now. He grabbed two marijuana plants, one in each hand, and ripped them out of the pots. He tossed the plants onto the rug outside the door. He pulled out every one of them, two at a time. The more he destroyed, the hungrier he grew for destruction.

One thing led to another.

Nicky threw the pots out onto the rug. Pots cracked open. Dirt scattered. Nicky was satisfied. Now he could leave.

Nicky climbed Mayflower Avenue and reached Summit Avenue, and to him the yellow lights of Eggplant Alley seemed as warm as his mother's eyes. Nicky heard Mr. Storch's xylophone and televisions going and water running. The noises were as soothing as a lullaby. He knew he was home, and he shocked himself by thinking, "The finest place in the world."

Nicky's legs were weak. He shuffled up to the second floor. He could barely walk. He needed help. He knew that his best friend Lester was the only one who could help him. Lester was the only one who knew about the letter that Nicky threw down the sewer. The letter that would have kept Roy out of that airplane. If only Nicky hadn't thrown it down the sewer.

Nicky knew Lester would help.

He thanked the Lord for Lester and rapped on 2-C. The door flew open and Nicky looked up into the face of a middle-aged black man, his hair speckled with gray. Nicky's brain flashed: "What's going to happen next?"

Nicky shot a look at the door number. He was tired and frazzled. His eyes were watery. He thought perhaps he had knocked on the door to the wrong apartment.

The door lettering said 2-C.

"Can I help you?" the black man said.

Nicky breathed hard. Lester must have moved. He said stupidly, "Does Lester Allnuts live here?" And as he spoke, Nicky saw something familiar in the black man's face. It was the eyes. Nicky had seen these eyes somewhere before. A million times before, behind the thick lenses of black-rimmed nerd glasses.

"Why, sure," the black man said. "He's my son. Let me guess—you're Nicky."

The man stuck out his hand. Nicky limply shook the hand.

"I'm John Allnuts. I just got in a couple hours ago. I've heard a lot about you. Come on in."

Nicky stepped into 2-C and immediately saw why Lester never wanted him to enter 2-C. On the wall inside the door was a framed portrait of Mr. Allnuts, black face smiling, resplendent in his army dress uniform. Nicky noticed the picture frame was scratched, as if the portrait had been hastily thrust into a closet many times.

"Lester is in the shower," Mr. Allnuts said. "I hear your brother is in the army, too."

"I have to go," Nicky said.

Nicky ran up three flights of stairs and burst into the apartment. Mom and Dad were still on the couch, still in their winter coats, now in the dark. Nicky hurried to his room and dropped to his knees at his bed.

He slipped a hand under the mattress and produced the composition notebook left over from first grade. He flipped to the page that listed the five things that ruined his childhood. He slowly ripped out the page. In his silent dark room, the tearing of the paper was like a whisper. Nicky calmly shredded the list into tiny pieces and threw the pieces out the window. The bits of paper fluttered in the courtyard air like confetti. Nicky watched the paper fall and muttered, "Kid stuff."

39
Turning Blue

Days and days passed, but Nicky no longer looked at the calendar. There wasn't a single date worth circling.

Days and days passed, and Mom clammed up and kept busy, working hard at Gimbels, working hard at home. She scrubbed, she scoured, she polished, she baked, she laundered. She organized the button box, rolled pennies, alphabetized the record albums. For the first time in Nicky's life, she knitted (she produced a toaster cover). She strung beaded bracelets again, this time not for the money, but for the distraction. Mom was determined to never sit still, not for a minute.

Days and days passed, and Dad sat still, every chance he got. Dad took the zombie option. He got up, he went to work, he came home and sat in his chair with the *Daily News* in his lap, but he didn't read the *Daily News*. At supper time, Dad ate without appetite. Mom had to encourage Dad to finish his meals, which was a first.

The only sign of life from Dad came once a day, at the moment he walked through the door from the Yum-E-Cakes route, and he sought out Mom or Nicky, and he asked, eyes hopeful, pleading, "Anything?"

Then there was Lester.

The day after the bad news arrived about Roy, the day after Nicky met Mr. Allnuts, there was a shave-and-a-haircut rapping on Nicky's door. Nicky heard the knocking and froze, still as a statue, on the sofa in the empty apartment. Nicky held his breath, so he would not be heard. He did not make a sound, as Lester knocked and knocked.

The knocking grew rapid and desperate, and Nicky played over and over in his mind all the terrible, hurtful, bigoted, hateful, racist things he had said to Lester. Nicky had stuck a million daggers into Lester, and even though he didn't mean to hurt Lester, Nicky had hurt him and he felt vile for it. And Nicky did not know how to face up to his vileness.

The knocking tapered off, weak and futile, then stopped. Then Nicky heard sniffling and sneaker steps clomp across the hallway and fade down the staircase.

The next day, Lester returned and knocked on the apartment door. This time Nicky was at the kitchen table, eating a Yum-E-Cake, and he stopped chewing at the knocking. He heard Lester call, pleading, "Nick-eee, are you in there? Come on, Nicky. If you're in there, please. Open up."

Nicky closed his eyes. He thought about the word *mulignane,* and the thought made him shiver and wish he could—poof—just disappear from the face of the earth. Then he thought of the joke about the black man who found the genie's lamp, which made him remember the black kids in the sandbox joke. Nicky felt the Yum-E-Cake trickle up the back of his throat.

"Nick-ee," Lester called, now begging. "Nick-ee, are you in there?"

Nicky sneezed—he couldn't help it—splattering half-chewed Yum-E-Cake across the table.

Lester fell silent in the hallway.

"I heard that," Lester said. He pressed his mouth to the door-jamb, and his voice sounded whispery and haunting through the crack. "Nicky. I know you can hear me. Nicky, I'm sorry I hid who I really am. I want you to know that. And I want you to know I'm proud of who I am. That's it. And I guess I won't be coming up here anymore."

Then there was the sound of slippers shuffling, leaving, fading down the staircase.

Nicky clonked his head onto the kitchen table. He needed a mountain of forgiveness from Lester. And Nicky had no idea how to ask Lester for that much forgiveness. It seemed like too much to ask. It would be like asking someone for his dog.

Days and days passed, and one Friday afternoon, Nicky was on his way to the lobby for the mail when he veered left on the second floor and marched up to 2-C and knocked. It was a spur-of-the moment-move, an impulse, like suddenly leaping into the pool to simple get it over with.

Nicky knocked, with no idea about what he would say to Lester. Nicky knocked and hoped something would occur to him.

There wasn't a peep from inside 2-C.

Nicky returned to 2-C every day for a week. No one came to the door. There was no sound from inside, no shadow under the door.

One afternoon, Nicky brought a Band-Aid to the door of 2-C. He had picked up this trick from a TV cop show. He adhered the Band-Aid to the door and the doorjamb. If someone ever opened the door, the Band-Aid would fall away. Nicky monitored the Band-Aid for a week. The Band-Aid stayed exactly where he had left it, stuck tightly. No one had gone in or out of 2-C.

Nicky searched Eggplant Alley and found Mr. Misener in the basement of Building A. The superintendent was fixing the handles on garbage cans. Nicky asked Mr. Misener if the Allnuts family in 2-C, over in Building B, had moved out.

"How do I know?" Mr. Misener said. "What am I, an information booth?"

One day in the middle of March, Nicky walked home from school, under powder-blue skies, in beautiful bright sunshine. And he wished the warm, spring-like weather would go away and stop breaking his heart.

"I can't wait for winter," he grumbled.

He climbed the steps into Eggplant Alley. A man in a Western Union uniform scampered down the steps. The man tipped his cap at Nicky. Western Union was the company that delivered telegrams.

Sometimes they brought good news. Sometimes they brought bad news.

Nicky took the stairs two at a time, glancing at the quiet 2-C,

Band-Aid still on the door, as he scurried along the second floor, cursing the heavy textbooks in his book bag.

He was breathless when he reached the fifth floor and spotted a yellow envelope under his apartment door.

His heart thudded as he tore open the envelope and read:

To Mr. and Mrs. Salvatore Martini,

Although United States officials are making every reasonable effort in behalf of the Americans missing or detained in Vietnam there has been no new information since our last contact. Army officials continue to hope that the status and whereabouts of your son can soon be determined. My continued sympathy is with you.

Sincerely,
Sterling Gentry
Major General USA

Sometimes Western Union brings no news at all.

When Mom came home from work and read the telegram, she said, "No news is good news. In a way."

That night after supper, Dad sat in the living room with the television tuned to *The Music Man*. Nicky was at the kitchen table, eating Yum-E-Cakes.

In the living room, Mom said to Dad, "I like musicals, but this one gives me a headache. How can you watch this?"

A lovely warm breeze rippled the kitchen curtain and softly brushed Nicky's neck. Out on Groton, the tenements glowed orange in the dusk. The loveliness made Nicky's eyes ache and sting, and Mom entered the kitchen and caught him crying.

"I wish it would snow," Nicky sobbed, his mouth filled with dessert pie.

"Don't cry, honey," Mom said. "Count your blessings. At least we have hope. Some families have no hope at all."

Nicky sniffed and said, "Dad doesn't seem to be counting his blessings."

"Never mind what your father is doing," Mom said. She squirted soap into the sink and ran hot water into it. "Worry about what you're doing. It's different for your father."

"What's that mean?"

Mom leaned both hands on the sink while a mountain of soap bubbles formed under the rushing water. "Your father thinks he should have . . . He could have . . . He might have . . ." Mom shrugged. "Anyway, I think your father is going to hold his breath until Roy comes home. Until he turns blue."

Nicky blurted, "That was my plan. I'm the one responsible. Not Dad." The words came out like a violent belch.

Mom turned off the faucet and the fresh soap bubbles made a ticking sound. She looked over her shoulder at Nicky and said, "You? You're the least responsible one of all."

"Oh, no, I'm not. No, I'm not," Nicky said, sweating.

And then he felt three years old again, hopeless except to his mother, and the tears and his terrible story poured out of him. How Dad had written the letter to Roy to order him to stay out of combat and to stay out of airplanes. And how Nicky had thrown the letter down the sewer. How one thing led to another, and so it was because of Nicky that Roy went off in some airplane and went missing.

Mom nodded as she placed the dirty dishes and glasses into the sink water.

"So you threw that letter away, huh?" She spoke carefully and casually without looking away from the water. "I kinda knew you did something like that. But I don't see how that matters. Let me tell you a story. When your dad was a boy, one of his friends was spitting off the roof of his tenement. Spitting on people walking by. Being a brat. And this kid, this friend of your dad's, fell off the roof. So your father had a thing about roofs and such."

"But if I didn't . . ."

"Just listen."

"But it's my fault . . ."

"Listen to me. You know how many times Dad told Roy to never, ever, ever, EV-ER, throw water balloons off the roof? A million times. Do you know how many water balloons Roy threw off the roof? Zillions of them. So my point is, Roy didn't mind his father about water balloons. He would not have minded your father about airplanes." All this while washing dishes and stacking them in the drainer.

Nicky felt his chest lighten. A pleasant breeze fluttered the curtains and dried the tears on his cheeks and chin.

"Blame," Mom said. She wiped her forehead with the back of her soapy hand. "How can people expect to be forgiven when they won't forgive themselves? You want to blame someone, blame me. Or Margaret Mitchell. The one who wrote *Gone with the Wind*."

Nicky laughed at the joke.

"I'm not joking," Mom said. She worked a steel wool pad into a crusty broiler pan. "You don't know this story."

Mom said that when she was pregnant with Roy, in the ninth month, she started reading *Gone with the Wind*. She was crazy for the book. She couldn't put it down. She was determined to finish it before the baby came, because everyone knows there's no time for book reading with an infant in the apartment.

So one chilly night she stayed up till three in the morning and finished *Gone with the Wind*. And at 9 AM she went into labor. She was in labor all morning, all afternoon, deep into the night. At three minutes until midnight, old Doc Rosenberg told her "just one more big push, and the baby will be here." But Mom was beat. She had stayed up all night reading *Gone with the Wind*. She didn't have the energy for that push. Not right at the moment. She begged for a rest. A contraction passed. She rested. Another contraction came and went. Doc Rosenberg said no more resting. Mom said, "Tomorrow is another day," and pushed, and Roy was born at 12:01 AM on November 21.

"So what?" Nicky said.

"So, remember the draft lottery? Remember what number Roy's birthday drew in the draft lottery? Number one. November twenty-first was number one. If you were born on November twenty-first, you were guaranteed to get drafted. And he was." Mom made a face at the broiler pan. "And guess what about November twentieth? Dead last—three hundred and sixty-five," Mom said. "Roy would have never left home."

Years later, Nicky wondered if the *Gone with the Wind* story was true. Not that it mattered. He loved his mother for telling it.

"I'm sorry for crying," Nicky said.

"Don't be sorry," Mom said, washing. "Sometimes I feel hopeful. Sometimes I cry, too."

"What makes you hopeful?"

"Knowing that Roy is out there somewhere."

"What makes you cry?"

"Knowing that Roy is out there somewhere."

She plunged her hands into the sink. "I just pray he has dry socks."

Nicky wiggled his toes in his sneakers.

"Ma," he said.

Mom swirled a sponge in a soapy glass and said softly, "Don't you dare hold your breath. Stay alive, Nicky. Enjoy. Play. Say a rosary. I do, every night. Light a candle. I do, every week. Count your blessings. Do you know what I'm going to do tonight? I'm going to make a big batch of eggplant parmigiana. I'm going to put it in the freezer for when Roy comes home. Maybe it's silly. Maybe not. Know what, though? It feels good to do something for him."

Nicky didn't say anything.

"You know how I am about cooking," Mom said with a smile, and Nicky thought he was going to have to grow another heart just to hold his love for his mother.

Mom pulled the plug in the sink. There was a draining sound while Mom said, "I want to have all these nice things waiting for him when he comes home. You know how your brother loves eggplant parmigiana. Don't underestimate eggplant power. It is one of his favorites. My mother always said good things bring goodness. Maybe the smell of it will lead him home." She chuckled once and closed her eyes for a moment. The sink finished draining and emitted a raspy slurp.

And Nicky heard sweet sounds through the kitchen window, out of the orange dusk.

Thwock.

Clatter.

Jangle.

He took these sounds to bed with him.

40

The First Day of Spring

Nicky was awakened by the sound of singing in the courtyard. One of the old love songs. The voice belonged to Mr. Misener, the grouchy superintendent. The morning was so sunny, so warm, so fragrant and dreamy, even the meanest man in Eggplant Alley burst into song. Nicky listened and a feeling washed over him, starting at his toes and finishing at his scalp.

Life was going to change today. For the better.

Mom and Dad sat at the kitchen table. Mom shuffled coupons. Dad stirred his coffee, spoon clanging. The stirring was odd, because Dad took his coffee with no cream, no sugar. There was nothing to stir. But Nicky expected this sort of thing from Dad on this day.

Nicky settled down at the table and noticed the calendar was gone from the refrigerator.

"Sal, did you remember about the cake?" Mom said.

Dad said, "Yeah, I gotta go down there today anyhow. I'll stop by Orzo's."

Nicky sipped Tang and stared out the kitchen window at the PS 19 schoolyard. The schoolyard was streaked with sunshine and shadows, but it was empty. Nicky stared until his eyeballs hurt.

All he got was achy eyeballs. The schoolyard was empty. He did not see old things.

"Know what?" Nicky said. "Today I'm going to start up a stickball game."

Mom sorted through coupons and said, "Nobody plays stickball around here anymore."

Nicky said. "Well, I'm going . . ."

Dad said sharply, "Jesus H. CHRIST, Nicky. Not today."

The kitchen was quiet except for the boink-boink-boink of the leaky faucet.

"Especially today," Nicky said. "Don't you know? Today's the first day of spring."

Mom rushed out the door for her Saturday shift at Gimbels. Dad grabbed his keys and mumbled about Orzo's. Nicky imagined a trip to Cherry Street would do Dad some good. For Dad, going to Cherry Street was like going to the roof.

Nicky fetched his B-4000 mitt, Roy's old mitt, and the yellow stickball bat from the bedroom closet and placed them on the coffee table in the living room. He parted the curtains. He scanned the PS 19 playground. Not a soul in sight. Not even a pigeon.

Nicky wandered the apartment. He stared at the living room sofa until his eyeballs ached. He did not see old things. The sofa remained empty. He stared at Roy's bed until his eyeballs ached. He did not see old things. The bed stayed empty.

He stared out the bedroom window. Tender lime-green grass was sprouting in the courtyard. Nicky stared at the courtyard until his eyeballs ached. And he saw a young man in an army uniform. The young man climbed the steps from Summit Avenue, into the shadow of the archway, out of the shadow, into the courtyard of Eggplant Alley.

Nicky yanked back his head like a frightened turtle. Was that person in an army uniform, that man about the size and shape of Roy—was that an old thing?

Nicky's heart raced. He sweated. He did not look out the window. He listened closely. He clearly heard army shoes clonk on the courtyard walkway.

Nicky held his breath. He heard the door to Building B creak open five stories below.

Nicky tiptoed to the apartment door. He tiptoed because he did not want to disturb whatever was happening. It was like a great dream. He didn't want to chance waking up.

Nicky stood at the door and clenched shut his eyes and listened. The elevator thumped on the fifth floor. The elevator door crunched and rumbled open.

Army shoes clonked on the hallway tile. The steps faltered. The steps stopped.

The footsteps in the hallway moved briskly and surely and softened on the welcome mat, on the other side of the apartment door. Nicky saw a shadow under the door. He heard familiar breathing. And his head swooned at the odor of Old Spice after shave. It was a miracle.

Nicky threw open the door.

"Well, hey-lo," the young man in the army uniform said. "I'm Manuel Rivers."

Nicky's bottom lip stuck out.

The man said, "You must be Nicky."

Nicky didn't say anything.

"I know your brother, Roy."

Manuel Rivers sat on the sofa, on the plastic slipcover, and spoke of Roy.

He told Nicky that Roy was a great guy, a hard worker, and a fabulous stickball player. He said Roy often talked of Eggplant Alley and his family.

"He said this was the finest place in the world," Manuel Rivers said. "He told me all sorts of tales about you guys. That reminds me, how's the dog?"

Nicky shrugged.

Manuel Rivers said he had no idea what Roy was doing in the observation plane on the day he went missing. He said Roy might have been helping out the pilot, who sometimes had trouble finding observers when he was ordered on routine, mostly unnecessary scouting missions. He also said Roy might have been merely taking a joyride.

"The only ones who know are Roy and the pilot," Manuel Rivers said. He paused and looked at the rug. "The pilot didn't make it."

Manuel Rivers said a search party found the wreckage of the plane three days later. He said the pilot's body was found in the wreckage. He said there was no trace of Roy.

"They went down in Vietcong territory," Manuel Rivers said. "That's good news and bad news."

"Bad news?"

"The VC don't report who they have taken prisoner. So anything could be possible."

"Good news?"

"The VC don't report who they have taken prisoner. So anything could be possible."

Nicky nodded. "So there's hope?"

Manuel Rivers said, "Oh, there's hope. Don't ever forget that."

Nicky didn't say anything.

Manuel Rivers said, "You'd be a real numbskull to give up hope."

"Roy always said I was a numbskull."

"Yeah," Manuel Rivers said, grinning for the first time. "He told me."

Manuel Rivers shifted his feet. He looked at the ceiling. He studied his fingers. He was a man out of things to say. His eyes fell upon the baseball mitts and stickball bat on the coffee table.

"Hey, nice mitt," he said. "Is that the B-4000? Very cool. Gotta game today?"

Nicky said, "Yeah, I do."

Nicky and Manuel Rivers walked downstairs together. As they passed the second floor, Nicky glanced as always at 2-C.

The Band-Aid was gone from the door.

"Very interesting," Nicky thought.

Nicky and Manuel Rivers walked out the back door of Building B, along the walkway in the cool shadows, and into the warm sunshine of the PS 19 playground. The beautiful spring day had finally drawn people outside. Fishbone, Icky, Skipper, and Bob smoked cigarettes on the short wall. Residents of the tenements on Groton Avenue were spread along the stoops. A tinny radio was playing somewhere.

Nicky glanced up at Building B as he walked. He counted the windows—six over from the left, two up from the ground floor. He picked out Lester's kitchen. The window was closed. The lights were out. The lace curtain was drawn.

Nicky and Manuel Rivers approached Icky and the old gang. Nicky made introductions.

"Any sign of Roy?" Icky said.

"Not yet," Manuel Rivers said.

Nicky held up the stickball bat and the gloves and said, "Anybody interested?"

Icky scowled.

Manuel Rivers said. "I hear you guys have some pretty smoking stickball in this neighborhood." He nodded at Icky. "And you—I heard you got a pretty nasty drop pitch."

Icky shrugged, clearly pleased.

"So bring it on, man," Manuel Rivers said. "I mean, look at this day." He turned his face up to the sun. "Perfect for stickball."

Icky said, "Nobody plays stickball around here anymore."

But Fishbone and Skipper and Bob looked at one another and shrugged. Fishbone shrugged again and said, "I'll play, if anybody wants to. Who's got a ball?"

Nicky did not have a ball. He had planned to go to Popop's for a new Spaldeen. Then he got busy looking for old things, and the morning flew by.

"I ain't got a ball," Nicky said quietly, sadly, and he looked down, feeling like a numbskull. His eyes were drawn to the dirty bottles and rusty cans and yellowed newspapers gathered at the base of the low wall. He spied something round. It looked like a rotten tangerine. Nicky toed his sneaker at the object. It was Roy's old Spaldeen, mottled green by the months since the stickball game in the snow with Lester.

"Mud-dun, we can't play with that cruddy thing," Icky scowled.

Manuel Rivers said, "Gimme that."

He squeezed the ball like a lemon. The green outer membrane of filth fell away in chunks. He squeezed some more and flakes fell away and the Spaldeen turned freshly pink, good as new.

"Batter up," Manuel Rivers said.

The gang walked onto the schoolyard, out of the long shadows, into the sunshine, onto the concrete diamond. Icky lagged behind, hands in his pockets, head down.

Manuel Rivers counted out loud. "Only six," he said. "Roy went on and on about how you guys played with full teams. Where is everybody?"

"That was the good old days," Fishbone said.

Manuel Rivers said, "There's gotta be more guys than this around."

Icky shook his head. "I was just over on Summit. I didn't see nobody on the steps."

"How about them?" Manuel Rivers said. He nodded toward four black boys reclining on a front stoop across the street. The boys were listening to music from the tinny radio.

"I don't think so," Fishbone said, smirking.

"Why not? Let's ask them," Manuel Rivers said.

Icky said to Nicky, "Tell this guy the way it is around here."

Nicky turned his back on Icky and said to Manuel Rivers, "All right, let's ask them."

Icky stepped back and said, "Flub this. I don't need the aggravation." He thrust his hands into his pockets and strolled, muttering, off the PS 19 playground and into the shadows of Eggplant Alley.

Fishbone tucked his hands into his back pockets and shrugged. "I don't care in one case or the other. But you gotta do the asking, not me."

Nicky and Manuel Rivers walked to the fence on Groton Avenue. They carried the gloves and the bat and the ball, clear signals of peaceful intentions. The groan of a window sliding made Nicky look up at Building B. Lester's kitchen window was open. Nicky was sure he saw nerd glasses behind the rippling lace curtain.

Nicky and Manuel Rivers hooked their elbows on the top of the fence. Manuel Rivers called to the four black boys on the stoop, "Yo. You guys wanna play?"

A short stocky boy, draped lazily on the steps, leaning way back on his elbows, snorted loudly and made a P-U face. He said, "Not interested, GI Joe."

A boy with a magnificent Afro, his long legs stretched out on the stoop, turned his face toward his companions and then back at Manuel Rivers. The boy shrugged. He was thinking about it.

Nicky held his breath. He thought of dominoes. He thought of talking Mom and Dad into a puppy. He thought of the lacy kitchen curtains parting, two stories up. He thought of taking in a Yankee game with Dad and Lester and Mr. Allnuts. He thought of pushing the doorbell at the Only House With Trees, stone lions smiling at him, good news written all over his face. He thought of a lanky figure in an olive uniform strolling through the courtyard in a cloud of Old Spice, duffel bag bouncing on his shoulder, face turned up to the sun, under a sky perfect for stickball, the face calling out, "Hey-lo, Eggplant Alley."

"Come on, play," Nicky whispered, exhaling softly.

The boy with the Afro stood. He stretched his arms over his head. The boy turned his face to the sun and said, "It's a great day for stickball, sports fans."

The boy extended his hand. Nicky gently gave him Roy's old glove. Nicky had never seen a happy ending, but he still believed in them.